TYRANTS, TORMENTORS AND THE TIARA

JAMES J. MEADOWS III

Copyright © 2012, 2014, 2023 James J. Meadows III.

All rights reserved. No part of this book may be reproduced, stored, or transmitted by any means—whether auditory, graphic, mechanical, or electronic—without written permission of both publisher and author, except in the case of brief excerpts used in critical articles and reviews. Unauthorized reproduction of any part of this work is illegal and is punishable by law.

ISBN: 979-8-89031-637-0 (sc)
ISBN: 979-8-89031-638-7 (hc)
ISBN: 979-8-89031-639-4 (e)

Because of the dynamic nature of the Internet, any web addresses or links contained in this book may have changed since publication and may no longer be valid. The views expressed in this work are solely those of the author and do not necessarily reflect the views of the publisher, and the publisher hereby disclaims any responsibility for them.

One Galleria Blvd., Suite 1900, Metairie, LA 70001
(504) 702-6708

CHAPTER

1

Clement's eyes shone like embers beneath the hood of his robe, watching the fire in the hearth fade to nothingness. He didn't need the light, and there was no one else in the cabin.

An exile imprisoned deep in the confines of an ancient forbidding forest, Clement had only his hatred to keep him company. No strangers traversed the deadly maze of overgrown firs and spruces looming outside his locked door. No adventurers scaled the treacherous cliffs or ascended the slick, icy walls to reach the barren plateau upon which dwelt his gloomy home. Evil spirits and monsters inhabiting the cursed land kept far from the dark abode as though fearing the wrath of the greater terror lurking within. Only the pale rays of the moonlit sky dared venture toward his desolate lair.

Clement remained a ruin of his former glory. Gray streaks adorned his cropped brown hair. Deep lines cut a winding ravine down his weathered face giving the illusion of greater age to a man only in his mid-thirties. Rips and tears decorated a stained brown robe, its vanished splendor once displaying the skill of the land's greatest artisans. But smoldering blue eyes showed the power and life still burning within the sorcerer whose tyrannical fist once grasped the largest country in the continent of Aurba.

The once mighty tyrant wasted away. For seven years, he sat, ate, and slept within the walls, rarely rising from his rotting chair except to seek the replenishment of his provisions.

Like water disturbed by the ripple of a fish passing beneath, the air changed. Clement's head rose as he felt the alteration in the room. The magic surrounding him swirled and tingled in reaction to a conflicting energy source. Someone had entered the cabin. A smile crossed Clement's lips as he rose from the chair and turned to face the thick shadows masking the corner behind him.

"Welcome, Darien," he said. "I'm glad you could come."

The shadows split apart as a tall green-cloaked man emerged from their depth. Hatred oozed from his every pore like pus. He was a tall man, powerfully built with large muscular hands protruding from long emerald sleeves. He possessed an unkempt appearance, wild scraggly beard, and dirty, knotted hair. His disheveled exterior gave the impression of a mad man, but the strength in his steady brown eyes dispelled the illusion as they focused with unwavering intensity upon Clement.

"Please, sit," Clement offered, waving his hand in a circular motion.

The shadows in the room swirled like a strange fog before congealing into a plush black armchair. Clement motioned for the big man to take a seat, but his visitor ignored the gesture. Instead, he ran his eyes up and down

Clement's frame, scrutinizing his host with disdain. His lips curled into a malicious grin.

"Well, well," he said, slipping in sarcasm, "Clement the Great. Not looking so great now, are we?"

Clement's eyes narrowed at hearing his old title used in such a disrespectful manner. His name once inspired fear in the hearts of the most hardened warriors. For more than ten years, lords and ladies offered their finest wealth to curry his favor. Would-be apprentices swore their souls to his service just to glimpse his power. Opponents forfeited their lives to placate his wrath.

Only three sorcerers dared to defy him. Equally powerful and corrupt, they forged their own empires in a war for supreme dominion over the embattled land, but their kingdoms never matched his size. Their wealth never equaled his splendor. Their magic never rivaled his might. And their reputations paled before his greatness.

Clement gave a harsh laugh, surveying his mocker. "Ha, you should look in a mirror. From where I stand, you don't look so good yourself."

Darien too had fallen far from his previous glory. He was one of the opposing sorcerer lords, once ruling the second-largest kingdom on the continent. His empire spanned most of the wild and untamed northeastern tundra while Clement controlled the resource-rich northwestern forests.

Darien ignored the jab. Drifting behind the chair, he ran his fingers along the top.

"I would have thought," Darien stated, "someone cunning enough to poison and murder half the population of my capital would devise a better way to kill himself than wasting away like rotting fruit."

"And I'd have thought someone who once bewitched the children in his kingdom to instantly age to adulthood to fuel his army could enchant himself to not smell like a walking outhouse. You could at least look like you shaved once in the past seven years."

Darien's hand shot to his face and stroked the dilapidated web of neglected strands and matted fur.

"Enough of this. I received the bauble you sent requesting a meeting. I would normally ignore such a message, but the obvious risk you took intrigued me. Someone could have intercepted your spell. And to bring me past all of your defenses? I had to know why."

"The risks were necessary," Clement said.

"Indeed. But to what end?" Darien asked.

"If you sit down, I'll explain everything."

The tall man glanced at the chair apprehensively. He moved around the seat, his keen eyes inspecting every inch. Finally, he lowered himself onto the cushions, but his body remained tense.

Grabbing the arm of his rocking chair, Clement spun the seat to face the enchanter. He attempted to act calm and unbothered by Darien's presence, yet he felt anxious and noticeably avoided turning his back to the visitor for even a second.

"Come now, Clement," Darien said. "Surely you do not confess to being afraid of me."

"Even the smallest viper is deadly if given the chance to strike," Clement said, taking his seat.

"Perhaps. But, unlike some people, I have honor. I do not strike when someone's back is turned."

"Indeed, your lack of subtle cunning remains your greatest weakness. Still, your misguided self-righteousness, although deadly for so many innocent citizens, is part of the reason I called upon you for help."

"Help?" Darien repeated, ignoring the rest of the statement. "You called me here to ask for help?"

Clement scowled.

"Trust me, I'm not excited about the idea either, but where else can I go? My apprentices are all dead. I have no friends. Though neither of us doubts our feelings toward each other, of all our enemies, I suspect we hate each other the least."

"That is not saying much," Darien mused. "Regardless, if given a choice between helping you and killing you, why should I choose the first?"

"Aside from the obvious fact that you're no match for my powers," Clement said, "the answer is simple. You need my help."

"And why do I need your help?" Darien asked.

"Because, beneath all your egotistical arrogance, you are nothing! A worthless, disgraced, and fallen nobody!" Clement's voice rose as he abandoned his forced restraint.

Darien leapt to his feet in fury. Clement sprang up as well, his arms gesturing for emphasis.

"You're an outcast! A failure! You stand here in your self-righteous haughtiness, but in the end you're no better than me: a relic of a bygone age with no home, no family, no kingdom, and no hope."

Darien and Clement breathed heavily as they squared off against each other. Their wrath grew more intense with each second as they gazed unblinking into one another's eyes. A chill coursed through the cabin as they summoned their magic until the room crackled with building energy.

Then Darien relaxed, allowing his magic to disperse. Sensing the change, Clement did the same, resuming his seat. Darien reclined into the armchair, his hands crossed in deep thought.

"You are right, of course," Darien said, resuming his typically stoic manner. "And I can no more help myself than you can help yourself. What help do you think we can provide to each other?"

"Like the hydra, many heads combined can achieve what one alone cannot," Clement said, "Together, we can do what no one of us can do alone."

"Which is?"

"Kill Queen Sylvia."

The mention of the name brought an instant reaction. Darien's face darkened, and his lips curled into a snarl. Sylvia represented the source of all their suffering. Just when Clement, Darien, and the other tyrants had reached the pinnacle of their power, the young sorceress appeared. Like the sun splintering the gloom of an endless night, she arose from an obscure existence as an unknown healer to shatter the tyrannical reign of the four rivals.

Rallying the citizens behind her banner of freedom and justice, she scattered armies and toppled thrones. She crushed the tyrants beneath her heel, exiling them to the distant reaches of civilization. Clement's kingdom fell last. Darien's the next to last.

As quickly as the darkness fell over Darien's countenance, it vanished. A bemused smile crossed his lips.

"Is this why you called me here? You want me to help kill the empress?" Darien shook his head. "Sorry to disappoint you, but despite my lowly station I have not despaired to suicide. I have watched Sylvia. Her powers grow with each passing day beyond anything I ever imagined. Even you and I combined are mere bugs to be crushed before her."

"Perhaps," Clement acknowledged, "but I have something that can turn the tables. Something even her formidable powers can't resist."

"What?"

"This," Clement reached into his robes and pulled out a small orb made of a deep-blue crystal with a dark-red tint.

The gesture brought an immediate reaction. Darien leapt to his feet, sending the chair cascading to the floor. Retreating as quickly as possible, he backed against the cabin wall. His face was flushed with terror, and he pointed at Clement. Magic surged into the extended fingertips.

"Wait," Clement shouted, holding up a hand, "the orb isn't for you. It's for Sylvia alone."

Darien breathed heavily, his body tense. "Place it on the chair," he ordered.

Clement did so. He moved slowly to avoid alarming his rival. He straightened the armchair, placing the fist-sized jewel onto one of the cushions and stepping backward. He thought about summoning his magic for defense but rejected the idea. He needed Darien's trust. At this critical stage any potentially aggressive movement could ruin everything.

Darien's arms remained raised as he advanced. He surveyed the glimmering stone. The crystalline object radiated a dim inner light from deep inside its glossy depths. Darien stared in awe.

"Violet quartz crystal. I have not seen one of these since . . ."

He fell silent, his face mask-like as he stared for long minutes at the stone. Clement let him stare, saying nothing as the minutes passed. Inwardly, he breathed a sigh of relief. Pulling out the gem without some sort of advanced warning was a mistake. He couldn't blame Darien for reacting in such a manner.

Violet quartz crystals were the most dangerous objects in all of existence. The innocent-looking stones served as a receptacle of magical power, possessing the ability, if activated by the correct enchantments, to rip the very essence of life from a foe and leave them an empty shell. The unfortunate enemy's life force became sealed inside the crystal, while the mindless corpse rambled on. The fate was not a desirable one.

Darien lowered his arms, his eyes narrowing as he studied his host.

"Where did you get this?"

"I stumbled upon it while wandering the mountains."

"This is your plan?" Darien scoffed. "You are mad. Sylvia will never allow you to complete the spells necessary to activate it. How do you know it will not explode?"

The question was a reasonable one. Each violet quartz crystal only held a limited amount of power. If the essence going into the gem exceeded its capacity, the stone exploded in a shower of tiny shards, dooming anyone unlucky enough to be nearby. Charged crystal shards were instant death to anything they touched.

"The High Mage Nilliath trapped the Dread Lord Ithos's power in a crystal smaller than this," Clement answered. "I'm confident this crystal is sufficient to hold Sylvia's essence. As far as casting the spell, I'll give you cover while you cast it. I may not be able to defeat Sylvia, but I can hold her off long enough. If you don't know the spell, I can teach it to you."

Darien gaped in disbelief.

"First of all," he said, "I know how to cast the spell. Second of all, are you out of your mind? Who would teach another sorcerer a spell like that? How do you know I am not going to use the orb on you?"

"Because violet quartz crystals are only good for a single absorption. Everyone knows that. You hate Sylvia as much as I do. Between taking down each other or Sylvia, we'd both choose to destroy her. After the disgrace we suffered at her hands, after the exile we still suffer at her hands, her death is the only thing that matters!"

"Perhaps," Darien said, "but I am no fool! The theft of essence can be reversed and the stolen power absorbed into the body of another. Do you think I am going to let you steal Sylvia's powers and make them your own? I will see you dead first."

"Don't be an idiot," Clement said. "Do you think I'd to try reversing her power into myself? Everyone who has ever tried to absorb the powers of violet quartz has died. Remember Allidian the Lich or Cormorthian the Blade. They were the greatest wizards of their time. Even Nilliath failed to get the spell right!"

It might've been an exaggeration, but Clement had never heard of a single successful instance of the ritual being performed. The spell for absorbing stolen essence from a crystal required twenty-four hours of unbroken concentration. The legends of famous wizards and witches who died attempting the spell formed a common part of magical lore.

Allidian rushed the ritual, absorbing the powers too fast. He exploded. Cormorthian failed to concentrate hard enough and died when the crystal exploded. The legendary High Mage Nilliath died trying to complete the ritual when a sneeze at an untimely moment caused him to spontaneously combust.

"Can you think of anyone who cast the spell and lived to tell the tale?" Clement asked.

Darien turned away, gazing down at the floor. "Just one," he mumbled.

"Look," Clement said, "if you're so worried about the orb, we can destroy it afterward."

"And then what?" Darien asked, his features darkening as he looked back at Clement.

"What do you mean?"

"After Sylvia is dead, what then? You go off and rebuild your empire, and we spend another ten years trying to kill each other. No, I do not think so."

"You prefer to remain an outcast?"

"You are such a liar. You do not share power. The moment Sylvia is dead, you will turn on me like a predator battling over his prey."

A cold, cruel smile crossed Clement's lips.

"Come now, would you really have it any other way? We didn't spend ten years marching armies across each other's lands, slaying each other's apprentices, murdering each other's families, and butchering each other's citizens just to see the other return to power. Now we can end the conflict with one quick battle, a single duel to the death, you versus me."

Darien gave an equally cruel smile. "Agreed," he said, his eyes glittering.

"Then you'll help?"

"Yes," Darien answered, "but we must take a blood oath first."

"Why?" Clement asked, his smile vanishing. Clement hated blood oaths. The complex and disgusting rituals revolted him and involved nasty complications if broken.

"For my piece of mind," Darien said. "I want to know that I will not have to watch my back while we travel together, and I want to know the crystal is going to be destroyed. We will take an oath that neither of us will kill the other until the orb is destroyed."

Clement failed to understand the need for the oath. He wasn't going to jeopardize his own plan by attacking Darien prematurely. Furthermore, he possessed no desire to steal the powers from the orb. Nor did he believe anyone else foolish enough to try. Still, he lacked a reason not to take the oath. Should he be severely weakened during his battle with Sylvia, the delay might give him time to recuperate before battling Darien.

"Very well," he said, "we'll perform the ritual tonight and set off in the morning. We have about three weeks of steady travel ahead of us. We'll fine-tune our plan along the way."

"So be it," Darien said.

Clement smiled. Sylvia's death awaited at the hands of an alliance she could never have imagined.

CHAPTER

2

Three weeks later, the majestic city of Rhoria shimmered beneath silvery moonlight. The soft glow of the celestial orb illuminating the night sky reflected off stone streets and rooftops, bathing the town with an ambiance of pleasant serenity. Yet, inside the queen's bedchamber, where the beams glistened off beads of sweat coating Sylvia's face, neither peace nor rest could be found.

She thrashed violently, her silken sheets and long blonde hair going in all directions as she fought against the nightmares bombarding her sleep. Her breaths came in harsh gasps as her long nails tore across the sheets. Inaudible screams and sobs issued from her lips as she struggled against the dark visions. A silver tiara with violet gems clung tightly to her head as if fearing the violent fit might fling the enthroned jewel from its lofty perch.

Mere yards from the dreaming queen, a shimmer passed across the large circular balcony. Imperceptible to all but the sharpest eyes, the outline of a cloaked figure drifted across the window. Only the strange displacement of the stars, akin to light seen through water, gave any indication of the mysterious presence.

With slow, measured movements, the intruder crept across the parapet toward the glass double doors in the middle of the balcony window. The well-fortified portal stood armed with multiple inner latches above a sturdy lock, but the spectral form appeared unconcerned. It approached the door with graceful stealth until only inches separated the clear glass from the equally transparent trespasser.

A distortion in the upper part of the figure gave the impression of a head rising in astonished surprise. The unseen shape dashed out of sight, hiding behind a small alcove on the far side of the balcony. At the same moment, Sylvia awoke.

She sat upright, unaware of what woke her, but an uneasy feeling gripped her mind. She sensed the room had changed and gazed around. Her quarters were massive. Even with the moonlight from the nearby balcony, she saw very little beyond her immediate surroundings. Yet, everything appeared normal.

Sylvia turned her attention to the balcony, scanning the stone outlook and the sprawling city beyond. Again, everything appeared as it should. Still, the vague uncertain feeling of discomfort lingered. She considered calling for the guards but dismissed the idea.

She was being silly. There was no threat the guards could handle that she couldn't. Besides, the bed chamber was surrounded by a web of formidable enchantments. None but the greatest sorcerers could dream of penetrating it. The magic tingled in the air around her. Basking in the feel of the familiar enchantments, Sylvia eased back onto the bed and closed her eyes.

As her golden hair fell upon the pillow, her eyes flew open. She recognized the source of her discomfort. The spells encasing the bedchamber weren't hers. Nor were they any form of defensive enchantment. She was enclosed within a massive sink field, a network of enchantments designed to suppress a spellcaster's magical energy. She couldn't guess how such a feat had been accomplished but knew she needed to get out of the room.

"Arthur! Marek!" she screamed. She sprang from the bed and dashed toward the door. She never reached it. A towering black figure emerged from the shadows to block her retreat.

"Arthur," she cried again. "Marek."

No sounds came from the distant hallway. Sylvia stared at the intruder. Eyes like red orbs peered from vast hollow sockets. Green scaly skin covered immense muscles. Powerful arms the size of tree trunks ended in sharp, deadly claws. Rows of razor-sharp teeth adorned an unnaturally wide mouth. Large bat-like wings protruded from the middle of his curved back. Sylvia was no expert on mythic beasts, but she could recognize a demon.

But demons were extinct. She dismissed the thought. Now wasn't the time to dwell on such matters. She needed to reach the door, demon or not. She summoned her magic. Energy rose to her fingertips, but the sink field pulled back. Normally her power glowed with the light of the sun. Now, though she strained with all her might, the chamber only crackled and flashed like clouds during a lightning storm. Still, her power remained greater than most spellcaster's unhindered.

Her mind raced through various spells and incantations. She needed one powerful enough to disable her foe but simple enough not to drain her strength if the fight became prolonged.

"Kalecheet," she shouted, raising her hands.

She focused on the word, allowing the sound to alter the magic flowing through her. As the vibrations reshaped her energy, she visualized the goal of the spell. The vibrations and concentration united to give life to the sorcery. It burst from her fingers in a beam of pulsating orange light. The spell struck the abomination with all the force she could muster. The burst sent shock-waves rippling through the air powerful enough to evaporate a dozen men. It struck the demon directly in the chest with a resounding blast. The beast appeared unfazed. The spell didn't even leave a scratch.

Sylvia gaped. Goosebumps rose on her arms. A feeling of panic gripped her as she reeled from shock. Her instincts screamed to run, and her resolve vanished. How could she defeat an impregnable foe?

The demon launched itself at her. Sylvia attempted to dive out of the way, but her opponent proved swifter. It seized her body in its enormous left hand, long fingers wrapping around her slender waist. Before she could react, its right hand flashed across the air in front of her. With both surprise and horror, Sylvia felt the claw snatch the silver tiara off her head.

"No!" she shouted, her hands flailing in an attempt to retrieve the stolen crown.

Sylvia wondered how the beast knew to target the jewel. Then she found herself soaring through the air. She crashed into the wall of her chamber with a sickening thud. Everything went dark.

Seconds later, the balcony window exploded in a shower of splintered wood and broken glass. The demon burst from the room, soaring through the air at an incredible speed. Soon, it became indistinguishable from the dark sky above. Sylvia and the tiara vanished with it. Crouching upon the balcony below, the cloaked figure watched them disappear.

"An entire plan built around accessing a secret passage, and you did not even have the common sense to figure out where the entrance is located?"

Darien crossed his arms irritably. Clement said nothing. Any attempt to defend himself would only exacerbate the enchanter's already sour mood. Clement was determined not to fuel his antagonist's diatribe. Besides, he needed to concentrate.

They stood in a deserted corridor stretching far into the distance and intersecting with various halls and empty rooms. Prior to the meeting with Darien, Clement had spent several weeks scrying, a skill he mastered years ago. A talent not possessed by all mages, scrying produced all the benefits of monitoring another person's every action without being there physically.

He employed this method of spying to watch people traveling to and fro inside the castle. The fire in his fireplace served as the medium through which these visions passed. He spent many nights supervising the activities of the palace denizens, particularly those of the queen's closest advisor and confidant, the high mage, Cornelius.

From the high mage, Clement learned of a network of secret passages Cornelius used to enter and maneuver through the palace without encountering guards and fellow bureaucrats. The most important passage was a secret doorway triggered by a suit of armor and leading almost directly to the queen's bedchamber. Clement had not made particular note about which suit of armor triggered the door. He knew what the decoration looked like. How many such suits of armor could there be in one hallway?

Clement looked back at the two-dozen suits of armor they'd already passed and gazed ahead at several dozen more still awaiting them. Each coat looked identical. He pressed onward, examining the next suit and then the next despite the loud exasperated sighs of his companion.

Clement was growing irritated. So far, the combination of secret tunnels and passages had enabled him to avoid any guards or servants. But, if they lingered much longer in the hallway, someone was bound to see them. This and his growing desire to make Darien shut up wore on his nerves.

Finally, Clement's eyes lit up as he spotted the small trigger inside a coat of arms. Darien seemed to notice the change.

"Have we found the 'chosen one' at last?" he asked.

Clement lifted the suit's visor and lowered it. A blue dot, no bigger than a standard coin, appeared on the wall beside the decoration. If Clement wasn't looking for it, he probably wouldn't have seen it. He pressed his left index finger against the small dot. Responding to Clement's touch, the wall dissolved, revealing a long staircase stretching upward. A small landing at the foot of the staircase contained another coat of arms. Clement advanced toward it, but Darien hung back.

"Did you want to clean your smudge off the armor before we continue," Darien asked, gesturing at a set of fingerprints adorning the polished metal.

"No," Clement said, "I'm not worried about leaving evidence of our presence. Sylvia's corpse will give the secret away."

With a shrug, Darien followed into the passage. The suit of armor on the landing looked identical to the ones in the hallway. Clement raised and lowered the visor of this suit, and the wall reappeared, sealing them inside. A soft blue light radiating from an unseen source provided visibility, and the staircase ascended at least two stories. At the top, another landing held another suit of armor.

"Here we are," Clement said, looking around with pride.

He wasn't expecting praise and therefore wasn't disappointed.

"I am glad to see dumb luck compensates for incompetence," Darien said. "Shall we ascend?"

Clement scowled for a moment before a cold smile crossed his lips.

"Of course, I'll lead so I can check for traps."

Darien raised an eyebrow, but he motioned Clement ahead. Clement proceeded up the staircase, muttering spells beneath his breath and examining each step. He felt Darien summon defensive spells to protect against any plot Clement might be brewing. But Clement was too crafty for any direct form of revenge. He moved up the stairs still muttering spells, but they weren't charms for detecting traps. Clement didn't need to search for traps. He already knew where there was a trap.

About halfway up the staircase, Clement spotted the trick step. He knew the step was trapped because the high mage avoided it every time he ascended the passage. As gifted as the high mage might be in the magical arts, he obviously knew little about defending himself from scrying spells. This failure allowed him to reveal vast amounts of useful information to Clement's prying eyes.

I'll have to thank his corpse after I kill him, Clement mused. *It's the least I can do to show my gratitude.*

As Clement reached the trick step, he completed his spell. A transparent film covered the stair, providing a solid surface. Clement glanced to make sure Darien didn't notice before stepping upon the stair in the same manner as any other. The enchanted surface easily supported his weight, preventing him from triggering the trap. Darien followed, also stepping on the magically coated stair, unaware of Clement's deception.

Clement secretly dismissed the spell. He and Darien planned to escape back through the same tunnel. After Sylvia's death, the stair would be waiting. Since Clement wasn't taking any direct action to kill his companion, the blood oath wouldn't be broken. They reached the upper landing a few minutes later. Clement stopped and turned to face Darien.

"You remember the plan," he said. "We must take out the guards at the door before they can squeeze the alarm amulets around their necks. A suit of armor on the other side opens the door. Don't forget, we must move swiftly. Are you ready?"

Darien nodded. Clement raised the visor and dropped it. A blue dot appeared, and a section of wall slid silently away at Clement's touch. He listened for any sound or movement to indicate someone spotting the opening. None came. Everything was going according to plan. Then everything went wrong.

"Arthur! Marek!" a female voice screamed in alarm.

Clement's heart leapt in terror. The voice belonged to Sylvia. Somehow, they'd been spotted. He hesitated. Should they continue with the attack or flee?

"Arthur! Marek!"

The cry sounded again, but no alarm greeted their ears, and they saw no movement in the hall. No one was responding. Something was wrong.

"Kalecheet!"

Clement's eyes widened as the sudden realization sank in. Sylvia was attacking someone. Somehow, someone or something had beaten them to the queen, and no one was coming to her aid. Fate smiled upon them this night. There might never be a better time to carry out their plan.

The pair dashed into the hallway. A muffled shout came from the queen's room, but Clement couldn't make it out. Ahead of him, two guards stood at attention. Darien raised his arms to fire a spell, but Clement grabbed him.

"Why aren't they moving?" he asked.

Hurrying up to the guards, Clement and Darien examined them. The men stood perfectly motionless, like human statues. Only their eyes, darting around in panic, gave any indication of life. Yet, even they appeared to be covered with a strange white glaze.

"They are dying," Darien observed. "Someone . . ."

Before he could finish, a loud crash of shattering glass and splintering wood sounded from the bedchamber. Forgetting the guards, Clement seized the door handle. The knob didn't turn. Darien reached for the keys, but Clement didn't wait.

"Beetseeya!"

The door burst into splinters. Clement charged forward, Darien behind him. The room was empty. Shattered wood littered the deep-red carpet, and mounds of broken glass rested where a large balcony window once stood.

"They are gone," Darien gasped.

"Glad you noticed," Clement replied.

"But who attacked her?" Darien continued. "Where did they come from? If they bewitched the guards and entered from the hall, why was the door locked and closed? If they did not, how did they enchant the guards?"

"I don't know," Clement responded, examining the room. "Based on the blankets, the attack came while she slept. She threw the sheet aside in a hurry. What interests me more are the enchantments. Feel the room. Someone created a power sink. No one could cast these spells without awakening her. What?"

Darien had dashed over to the mattress. A tattered cloth covered with archaic symbols sat atop a pillow. Made from a rough discolored fabric, it clearly didn't belong with the other blankets. Darien held up the cloth, and Clement examined the markings.

They resembled an ancient coat of arms. Inside the outline of an elegant shield was a fancifully drawn arcane symbol composed of ten emerald crescent moons revolving around a large red claw. It possessed no innate magical properties, and Clement was unfamiliar with the design. He looked at Darien. The enchanter wore a grave expression.

"Darien, what . . ." Clement began.

"Arthur, Marek," an authoritative voice boomed down the hall. "What's going on?"

"Guards!" Darien said. "We must get out of here."

Clutching the cloth, he made for the door. Clement started after him then stopped.

"What?" Darien began, but Clement held up a hand.

He stood still, listening. He turned toward the shattered window and stared into the balcony beyond.

"I thought I heard footsteps," he answered. "On the balcony..."

A guard burst into the room with sword in hand. He stood over six feet tall with a large chest, powerful arms, and shoulder-length brown hair. He wore thick chainmail underneath a leather jerkin yet moved with the gracefulness of a cat. Scanning the room, the guard took in the broken window, missing queen, and sorcerers standing beside the bed. He displayed no signs of fear and wore the determined look of someone prepared for battle.

"Where is she?" he demanded, reaching for an amulet around his neck.

Clement recognized it as an alarm broach worn by Sylvia's private guards. Reacting quickly to prevent him from triggering the alarm, Clement shouted the first spell to come to mind.

"Molnia!"

Bright streams of dazzling white lightning burst toward the soldier and smashed into his chest with a deafening blast. The spell fizzled. The man stood completely unscathed. Clement gaped in astonishment. No normal person could survive such an attack, even inside a power sink.

The warrior squeezed the pendant, and the wails of a woman shrieking filled the palace. It grew louder and quieter at regular intervals, and the walls changed colors in rapid succession from blue to red to green and back to blue. Without another word, the guard charged. Raising his sword, he brought the blade down in a deadly arc toward Clement.

"Dveshenie!" Clement said, batting his hand as though swatting a mosquito.

The warrior's sword seemed to take a life of its own, spinning and bobbing in his hands before launching him headfirst into a wooden nightstand. Without further delay, Clement dashed from the room and made for the secret passage. Darien raced close behind, and Clement saw him carefully stuff the strange piece of cloth into a pocket of his robes.

Turning the corner into the passage, Clement spotted the guard chasing behind. Distant shouts and clanking armor warned of more reinforcements coming. Hoping to thwart their pursuers, Clement triggered the armor inside the passage as he raced past. The secret door slid back into place, but not before Darien and the guard slipped inside.

The tenacity of their pursuer worried Clement. Searching for some way to lose him, Clement remembered the trick stair. If Darien triggered the snare, the enchanter would be caught. The distraction might buy Clement time to escape. He rushed ahead, imagining the look on Darien's face when the big man fell for the ploy. At that moment, he heard Darien shout behind him.

"Smazka!"

A slimy liquid appeared on the stairs beneath Clement's feet. He slipped, his legs flying into the air, and he fell careening onto the hard stone. Landing on more of the slick ooze, he slid several steps before coming to a stop. Darien raced past, grinning.

The smile vanished, however, as his foot sank into the trick stair. A bright flash of light filled the hallway. Thick blue walls of flickering energy blocked the corridor, preventing anyone above the step from descending and anyone below from ascending. Darien was snared. Unfortunately, Clement was little better. Looking up, he saw the guard charging.

"Stradat!" Clement shouted, pointing at the guard.

A cylindrical beam of swirling black light erupted from his hand and slammed into the guard. Again the seemingly invincible warrior remained unaffected. The guard raised his sword to strike. Clement focused his energy into a shield around himself. While he doubted the hastily constructed barrier could completely deflect the attack, he hoped it might absorb enough of the impact to prevent a fatal wound.

The sword plunged downward, but Clement was spared the blow. The guard lurched forward as though struck hard in the back. Losing his balance, he fell through the air, tumbling almost a dozen steps before crashing into the magical barrier with a sickening crunch. Stunned, Clement stared down at him. He was unconscious.

Clement glanced up the stairs. No further pursuit appeared forthcoming. Clement sprang to his feet. Looking down, he discovered the barrier was gone. Darien's puzzled expression showed he had not disarmed the trap. But who did? Lacking time to dwell on the strange stroke of fortune, Clement hurdled the unconscious guard and hurried down the stairs. At the bottom, he caught up with Darien.

"I suppose the grease was meant for the guard!" Clement said, his face flushed with anger.

"Yes!" Darien snapped back. "And I am sure telling me about the trapped step just slipped your mind!"

Darien crossed toward the suit of armor. He grabbed the visor but hesitated. "Is it safe to exit?"

"I don't know, but we can't stay here," Clement replied. "I believe only the high mage knows about this passage, and he lives at the academy. We will be gone by the time he arrives. The main guard won't know about the tunnel, how to open it, or where it leads. They'll likely be searching for us along the main passages. The hallway outside is far enough from any known exits to escape notice."

Darien nodded and activated the door. As predicted, no soldiers patrolled the hall. Checking both directions, they left the passage and made their way sneaked the palace. Retracing their steps, they weaved down deserted corridors and past empty rooms before reaching a large mural hanging on the wall. The painting hid a secret hallway. Stepping through the illusory canvas, they vanished into the tunnel.

After several more twists, turns, and secret corridors, they reached their destination: a small closet filled with various rags, buckets, and other cleaning supplies. The apparently insignificant room possessed a dark secret crucial to their mission. The blank wall on the right slid away, providing discrete access to the royal park. An illusionary wall of thorn bushes concealed the camouflaged doorway, making it the perfect tool for someone to enter or exit unseen.

Of course, entering and exiting the bushes involved some risk. The park was next to the academy, and many apprentices took refuge there when studying, practicing incantations, or involving themselves in illicit fraternization. Fortunately, once beyond a hundred yards, they could easily disappear into the sprawling alleyways of the city.

Clement and Darien pushed aside the sliding wall and climbed from the portal. A small alcove separated the door from the row of fake plants. Flipping up the hoods of their cloaks to maintain some anonymity, they dashed through the false shrubbery. After only a few short strides, they sprang forth from the concealing bushes and almost collided with High Mage Cornelius.

He was a tall, strikingly handsome man in his upper twenties. Wrapped in a long golden cloak, he sported a broad chest, short-cut black hair, a neatly trimmed goatee, and penetrating blue eyes.

For a second, they stood facing each other. Then Clement saw the color drain from the high mage's face. He wasn't looking at Clement. His frightened eyes were fixed upon Darien. The enchanter's face flushed with unsuppressed fury, exceeding even his hatred for Sylvia. Murder shone in his eyes.

"You!" Darien growled through gritted teeth. "Desecria!"

The enchanter screamed the spell, launching his hands toward his victim. Massive tendrils of black lightning spewed from his fingers. Like a swarm of snake-like voids, the spray of deadly energy sucked the light from the surrounding air. A deafening crackle resounded through the park as the incantation tore through the night.

Desecria represented the most powerful and deadly spell known to wizardry. Dating back to before written records, some speculated it might be the most powerful destructive incantation known. The charm existed for only one purpose: complete and utter annihilation. Extremely advanced and difficult to learn, the spell remained a necessity for any spellcaster. Few spells unleashed more devastation upon one's enemy.

More than any other spell, Desecria drew power directly from the life force and mental fortitude of the welder. Employing it was dangerous, because depending upon the amount of power directed into the charm it left the caster physically weakened to the point of exhaustion. Occasionally spellcasters even died from casting it. To a strong sorcerer, the draining effect only became overtly crippling if they casted it too many times in a single battle or channeled too much of their own energy to increase the potency. Still, most sorcerers saved the incantation as a last resort or to obliterate an opponent with one powerful single-minded attack. Clearly, Darien intended the latter.

Cornelius summoned his magic, focusing the energy into a shield around him. The lightning ripped through the shell, tearing the defense to pieces. Still, the buffer deflected the bolts just enough for Cornelius to dive beneath. He recovered quickly, tumbling back to his feet but didn't counter-attack. Instead, he assumed a defensive posture.

"Darien, we must leave!" Clement shouted.

Darien ignored him. Stumbling forward, his strength drained by the Desecria spell, he wasted no time renewing his assault.

"Zemliya," Darien shouted, clapping his hands together. Again, the high mage summoned his magic around him. A shower of needle-like stones erupted from the ground, pummeling his defenses. The loud crash of the rocks exploding against the hastily summoned shield echoed through the courtyard.

"Darien, he's stalling for reinforcements!" Clement screamed. "The academy is just yards away. We must get out of here!"

Darien either didn't hear the warning or didn't care. He strode toward his adversary focused on maintaining the deadly barrage. With each second, the pummeling became more intense, and the high mage's face turned red with the effort of keeping the shield steady against the onslaught.

"He is weakening," Darien shouted, "Help me!"

Clement looked around anxiously but realized that Darien wouldn't leave until the battle was over.

"Razreevat!" Clement shouted.

A series of thin silver streaks burst from his fingers in rapid succession. With a loud blast, the projectiles whipped toward Cornelius with frightening speed and accuracy.

"Rasseyat!" screamed a female voice about two dozen yards to the right.

A blue streak of light collided with Clement's spell. The silvery beams scattered, splintering off in random directions before fizzling out of existence.

Clement turned and saw a teenage girl with short black hair charging toward the battle. Behind her followed several others. All wore the flowing silver robes denoting their status as apprentices. Still, they raced valiantly to the rescue of their esteemed headmaster. Dispatching them would be an easy task, but the youths likely represented only the beginning of the reinforcements. He and Darien could probably win a prolonged battle, but that wasn't why they came.

"Time to go. You can stay if you want, but I'm leaving!"

Surrounding himself in a bubble of defensive magic, Clement raced for the nearby city streets. Looking back, he saw Darien cast a last contemptuous look at the struggling high mage before following Clement's lead. Spells bounced harmlessly off Clement's shield. The apprentices lacked the power to pierce their defenses, and the high mage remained temporarily weakened. Clement didn't give him the chance to recover. Reaching the nearby street, Clement raised his arm, crying, "Timan!"

The air crackled. Gray misty bubbles appeared, hovering over the street and park. An instant later, they popped in unison, wrapping the entire area in thick fog. The mist grew, expanding to cover the entire northern section of the city. Clement heard the high mage shout spells to disperse the fog, but the counter charm took several minutes to cast. By then, he and Darien would be gone.

CHAPTER

3

Clement and Darien raced down the street searching for a place to hide. They needed to get out of the open before the high mage could disperse the fog. Spotting a shabby stone house to the left, Clement grabbed Darien's arm and gestured toward the run-down building. Darien nodded, and they hurried for the door.

"Otkreeteeyay!" Clement shouted, pointing at the handle.

A loud gust of wind swept from his hand, striking the door. The barrier thrust open. Clement and Darien leapt into the house. Darien slammed the door behind them, barring and locking the passage.

An elderly couple sat in front of a fireplace in the hut's lone room. They wore dirty, ragged clothing. Their leathery skin was wrinkled and weathered. They looked up in terror as the cloaked figures burst into the house. Clement strode toward them. The woman, knitting in a ragged old armchair, held up her yarn and gave a feeble shriek. The elderly man, whittling in an old rocking chair, tried to rise.

"Zaseespat!" Clement said.

He held out his hand with the middle fingers curled down. His index finger pointed at the man. The little finger pointed at the woman. Two beams of pale-blue light shot from the outstretched tips, striking the couple. The old lady's half-knitted sweater fell into her lap, and her head dropped onto her chest. The man collapsed into the chair, the block of wood and whittling knife falling from his hand. His head reclined backward, and a loud snore escaped his lips.

"You did not kill them?" Darien asked, surveying the sleeping couple.

"No," said Clement, "I didn't come here to murder helpless citizens. The man and woman will wake up tomorrow and think our visit was a dream, if they remember at all."

Darien gave a quick smile but hid the expression behind an emotionless mask. Nodding, he strolled to the window and gazed into the darkness.

"The fog is dispersing," he observed. "They will be moving down the street within the next few minutes. We might do well to put up some concealment spells."

"True," Clement agreed. "Know any good ones?"

"I do," said a female voice from the fireplace, causing both men to jump.

The air in front of the hearth shimmered. Before their astonished eyes appeared a young woman barely older than thirty. She wore light-blue robes, inner garments wrapped tightly around her lithe, shapely body. She reclined leisurely, her left arm resting on the mantle as she stared at them in amusement.

Exceptionally blonde hair reached past her shoulders to the center of her back. Her eyes were an enchanting green and seemed to glow like a cat's. Her silky skin lacked the slightest blemish to tarnish her delicate features. Altogether, she possessed a simple and alluring beauty most men would find attractive. Clement wasn't one of them.

"You!" he hissed.

His arms shot toward her. Energy surged to his hands. A deadly spell sprang to his lips. The woman smiled smugly, taking no actions to defend herself. Darien dove in front of Clement, grabbing his arms.

"No, someone will hear you! We cannot afford to give away our location over this rat!"

Clement stepped back, yanking his arms free. He glared menacingly at the woman. She gave an arrogant smirk, holding her head high as she gazed down her upturned nose. Darien looked at her, his eyes narrowing as he studied her haughty expression.

"So," he said, gazing at her like filth on his shoes, "Lillian the Insidious returns home."

Lillian's smile dropped.

"Don't call me by that name," she hissed.

"What?" Darien said in mock surprise. "You do not like your 'insidious' title? You were not ashamed of having the smallest kingdom, the weakest army, and the feeblest powers. Why should you be bothered by a name?"

"Men," Lillian said, "so obsessed with size. And yet your inflated militaries and massive territories proved helpless against my network of spies and assassins. While you murdered loyal advisors and friends to weed out my agents, I held your kingdoms locked within the clutches of my invisible hand. I possessed true power. All you cared about is being the biggest. Compensating for something, I suppose."

"How would you know?" Darien retorted. "When were you ever with a man, excuse me, I mean a man who did not suddenly die a horrific death the moment you started feeling the slightest love for him? How sad that all your spies and plagues and access to the complete writings of the magical academy still left you helpless to break my curse as your paramours died one by one before your eyes."

Lillian lifted her head high.

"It taught me a lesson. There's no place for emotion in the life of a ruler."

"Except fear, you mean," Darien said. "After all, oh cowardly one, it was you who hoisted the white flag above your castle the moment Sylvia's forces set foot upon your land, fleeing your kingdom like a scared child!"

"All of these insults and attacks, so ungrateful after I saved your lives."

"What are you talking about?" Darien asked.

Clement shook his head. He knew exactly what she was talking about. And he now knew who he had heard on the balcony outside the queen's bedchamber.

"Oh, seriously," Lillian said. "Even you're not naïve enough to believe the guard tripped over his own feet before hacking Clement to pieces. Or, maybe you believe the magical barriers disappeared on their own."

"No," Clement said, advancing toward her, "but neither are we 'naive enough' to believe you saved us out of generosity! You always have ulterior motives. Regardless, if you're going to enchant the house, you better do so! At least we can find out what you want and get rid of your nauseating presence!"

Lillian made a "Humph." Lillian threw her long hair behind her head. She closed her eyes and waved her left hand, palm outward, in an arc before her.

"Prayat," she sang in a melodic voice.

The room filled with a thousand swirling pin pricks of light no bigger than a marble. The luminous orbs hovered like stars in the night sky, spinning softly. With each rotation, the balls grew smaller until completely vanishing.

"There," Lillian stated.

Clement frowned. He recognized the spell from previous dealings with spies and provocateurs. It concealed the presence of anyone inside the room from all attempts to discern their location. Further, the enchantment prevented itself from detection. It remained a favorite among suspicious individuals because the spell collapsed if anyone other than the caster summoned magical energy inside the protected radius.

"How clever," Clement scowled. "Casting an incantation effective only as long as we don't attack you."

"I'm no fool," she said. "We all know how we feel about each other, and none of you are above blasting me in the back the moment my head is turned. Caution is reasonable."

"You mistake us for yourself," Clement said. "We fight people head on. We didn't need to degrade ourselves by resorting to underhanded means to build our kingdoms."

"Underhanded," Lillian said in airy disbelief, crossing her arms. "I have no clue what you're talking about."

"Using a plague to wipe out every nobleman and royal ahead of you in line for the throne?" Clement asked. "You don't call that underhanded?"

"I call it resourceful," Lillian answered loftily.

"And murdering your father in his sleep?"

"Opportunistic."

"And framing innocent apprentices for his death?"

"I pardoned them a year later."

"I'm sure that provided great comfort during the year they stewed in your dungeon."

"Oh, what do you care about some stupid apprentices?" Lillian burst out. "And what do you care how I killed my father? He's the one who expelled you from the magical academy just because you were poor! You should thank me!"

"Thank you?" Clement fumed. "You robbed me of my victory."

At the time of Lillian's rise to power, Clement's armies were moving steadily southward. His plan put him on pace to conquer Rhoria within months. Revenge against his former master, Lillian's father, Sorin was within his grasp, along with control over all western Aurba. Lillian stole both.

"Regardless," Darien interrupted, "none of this has anything to do with why we are here."

"True," Clement agreed still addressing Lillian, "what do you want? Why were you on the queen's balcony tonight?"

"The same reason you were," Lillian answered. "Revenge."

"Going to murder her in her sleep?" Darien scoffed, "I am not surprised. You never had the guts to face someone capable of fighting back."

"My way is twice as clean and just as effective. Perhaps if you didn't have all the subtlety of a raging rhino, you could try it yourself."

"Anyway," Clement interrupted, "back to the point at hand. Why'd you follow us, and what do you want?"

"You're supposed to be smart," she said. "Why don't you put that hollow cavity between your ears to work and answer the question yourself?"

The answer required little thought. She obviously wanted something they possessed. Not a physical object, which she could simply steal after their deaths. Rather, she desired information. She had not come to them before they entered the queen's room but followed them afterward. So, the information must be related to something inside the room.

"The cloth," Clement said, "you wish to know what it means."

"I do."

"Well, Darien, as much as it pains me to agree with her, I'd also like to know what it means. But first," he added, turning back to Lillian, "tell us what happened in the queen's room tonight."

"No, that's my bargaining leverage. Once you tell me about the cloth, I'll tell you what happened in the room. Besides, I've already made the first compromise by casting the concealment spell. You can make the second."

"Fine," Darien answered, ripping the fabric from his pocket and tossing it onto the ground. "Here it is."

Lillian picked up the cloth, examining the symbols.

"What does it mean?" she asked.

"How should I know?" Darien answered, moving the curtain aside and glancing out the window.

"I swear you're the world's worst liar," she said, shaking her head in condescension. "I saw your face when you looked at it. You recognized the symbol immediately."

"All right," Darien said, turning from the window. "The symbol is a coat of arms belonging to the descendants of an ancient bloodline. The name of the family is Junlorace. They dwell in a secluded fortress hidden deep in the Blood Fang Mountains, along the southeastern border of my former kingdom. According to rumors, the family and the keep have existed for over a millennium, protecting the land from the powerful and ancient lord of the demons, Darlyth."

"Darlyth?" Lillian repeated, "I thought Darlyth was dead."

"No," Clement corrected in a sarcastic tone. "Seriously, your father was the kingdom's foremost expert on the history of the Demon Wars. Did you never listen to anything he taught? Or is that why he refused to take his own daughter as an apprentice?"

Lillian's eyes flashed. She glared at Clement but he ignored her.

"According to legend," Clement began, performing an accurate, but mocking impression of Lillian's father, "Darlyth was the lord of the demons and the only demon capable of using magic. His magic was so powerful that no mortal could stand against him. A thousand years ago, he led his creations on a quest to conquer humanity. The ten greatest sorcerers of the age, led by the legendary Kendross, crafted two enchanted spheres and placed Darlyth into a deep slumber. As long as the spheres remain intact, the demon lord and his minions remain imprisoned. The orbs rest to this day, guarded by the most devout warriors. No demon has been seen since that time."

Clement finished and gave Lillian a smug look.

"Your information is outdated," she replied. "A demon has been seen since that time."

"When?" Clement challenged. "By whom?"

"Tonight. By me. That's what happened in Sylvia's bedchamber. A demon kidnapped her. I was about to break into her room when I felt the power sink. I looked up and saw a demon materialize out of thin air. I'm lucky I didn't get cut to shreds as he escaped through the window."

"So, you're telling me the demons have broken free from their slumber," Clement said in disbelief.

"I am not surprised," Darien said. Clement and Lillian stared at him. "Prior to Sylvia's rise to power, I received reports indicating corruption among the guardians of Junlorace Keep. Apparently centuries of confinement coupled with a lack of new recruits drove them to desperate means for survival."

"Countless generations isolated inside an aging fortress in an impassable and monster-infested wilderness will do that," Clement mused. "After seven years in a similar situation, I should know. We can assume the same fate befell whoever guarded the other orb."

"But how did you find out?" Lillian asked. "Surely you had other things occupying your time without worrying about the events of a random keep in the middle of the Blood Fang Mountains. And why did my spies never report this news to me?"

"Indignant that I slipped one past you?" Darien asked. "Perhaps your spies did not have my kingdom 'down upon its knees' as much as you thought."

"Don't kid yourself," Lillian snapped. "My spies held you like a vise. You couldn't even sneeze inside your castle without my knowing!"

"And yet you completely missed over a month of secret operations within the Blood Fang Mountains involving more than a dozen of my highest-ranking generals and apprentices."

"What happened?" Clement asked, interrupting the sparring match.

"Toward the end of my reign, I sent a scouting party into the mountains to monitor for signs of invasion. Although I doubted anyone was foolish enough to march an army through those forsaken lands, I could not completely rule out the possibility of such an attack. So, I occasionally sent patrols of soldiers, who I disliked or wanted eliminated, to scout the land looking for hostile forces. Once in a while, one of the patrols even returned."

Darien shook his head in bewilderment at how such a bizarre and unfortunate event could happen.

"Anyway," he continued, "this particular patrol found a weak and tired man wandering the woods. He begged to be taken before me. I granted him an audience, and he told me the most remarkable tale. He claimed he escaped from Junlorace Keep, one of the two ancient fortresses holding the golden orbs imprisoning the demon lord. He further explained that his family had served as guardians for many generations. But now, he said, a powerful cult of madmen and insane sorcerers was gaining power over the keep. The group, he explained, planned to destroy both orbs, thereby freeing the demon lord from his sleep. He warned me about the danger and told me I could identify the servants of the cult by the Junlorace family coat of arms worn on their tunics. The symbol is the same one adorning the cloth."

Clement and Lillian listened intently, waiting for him to continue.

"I was intrigued by the report, although I could not be sure it was not a trap. I offered him food and rest, intending to speak to him more on the subject later. However, he died mysteriously in his sleep the following night. I was rather alarmed for a guest to die under the shelter of my own roof without me being the killer, so I sent a group of agents to the fort, under the guise of ambassadors, offering to provide them assistance and help in the protection of the orb."

Clement gave a loud groan, burying his head in in his hands.

"Oh, give him a break, Clement" Lillian said, smiling in amusement. "Stealth and subterfuge were never Darien's strongest talents."

Darien gave Lillian a withering look. He started to retort, but Clement jumped back into the conversation.

"After they all vanished never to be heard from again, what did you do?"

"I waited to hear back for two weeks," he said, beginning again.

If he was irritated by Clement's ability to predict the result as though the end was obvious, his irritation only increased when Clement reacted by burying his head in his hands again. Even Lillian shook her head in disbelief. Darien's voice grew in volume as his face turned red.

"Then I dispatched a group of my most skilled apprentices and thieves to infiltrate the keep. I ordered them to scout the area secretly, gathering as much information as possible. If necessary, I planned to steal the orb before its destruction. Unfortunately, I became distracted by the swift and sudden rise of Sylvia. Within the next few months, my kingdom came under attack, and I was over-thrown. Thus, I never finished my plans."

"You don't need to worry about the orbs anymore," Lillian said. "From what I saw, they are destroyed and the demons are free."

"But," Clement interjected. "If Darlyth is free, why hasn't he revealed himself? Darien learned about the cult and their intentions seven years ago. Why has he made no move before now?"

"In the Demon Wars, Darlyth was defeated by powerful wizards," Lillian observed. "He may fear such a fate occurring again."

"Perhaps he fears Sylvia's growing power," Clement suggested, "He may want to eliminate her before she can become a threat."

"I don't think so," Lillian replied. "If the demon wanted to kill Sylvia, he could've done so. Instead, he kidnapped her. I suspect he was targeting her tiara."

Clement looked at Lillian in blank confusion.

"Why would the demon target a headband?" Darien asked.

"For the same reason I was," she responded, smiling at their bewildered faces. "Her tiara is the source of her might. You see, I knew Sylvia before her rise to power. She and I attended the academy together and apprenticed under the same master. We hated each other. She was an annoying goody two-shoes, too weak to pursue the avenues of true power. I daresay I had a good assessment of her capabilities. She was an above-average sorceress at best. Even that may be giving her too much credit. The powers she displayed in her battles against us were far beyond anything I believed her capable of wielding. During exile, I found myself questioning her changed nature. How did she quadruple her strength in such a short period of time?"

Clement listened with interest. He had wondered the same thing many times himself.

"Then I thought about the tiara. After her rise to power, she wore the headband constantly, even in her sleep. Yet, I couldn't remember seeing Sylvia wear any piece of jewelry on her head, even so much as a hairpin, during her entire apprenticeship. The development seemed suspicious. I began investigating the history of the object.

"I knew I could be wrong. But after researching, bribing, and extorting information from every vulnerable source, I managed to gleam a few details concerning its history. Apparently, it was crafted shortly after her husband's death."

"She was married?" Clement asked.

"Oh yes. Before her rebellion against our kingdoms, her husband Robert was a teacher at the academy. He died about a year before her rise to power, bitten by a death spider."

Lillian shot a look at Clement, who smiled. Death spiders represented the pinnacle of his creative skills. Through a combination of breeding and magic, he forged them. A spy released them into Lillian's palace. The poisonous pests failed to kill the spymaster but spread like fire throughout the city. Lillian never truly eradicated the infestation, although sightings and deaths dropped significantly after her palace burned down.

"I guess I know why Sylvia hates me so much," he said smirking.

"I doubt she felt positive feelings for any of us," Lillian replied. "As an apprentice, she always spouted idealistic rubbish about honor, virtue, and other stupid stuff. I wanted to gouge out my ears just to escape her speeches. Anyway, I learned the crown was forged by her children."

"Her children," Darien and Clement exclaimed in unison.

"Yes," she said, waving in a dismissing gesture, "she had three children. According to my research, they were extremely gifted young prodigies. They forged the crown as a gift. It enhances her magical powers to incredible levels."

"So," Clement said, "you planned to steal the tiara to enhance your powers."

"I doubt the process is so simple," Lillian said, shaking her head. "Sylvia isn't a fool, and though her children were young they weren't fools either. I'm confident the crown is protected with a self-charm."

"That's why the demon kidnapped her," Clement said, understanding dawning. "Only she or someone she gives it to can use it. The demon lord needs her to willingly give him the crown."

"Exactly," Lillian agreed.

"But why were you after the crown if it is useless to you?" Darien asked.

"Isn't it obvious?" Lillian said, rolling her eyes. "I want to steal the crown so she can't use it. Without the tiara, she can't maintain control of her kingdom and suppress the corrupt political forces lurking within. In time, her empire will fall, and I'll have my revenge."

"Nice," sneered Darien. "Just grab the headband and run away like a child. Let others do your work for you. Good to see exile did not change you."

Lillian opened her mouth, but Clement spoke first. "Where are her children now?"

"I don't know," Lillian responded, taking her eyes off Darien. "No one knows. I can't find a shred of information concerning their whereabouts. In fact, I can't find a single reference to them or a single person who has seen them since before Sylvia's rise to power. They appear to have vanished completely!"

"Strange," Clement mused. "Three children capable of forging a legendary artifact at a young age must be growing stronger. Their skill and fame should be hard to keep secret."

"Regardless," Lillian said, "right now we have more pressing issues. If Darlyth gets a hold of the tiara and his already legendary powers are multiplied more than threefold, all the wizards in the world won't be enough to defeat him."

"Does he really think Sylvia will give it to him?" Clement wondered aloud.

"Everyone has a breaking point," Darien said, shrugging. "We know as well as anyone about the power of torture."

"What I don't understand," Lillian interjected, "is why they left behind the cloth. Why do they want people to know they kidnapped her?"

"Maybe they always leave evidence behind," Clement suggested. "There are cults who perform such actions. They may not believe anyone will recognize the symbol. Without Darien, you and I wouldn't understand its meaning."

"They may not care," Darien said. "With Sylvia gone, who will stand against him? The high mage? The demon lord can crush him without a thought."

"Perhaps," Lillian acknowledged, "but something doesn't feel right."

"I agree," Darien said. "If Darlyth is the only demon capable of using magic, who created the power sink? Who paralyzed the guards? How did the demon get into her room without anyone noticing?"

"I don't know the answer to any of those questions," Lillian said.

"Me neither," Clement replied. "But I do know one thing. I have no intention of letting Darlyth rise to power."

Lillian and Darien looked at Clement in surprise. He smiled maliciously.

"This world is mine," he declared. "I didn't spend years building power to waste my life enslaved to some demon with a stupid piece of headgear!"

"Surely you are not telling me," Darien said. "You are going into the heart of the Blood Fangs to save Sylvia from the demon lord."

"I am," Clement acknowledged. "And after I save the queen, I'm going to kill her! I want to see how tough she is without her hat."

"Uh, Clement," Lillian said, "you know your powers are no match for the demon lord right? Don't get me wrong, I've got no problem with you getting killed. And I regret not getting to watch. But you do realize you're going to die!"

"Yes," Clement said sarcastically, "because I'm really planning to fight him one-on-one! Come on! I'm going to do exactly what you wanted to do tonight. I'll sneak into the fortress, destroy the crown, and kill Sylvia. Then I'll sneak out again."

"Right," Lillian said with equal sarcasm, "because you're so stealthy! You'll be lucky to get within ten feet of the castle."

"Well, if you're so good, you can come watch. You'll get your wish of seeing me die, and we can find out if you have enough guts to make your own attempt," Clement said.

Darien laughed. "Lillian never kills anyone who is not already asleep!"

Lillian smiled as though the observation were a compliment while Darien turned to Clement. "Do not pretend you can kill Sylvia! Everyone knows the story of your last battle. Your best option remains using the orb. To do so, you need my help. Besides, I cannot kill you until we destroy the orb!"

"And whose brilliant idea was making that oath?" Clement exclaimed.

"Great!" Lillian rejoined. "You're exactly who Clement needs. You couldn't be stealthy if your life depended on it. Which, by the way, it will!"

"Fine, when Darlyth takes over the world, you can sit around thinking about how right you were. Maybe Darlyth needs concubines," Darien mumbled.

"I don't think your curse will work on him," Lillian responded. She turned and headed toward the door. Grabbing the handle, she looked back toward them. "If we're going, we better leave soon. We can get out of town more easily under the cover of night. Besides, your sleep spell won't hold the couple forever."

"Wait a minute," Darien protested, "who invited you along?"

"Clement did," Lillian answered.

Clement opened his mouth to object, but Lillian cut him off.

"You said I could tag along and watch you get killed. Sounds like fun. Besides, I came here to destroy the tiara. I can use the time while the guards kill you to complete my task. At least your deaths won't be in vain. Darlyth will kill Sylvia once the tiara is gone. So, your actions will bring about the queen's death. You see, we have a win-win situation!"

Clement and Darien looked at each other. Lillian was a conniving and dangerous opponent, but she knew their plans. If she was traveling with them, they were in a better position to watch for any treachery.

"Very well," Clement said, "I would demand a promise that you won't do anything to jeopardize our mission, but since I've no desire to take a blood oath, and you've no honor, the point seems mute."

"Good," Lillian answered, "glad to see we can skip the formalities."

Clement continued. "If I see the least sign of treachery, I know six hundred ways to kill a person, and I'll make sure you experience at least one of them if it's the last thing I do."

"It would be," she said.

She opened the door. Peering outside, she moved into the night. Darien followed, but Clement held back. He glanced at the elderly couple, his eyes taking in their ragged clothes and dilapidated home. He pulled three gold royals from the pocket of his robes and tossed them onto the floor.

"For your troubles," he whispered and hurried away.

CHAPTER

4

Rhoria was the second-oldest city in Aurba and the most poorly designed. The streets were small and cramped. Numerous alleyways intersected the tangle of crisscrossing avenues to form a web of random passages even natives struggled to navigate. The architectural nightmare played well into the hands of the criminal element and allowed the neater city of Rayessburg, once Clement's capitol, to dominate trade on the continent.

Still, Sylvia chose Rhoria as her capital, and the town remained the center of magical study and military might. Clement was thankful for her decision. Escaping unseen through the streets of Rayessburg would be virtually impossible. But with Lillian's help, they managed to maneuver unseen through Rhoria's maze of avenues and back roads.

Apparently the guards concluded Darien and Clement had already escaped. As time passed, the number of search parties dwindled to only a few patrols. The hour was well past midnight. Lights in most houses and streetlamps were burnt out, and a powerful snowstorm sweeping through the city aided the covert journey. The biggest challenge remained escaping through the outer wall without being spotted by watchmen. The stone fortifications stood over fifteen feet high, and sentries patrolled every few yards. Lillian assured her companions she could get them out with minimal fuss.

Darien wrapped his cloak tightly around himself, and Lillian muttered quietly. Clement suspected she was uttering warming spells, protecting herself from the cold. After hours of walking, they reached the outer wall. Lillian directed them toward the nearest gate. Before they took four steps, Darien stopped. The enchanter stared behind them, his eyes fixed on a strange shape moving through the hazy darkness. Observing Darien's bizarre behavior, Lillian and Clement stopped as well. Following his gaze, they discerned the form of an old woman.

She hobbled toward them. Her body bent low over a rickety wood cane as she slowly and seemingly painfully limped their direction. She wore a thick black woolen cloak with a hood pulled over her head, shielding her aged frame from the freezing winds. Beneath the hood, they saw the ancient face of a weary wanderer. Her skin was wrinkled and cracked from too many days spent in bad weather. Her ancient lips formed a crinkled scowl, curving inward as though lacking teeth. The most notable feature, though, remained her eyes. The milky balls shone bright in the wintery sky, clear and unseeing. She was blind. But she stared ahead at where they stood. In her left hand, she held a begging cup indicating a wordless plea for alms.

Darien stared at her, contempt slicing a path across his normally placid face. Lillian looked bewildered. Clement couldn't blame her. Rhoria boasted a population of more than three thousand citizens. Beggars weren't uncommon. Some elderly transient spotting the company was inconsequential, a blind beggar even more so. But Darien stood rooted to the spot, glowering at the aged vagabond. Waves of intense loathing radiated from his body like a venomous ooze.

Clement's surprise turned to irritation. He didn't understand Darien's aggressive stance toward the woman. Whatever the cause, the delay was slowing their progress. If the enchanter wanted to kill the old hag, he needed to do so. At the very least, they couldn't afford to linger any longer.

"Darien..." Clement began.

Before he could get any further, his companion cut him off. The enchanter started shouting in the quiet night air.

"I know who you are, witch!" he declared. "Your disguise does not fool me. What do you want?"

The woman stopped in her tracks. The milky white eyes shimmered, revealing two round black pupils. The ebony orbs stared straight at them. The lips of the wrinkled face curled upward into an evil toothless grin. The stranger knew who they were and didn't fear them. The begging cup in her hand vanished in a small wisp of swirling blue smoke. The now-empty hand gestured toward a blank wall to her left. Responding to the motion, the bricks started shifting. A doorway manifested in the middle of the formerly blank façade, casting warm streaks of bright firelight through the opening. With a flick of her wrist, the begging cup reappeared in her wrinkled hand. The black-cloaked stranger stood motionless, waiting for them.

Lillian hesitated. Clement glanced at Darien. The enchanter ignored them, not taking his eyes off the mysterious woman. Striding across the building snow, he headed toward her. Exchanging a quick look, Lillian and Clement followed.

"Darien," Clement said catching up to him, "what in the world?"

"Xanaphia," Darien said, the name escaping his lips in a hiss.

Stunned, Clement slowed his pace. Xanaphia was a name he knew only too well. The sorceress was the first of the four tyrants to forge her kingdom and also the first to fall. Xanaphia forged an empire easily as large and powerful as either Darien or Clement. She was a master of necromancy, arguably the greatest expert on death magic to live in the modern age. Armed with hordes of monstrous undead abominations, the "Dark Queen of Suffering" marched armies across the land with unrestrained brutality. Clement vividly remembered many bloody battles fought against the merciless foe.

Clement always felt glad her kingdom shared a larger border with Darien. The conflict between Darien and Xanaphia was legendary. They often led armies against each other. Minstrels across the land still sang ballads about their duels. Sources claimed Darien feared Xanaphia more than Clement and Lillian combined.

The necromancer awaited the arrival of the company. Once Darien approached within a dozen yards, she stepped into the doorway, disappearing from sight. Darien followed, but Lillian didn't. Her eyes wide with curiosity, she paused to examine the doorway.

"What a unique spell," she muttered to herself. "This could be useful to me. How to strip the secret from her . . ."

"That," Clement sneered, "requires a combination of brains, which you lack, and brawn, of which you have even less. You might do better to steal them from Sylvia. I hear she thoroughly looted Xanaphia's library after her victory."

"I didn't think there was much left of her library after your arsonists burned down the building," Lillian said, straightening up.

"She managed to salvage some of her materials," he said. "Although she was pretty upset. Serves her right though, after she transformed so many of my apprentices and mistresses into undead monstrosities, still alive and screaming during the ritual."

"Any woman who sleeps with you deserves a horrific death," Lillian responded. "Besides, I suppose it was just coincidence that the spell for unquenchable fire you used on her library was later used by her on my palace."

"Ah, yes," he sighed, "it was one of the happiest days of my young life."

He strode through the portal without looking to see her reaction, finding himself standing in a small room with bright flames issuing from a large fire pit in the middle of the floor. The walls were completely blank. A small wooden table sat in the far corner with several loaves of sourdough bread and a few canteens resting on top.

He could see the old woman standing beside the fire opposite the doorway. Directly across from her stood Darien. They glared so intently at each other that neither noticed Clement's entrance. This pleased him, and trying to remain insignificant he quietly took a seat to Darien's right.

Lillian entered the room shortly thereafter. She lingered momentarily, appraising the situation. Noting where everyone stood, she crossed the room, taking a spot opposite the fire from Clement. Lillian reclined against the wall. Placing her hands behind her head, she stretched her legs looking perfectly at ease. Her casual manner caught the attention of Xanaphia. Taking her eyes off Darien, the necromancer scowled at Lillian before turning to Clement. She scrutinized him, giving a short derisive snort before returning her attention to Darien.

The entryway dissolved, replaced by a thick brick wall. Standing before the assembly, the old woman reached up. With a flourish, she yanked off her cloak. As it whisked off her body, her image grew blurry. When the haze cleared, the old woman was gone.

In her place, a woman in her late thirties stood towering above the company. She was incredibly tall, even taller than Darien, with a strange, unnatural beauty, more unnerving than attractive. She possessed smooth, flawless skin. Yet the skin possessed an unnatural shade of white, as pale as the snow falling outside, and had a waxy appearance. She possessed deep, penetrating eyes. But the pupils of the eyes were pure black, lacking irises and bright red veins stretched across the outsides. Her dark black hair hung long, but the dark strands swayed with their own life, as though agitated by hot steams rising from a furnace. Her thin black lips stood in stark contrast to her white skin, adding to the ominous appearance.

Clement, who'd never seen Xanaphia without the cloak, was caught off guard by the transformation. He tried to hide his surprise, but Xanaphia noticed the flicker of astonishment. Glancing at him, she gave a small self-satisfied smirk.

Lillian, reclining on the floor, seemed amused by the change. She apparently possessed enough agents in the witch's kingdom to have a solid knowledge of her enemy's true appearance. Darien, who knew Xanaphia well, was unfazed by the alteration.

Staring at his enemy's true form, Clement saw Darien's anger swell. Standing before him was the one person Darien hated more than any other. Xanaphia and he had apprenticed together under the same master at the Rhorian Academy. They initially became friendly rivals, competing for the attention and praise of their mentor. It wasn't long before the competition escalated into all-out war. Xanaphia transformed Darien's familiar and pet cat into an undead zombie. Darien responded by poisoning Xanaphia's food. The healers saved her, life but the concoction altered her body forever. The chemicals turned her skin a pale wintery white and distorted her eyes to be forever black. Afterward, she created the magic cloak, concealing her true appearance.

After their master broke up the fighting, the rivals ignored each other for the next two years. Then Xanaphia approached Darien. She apologized to him, suggesting they forget the past and start over. For a while, they became very close. Many in the school commented with surprise on the newfound friendship, which soon blossomed into romance. Still, Darien never completely trusted her, and his suspicions proved correct. One night, Xanaphia seduced him, lured him into bed, and attempted to kill him. Only a combination of quick reflexes and quick thinking saved his life.

Alarmed by the sounds of battle, their teacher came to investigate. Hearing the master coming, Xanaphia stopped her attack. Darien didn't. In his rage, he fired a powerful killing spell at her back. Xanaphia sensed the danger and dove out of the way. The spell rebounded off a wall, striking the aged teacher, killing him instantly. Hearing the footsteps of the other students and teachers coming, Darien leapt from his tower window, using his magic to soften the landing.

With no clothes and only a few possessions, he fled the city. Fearing blame for her instructor's death, Xanaphia also fled. The two never returned to the academy, and both blamed the other for their teacher's death. Xanaphia blamed Darien for casting the spell. Darien blamed Xanaphia for starting the fight.

"We are all together now," Xanaphia said. She had a shrill, unnatural sounding voice as a result of the poisoning, which she could also mask with the cloak, though she made no effort to do so now. "Kind of like a family gathering, don't you think?"

Clement gave a derisive snort. "Maybe, if your family consists of a bunch of psychopathic killers who would just as soon murder each other as look at each other."

"Do not rule out the possibility," Darien said. "Such an upbringing might explain how she grew up to become a monster!"

Lillian gave a laugh.

"Why're you laughing?" Xanaphia sneered. "Your family is the epitome of Clement's description. By the way, I hear they took down the statue of your mother. You know, the life-sized one that mysteriously appeared in the middle of town after she accused you of murdering your father."

Lillian shrugged.

"I told her to keep her mouth shut. She said, 'make me.' So I did."

Clement looked at Lillian. "I thought her mouth was open in the statue."

"Yeah," Lillian replied, "the spell took longer to cast than planned. Some things are all about timing."

"Anyway," Darien interrupted, "what do you want, Xana?"

Clement's eyes widened at hearing Darien use a nickname. Lillian too looked astonished at Darien's audacity. Xanaphia's eyes flashed, and her pale face flushed with rage.

"Where is she?" Xanaphia hissed at Darien through gritted teeth.

"Where is who?" Darien retorted.

"Don't play coy with me! The word is out all over the castle. You kidnapped Sylvia. I want to know where she is."

"Why?"

"Because I didn't come all the way up here just to be robbed of my vengeance by you scum!" Xanaphia declared angrily, her hair whipping as though caught in a typhoon.

"Wait," Clement said, "you came to Rhoria tonight with the intention of getting revenge against Sylvia too!"

"Yes!" she snapped. "Unlike you three, I plotted revenge on my own!"

"Please," said Lillian, "like I would plot my revenge with these buffoons! I came here on my own too!"

"Wow! The stars really aligned against Sylvia tonight," Darien observed. "Four separate plots launched on the same day within mere hours of each other."

Xanaphia held up a hand. "Wait a minute. Are you telling me each of you arrived independently to launch an attack against Sylvia on the same night?"

"No," Clement responded. "Darien and I came together."

"My plot, Lillian's, and the men's," Xanaphia said ruefully. "I suppose the fourth plot will answer my question concerning Sylvia's location."

"Perhaps," Darien shrugged. "But why should we tell you? Even if we know where she is, what makes you think you can get to her? And if you do, what could you hope to accomplish?"

"I agree," Clement said. "Darien and I recognized our limitations and worked together. Lillian recognized her limitations and tried to reach Sylvia in her sleep. But you don't have Lillian's stealth and you appear to be working alone. What do you hope to achieve when you find her?"

"My plans are none of your business," Xanaphia spat.

"Sylvia's whereabouts are none of yours," Lillian replied. "What do we care if you get your revenge? We have enough troubles trying to carry out our own vendettas without worrying about yours."

Xanaphia glared at Lillian. With a quick angry gesture, she reached for the shining blue handle of a dagger sheathed on her right hip. Yanking the weapon from the holster, she held the dazzling turquoise and red stone blade into the firelight. She pointed the weapon directly at Lillian, who scrambled backward in alarm. The knife was only about a foot long and extremely thin. It looked both fragile and deadly. Darien's eyes narrowed.

"Is that a violet quartz crystal dagger?" Lillian asked, her voice filled with a mixture of shock and awe.

"Yes!" Xanaphia said. "I intended to use the weapon on Sylvia. Yet, I can satisfy myself by employing it on one of you!"

"You can try," Clement responded. "Do you really think we're going to let you cast the absorption spell? We'd kill you the moment you started casting."

"She does not need to cast any spell," Darien said. "The dagger is enchanted. All she has to do is stab her enemy. The spell activates immediately."

"Incredible!" Lillian marveled. "Have you spent the last seven years in exile making this one deadly trinket?"

Darien interrupted again. "No, she stole it from Sylvia's treasury."

"How do you know?" Clement asked.

"Because Sylvia took possession of the dagger after defeating me. It is mine!"

"No!" Xanaphia screamed furiously. "It's mine! I made it!"

"And I killed the assassin you sent to use it against me!" Darien shouted back. "To the victor go the spoils."

"Regardless," she responded, "the dagger is mine. I regained possession. I'm the victor now!"

"You broke into Sylvia's treasury and stole the dagger?" Lillian asked. "How did you pull that off?"

"I may not be the cowardly master of stealth magic," Xanaphia said, "but I don't need to turn invisible to access forbidden places."

Waving her hand, she summoned her cloak off the floor. The robe wrapped itself around her. A moment later, Sylvia stood before the company wearing a hooded nightgown.

Lillian scrutinized the queen's doppelganger. "You don't have her tiara."

"You don't have her tiara," Xanaphia mocked, resuming her true appearance. "Who cares? The guards didn't. The fools deserved the death they received."

"If your disguise was so good, why'd you kill them?" Clement asked incredulously.

"Because a bunch of idiots caused the alarm to go off. I was about to leave and head to her room when the wailing started. The guards realized something was amiss and attempted to waylay me. Their remains will never be found!"

Clement reflected upon these words. "So, you stole the dagger, planning to kill Sylvia. Not much different than our own plan."

"Except we are going to destroy our orb," Darien interjected. "She wants to actually steal Sylvia's magic for her own!"

"Really?" Clement said with obvious amusement. "Shame she didn't succeed. I'd love to see her blow herself up."

"Yeah." Lillian smirked. "No one has ever succeeded in casting the absorption spell. What makes you think you will?"

"She has already succeeded!" Darien answered.

Clement and Lillian both gazed at him in shock. Xanaphia gave a smug smile. Suddenly, everything made sense to Clement. Darien mentioned knowing one person who succeeded in absorbing powers from a violet quartz crystal. He was referring to Xanaphia. That explained why Darien was so adamant about destroying the orb. He wasn't worried about Clement taking Sylvia's powers. He wanted to make sure the person he hated the most in the world, Xanaphia, didn't get them.

"There," Xanaphia said. "You know my story! Now, where is she?"

"Ha!" Darien snorted. "I do not fear you! Do you think I will let you steal Sylvia's power? Over my dead body!"

"I'm fine with that arrangement!" Xanaphia said, raising the dagger.

"Wait!" Clement interrupted, holding out his hands. "Stop, both of you!"

They turned to face Clement, their eyes blazing.

"Look, Darien!" Clement said. "We're a long way from worrying about her stealing Sylvia's power. If we don't hurry, Sylvia won't have any power left to steal. If that happens, she can use the dagger on whoever she wants. Doing so won't save her!"

"Save me from what?" Xanaphia asked.

Lillian, Clement, and Darien exchanged glances. They only confided in each other because each possessed information necessary to solve the puzzle surrounding Sylvia's disappearance. Xanaphia brought no such information to the table. Clement felt unsure how much to reveal.

"Before we reached Sylvia's room," he began, "Sylvia was kidnapped. Lillian watched the battle from the balcony."

"Why did none of the guards see the kidnappers?" Xanaphia asked. "How'd they kidnap her? She must've put up a fight."

"Fight is not the right term," Lillian said. "Massacre makes more sense. The enemy beat her swiftly and thoroughly."

Xanaphia appeared to blanch, although her skin was so white already one could hardly tell.

"They wanted her tiara," Lillian continued. "The tiara enhances the magical powers of the wearer."

"How do you know?" Xanaphia asked.

"Research," Lillian responded. "In any case, someone else found out also."

"Who?" Xanaphia demanded.

"A group of cultists," Clement said. "They operate out of a small fortress in the Blood Fang Mountains."

"These two morons are going after them, and I'm tagging along to watch them die. Oh! I'm also going to destroy the tiara," Lillian said.

Clement rolled his eyes, but Xanaphia seemed interested.

"Excellent," she said. "I will come too!"

"No, you will not!" Darien shouted.

"Try to stop me!" Xanaphia retorted. "If you think you can kill me, then do so. If not, you can't stop me from following!"

"But why do you want to come at all?" Clement asked. He was getting frustrated. The group seemed to be growing at an exponential rate.

"I traveled for weeks on a mission to kill Sylvia!" Xanaphia said. "I'm not stopping just because someone arrived first. Plus, I don't want to see Sylvia's powers in the hands of some unknown threat. I don't trust the feeble powers of you three weaklings to end the danger!"

Darien glared but said nothing. Lillian appeared lost for words. Clement gave a defeated laugh. He never imagined his quest for vengeance resulting in a long and perilous mission with three of the four people he hated the most in the world.

Lillian found her voice. "That's all fine and dandy, but we're about to embark on a weeklong trek. At some point we'll need sleep. Is there really anyone here willing to sleep within a mile of each other?"

The four companions eyed one another suspiciously. The long silence left no doubt regarding the answer.

"I am not sleeping anywhere near her!" Darien said pointing at Xanaphia.

"Her?" Clement exclaimed. "Lillian is the one who kills people in their sleep."

"All right! All right!" Xanaphia said. "Why don't we just take a blood oath?"

"No!" Clement snapped. "A four-person blood oath will take days to cast."

"Fine," the necromancer responded. "I'm guessing we've all trained our minds and bodies to survive on little sleep. Therefore, we'll sleep in four hours segments. During the first four hours, Clement and Lillian will keep watch to make sure we don't kill each other. During the next four hours, Darien and I will keep a watch on each other. How is that?"

Darien, Lillian, and Clement looked at each other again. Finally, they broke eye contact, giving shrugs. Xanaphia seemed determined to come with them, and they were determined to continue with each other. No one liked the alliance, but each recognized the usefulness of the other being at their disposal.

"All right," Darien said. "But we need to get moving. We would do well to be out of town before light."

"No need," Xanaphia said, "My magic room will stay intact as long as we're inside. No one can enter without my permission. Further, we don't want to be caught sleeping or resting outside of town. The palace dispatched a number of heavily armed and magically trained search parties. They're hunting for you."

"How do you know that?" Lillian asked.

"The same way I knew Clement and Darien set off the alarm. I disguised myself as a guard and investigated. I heard Generals Gaheera, Cordor, and Cornelius discussing the rescue plan."

"Okay," Clement said, "but if we rest here, how will we get out of town."

Xanaphia smiled.

"The wall we're in is part of the outer battlements, and I control where the doors appear."

When she waved her hand, a door appeared on the opposite wall from where they entered. Looking through, they saw the thick trees and forested wilderness surrounding Rhoria. The snow still fell, accumulating upon the thick brambles lining the outer wall. Xanaphia duplicated the motion to make the doorway disappear.

Satisfied, Lillian said, "Well, then, looks like we're camping here for the night! In the morning, we depart for the Blood Fangs!"

She rolled onto her side. Muttering self-defense spells, she closed her eyes to fall asleep. The others stared at her.

Clement smirked and performed a mocking imitation of Lillian's voice. "Well, then, looks like you two have first watch!"

Clement lay down on the floor. Following Lillian's lead, he conjured a few defensive enchantments of his own. The day had not gone the way he hoped. Not only was he unable to destroy Sylvia, but now he was stuck with these scoundrels for the next week.

CHAPTER

5

When Sylvia regained consciousness, she thought someone had burned out her eyes. After feeling her face, she concluded the darkness was so overwhelming her enhanced senses couldn't detect any light. Cold iron manacles attached to a slab in the floor gripped her arms and legs. The chains were short and provided little room for mobility.

"Soboda," Sylvia said, tapping the shackles.

To her surprise, the spell failed to unlock her bindings. Her magic didn't even rise to her command. She hesitated.

"Osvashat," she tried again, placing her hands together and swinging them apart. Her summons produced no energy.

Wherever she was, a barrier surrounded the room blocking all magic. Sylvia was unaware of any power capable of completely negating magical energy. She knew about power sinks, creatures with strong magic resistances, and even rare humans born with a complete immunity to spells. But a force capable of preventing a spellcaster from summoning their powers was foreign to her.

Defeated in her attempt to cast spells, she considered her predicament. The outlook wasn't good. She found herself in an unknown place, deprived of power, and kidnapped by a mythical creature. Sylvia had never paid much attention in history classes. Though the Demon War remained the most pivotal event in the history of mankind, she could recall very few facts about it.

The only thing she knew for certain was that the demon targeted the tiara. How it knew about the tiara, she couldn't guess. It, or whoever was controlling it, also knew about the self-spells protecting the crown. Otherwise, she would be dead. Eventually someone would come to convince her to relinquish the prize.

As if in answer to her thoughts, she heard the distant noise of keys jingling, followed by the scrape of wood against stone. Torchlight appeared in the distance, revealing a long set of stairs to her left leading upward through a stone archway.

Three figures passed through the archway. The foremost was a man wrapped in a hooded white cloak. A man and woman followed behind, flanking him. They wore thick armor with short swords sheathed to their tunics. They held torches in their hands and appeared to be guards. Both bore symbols on their breastplates consisting of swirling crescents and a clawed hand.

The torchlight filled the dungeon, and Sylvia surveyed her surroundings. She sat in the middle of a large cell with thick metal bars. There were five more cells of relatively equal size. All were empty. She occupied the last cell on the right side.

The cloaked man approached Sylvia's cell. His hooded forehead almost brushed the seven-foot-high ceiling as he walked. He placed a torch in an iron rack affixed to the wall and stood looking down at her. She gazed back at him, unafraid and unwavering. Beneath the darkness of the hood, she saw him smile. Long, slender fingers emerged from the robe and lowered the hood to reveal her captor's face.

He was young, either in his upper teens or early twenties, with shoulder-length black hair. His skin was unnaturally pale with an almost greenish hue and his thin limbs and face gave the impression of severe emaciation. He appeared frail and sickly. Only his eyes revealed the truth behind the otherwise fragile façade. His deep-set sockets glowed a dark crimson, piercing the darkness of the dungeon like tiny candles. They were not the eyes of a human.

"Jason, Amanda, leave me."

He possessed a strong authoritative voice. The guards bowed. Backing up several paces, they proceeded up the stairs. The man waited until they were gone before speaking.

"Welcome, Queen Sylvia, to Junlorace Keep."

Sylvia's mind raced. She'd heard the name Junlorace Keep before. She had not heard it in school, but it sounded familiar. How did she know it? The man stared at her, apparently waiting for her to say something.

"Who are you?" Sylvia said at last.

"My name is Cyril Junlorace. I'm the last living descendant of the Junlorace family and the ruler of this keep."

"What are you?" she asked, her attention riveted by his glowing eyes which randomly flared and faded.

"I'm a kefling. I'm the first such creature born in a millennium. A kefling is a child conceived of two parents performing an ancient demonic ritual. I'm part demon from the blood ingested during the ceremony. I'm part human, from my human parents, and I'm part magic, composed of the spells performed during conception. Are you confused yet?" he added with a chuckle. "I know I am."

He leaned against the bars of the cell opposite her.

"I know you're after the tiara!" she said. "You can't have it!"

"I'm not surprised by your defiance. You've been through a lot since last night. I'm sorry you must endure this nightmare. But we're both pawns in a much bigger game. Stubbornness won't serve you well."

"Perhaps you'd care to explain this *game* to me" Sylvia said, annoyed by his casual manner.

"I assumed you'd already surmised the answers. Did a demon not snatch you from your room last night? Do you not know what that means?"

"It means you're an evil and arrogant man with great resources. It means you want my tiara and will stop at nothing to get it."

Cyril gave a mirthless laugh.

"Sorry to disappoint you, but you couldn't be more wrong. There are many villains in this story, but I'm not one of them. You, on the other hand, are."

"What?" Sylvia exclaimed.

"Darlyth, the demon lord, has risen from his slumber. Ten of the greatest wizards to ever live sacrificed their lives to imprison him. Now, because of people like you, he has been allowed to return."

Cyril no longer leaned on the prison bars but paced between the cells. His fiery eyes and voice grew fiercer with each step.

"For a millennium, my people protected you," he said. "We sacrificed our freedom and ambitions to ensure your safety. You and your people sat around in lavish homes, interested in nothing but gain and glory. Political leaders and nobility claim to care about their people. In truth your only motivation was furthering your own interests. You and your ancestors enjoyed the freedom and safety we provided, yet ignored us when needed help and called for assistance. We couldn't give you wealth and power, so, you turned your backs on us. My own parents, driven to despair, released the demon lord in the vain hope of freedom and reprieve.

"You are the villains, all of you. But you don't have to be a villain anymore. You have a chance at redemption. You have a chance to correct the errors of your negligent ancestors. You have a chance to give me the tiara."

Sylvia folded her arms, looking at him with disdain.

"A lot of hollow words," she said. "Perhaps you'd care to explain what part my tiara plays in this fascinating story."

"The demon lord wants it. Mankind is only a shadow of its former glory, and there may be no sorcerer capable of standing up to him. Still, he remembers his previous defeat. He won't take the risk of losing again. With the crown, no one can stand against him."

"And I'm supposed to become a hero by giving him the crown?"

"No, you're supposed to become a hero by giving the crown to me!"

"How are the two different?"

"Because I can slay the demon lord."

"Great, then do so. Why do you need the tiara?"

"Because I can't kill him without it," he said. "I'm a kefling. I'm part demon. I have the strengths of a demon, but I also have their weaknesses. One of those weaknesses is the inability to defy the orders of the demon lord. I must obey whatever he tells me to do."

"Then how does the crown help you?"

"Because I'm also part man. I have the strengths of a human, including the ability to weld magic. With the crown, my powers will be sufficient to resist his will and topple his throne."

"Why would you do that? I thought my people were villains, monsters who set the demon lord free. Now you want to save us?"

"No," he said, his voice growing menacing, "I want to rule you!"

"So you'd become the new demon lord, taking his place upon the throne."

Cyril crossed his arms and leaned casually against the prison bars behind him.

"Does it surprise you to hear me say so? I feel no need to lie. Demons feed off human blood. The demon lord will turn mankind into cattle to satisfy his hungry hordes. Humanity would be better off under me. At least I'm a man."

"Only half of one. You're also half demon and, from what I can tell, all monster." Sylvia rose from the floor to face him. "One dictator is the same as another. I sacrificed everything to stop tyranny. I've spent my life opposing tyrants! I'm not going to throw away everything by creating a new one!"

Cyril shrugged and rose upright. "I understand you're upset. You've heard many things and need time to digest them. Perhaps after thinking over what I've said you'll see reason."

Cyril withdrew the torch from the iron fastening. In a blur, he flashed from the front of her cell to the archway at the bottom of the stairs. Sylvia couldn't imagine how anyone or anything could move so fast.

"I've given you a chance to escape torture and save the world," Cyril's voice boomed. "I'll give you another. Reconsider my offer. A time is coming when you'll wish you had."

In another blur, he vanished up the stairs, the torchlight fading with him. Sylvia heard a door slam and a key turn. Silence followed. Like the jaws of a massive monster, blackness swallowed her solitary form, engulfing her within a sea of darkness. She again found herself imprisoned within a world of endless nothingness.

She sat alone with no company save her thoughts. She heard her stomach rumble with hunger. She wondered if someone would bring her food and water. If the goal of imprisonment was to force her to cede the tiara, they might choose to starve her. Even if they brought refreshment, the food and drink might be laced with a drug. She couldn't risk eating or drinking anything they provided.

Sylvia considered her chances of rescue. Her people would search for her. But she doubted anyone at the palace knew of Junlorace Keep. She wondered if anyone had seen the demon. She didn't know how it kidnapped her. She went unconscious after hitting the wall. There was a chance someone spotted the fiend as it escaped. If so, a history teacher at the academy might be able to connect demons with Junlorace Keep.

On the other hand, the dark-skinned demon kidnapped her in the middle of the night. It entered her room without being seen. It might have exited the same way. Even if it took to the skies, the night was overcast. The demon might blend into the clouds, escaping unnoticed. Even if the creature was seen and one of the professors happened to know about the keep, would they really have reason to look for her there?

Sylvia didn't know how far away Junlorace Keep was from Rhoria. The demon possessed wings. If it could fly, it could cover ground swifter than someone on foot. The distance between Rhoria and Junlorace Keep could require weeks of travel for an ordinary person. Altogether, the chances of rescue seemed slim.

She didn't know much about the demon lord. If ten wizards gave up their lives to imprison him, he must be incredibly powerful and evil. Perhaps he could force her into surrendering the crown. Without hope of escape or rescue, the choice came down to either giving the tiara to Cyril or the demon lord. She didn't like either option.

Cyril could be lying to her. He seemed passionate when he spoke but could be a talented actor. He might hand the tiara to the demon lord. Even if he didn't, he seemed incredibly arrogant. He might not be powerful enough to defeat the demon lord, even with the tiara.

He might be lying about a demon lord. She possessed no way to verify or refute his claim. Cyril himself might be the demon lord for all she knew. If the demon lord wanted her crown, why not confront her directly?

Ultimately, Sylvia knew she could never willingly hand over the tiara. As she told Cyril, she had lost everything in her battle to free Aurba. True, she gained a kingdom and great glory. But she never wanted those things. She wanted to be free and see her people free. In so doing, she lost more than she could ever regain. She gave her people the gift of independence and would endure any suffering to ensure they kept it.

Sylvia tested the chains. There was sufficient slack to permit her to assume a fetal position. It wasn't comfortable, but at least she could pass some time lost in sleep. Sylvia closed her eyes. Her dreams wouldn't be pleasant. They rarely were. But she suspected tonight's dreams would be particularly horrid. Maybe when she awoke, her mind would be sharp enough way to solve her dilemma.

Xanaphia watched with growing frustration as her companions rubbed their sleep eyes. They were supposed to be her equals, legendary sorcerers whose magical powers allowed them to transcend human limitations. Yet, she owned zombies who looked more energetic and alert. The party had woken up more than an hour ago and, in her mind, planning their route shouldn't have taken ten minutes.

"The snow is still falling," Clement said, yawning. "It must be at least two feet deep."

"We'll push through," Xanaphia said, silently vowing to attack the next person who yawned. "My concern is our path. Based upon Darien's descriptions, we have three options available. We can take the Queen's Road to the east and enter the Blood Fang's from the south . . ."

"No good," Lillian said, "the east is open plains. We'll be sitting ducks. Besides, there are no good entry points from the south except through Buried Grove . . ."

"Unburied Grove," Darien corrected her.

"Whatever," she said, "we lose almost two days going that way."

"The smoothest path is from the north," Xanaphia continued. "We can keep to the forests until we cross the Blackguard River. There are numerous roads running the expanse of the valley. We can keep to the edge until we reach the Northern Blood Fangs and then move south."

"Again, we lose too much time," Clement said. "The diversion to the Blackguard requires at least an extra day of traveling. Entering the mountains from the north is easier, but we can't afford to give up two or three days for the sake of smoother ground."

"That leaves the path northeast," Darien said.

"Exactly," Xanaphia confirmed. "We can head for Riddian's Pass. There are no roads. The terrain is wild and the forest overgrown. Plus, we pass through the Shattered Canyon. That's the most direct route."

"The Shattered Canyon and Riddian Pass are great places for an ambush," Darien observed.

"Let them try it," Xanaphia said. "We're the four deadliest sorcerers of our generation. If I could feel pity, I'd feel it for anyone who gets to our way."

Clement nodded, "Let's do it."

Without further conversation, the company headed out the door. At first, the march moved at a fast pace, but the deep snow and thick forest steadily wore down the hardy travelers. Only Xanaphia remained immune to the treacherous conditions.

She strode ahead of the company, plowing through the knee-deep ice. She didn't really expect the others to keep pace.

Despite her lanky appearance, she possessed supernatural physical strength and resiliency. Her years of constant necromantic experiments and magical enhancements altered her body to a level beyond the range of mere mortals. She was more like her undead creations than a human being. She hardly smelled the refreshing scents of the surrounding spruces. She barely felt the chill of the freezing winter winds. When she ate and drank, she hardly tasted the flavors.

She pondered the nature of her power as she walked. Was she losing herself? For years, she had transformed her mind and body with the conviction that the changes were necessary to defeat Darien. Yet, not only did she fail to defeat Darien, she couldn't even defend her kingdom against Sylvia. The only thing her alterations achieved was the gradual loss of her humanity. She wondered if the true reason for her transformation wasn't simply because she was addicted to power.

She glanced back at the company. Clement and Lillian trudged several yards behind, their heads bent low against the frosty winds. Behind them, Darien marched, his eyes locked upon Xanaphia. She suspected he drew strength from visualizing her death.

She longed to draw her dagger and thrust herself upon him. But only he knew the way to Junlorace Keep. She needed him. She disliked the thought. Even more, she disliked knowing he didn't need her. None of them wanted her to come. She suspected they were keeping secrets from her, and they held all of the cards.

They didn't want her to gain Sylvia's powers, but she wasn't giving up on her plan to use the dagger. They would steal Sylvia's powers if they could. It wasn't Xanaphia fault they lacked the necessary skill. She had spent years honing her powers of concentration to levels unequalled by any other mortal. And she alone had managed to successfully cast the absorption spell, perhaps the only person in the modern age to achieve the feat. She deserved the essence she stole, or so she told herself. Again, Xanaphia wondered if she was merely addicted to power.

Her thoughts drifted like snowflakes across the expanse of her mind as she continued onward through the endless trees and snow.

CHAPTER 6

No one saw the attack coming. Xanaphia didn't even see the dead bodies scattered around the clearing until a bright red glint drew her thoughts back to the present. A crimson liquid ran along the ground, staining the white snow beneath. Her eyes absently followed the trail to a horribly disfigured body wearing wizard robes. The sight snapped her mind back to attention. Her eyes shot up. She started to yell a warning, but the words never escaped.

A massive form slammed into her, lifting her off the ground. She screamed as sharp three-inch-long claws buried themselves into her flesh. Her attacker hoisted her into the air for a second before throwing her aside like a doll. Xanaphia flew several feet before skidding to a stop. There she lay in shock, overcome by the pain from the bloody gouges in her stomach.

Fortunately, the scream alerted Clement and Lillian. They looked up in time to see the beast fling the necromancer aside. Their attacker stood over eight feet tall and almost as wide with bright red eyes. The upper body was man-like with a powerful chest, muscular arms, clawed hands, and dark scaly skin. The grisly mockery of a centaur possessed the lower body of a spider. Eight hairy protrusions connected to a large furry torso and raced across the ground at an incredible speed.

Clement and Lillian barely summoned their energy before it crashed through their ranks. Charging between them, its massive arms swung outward. The left fist hammered against Clement's hastily summoned shield knocking him into the middle of a large thorn bush. Its right arm collided with Lillian's shield, smashing through her defenses and slamming into her chest. Waves of agony shot through her body. The force of the blow sent her crashing to the ground, where she disappeared beneath the snow. Next, it charged Darien, but his distance from the rest of the company gave him time to counterattack.

"Moroshnoye!" he shouted, slamming his hands together.

The snow around his adversary congealed into large walls of solid ice, which collided together like a wintery Venus fly trap. Large chunks of icy shrapnel tore into the beast's flesh, but it seemed unfazed. It continued charging, ignoring the icy walls crashing into him.

Darien attempted to dive away, but the monster's claws caught him, slicing into his left arm and spewing blood across his robes. The attacker's momentum carried it past Darien, but it whirled around for another attack. Leaping into the air, the creature raised its arms above Darien's fallen form, preparing to impale him with its razor-sharp claws. The enchanter conjured his magic in a desperate attempt to block the attack, but before the blow fell a shout rang through the air.

"Nasekamoye ebevat!"

It came from Lillian. She had managed to raise herself into a crouching position and held her right hand toward the creature. A dark, lime-colored streak of light issued from her fingertips, striking the spidery abdomen.

The creature froze mid-attack, as the strange green light bounced off it without doing the slightest damage. Still, Lillian had succeeded in getting its attention. Forgetting Darien, the creature sprang into the air, landing only inches away. Lillian tumbled to her left, staying low to the ground to remain a smaller target, but the monster's arm plowed through the snow, scooping her up and launching her into a nearby tree. She smashed into the trunk with a sickening crunch and crumpled to the ground.

Before it could finish her off, another spell from Darien distracted the beast, and it leapt back toward the enchanter, leaving Lillian writhing in pain. Beside her, Clement fought to get untangled from the thorn bush the creature had thrown him in. With a jerk, Clement ripped free, tearing several more holes in his already damaged robes, and glared at Lillian.

"Nasekamoye ebevat?" he shouted, his voice a mix of anger and sarcasm. "Were you trying to swat a mosquito off of him?"

"First spell . . . came to mind!" she wheezed, striving to regain her breath. "Didn't see . . . you do . . . anything!"

The creature had charged Darien. This time, Darien was prepared. He had enchanted himself with a leaping spell and sprang into the air, soaring over the head of his stunned adversary and landing on the edge of the clearing near Xanaphia.

With an angry roar, the beast spun, chasing after him. The charge drew the creature directly in front of the waiting Clement.

"Desecria!" Clement shouted.

Black lightning burst from his hands, striking the creature directly in the chest. The beast released a shriek of pain, the spidery legs giving way beneath it. Green blood burst from its sides. For a moment, Clement thought it was down.

But the next second, the beast was back on its feet. Recovering quickly, it whirled toward Clement. Weakened by the Desecria spell, Clement could only stumble backward as the creature's claws raked across his body. Blood coated the ground. Clutching his side, Clement collapsed into the snow. Healing spells issued frantically from his lips.

"Moocheetseeya!" Lillian's voice rang out.

She was back on her feet, leaning against a tree for support. Orange light burst from the creature's wounds. The monster staggered away from Clement, howling in agony. At the same moment, another spell blasted toward the creature. Xanaphia was back on her feet.

"Perelome!" she shouted. Purple light burst from her hands.

Darien simultaneously released his own spell. "Napadat!"

The spells barreled down upon the monster, but the creature would not go down that easily. In an amazing display of agility, it collapsed into the snow, curling into an unnaturally small ball. The spells soared above its head, and it rolled away from them.

Resuming its full size, the creature reared up on its back legs, facing Lillian, who opened her mouth to cast another spell. Before she could, an enormous net of rope-like materials spewed from its belly. The web caught Lillian in the chest and blasted her backward into the tree. Sticky strands spun around her body, pinning her to tree, and foul tasting webbing shot into her open mouth, choking her. Struggling for air, Lillian writhed against her bonds but could do little more. Satisfied that she was helpless, the beast charged toward Darien and Xanaphia.

"Shech," Darien screamed, red light flashing from his hand.

"Kalecheet," called Xanaphia, an orange beam flaring from hers.

The creature leapt above the spells, performing a summersault as it raced along invisible webs in the trees above. Then, the beast pounced upon Darien, snatching him from the ground and slamming him against a tree. The sounds of cracking ribs filled the clearing as his body collided with the piney wood. The monster gave a snarl, tossing him away dismissively and turning toward Xanaphia, who had retreated further into the clearing.

With a bound, the creature sprang upon her, but Xanaphia had anticipated his movements. Aiming her hands into the air, she shouted, "Perelome."

Purple light burst from her hands, shooting into the sky. The creature's leap carried it right into the beam, and the two collided with such force that the beast's torso was blasted backward, causing it to flip as it spun through the air. The creature crashed upon the ground in front of her, shaken but not defeated.

She tried casting another spell, but the fiend was too fast. Recovering quickly, the beast scuttled across the short distance separating them with ferocious speed. Swinging its clawed hands together, the creature tried to smash her. But Xanaphia's arms shot out, grabbing its wrists and pinning them away from her.

For a moment, the two stood locked in a deadly stalemate, the brute's demonic strength against Xanaphia's super-human might. The beast was badly injured, but so was Xanaphia, and the creature was more than five times her size. Already she could feel her strength giving way. A sadistic smile crossed the creature's lips, and its claws turned inward. They were just inches away from Xanaphia's face and closing fast.

Clement rolled onto his stomach in a desperate attempt to help, but the pain was too much. He would never get a spell off in time. Out of the corner of his eyes, he spotted Darien. The enchanter had scrambled up the tree and regained his footing. Turning back to the scene, the enchanter raised his hands, summoning his magic. But no spell came forth. He just stood there, hesitating in apparent indecision. Finally, Clement could take it no longer.

"Do something!" he shouted.

That roused Darien from his trance. A look of fierce determination lined his face, and he launched his hands toward the fight.

"Desecria!" he shouted.

The stream of crackling black lightning burst forth from his hands and shot toward the combatants. At the same moment, Xanaphia's strength failed. The monster's left hand broke from her grasp. The claws raked across her face, spraying blood across the clearing as she collapsed into the snow.

Darien's spell flashed above her fallen figure, slamming straight into the beast. With a blood-curdling shriek, the beast stumbled backward, writhing against the tendrils of deadly magic. Clement saw the body go limp, and with one last wavering step the massive body fell, scattering snow and ice into the air. A moment later, the beast's spidery legs curled inward, and everything became still.

Darien collapsed into the snow, panting for breath. For several minutes no one moved as each muttered self-healing spells. Almost every magic user knew at least one spell designed to regenerate their wounds, even if they knew none for healing others. The spells worked quickly, and Clement could feel his wounds sealing. Pushing himself off the snow, he climbed gingerly to his feet, a little dizzy from loss of blood, but otherwise alright.

Beside him, Lillian had managed to spit out most of the web from her mouth and was now busy disentangling herself from the tree. Xanaphia was also back on her feet, and she looked furious. Turning toward Darien, she marched across, her expression livid. Darien watched her approach, rising to his full height, which put him at eye level with the approaching necromancer.

She approached until her face was inches from him. She was covered with blood and sweat from the battle. Her breaths came in hard gasps. Yet, she stood aggressively before him, her eyes flaring.

"What took you so long to cast the stupid spell?"

"I could not decide whether to cast the spell on the monster or on you!" Darien answered.

Xanaphia glared at him. Then her body relaxed. The tension drained from her muscles as she cast a contemptuous look.

"I'm surprised you chose to target the monster."

"He didn't, you ditz!" Lillian interjected as she walked by, now free from her cords. "He fired the spell at you. The monster knocked you down at the wrong time."

Lillian walked off toward the body of the fallen beast. Darien held his head up high and strode past Xanaphia, slamming his shoulder against hers. Xanaphia's smirk grew, and she gave a satisfied nod.

"Makes sense," she said. "I'd have done the same thing."

Turning around, she followed after them. Clement did not. He wasn't interested in the monster. A short distance away, a collection of human remains lay on the ground. The bodies were badly mutilated, but Clement recognized Queen Sylvia's insignia on their garb. He guessed they were one of the parties pursuing him and Darien.

He crossed the clearing to examine them. The mangled and disfigured corpses had perhaps been there since last night. Most appeared to be soldiers, but two were not. Their robes marked them as high ranking members of the Rhorian Magical Academy. One was a female. The other was mutilated beyond identification of gender.

Each possessed shoulder bags. The unidentifiable figure still wore one, but the woman's bag was resting on the ground. Apparently, she threw off the pack during the battle. Deep tears and gouges indicated she had used it as a makeshift shield. Resourceful, thought Clement, but futile.

He lifted her right hand. When he was young, Clement developed an expertise in magical identification. The rare skill allowed him to recognize spells cast upon an object by its markings and enabled him to identify spells cast by a sorcerer through magical residues. Clement spread apart the fingers of the dead sorceress, feeling the tips and running his hands along her fingers. He felt a number of uncommon and powerful spells clinging to her skin. She was clearly a learned battle mage and had put up quite a fight.

Clement lowered her hand and picked up the shoulder bag. Water dripped from the bottom, and he observed a shattered glass canteen resting inside. He rifled through the contents: a folded letter, a small circular wooden box, and a pile of wet parchment.

He pulled out the wooden box and removed the lid. Inside was a thick green goo, like an emerald mud. A strong nauseating smell radiated from the mixture. Clement moved the stuff away from his nose, replacing the lid.

"Magic healing balm?" Lillian asked.

Clement looked up to see her standing over him. Apparently done examining the monster, she had wandered over. Darien and Xanaphia were still examining the beast.

"I guess so," Clement said with a shrug. "I've never made the stuff, but I've read about the potion. This matches the description."

Pocketing the balm, he reached into the bag to examine the other items. Lillian strolled over to the other bag. Removing the strap from the dead spellcaster's neck, she joined Clement in rummaging through the dead party's possessions. Clement pulled a handful of papers out of his bag. They appeared to be magic scrolls. With a loud rustling, Clement vigorously shook the papers, attempting to get the water off.

Darien turned toward the noise, and Clement saw him scowl. Abandoning his examination of the monster, Darien crossed toward the scavengers. Xanaphia looked up too but merely smirked at the pillaging before resuming her study of the corpse.

"Anything good?" Darien asked, a hint of accusation in his voice.

"I'm finding out," Clement said unabashed.

He tossed the miscellaneous scrolls toward Darien, who caught them. Clement reached back into the bag, withdrawing the folded letter. Unfurling the document, he scrutinized the contents. It appeared to be nothing more than a simple decree ordering an unnamed general to lead a group of soldiers in search of Darien and Clement, yet something wasn't right. The paper was the only thing in the bag that remained dry.

Phelidius paper, Clement realized with a smile.

The arch mage Phelidius designed the enchanted paper during the Obsidian Wars to allow nobles to secretly communicate with their generals. To the unsuspecting reader, the letter contained only a simple message of the writer's design. To someone capable of recognizing the parchment, the text contained a more sinister secret.

"Fahkoose," Clement whispered.

The writing grew blurry and out of focus. A second later, the original text had vanished, replaced by a long letter written in a hasty scribble. Clement scanned the document.

"Pretty basic scrolls," Darien said, oblivious to Clement's discovery. "Only of use to weak or moderate spellcasters."

"They're perfect for you," Xanaphia jeered, now joining the others.

Darien ignored her. "Here Lillian, a gift."

He tossed the papers to the spymaster. She gave a Xanaphia-like smirk but said nothing.

"Listen to this," Clement declared, leaping to his feet. Clement held up the letter, reading in an official tone.

General Gaheera,

Before beginning your quest, I must inform you of suspicions brewing in my mind. I confirm I lack the magical powers possessed by you or Cornelius. Nevertheless, I'm convinced not everything is right at the castle. When I found Darien and Clement in the queen's room, Sylvia was nowhere to be seen. The window to her room was blown out, and they appeared to be examining a strange cloth. The high mage theorizes they destroyed the window, sending the queen through the portal. But why would the wizards not escape through the window with her? What was the strange cloth stolen by Darien the Dark? Cornelius explains away my questions saying the ways of evil are strange. Yet it still doesn't make sense.

The guards were frozen in place to give the impression they were keeping watch. If Darien and Clement planned to fight a loud battle and blast open a window for everyone to see, why not simply kill them instead of giving the illusion that all is well. I suspect someone inside the castle had a hand in Sylvia's capture. I question whether the queen was really taken by Darien and Clement at all.

I think someone beat them to the queen. The cloth might be some sort of ransom note. Perhaps Darien and Clement are using it to track the true thief for their own devious ends. In any case, I believe someone inside the castle paralyzed the guards. Cornelius feels we should focus on an enemy we know rather than speculating about some unknown threat. I admit my theory is a stretch. Perhaps I'm just paranoid. Still, if you're able to apprehend Darien and Clement, please search for the missing piece of cloth. Second, if you recover the queen, please alert her to the potential dangers waiting inside the castle. I sent similar letters to General Andrus and General Alexis. I myself will be in the traveling party with Cornelius. Best of luck be with you, Commander.

—General Cordor, Head of the Queen's Personal Guard.

Clement lowered the letter.

"Wow!" Lillian said. "He's sharp!"

"Indeed," Darien agreed. He took the letter from Clement and scanned it. "So, the man chasing us was General Cordor. I have heard many things about him."

"Me too," Xanaphia said, no trace of a smirk on her face. "I'm not comforted knowing he and Cornelius are working together."

"I hear he is a Morodin," Lillian said, checking her newly acquired canteen for cracks.

"What is a Morodin?" Darien asked.

"A human born with a bizarre abnormality making them immune to all magic," Clement answered. "They're extremely rare. Less than one is born each generation."

"That explains why he was not affected by our spells," Darien observed.

"Morodins are easy enough to defeat," Xanaphia said. "Just cast spells on the things around them rather than on them. I wouldn't be worried about him or Cornelius alone. But a Morodin and a powerful sorcerer working together can be a lethal combination. Each can compensate for the other's weakness."

"I wouldn't worry too much," Lillian said, picking up the scrolls and flipping through them. "They're looking for Darien and Clement. If we vanish before they see us, we don't need to get involved."

Xanaphia looked at Lillian with disgust. "I swear you're the most spineless brat I've ever seen!"

"Brave is just another word for suicidal," she replied.

"And what if they see us first?" Xanaphia asked. "The searchers will assume we're in league and come looking for us after they finish off these dim-wits."

"Nice insult coming from a talking zombie," Darien said.

"When they find us, I don't want my only support to be a pathetic weakling like you!" Xanaphia finished, ignoring Darien.

"Hopefully, their party went south or west," Clement interrupted. "These corpses are probably the only party sent north."

"Probably," Lillian agreed. "But they likely sent a party east also. They might head for the Pass of Riddian."

"I doubt they'd go there," Clement said. "They have no reason to enter the mountains. They probably followed the main road toward Buried Grove."

"Unburied Grove," Darien corrected.

"Would you stop that?" Xanaphia snapped.

"How many search parties were sent after us?" Lillian asked, looking up at Xanaphia.

"When I left, the plan involved sending four."

"One going each direction," Clement observed. "Each led by one of Sylvia's mightiest generals."

"None are a match for us though," Darien said. "And I would not mind facing General Alexis. She is the only person to ever outmaneuver me on a battlefield. I owe her one."

Clement glanced down at the corpse resting at his feet.

"This was General Gaheera," he said. "She led a powerful assault force through the southern part of my realm during Sylvia's invasion."

"She was a powerful sorceress," Lillian said, standing up. "And Sylvia's oldest friend. She was present at my surrender and very civil to me."

"Whoever the traitor is, they were clever to split up the search parties," Darien observed. "Together, Gaheera, Andrus, Cornelius, and Alexis would be a powerful force. Divided, they are vulnerable."

"I doubt they were powerful enough to defeat this creature, even together," Clement said. "What was that thing, anyway?"

"Not sure," Darien said. "I have never seen anything like it."

"Whatever it was, it wasn't here by chance," Clement said. "Notice how none of the bodies show signs of being eaten. The creature ambushed them, made sure they were dead, and went back into hiding."

"That's not entirely accurate," Xanaphia replied. "The bodies aren't eaten, but there isn't as much blood as I'd expect. The creature was probably feeding on their blood."

"Very likely," Darien agreed. "With that and the monster's unique magical properties, I suspect we are looking at some kind of demon."

"What?" Xanaphia exclaimed, staring a Darien. "Demons haven't been seen in millennia."

"They have now," Lillian said.

"Such a keen observation," Xanaphia scoffed. "If that's the limit of your intellectual brilliance, I can understand why you don't own a single scholastic award. Pretty pathetic for a headmaster's daughter."

Lillian opened her mouth to retort but Xanaphia continued on, pointing at the letter in Darien's hand.

"Perhaps, instead of idiotic remarks, I deserve an explanation regarding this 'mysterious cloth' and the true nature of the threat facing us."

Lillian and Darien both glanced at Clement. He shrugged.

"I suppose so," he said. "But the explanation is long, and I don't want to lose any more time. As I remember, the Armored Plains are just a few hours away. The Shattered Hills are only five or six hours from there . . ."

"You should know, as many times as you invaded me through them," Lillian muttered.

"They're a good place to camp unseen," Clement continued. "Once there, we can find a safe place to talk."

Xanaphia clearly disliked the idea of waiting, but she didn't push the matter. Without a word, she whirled around, marching away in the direction of the Armored Plains. Darien also turned northward, following a short distance behind. Lillian remained. Clement watched her scan the bodies like a vulture, looking for anything else she might consider valuable. Then she checked her newly acquired shoulder bag before following the others. Clement took up a marching position behind her, and together the company departed the clearing.

CHAPTER
7

Sylvia awoke to a sudden light filling the dungeon. Her cramped muscles ached as she stretched from her uncomfortable sleeping position. She had a terrible crick in her neck and tried turning her head left and right to loosen the tendons. As she did so, she spotted Cyril standing at the door to her cell. He held a tray of food covered by a metal lid. Unable to stand comfortably, Sylvia sat upright facing him.

"Food and water, Your Majesty," he said, giving a respectful bow.

He lifted the lid on the tray and slid the dish, along with a canteen of water, through a small opening at the base of the cell. The plate contained a large loaf of bread and a block of some white glistening substance. Her stomach ached and her throat burned, but she eyed the dish suspiciously.

"Are they safe to eat?" she asked.

Cyril smiled. "If I wanted to poison you, do you not think I could just force it down your throat?"

Sylvia acknowledged there was no reason for him to be subtle. With some relief, she reached for the canteen. She was thirstier than she could ever remember being in her life. Unscrewing the lid, she took several gulps of water before lowering the canteen. She was about to reach for the food but noticed Cyril watching her.

"Are you going to stand there the entire time I eat?"

Cyril laughed like someone unaccustomed to the act.

"If you want solitude, you'll get plenty," he said. "Are you not glad for some company?"

Sylvia glanced down at the strange white block. The food resembled discolored string cheese.

"What is this?" She asked.

"Wingham cheese," Cyril answered, taking a seat on the floor.

Winghams were a unique breed of carnivorous flying reptiles native to the far northeastern regions of Aurba. They resembled dragons in appearance but were closer to Wyverns in size. Sylvia had never seen one.

"I thought Winghams were extinct," she said. "Darien the Dark led a campaign to wipe them from the world."

"And he succeeded, for the most part," Cyril replied, "but Darien's hunting parties never came this far south. They were fortunate. We've bred Winghams for generations and would've fought hard to protect them."

Sylvia lifted the cheese to her mouth and nibbled cautiously. It had a sweet flavor, reminding her of vanilla. The taste was a pleasant break from the flavorless bread.

"Do you like it?" Cyril asked. "I was told to give you bread and water, but I suspected you'd never tasted it. I thought you might enjoy some."

Sylvia placed the cheese back on the tray.

"Why're you being nice to me?" she asked.

"I've nothing to lose by being nice. If you're asking whether I'm being nice for personal motives, my answer is yes. I want the tiara. I'd rather see the crown in my own hands than the hands of the demon lord. Further, I'd like to slay the demon lord. He killed my parents. I don't pretend I wouldn't forge my own empire and punish the people of this continent for the injustices they performed against my ancestors, but I maintain that my actions would be the lesser of two evils. If you understood the demon lord's plans, I think you'd agree."

"You keep speaking of this demon lord," Sylvia said. "How do I know he's real? He could be a lie you're using to convince me to hand over the crown."

Cyril smiled sadly.

"Alas! How comfortable would be the world if there were no demon lord. Did you not see a demon yourself? Did you not get kidnapped from your bed by one?"

"I did," Sylvia agreed. "And he brought me to you! Why would he bring me here rather than to his master? How do I know you're not the demon lord in disguise?"

"Valid questions," Cyril said, rising to his feet. "As far as proving I'm not the demon lord, have you not seen a demon? Do you not have reason to believe I'm not one? No doubt you know from your history lessons that Darlyth was the first demon, and his appearance . . ."

Cyril stopped, looking at the expression on Sylvia's face.

"Do they not teach the history of the Demon Wars at the academy?"

"They do," Sylvia conceded. "But they don't test on it. I never paid attention."

Immediately, Cyril's eyes glowed with anger. Rage and resentment burned a path across his face. His hands clinched into tight fists. His body trembled in fury, and for a moment Sylvia feared he might throttle her through the bars. With obvious effort though, he regained his composure. He raised his hands in front of his body, lowering them as he took several long slow breaths. After a moment, he continued speaking in a tone of forced calmness.

"You were brought here because of me," he explained, skipping to the second question as though the previous exchange never happened. "Kendross Keep is the fortress built atop the demon lord's home. All the humans there were transformed into monsters. I convinced the demon lord you might surrender the tiara more quickly if surrounded by humans than demonic entities. The suggestion was dangerous. If Darlyth suspected my plans, I would've died. Nevertheless, the potential reward was worth the risk. That's how I obtained my chance to destroy him. You too have your chance, a chance to save the world."

"If you wish to destroy your master, give me the tiara," Sylvia urged. "We can destroy him together."

Cyril hesitated.

"I haven't forgotten my ancestors' vows to keep the world free of Darlyth's evil," he said. "But even with the tiara you're not powerful enough to defeat him. You couldn't even slay the demon in your bedchamber, and Darlyth is a hundred times mightier. I *can* kill him, but not without the tiara. I have not the power to resist his will. Only with the tiara can I be free.

"I've also not forgotten the pain your people inflicted upon my ancestors," Cyril continued, his red eyes burning in the torchlight. "I'll never forget the neglect and cruel injustices suffered at the hands of your ancestors. They cannot go unpunished!"

"You can't punish people for the mistakes of their ancestors," Sylvia argued.

"Why not?" Cyril asked. "People suffer all the time for the mistakes of their ancestors. Households live in poverty because predecessors squandered their wealth on drinking and frivolity. Children and their children endure curses for countless generations for crimes of long-deceased relatives. Former noble families live in disgrace because a distant head of house once fell out of favor. These things happen all the time."

"We aren't talking about poverty and curses," Sylvia protected. "We're talking enslavement!"

"You may think me just another tyrant," Cyril replied. "Maybe I am. But remember Kendross Keep. The men and women there broke the vows their ancestors honored for a thousand years. They set Darlyth free. He rewarded their loyalty by twisting them into deformed monstrous servants. He'll do the same to your people! Others he'll force into camps like farm animals to feed his hungry hordes. Do you wish to see that?"

"What would you do?" she asked. "March armies across the land? Kill thousands? Inflict vengeance upon people who don't even understand why they're suffering?"

"I would dispense justice," he said. "Yes, I'd punish them. I have a right to do so. When you overthrew the tyrants, did you not punish those who helped them rise? Have I not the same right? Your people's ambivalence makes them accomplices to evil! Their neglect allowed Darlyth to rise. If they're never punished, they'll never learn the error of their ways!"

"Who're you to judge them?" Sylvia demanded. "Your parents helped set him free. You serve him! You're a servant of evil wanting to punish others for not stopping the evil you serve. You're a hypocrite."

"As are you," he said. "You judge me for serving evil, but I have not the choice. I'm half-demon. I lack free will. You've always had free will, and you used it to ignore your history lessons. When your professors told you about an ancient evil threatening the world, you yawned and said 'boring.' You profess yourself a hero of the people while your apathy furthers their demise."

"They were taught as legends," Sylvia said. "I didn't know they were real. The stories were outlandish. Some scholars claimed they were myths, like the barbarians' tales of their gods, created when civilization was born to explain the mysteries of the world and give a united cultural identity. Without knowing they were true, no one would send soldiers searching the continent for a possibly non-existent keep protecting against a potentially non-existent threat."

"Darien did!"

Sylvia stared in surprise. Cyril smiled at her stunned expression.

"Oh yes," he said, pressing his advantage. "The same 'heartless tyrant' that you insult sent an envoy of soldiers and supplies to help us. You, in all your righteousness, never sent a single troop. Only Darien, who you overthrew, took the risk to safeguard his citizens."

"What happened to them?" Sylvia asked.

Cyril hung his head.

"My parents were already scheming to release the demon lord at that time," he answered. "They killed everyone who wouldn't join their cause."

Cyril froze with a horrified expression, as though he had said too much. Sylvia felt a rush of excitement. The possibility that Darien's former advisors and soldiers might know about the fort brought a glimmer of hope to her otherwise desolate situation.

She glanced back at Cyril. He was gone. She spotted him standing in the archway.

"The torch is almost burned out," he said.

She looked at the torch on the wall. The fire was indeed getting dimmer.

"I recommend finishing your food and water. I'll send a guard down shortly to collect them. In the meantime, think about what I've told you. I'll grant you one last chance to give me the tiara. After tomorrow morning though, I can no longer protect you."

Cyril disappeared up the stairs in a flash of movement. In the distance, she heard a door slam. She was alone, again.

The Shattered Hills were the most mysterious structure in Southern Aurba. At first glance, they appeared to be little more than a wide expanse of open plains covered with random hills. A closer examination revealed the more bizarre characteristics. Each hill stood identical in size with ridges rising exactly five feet off the ground. Even more unusual were the triangular fissures running like cracks through the northern side of each mound.

These unique mini-cliffs formed a sort of trench system from which the Shattered Hills drew their name. The reason for the mysterious hills and accompanying holes remained a mystery. No one could provide a natural explanation, and most people believed the affect was manmade. Yet, even the oldest known histories and legends provided no clue as to who or what had created the depressions.

Clement located a large triangular alcove in one of the hills. The indention was wider than the others and provided plenty of room for the four travelers to sit. With some reluctant assistance from Lillian, Clement soon transformed the alcove into a suitable campsite with a blazing fire. Everyone took positions inside.

The winter winds whipped over the mound. Darien, whose skin was turning a noticeable shade of blue, took the position farthest inside the alcove. There the angled walls protected his back and sides from the strengthening gale. Lillian positioned herself to his right, where she reclined with her hands behind her head in her usual nonchalance. Taking a post opposite the spymaster, Clement waved his hand, shaping the dirt into a makeshift stool. He took a seat, warming his cold fingers in the nearby flames.

Xanaphia didn't rush into the fissure with the others. Displaying an obvious ambivalence to the weather, she took a post at the entrance. A short snowy barricade lay across the opening to provide protection from the wind. Xanaphia sat atop the mound like a chair. She crossed her fingers, rested her hands in her lap, and stared at the company with an expectant look.

"Well?" she said.

No one spoke. To Clement's annoyance, he discovered both Lillian and Darien were looking at him.

"Fine," Clement snapped. "I don't know why I'm telling the story. Lillian saw the kidnapping, and Darien knows about the keep. I suppose I can start the tale while they elaborate where needed."

Clement recounted the events surrounding Sylvia's kidnapping and the ensuing encounter with Lillian. Xanaphia seemed interested in Junlorace Keep and launched a barrage of questions. As Clement didn't know the answers to most of them, Darien took over the discussion, recounting his knowledge of the fortress and failed attempt to infiltrate the cult. When he finished, Xanaphia sat gazing at the snow.

Clement rummaged through a pocket inside his cloak. The hand sewn compartment was small and seemingly incapable of holding many objects. The appearance was deceptive. A spell woven over the fabric shrank any objects placed inside, allowing the apparently insignificant pouch to hold twenty to thirty pounds worth of random materials without added weight or bulkiness.

Clement produced a glass vial and a metal cup. Both enlarged to their normal size as they exited the pocket. Placing the vial onto the ground, he scooped a large amount of snow into the cup. He then held his right hand above it muttering, "Topat." The cup became encircled in the light and the snow melted into water.

Placing the cup down, Clement picked up his vial and removed the stopper. Tilting it over his cup, he carefully measured several drops of thick bronze liquid. As the droplets hit the water, a loud hissing sound filled the clearing. The water bubbled and smoked. When the smoke cleared, brown sludge filled the cup. Clement screwed the lid back on and returned the vial to his pocket.

Noticing Clement's actions, Darien also pulled a flask from his cloak and filled a canteen with snow. Xanaphia looked up from her contemplation, a smirk creeping across her face.

"You are drinking Valirian Food Potion?"

She shook her head in a condescending manner. Reaching into her own cloak, Xanaphia withdrew a leather pouch. Taking some powder out, she cast the dust onto the ground beside her. Clement shot her an ugly look.

"Interestingly enough, the focus of my magical studies wasn't wilderness survival," Clement said. "Maybe you knew your skills were too weak to stay in power forever and prepared for exile. I, however, was busy building an empire so powerful it made your kingdom look as pathetic and insignificant as the half-corpse ruling it!"

Clement could tell he'd struck a nerve. Xanaphia's smirk vanished, her eyes flashing.

"And how long did it take Sylvia to crush your army and rip your 'mighty empire' to the ground?" Xanaphia asked. "Two days? Three days?"

"Three weeks," Clement hissed.

"Oooh," Xanaphia said, "I'm so impressed."

"I lasted a lot longer than when you got your butt handed to you!"

"I can't be blamed if she targeted my kingdom first!" Xanaphia protested angrily.

"Really?" Clement replied. "I thought she was employing sound military strategy. Don't you always attack the weakest link first?"

Xanaphia leapt to her feet, her fists clinched.

"My armies dealt more destruction upon her forces than the three of you combined!"

"Don't delude yourself!" Clement said, also rising. "She lost more soldiers just crossing the Blackguard River than your pathetic creations dealt the entire war! You were, are, and forever will be nothing compared to me!"

"How dare you!" she said. "I could crush your pathetic soul any day of the week!"

"Bring it on!"

Clement felt Xanaphia summon her magic and conjured his own. The air crackled from the building power, and the wind increased in fury, howling with anticipation. The surrounding snow melted as their energy congealed into a ball of intense heat radiating from the combatants. The glow of the sphere soon outshone the fire. Battle seemed imminent, and the two spellcasters glared at each other waiting to see who would make the first move.

Out of the corner of his eye, Clement noticed a rabbit emerge from a mound a few yards away. It hopped toward them, sniffing the ground and air intently. It moved in an almost hypnotic state, like a warrior trapped in the grip of a siren's song.

Clement fought against the distraction. Concentrating on the coming assault, he returned his gaze to Xanaphia's murderous eyes. The whole world seemed to freeze in awkward anticipation. Then Xanaphia struck.

"Desecria!" she cried.

A ray of the obsidian lightning spewed from her hand, striking the rabbit. It collapsed, dead before hitting the ground. As though satisfied, she smirked, allowing her magic to fade.

Demonstrating fearless contempt, she turned her back to Clement and knelt down to pick up the rabbit's body. Holding it up, she gave Clement a side-long glance as though to say "that could've been you."

"Some of us don't need survival magic to get food," she said, resuming her seat.

Clement raised an eyebrow, thoroughly unimpressed.

"Some of us don't need Desecria to kill a rabbit," he retorted, sitting down and picking up his cup.

"Do not be rude," Darien said, his eyes sparkling maliciously at the small, malnourished mammal in Xanaphia's hands. "Let her enjoy her feast! If she only takes one bite, she might be able to save the other for tomorrow!"

Clement looked down at his drink, smiling at only the remark. The drink was nothing to smile about. On the upside, Valirian Food Potion filled a person as though they had eaten an entire meal. On the downside, it looked like mud, smelled like mud, felt like mud, and the flavor wasn't much better. He tried finishing the drink quickly before he could taste it and fought the urge to gag. Valirian was a sick man, he thought miserably.

Xanaphia looked equally unenthusiastic about her meal, gazing at her emaciated quarry with downcast eyes. Muttering spells, she removed the fur and skin in preparation for eating it. Several moments passed in silence as Darien finished mixing his potion and sat staring apprehensively at it. Clement placed his empty cup on the ground and noticed Lillian watching them all with obvious amusement.

"I studied survival magic," she said, breaking the silence in her arrogant tone.

All eyes drifted toward her. She placed her shoulder bag onto the ground and rummaged through it. At some point, Lillian must've emptied the pockets of her cloak into the pack, because when she sat upright again she held a small ceramic plate, which Clement knew wasn't inside when she picked it up. She placed the plate on the ground and retrieved a large glass beaker from inside her satchel. The corked bottled was filled with a bizarre multi-colored liquid that floated inside the container like living mist.

Holding the bottle at eye level, she swirled the liquid left then right, muttering phrases no one could hear. Lillian stopped churning the vial and removed the cork. She poured three drops onto the plate: the first at the top, the second on the bottom right, and the third on the bottom left. The droplets fizzled like water boiling on a stove. A puff of smoke arose. When the fumes cleared, a meal of various fruits, nuts, cheeses, and breads filled the plate to the brim.

Clement, Darien, and Xanaphia sat frozen, their food forgotten as they studied the lavish cuisine. Lillian said nothing, pretending to ignore their shocked faces, but her smile betrayed her. Clement could tell she was fighting not to laugh. He glanced at the others. Darien looked like someone had punched him in the stomach. His eyes shifted between her plate and the muddy potion in his hands. Xanaphia's eyes narrowed, and she whisked her body around to face away from Lillian.

Clement forced himself to look unimpressed. He muttered a cleaning spell on the cup and stashed it inside his robes. For several minutes, he watched the spymaster, who sat feasting haughtily on her plate of fresh foods. Her exaggerated sighs of delight as she savored her meal struck his nerves like a hammer. As she lowered a bunch of grapes into her mouth like a pampered queen, he couldn't contain himself any longer.

"You think you're so smart," he hissed. "If you spent more time studying real magic instead of those silly survival tricks, maybe you could've put up some resistance when Sylvia marched through your kingdom. Maybe you could've fought instead of hoisting the white flag outside the windows of your room as she approached!"

Clement saw Darien look up in interest and heard Xanaphia turn back toward to the fire to watch the exchange. Lillian froze mid-bite. Lowering the grapes, she met Clement's gaze with a hardened expression.

"Ah yes," she said. "Because your knowledge of six hundred ways to kill a man served you so well when Sylvia blasted you through two walls and into your courtyard."

"At least I fought!" Clement said, rising to his feet. "That's more than you can say!"

"At least I was smart!" Lillian shouted back. "That's more than you can say. Because I surrendered, I was able to leave the country under escort rather than getting banished to some forbidden region. I didn't waste the lives of my most loyal generals, and they smuggled powerful magical tools and equipment for me."

"I am surprised you trusted your generals with powerful magical objects," Darien said, jumping into the conversation with the apparent hope of distracting them. "What if they ran off and kept them?"

"Of course they ran off and kept them," Lillian said testily. "That's why I killed them afterward. But they served their purpose."

"I had to kill my best apprentice," Xanaphia said, her voice casual. "He snuck my cloak out of the castle at the last minute then fled with it. It took months to track him down and reclaim my prize."

"So, neither of you got the bright idea of sneaking your treasures out of the kingdom before her invasion?" Lillian jeered, looking at Darien and Clement.

"Nor would I if given the chance again," Clement said. "I didn't want to run. I wanted to fight. I wanted to kill her or die trying."

Clement was still on his feet and he looked down upon the others as he spoke.

"You may be a survivalist," he shot at Lillian. "But I'm not. I'm a warrior. I wanted to fight. If she was going to defeat me, I wanted to perish using every resource, power, and spell I owned. I wanted to go down in a blaze of magic and glory just like every wizard should!"

They were all staring at him. He turned away from them gazing into the hills.

"They say she 'showed me mercy,'" Clement said bitterly. "I didn't want mercy. I wanted her to finish me, and she knew it. She may have let you live out of mercy. She let me live out of spite. She loomed over my beaten body, blood coating her clothes and hair, looking down upon me with her self-righteous smile."

His companions, the fire, and the whole world seemed to fade around him. In Clement's mind, he was back at his castle. He could feel the searing pain issuing from his broken bones. He tasted the blood filling his mouth and stinging his eyes. He lay upon the cold icy snow inside his courtyard. Smoke filled the skies as his capital burned and his defeated soldiers stared in despair from the ramparts.

Sylvia's shadow fell across Clement's face. He pressed his arms against the ground to lift himself but his weary muscles no longer supported his weight and he collapsed. The battle was over. He was defeated.

He looked up into Sylvia's hate-filled eyes.

"Kill me!" he ordered, his voice ringing through the courtyard.

"No!" Her eyes flashed with sadistic joy. "Your reign of terror is over, and now you will suffer. You'll suffer like you made so many others suffer. You'll feel the pain you caused your people, weep the tears shed by wives whose husbands you took, and feel the loss of mothers whose children died because of you. Their pain is yours to share!"

Her insolence fueled his anger. Raising his hand, he sent a blast of magical energy at her, but she deflected the attack with ease.

"If you think this humiliation is bad, let me see you come into my kingdom again," she said. "I promise, you'll pray to the gods for the pain of exile after the suffering I'll bring upon you."

Sylvia leveled her hands at his face, as a cheer rose from her supporters.

"I was banished to the distant northwestern mountains," Clement finished, his mind coming back to the present.

He became aware of his companions sitting around him. They stared enraptured, like rats bewitched by a piper's song. His face turned red. He had exposed too much of his weakness. He sat back down and prodded the fire with a stick. He wished someone would say something. When no one did, he conjured a few pieces of wood and tossed them into the blaze.

"I had no one to take my valued possessions," Darien broke the silence. "My best generals and apprentices were killed investigating Junlorace Keep. The rest died during the war."

"Did any of your men return from the keep?" Xanaphia asked.

"Only one," Darien answered. "When I lost contact with my spies, I sent my most powerful apprentice, Corineous, to find them. I do not think he reached the fort though. He was captured by Sylvia's forces. He betrayed me, joining her army and becoming one of her most powerful allies."

"Corineous?" Clement said, searching his brain for one of Sylvia's generals with such a name. His eyes sprang open. "You mean, Cornelius, the high mage!"

"The same," Darien confirmed. "He changed his name after joining her forces. He wanted to leave his evil past behind. He picked a new name so he could claim a new start."

"How much does he know about Junlorace Keep?" Lillian asked.

"Not much," Darien said. "I instructed him to stay clear of the keep. His orders were to contact the other generals and bring them back in preparation for the war with Sylvia."

"But he knows the location," Clement said.

"He knows the general area. The soldier who escaped from the fort only gave me directions based upon landmarks. I described the Junlorace banner and told him to stay clear of anyone wearing it."

Clement and Lillian exchanged a look.

"What?" he asked.

"You were holding up the cloth when Cordor entered the room," Lillian said. "If Cornelius knows the symbol, they may be able to figure out where Sylvia is being kept."

Darien shrugged. "That is a possibility, but the theory involves a lot of ifs."

"Besides, based upon the letter, Cornelius isn't taking the cloth seriously," Xanaphia said. "Even if Cordor convinces him to take the cloth seriously and is able to describe the symbol to him, the high mage only saw the symbol once. What're the odds he would remember a random coat of arms he hasn't seen in seven years?"

Far to the southeast of the Shattered Hills, in the small town of Unburied Grove, General Cordor marched down the town's snowy thoroughfare. A winter storm was blowing in, and the wind grew more intense with each passing minute. Cordor picked up his pace, eager to rejoin his companions at the inn. He felt exhausted. Excluding a brief catnap, he had been awake since the previous night. His search party departed less than three hours after Sylvia's disappearance. Upon reaching the village, his company sought refuge at the local inn, but Cordor didn't. He was here to find the queen and refused to rest until he questioned the guards and militia.

The results weren't good. There was no sign of Darien or Clement. The news didn't surprise him. The sorcerers didn't have much reason to go this direction. The path north would be the most likely one for them to take. Their kingdoms were forged there. Besides, the city of Unburied

Grove offered little except empty, decaying houses, and those were plentiful in this war-torn nation.

Cordor glanced at the collapsed wall to his right. The fallen stone structure was all that remained of the once-proud fortifications that guarded the graveyard since the earliest days of recorded history. Now the cemetery was in disrepair, and the once vaunted defenses were little more than a ruin. Indeed, the last seventeen years were a sad story for the town.

Unburied Grove was once a proud theocratic city-state known as Buried Grove. The city was powerful and wealthy. The people there lived in splendor, and their town was the center of all commerce in southeast Aurba. The secret of the town's success resided in the land's religious teachings, which claimed anyone buried in the city's sacred soil would be blessed in the world beyond. All citizens desired to be placed within the graveyard, and wealthy nobles paid great sums for interment.

The city naturally attracted many necromancers desiring the corpses to fuel their devious ends. To prevent such defilement, an order of knights was formed to protect the cemetery. The knights proved successful in their mission, driving away many powerful foes and never suffering defeat at the hands of an enemy. No one could break their defenses.

Until Xanaphia came along.

She seduced the captain of the guard and infiltrated the cemetery. By the time the knights discovered her treachery, they were overrun by her newly created horde of undead monstrosities. In the morning, nothing remained of the fabled order except the ruined walls of the once mighty keep. The accumulated corpses of a thousand years became the unholy army with which she forged her empire. The town was decimated during the war, and the endless lines of unearthed tombs inspired inhabitants to sarcastically rename the town Unburied Grove. Xanaphia hated the name and attempted to outlaw it, but the title stuck.

Cordor alighted upon the doorstep of "The Inn of Sacred Rest." Striding inside, he was pleased to leave the cold night air and savor the warmth of the common room. The many hearths surrounding the vast chamber stood as a remnant of the glory days of the once-luxurious inn. Expensive chandeliers equipped with tiny mirrors reflected the fires' glow around a room once housing the wealthiest and most influential pilgrims. Now, the town's last remaining tavern was a simple gathering place where folk came to forget their troubles for a few pleasant hours.

Tonight, the inn teemed with young and old alike eager to bask in the presence of Rhoria's finest soldiers. Merchants sold trinkets to the visitors. Young men pleaded for tales of adventure. Young women battled for the attention of handsome warriors.

Amid the commotion, Cordor spotted Cornelius. The high mage was easy to find in a crowd. Just look for the man surrounded by all the women. Tall, muscular, and handsome, Cornelius was the epitome of everything women found attractive. Already he was encircled by a flock of google-eyed ladies, as he sat laughing, drinking, and recounting his exaggerated exploits.

Cornelius was in the middle of a laugh when he spotted Cordor. The high mage motioned to him, but Cordor shook his head. Instead, he crossed to a vacant armchair in the back corner and sat facing away from the revelers, grateful for the solitude.

He glanced idly at the hearth. A series of small depressions in the dust indicated footfalls had recently disturbed the floor. Judging from the size and shape of the steps, he was certain a child was the source. Very likely, one of the serving girls had recently replenished the wood in the fireplace. Judging from the amount of damage the logs had endured, he guessed the action must have taken place about an hour before.

Cordor felt pride in his powers of observation. As a Morodin, he was forced to develop them without any form of magical assistance. His talents impressed Sylvia, earning him a position as one of her bodyguards. In time, he became commander of her personal entourage.

A shadow crept across the floor toward the chair in which Cordor sat. He looked up to see Cornelius wrapped in his navy blue robes. The high mage placed his hand on the man's shoulder and gave a small squeeze. Then he crossed to an armchair where he sat facing the commander.

"I know what you're thinking," Cornelius said. "Stop berating yourself. Sylvia's disappearance isn't your fault. We're talking about two of the greatest wizards of the modern age."

"Her safety was my responsibility," Cordor said, staring into the fire. "Because of my failure, she is likely dead. Do you really think we'll ever see her alive again?"

"I don't know," Cornelius said, shaking his head. "The ways of evil wizards are mysterious. But I know Darien. He is man of action. If he wanted to kill the queen, then he'd do so. He wouldn't kidnap her unless he had a reason for wanting her alive. As long as he needs her, for whatever reason, there is a chance she remains alive."

Cordor nodded distantly.

"What did the town militia say?" Cornelius asked.

"No one reports seeing Clement or Darien," Cordor replied. "There are no sightings of either passing through the area."

"They have to be somewhere," Cornelius said. "One of our search parties will find them."

"I'm still not sure they're who we need to be looking for."

"Look," Cornelius said. "I've heard your theories and reasons. You're making things more complex than they need to be. We've clearly seen two enemies. We know they were in her room on the night of the kidnapping. They will be hard enough to find without chasing phantasms."

"But what about the guards?"

"There are many spells capable of paralyzing a person and draining the life from them while they're frozen," Cornelius said. "Even I know one or two. I'm confident Darien and Clement know some as well. Some say Clement knows six hundred ways to kill someone."

"But how did they get her out of the castle? And why didn't they go with her?"

"The ways of dark wizards are mysterious," Cornelius answered, annoying Cordor with the same sentiment he used to answer the question previously.

Cordor shook his head. Cornelius sighed in frustration. Sitting upright, he faced Cordor head on to get his attention.

"Look, Clement and Darien had good reason to stay," he said. "Remember the dead guards found at the treasury? While we weren't able to discern what was missing, I'm convinced they stole a powerful artifact. That explains why they stayed behind."

"What about the cloth?"

"How can I speculate about something I didn't see?" Cornelius answered. "I know nothing about the cloth. You're the only person who saw it, and even you admit you didn't get a clear look. Without any details, I can't include it in my calculations."

"What if I could describe the image for you?" Cordor asked.

"I thought you said you couldn't remember it."

"At first I couldn't. But I have replayed the scene a hundred times today. I even saw the symbol during my brief nap last night. Each time I think about the event, the image grows clearer. As if by magic, I could practically see the image swirling before my eyes as we marched here."

"If you're sure your visions are accurate, why don't you tell me?" Cornelius said. "I'm versed in most mystical symbols and designs. Perhaps I can shed some light on the mystery."

"I'm not sure if my dreams and recollections are accurate. My mind could be making up an image that wasn't there."

"Are the visions consistent?"

"Very consistent."

"Give it a go then," Cornelius said. "If the symbol is nonsense, I've lost nothing. But if your recollections are accurate, we may get an answer to the questions disturbing you."

"All right," Cordor agreed. He closed his eyes in concentration. "In my mind, I see Darien holding open the cloth as I enter the room. He releases the fabric, crumpling it in his free hand as he prepares to cast a spell. For the instant I see the cloth, I can make out what appears to be a shield with some picture on the front, kind of like a coat of arms. The picture is a large green clawed fist encircled by a bunch of small crescent shapes. I can't see anything else."

The high mage stared up at the ceiling in thought, stroking his goatee.

"A green fist surrounded by crescent moons on a coat of arms," he repeated. "That sounds familiar."

He rose from his chair and began pacing in front of the fire. Cordor watched him, hoping against hope.

"I know that symbol," Cornelius muttered to himself. "Where have I seen that before? When would it have been? I remember . . ."

For several minutes, Cornelius stroked his goatee, muttering to himself. Then, his eyes flew wide, mouth dropping open.

"It can't be," he said. "But it must be. That's the only reasonable explanation."

"What?" Cordor asked. "What is it?"

Cornelius ignored him, walking distractedly to the hearth and staring at the blank stones above the mantle.

"Of course," he said. "This explains everything. Why didn't I see . . . but after seven years . . ."

"What?" Cordor said, almost shouting in his excitement.

Several people in the common room looked over to the fireplace. Cornelius turned to Cordor. His expression was grave.

"Get the men," he said. "Tell them to go to bed. Then send a courier to get us supplies for traveling through the mountains. We leave in exactly five hours. I will explain later. Right now I need to send a message to Rhoria. I know where the queen is!"

CHAPTER

8

Anxiety gripped Sylvia's soul as fully as the oppressive silence gripped her senses. Trapped inside her lonely cell, she heard Cyril's voice repeat itself like a ghostly mantra haunting the corridors of her mind. He could no longer protect her, he had said. In her mind, that could mean only one thing: torture.

There were many forms of suffering in which the anxiety was worse than the event itself. Although Sylvia had never experienced torture, she doubted it was one of them. The prospect terrified her. She assumed it terrified any sane person. She had fought epic battles, led armies against overwhelming forces, and dueled against the greatest spellcasters of the age. But in all of those situations, the worst fate she could endure was death. Now, she faced the certainty of endless suffering until she surrendered the tiara, died, or was rescued. The prospects of the latter weren't good.

Devoid of means to determine the passage of time, Sylvia sat in eternal solitude awaiting Cyril's arrival. In some ways, she sought his presence as a freedom from the horrific and gruesome visions swimming before her eyes. In other ways, she dreaded his arrival as a herald of impending doom, bringing her worst fears to manifestation.

The gloomy vigil was broken by the jingling of keys and scraping of metal. Light filled the chamber, and Cyril appeared at the foot of the stairs, a torch held high in his hand. With measured steps, he advanced toward her cell. He appeared anxious. His eyes were dim, and his body language guarded. Sylvia knew he could be putting on an act to increase her anxiety. If so, it was working.

He approached until he stood before her. Sylvia gazed at him with stubborn resolve. Despite her nerves, she remained proud. She refused to let him see her fear. If she was going to be tortured, she would face the torture with the same strength and resolve that carried her through every challenge in her rise to power. Cyril studied her face and smiled sadly.

"I see you are determined not to give me the tiara. The end is inevitable, but I came to give you the chance, and so I shall."

He reached into his cloak, withdrawing the crown.

"You need only give the word, and the tiara will be mine," he said. "Do so, and I shall set you free. Do so, and you shall save your people. Do so, and Darlyth will die."

Sylvia's confidence swelled as she gazed upon the crown. It reminded her of her children. She could almost feel them in the room with her. She didn't know if she was imagining the sensation, but whether imagined or not it gave her strength. They believed in her. Surrendering the tiara meant betraying their trust.

"No," Sylvia said. "I'll never give up the tiara!"

Cyril sighed. "I'm sorry to hear you say so. I don't envy you the fate your stubbornness will produce. I pray your strength will hold. Perhaps tomorrow you will reconsider."

He turned toward the stairs.

"You're leaving already?" she asked.

"Yes," he said. "But, regretfully, I'm not leaving you alone."

Another figure passed in through archway. Sylvia recognized it as the female guard who had accompanied Cyril on their first meeting.

"Commander, they're impatient. They demand to come down!"

She spoke in an official tone but her voice trembled.

"So be it," Cyril said. "Allow them in."

A nervous expression flickered across the guard's face, but she hid her fright and turned to leave. Cyril called after her.

"Amanda!"

She looked at him uncertainly.

"You don't have to accompany them down," he said.

A look of relief crossed her face. She gave a small smile before hurrying up the stairs. Sylvia looked back at Cyril. A change seemed to come over him. The red in his eyes burned brightly, and his body tensed as though preparing for a fight.

Sylvia turned toward the archway. At first, nothing happened. Then she heard the noises. Deep, raspy, wheezing sounds like heavy rocks dragging against stone drifted down the stairs, echoing off the walls and getting louder. Sylvia's eyes strained to see the source, but no torchlight came from the stairs.

"What is that noise?" Sylvia asked.

"Former residents of Kendross Keep," Cyril said in disgust. "The demon lord considers human torture techniques too soft!"

Two figures appeared in the archway. Sylvia gasped in horror as the hairs on her arms rose. She couldn't remember seeing anything so hideous. She could tell the creatures were once human. They still possessed vaguely humanoid features. They had two arms, a head, and walked on two legs. The similarities ended there.

The creatures possessed awkward misshapen bodies covered with thick black fur. Their torsos bent low to the ground under the weight of humped backs, and their long arms dragged across the floor. The faces were bat-like with elongated noses and large pointed ears. The teeth were thin and sharp. The eyes were red and bloodshot. The wheezing noises proved to be the creatures' breathing, and Sylvia cringed each time they inhaled.

"What are they?" she whispered.

"I don't know if there is a proper name," Cyril said. "We call them grorgs."

The grorgs slunk into the room, gazing at her with wild feral eyes. She fought against her revulsion but soon succumbed to the disgust. She stared at the floor, unable to look at them any longer.

"She needs to be unshackled," one of them said.

The voice was as terrible as the breathing. The pitch was high like a child's but scratchy like an old man's and came out in one long hiss like a snake. She looked up to see the larger of the two grorgs pointing at her with a long, clawed finger. Its other hand held a brown sack concealing a number of various trinkets that poked against the outside.

Cyril pulled a key from his cloak. Unlocking the door, he proceeded into the cell. Sylvia held out her arms, but Cyril didn't look at her. He knelt down beside the metal slab affixed to her bindings. Touching the side, he revealed a concealed keyhole and twisted the key inside. The manacles on her hands and feet released, clattering to the ground.

She was free to stand upright and move around for the first time. She couldn't enjoy her freedom. The smaller of the two grorgs followed Cyril into the cell, advancing until it was almost touching her. She battled the urge to vomit as the creature's putrid breath blasted her face. She backed away, but the creature advanced, smiling maliciously.

The larger grorg gave a loud grunt, and the smaller one backed off. The larger companion reached into the bag and withdrew a pair of thin metal bangles.

"Hold out her arms," it ordered, looking at Cyril.

"Hold them out yourself!" Cyril snarled. "I'm not your servant."

The grorg growled, bearing its teeth, but Cyril didn't back down.

"Fine," it hissed, turning to its smaller companion. "Hold out her arms to me."

The smaller grorg advanced toward the queen, but Sylvia didn't want it touching her. She refused to be shackled against her will. Even in the face of extreme torture and horrific monsters, she would maintain her dignity. Sidestepping the advancing grorg, she strode toward the other, her arms outstretched. It looked shrewdly at her, smiling.

"So proud," it said. "But you might not be so eager to taste your fate in the days to come."

The grorg held up the bands, its bloodshot eyes sparkling with excitement.

"These are a special piece of magical jewelry," it said. "Let me show you how they work."

The creature pulled on the sides of the rings. To Sylvia's surprise, they opened in the center like manacles. The grorg snapped one onto each wrist then pulled hard to make sure they didn't reopen. Sylvia lifted her arms to her face, examining them with interest. They looked like plain bangles. The only remarkable characteristic was that they neither possessed keyholes nor any line to denote where they opened. They were thin, light weight, not connected to each other, and had no loops through which to connect a chain.

Sylvia failed to see their purpose. She looked at Cyril as though expecting some explanation, but the kefling had turned his back to her and was staring determinedly at the floor.

"Their powers won't function within the confines of the magical barrier surrounding this room," the grorg continued. "In order for you to see their full purpose, I must remove it."

The beast pulled a small pink rock the size of a marble from its bag. Holding the ball high into the air, its powerful fingers crushed the stone into powder. A dark-green light filled the dungeon for an instant before fading.

Suddenly, Sylvia's magic sprang to life. The effect blocking her spells was gone. She was free, at last.

Without thinking, she flung her arms toward the grorg. They had made a mistake lowering the magical defenses. Now she would make them pay. Even if they could defeat her, she preferred to go down fighting rather than subject herself to torture.

Her powers rose to her call, and energy surged to her fingertips. The excitement of battle flooded her senses. In the distant recesses of her mind, a voice cried out in warning but the invigorating sense of freedom blinded her to all thoughts of caution.

"Oustranyat!"

Magic exploded from her hands, sending strands of emerald light into the air. But the beams didn't fly toward the grorg. Instead, they fired backward, striking the bangles. The bands constricted, glowing red as they heated to inconceivable temperatures. Sylvia's battle cry quickly turned into a scream as the bracelets grew smaller and smaller, the metal burning through skin and flesh.

She fell to the floor, unable to do anything but scream. Gradually, the bracelets grew cool again. She looked down at her wrists. The bands had burrowed deep into her arms. Melted flesh oozed around them before solidifying, leaving the bracelets permanently welded into her body.

The smaller grorg seized her shoulder and yanked Sylvia to her feet. Lifting her arms to its ugly face, the fiend inhaled the smell of burnt flesh like a gardener savoring his roses. The larger grorg chuckled.

"Good," it said. "I had hoped you would assist with the demonstration. You played your part perfectly."

Sylvia glared.

"What've you done to me?" she asked, yanking her hands from the smaller grorg's grip.

"They're called burning bracers," the large grorg said. "Surely you've heard of them."

Sylvia fell to her knees, burying her hands in her face. While she had no way to know what burning bracers looked like, she still chided herself. She had learned about them while studying at the academy. They were dangerous objects created by an evil wizard to enslave his rivals. All spells cast by someone wearing the bracers were absorbed into the bands, rendering the spells useless and inflicting severe pain upon the wearer. All copies were supposedly destroyed after their creator's demise, but rumors claimed that former Headmaster Sorin owned a pair and put them on disobedient apprentices.

"I bet you've never heard of this though," the grorg continued. Sylvia looked up as the creature withdrew a small fist-sized rock from the bag. "Pretty, isn't it?"

Sylvia couldn't deny it. The stone had the size and shape of a river rock with a long oval body and glassy surface. The brilliant white stone resembled a misshapen pearl with a soft-white light radiating from the core. The light was gentle, calming, and quite pleasant.

"Do you like it?" the grorg asked. "It's called The Life Stone. It is one of the greatest treasures ever created for the benefit of humanity. Legend says it was crafted by an ancestor of the great Kendross himself!"

The mention of the name Kendross seemed to attract Cyril's attention. Sylvia saw him look up from the floor for the first time since the grorgs entered the room. Though he wasn't looking at them, she could tell he was listening.

"Any human touching the stone can't die from wounds no matter how severe," the grorg continued. "And, once a day, if the proper command word is spoken, it heals a human of all injuries, even regenerating detached limbs and body parts."

Sylvia stared at the stone in amazement, wondering why she had never heard of the object. Of course, almost all historical records predating the Demon Wars were lost, and history wasn't her subject. Still, such a powerful artifact should have stuck in her mind. Cyril also seemed interested in the stone. His brow furrowed in concentration, and she sensed his mind working frantically.

"You may be asking yourself what the stone means to you," the grorg said. It moved into the cell and bent toward Sylvia until their noses were touching. "It means you can't die. It means I can sever your head from your neck with my fingernails. As long as you hold this stone, you'll never feel the sweet release of death. It means you'll experience pain beyond anything imaginable and suffer it from now until eternity and never escape, unless you give up the tiara. That's what it means."

The creature backed away, allowing the implications to sink in.

"Take her to that cell," it ordered the smaller grorg, indicating the cell across from Sylvia. "Those manacles are better for chaining her spread eagle. That will make it easier to keep the stone on her."

The small grorg gave a cackle of delight, reaching for Sylvia's arm.

"Leave me alone," Sylvia snapped. "I can walk there myself!"

Rising from the floor, she lifted her head high and crossed toward the indicated cell.

"After you, Your Majesty," the large grorg sneered.

Sylvia ignored it, striding inside with as much dignity as she could muster. She laid down upon the cold stone floor, while the smaller grorg fit the manacles to her wrists and ankles.

"Are you going to stay and watch?" the larger grorg hissed at Cyril.

"No," he said. "I'm a warrior. Your disgusting sciences don't interest me."

She looked up in time to see him flash up the stairs. Then she turned toward the larger grorg, who entered the cell.

"Place the stone in her right hand and keep it there," it ordered the smaller companion.

The small grorg did as ordered, pressing the stone into Sylvia's palm and squeezing her fist tightly.

The large grorg grinned. "We can begin."

—⁂—

Cyril slammed the dungeon door shut behind him and locked it securely with the key before lowering a heavy wooden plank across the front for extra measure. Stepping back, he turned to the guards flanking the doorway.

"Amanda, Eustace," he said. "When they're ready to leave, come get me. *Do not* let them out of the room without my permission, do you understand? I don't want those *things* wandering my castle unattended!"

"Yes, sir!" they said, snapping to attention.

He gave a satisfied nod. As he turned to leave, the first sounds of blood-curdling shrieks issued from the depths below. He paused and turned back.

"If you need a break from the screaming, you can go to the surface for a few minutes, but at least one of you needs to remain on guard. Understood?"

"Yes, sir," they responded, their voices less certain as they listened to the cries.

Cyril darted down the hall and around a corner. At the far end of the corridor, a long stone staircase ascended for almost a hundred feet. The stairs were the first line of defense for anyone attempting to escape the dungeon. Long and steep, they were difficult to ascend or descend. Out of shape soldiers were often forced to climb them as a conditioning exercise. With his unique speed and unnatural vitality, Cyril ascended them in seconds.

At the top was a small landing with an archway leading to the courtyard. A blast of freezing wind and ice struck Cyril's unprotected face. The blizzard wracking the countryside was the worst Cyril could remember in almost a decade.

The storm didn't discourage Ladonna though. Cyril could see his zealous second-in-command standing knee deep in the snow as she led her soldiers through various drills. In the skies above, wingham riders fought the merciless winds as they drove their mounts through aerial maneuvers. Personally, Cyril thought they might benefit more from a warm day inside with their families. But he knew better than to argue with his feisty red-haired officer.

"Commander Ladonna," he shouted over the howling wind. She looked at him, leaning forward as she strained to hear. "I would like you to report to my office upon the conclusion of your drills."

"As you wish, My Liege!" she shouted.

Cyril turned away, strolling across the grounds at a walk. As he crossed the snowy grounds, Cyril surveyed the activity around the keep. In the distance stood the wingham pins. Caring for the reptiles was a central part of life at the keep. The inhabitants loved them like their own children. Even amid the storm, men, women, and children endured freezing temperatures and brutal winds to keep their beloved pets warm.

To his left, Cyril passed by the kitchens. The aroma of freshly cooked food wafted through the windows. He saw night watchmen finishing their meals in preparation of retiring. Other soldiers devoured their breakfast as the new day dawned. Farmers and laborers, done wintering the livestock, played games in the adjoining common room.

Cyril shook his head. The fortress was dying. Less than a thousand years ago, the structure housed almost fifteen hundred men, women, and children. In those days, it stood as the shining symbol of a new era free from the tyranny of the demon lord. Now, the fortress held less than a hundred and fifty inhabitants, many of them soldiers. Most could trace their ancestry directly to the original inhabitants. Others were reinforcements sent from Kendross Keep before the demon lord destroyed their home.

The citizens lived a hard life. From the moment they arose until the last hour before bed, which his ancestors declared an official and necessary period of rest, the citizens spent their entire day working. Cyril understood the rigorous and monotonous lifestyle. The Junlorace family stayed in power by sharing the same hardships as their people. Cyril could fight better than any soldier, cook and clean as well as any kitchen worker, plow the rocky fields with the farmers, tend the animals, and perform any other activity needed around the fortress. He always stood ready to assist his people whenever they called upon him.

But he and his people, like the keep itself, had outlived their usefulness. The keep was built to protect one of the golden orbs imprisoning the demon lord. Now the orbs were destroyed, and his people, like him, existed as nothing more than pawns in Darlyth's evil schemes. Still, the citizens remained. The keep was the only home they knew, and Cyril's devotion to the demon lord was the only thing keeping them alive.

Cyril stopped at a large wooden door and pulled on the cold brass handle. With a creek of iron and a crunch of snow, it slid open to reveal a short hallway with two doors on each side. The two on the left led to his family's sleeping chambers. Cyril never used them. He couldn't bear sleeping in the bed he once shared with his parents or sitting on the floor where they used to play.

His parents loved their people too. They saw the slow death the citizens endured in the quest to protect the orbs. Despairing from endless centuries of neglect, they became convinced only the demon lord could give them freedom. The decision cost them their lives. Cyril blamed both sides. He blamed the world for the neglect that drove his parents to madness. He blamed the demon lord for killing them.

He walked past the door leading to the library. For many centuries the room was in disrepair until Cyril's parents revived the upkeep of the texts. Ancient scrolls and histories predating the Demon Wars filled the room. The forbidden ritual for birthing a kefling was discovered within.

Cyril spent a lot of time in the room. He enjoyed reading old histories and researching arcane topics. The spells and manuscripts proved invaluable for developing his skills as a sorcerer. Yet, his greatest discovery wasn't made among the books or papers lining the dusty shelves. Beneath the floorboards in a back corner, Cyril discovered a secret compartment housing objects hidden by distant ancestors.

The most remarkable was the sword fastened to his belt. The magical blade remained impervious to age or rust. It first belonged to the general who led humanity against the demon lord in the final battle.

Cyril came to a stop at the last room in the hall. The door was open, and a fire burned in the grate, casting a gentle glow over a cluttered desk, two armchairs, and a small cot. The room once served as the office for the chaplain, but his family had died off many generations ago. Now, Cyril used the room as his own.

He crossed to the desk. As he walked around the back, his eyes fell upon the golden chalice resting in the middle of the oaken surface. His eyes glowed in the reflection of the shining metal as he gazed upon the cup. Someone had brought his daily drink.

His right hand shot toward the glass, but his left hand seized it by the wrist, pulling it back with an effort. Closing his eyes, he took several steadying breaths to suppress the waves of desperate hunger coursing through him. He must maintain control, he told himself. He must stay strong.

He opened his eyes again. In a controlled manner, he reached out, taking the glass in both hands. Lifting it to his lips, he drank the thick red blood inside. The warm, sweet fluid oozed down his throat, stimulating his senses and satisfying his lusts in a way no food could ever achieve. He drained the chalice until only the line of droplets sticking to the inside of the cup remained. Then he threw it away in disgust. He hated his drink but had no choice. He needed blood. He was half-demon. All demons craved blood and would go mad without it.

When Cyril was a boy, his parents let their blood for him. As he got older, they let the blood of their servants as well. Now, a rotation existed so every citizen gave a small amount of blood each week. Cyril hated asking them to do so, but they did the task cheerfully. They cared about him as much as he cared for them. They even went so far as to claim letting blood was healthy. Cyril wished he could reward them. If he could get the tiara, he'd find a way to repay their loyalty and punish those who had hurt them.

Cyril looked down at the papers covering his desk. He had spent all night reading them. Many were letters his ancestors sent to kings and nobles throughout the land at times of need asking for supplies, medicine, reinforcements, or other forms of assistance. The rest were rejection notices, refusals, and collections of various excuses for being unwilling to allocate any of their men or supplies to aid the survival of the isolated and politically unimportant keep. In time, his ancestors stopped sending the letters for fear of losing too many messengers to death in the mountains.

Outsiders wouldn't help them, only caring about increasing their political standing, gaining power, building allies, and enriching their coffers. They didn't care about the needs of an insignificant population hidden in the middle of nowhere, even if that population was the only thing standing between them and complete destruction.

Cyril's fists clinched in anger. They must be punished. They must see what happens to those who turn their backs upon his citizens in their hour of need. They must pay for their shortsighted greed and egotistical ambitions. And they would. They would suffer for their apathy, either at his hands or the hands of his demonic master.

With an angry swipe, he brushed the letters off the desk. As they floated to the ground, he heard a tap at the window behind him. He turned and flung open the shades. A powerful blast of cold air and ice greeted him as a white and gray pigeon swooped into the room and settled on his mantle.

Cyril scowled. He had expected to receive the correspondence yesterday. He fought to suppress his irritation as he untied the string. The bird sprang from the mantle and back into the night. Unfolding the note, Cyril examined the familiar writing of his long time correspondent.

We are coming. Be prepared.

Really? He thought. *That's it?*

No explanation of why they were late. No apology for the delay in contacting him. No discussion of timing, numbers, and anything useful. Cyril frowned and tossed the page into the fire. He rested his elbow on the mantle and stared at the blank wall before him. He remained lost in through until disturbed by the tinkle of a metal object.

He turned to see Ladonna placing the cup back on his desk. A surge of fresh emotions gripped him as he stared at her slender body and beautiful green eyes. Her hair was disheveled and covered with snow. Her face was coated with half-frozen sweat, and her skin had turned slightly blue. Yet, even now, she looked beautiful to him. He loved her dearly.

They had been together since childhood. She was the daughter of the former head guard, conceived during the keep's first attempt to create a kefling. The ritual failed. She wasn't a true kefling, but she wasn't entirely human either. Her hair was the color of blood and grew darker when she experienced strong emotions. Even more remarkable were the alterations bestowed by the demonic magic. Although one couldn't tell by looking at her, she possessed the inhuman strength, sharp senses, and lightning reflexes of a demon.

She was the perfect companion for him. Growing up, they were playmates and even promised to marry. It was a promise Cyril couldn't keep. The demon lord's rise haunted him, and his concern for his people came between them. He couldn't let himself be with her as long as his people remained in danger.

"Anything interesting?" she asked, pointing at the note in the fire.

"They're coming," he answered, taking a seat behind his desk.

Ladonna nodded. Crossing the room, she moved to the open window, closing the portal and sealing the chamber from the violent winds outside.

"The grorgs are in the dungeon with the queen, I presume?"

She spoke casually, but her face betrayed her disgust.

"Yes," Cyril confirmed.

"Do you really believe she'll give us the tiara?"

Cyril shook his head.

"Reason and diplomacy have failed," he said. "Perhaps torture will succeed where civility cannot. If the grorgs fail, we still have the last resort."

Ladonna sat down across from Cyril, gazing intently at him.

"And if that fails, what then?" she asked. "She'll be taken to Kendross Keep. We'll lose the tiara forever, and Darlyth will punish us for our failure."

"Possibly," Cyril said. "But the punishment won't be swift or harsh. I doubt he expects my plan to succeed. He went along for the sake of expediency but will still get the tiara even if my plan fails. He'll feel little need to make an example of us. He may not deliver any punishment at all."

"Cyril, this is madness," she said, rising to her feet. She bent over his desk her hair turning darker as she pleaded to him. "I know he killed your parents, but think of everything he has given you. Think of everything you'll lose if he learns of your betrayal. Think of all we gain by remaining loyal to him."

At the word "we," Cyril lifted his eyebrows. Ladonna blushed, and her hair turned even darker. Cyril knew her thoughts. If the demon lord took power and rewarded Cyril as promised, she believed they could finally be together. Cyril stared into her eyes. He knew how much he hurt her by distancing himself.

"Ladonna, you don't know the demon lord the way I know him," Cyril said. "You don't know demons the way I know them. There can never be hope or love in a world they rule. Not even for us!"

"At least there'll be retribution!"

Cyril nodded. Ladonna's parents had instilled in her the same anger and resentment Cyril possessed. The death of her parents had only solidified the feelings. But Cyril could not dwell on such thoughts. He had summoned Ladonna for a purpose. The sooner she began her mission, the sooner he could get the information he needed.

"I have an important assignment for you," he said, assuming a formal tone.

Ladonna apparently sensed the shift in his mood. She rose to attention.

"Yes, My Liege, I'm at your service."

"I need you to collect all literate soldiers and take them to the library," he said. "Search every book and manuscript on magical artifacts and relics. I need all the information you can find about an object known as The Life Stone."

"I shall do so immediately."

Ladonna turned and marched from the room. Cyril stared after her. She was right. He had a great deal to lose by treachery. Why was he risking himself for the people of Aurba? Not one of them had done anything for him.

He opened the large bottom drawer of his desk. A number of papers sat piled inside, but they were a ruse. He lifted the papers and the fake bottom to reveal a second chamber. Inside, sat a small wooden jewelry box. He withdrew the box, placing it on his desk.

He first discovered the box under the floorboards in the library. It was old and stained, but the sheet of gold affixed to the top remained in pristine condition. His hand ran across the plate, feeling the engraved letters to the ancient oath of Junlorace Keep.

I solemnly swear upon my blood and the blood of my children so long as my life and line endure, I shall do everything within my power to protect the world from the demon lord. To this duty, I dedicate all my thoughts, dreams, and my very existence from now until the end of the world!

No one had taken the oath for centuries, but Cyril knew the words by heart. He lifted the lid, revealing a pebble-sized fragment of gold on a velvet cushion. It was the last remaining piece of the golden orb of Junlorace Keep.

When the leaders of the two keeps completed the ritual to release the demon lord, Darlyth went on a rampage. Driven mad by bloodlust, he killed all of them. Only one person survived, Cyril. His speed had allowed him to find a hiding place. As he hid from the massacre, a small chunk of shattered orb kicked across the room. Instinctively, Cyril had picked it up and hidden it inside his pocket as Darlyth destroyed every other trace of the orbs. Cyril felt convinced the tiny fragment held the key to Darlyth's demise.

Cyril lifted the stone, turning it around in his hands. He knew every crack, crevice, and surface by heart from endless days and nights spent studying it. He felt a connection to it, as though they shared some inexplicable bond. He closed his eyes, savoring the strange connection. The stone's magic quivered at his touch. He felt sure the stone wanted to communicate with him, to pass on some secret revelation.

Approaching footsteps shattered his meditation. He placed the stone into the box and hurriedly returned both to the hidden chamber, slamming the drawer. A soldier strode in the room, holding a tray of eggs and bread.

"Commander Ladonna requested I bring food," he said. "She suspected you might not have eaten."

Cyril smiled. Ladonna was perceptive.

"Thank you, Jason. Just place it on the desk."

The soldier obeyed, giving a small bow and turning to leave. Cyril glanced at the fireplace. His eyes rested on the charred remains of the pigeon's note.

"Jason!" he called.

The soldier turned, snapping to attention.

"Once the weather dies down, take a message to Kendross Keep. Tell them the queen's rescue party is on the way. Request a demon be deployed to guard Spiked Canyon. I don't want to take any chances."

The guard nodded, but Cyril sensed his apprehension.

"Take two others with you for security," he added. "Dismissed!"

The guard left the room. Cyril looked at the tray of food. He'd been up for almost twenty-four hours without food or drink. The stress of the last few days had drained his appetite. He took the food over to his cot, where he lay down, intending to nibble on the bread and fell asleep within minutes.

CHAPTER

9

The march from the Shattered Hills was the most miserable day of travel Darien had endured since before his rise to power. His legs felt like lead as he marched against the gale force winds, and he ducked his head for protection from the pelting snow. He wasn't the only one struggling. Lillian and Clement muttered warming spells like mantras. Even Xanaphia strained against the tempest.

A shout made Darien look up. Lillian was calling to Xanaphia, who fell back to join the company. Darien rushed forward to join them also.

"I don't understand," he heard Xanaphia shout over the wind. "Why're we going that way? Riddian's Pass is to the northeast."

"I want to head for Southgrain," Lillian called back. "The town is a day's march east. I commissioned a road to carry supplies between there and Riddian's Pass. It was never finished, but we can make better time along the trail than trudging through this snow. Plus, the village is a good place to get food and provisions."

"Sounds good to me," Darien hollered.

"Southgrain it is then!" Xanaphia agreed.

The group turned and started walking in the indicated direction.

"I can't believe they rebuilt that stupid town," Clement shouted. "I thought I had destroyed the town forever after the forced relocation during my last campaign."

"I'm sure," Lillian said, her voice dripping with sarcasm. "But, incredible as it must seem, they decided to rebuild the town rather than remain in your labor camp."

"They were extraordinarily ungrateful," he said. "I put a great deal of work into making sure prisoners of war had nice facilities with good roofs over their heads."

"Since the mine was located in the arctic, having doors and windows might've been nice too," Lillian said. Clement ignored her.

"They had nice beds."

"Yeah, who doesn't like sleeping on straw mats?" Lillian retorted.

"And we shipped them almost one hundred pounds of food every day."

"To feed a population of more than five hundred."

"Not after the first winter," Clement protested. "Their numbers dropped substantially afterward."

"So did their productivity," Lillian noted.

"How do you know?" Xanaphia asked.

"Because the general in charge of the camp was one of my spies," she said. "He smuggled more than half the metals they produced into my kingdom."

"Makes sense," Darien said, walking past a suddenly immobile Clement. "Are you coming?"

Clement's eyes narrow, and his lips pursed. "That skunk, I could kill him."

"You already did," Lillian noted.

"True," he said, "but this time I'd have a good reason."

The trek continued in silence without stopping for lunch. By late afternoon, the storm broke, although the sky remained overcast. Darien studied the gray clouds overhead. Such weather characterized Aurba's typically fierce winter season. Still, Darien disliked the gloomy conditions. They reminded him of his flight from the academy.

Following his teacher's death, Darien had escaped into the rugged northeastern region of Aurba. No one would pursue him there. The icy wilderness was largely untamed, and the climate remained fixed in a seemingly endless ice age. No one would expect him to flee that direction, or so he thought.

In the far north, Darien was able to vanish and live in complete obscurity until Xanaphia rose to power. When she conquered the southeast and began expanding northward, Darien amassed an army to oppose her. Needing more soldiers, he subjugated the towns he passed through, forcing their citizens into service.

Some opponents suggested he was becoming just as evil as Xanaphia. They didn't live to make the claim twice. In Darien's mind, the suffering was for the greater good. When he destroyed Xanaphia, the people would thank him. But after Sylvia arrived, his ungrateful populace heralded her as a liberating hero. Her vilification of him wiped away everything he had done for his people and everything he had sacrificed to protect them. He hated her for it.

The group marched onward. Empty plains turned to thick forests. By the time the party approached Southgrain, Darien was exhausted.

Realizing they were close to the city, the company huddled to determine their next course of action.

"We still have several hours before we need to camp," Xanaphia said. "We should continue onward. We can't afford to lose time."

"I disagree," Darien said, his muscles aching. "We actually gain time by staying in town. Right now, we have to keep watch at night. We lose eight hours a day to sleep and another hour to set up camp and eat."

"He's right," Clement agreed. "If there's an inn, we can sleep in separate rooms. We won't need a watch. We can grab food and set off in the morning after a short rest."

"There used to be a small tavern," Lillian said. "I'm sure it's still there."

—⚅—

Twenty minutes later, they entered the town. Xanaphia walked behind the company. Everyone had taken actions to disguise their identities. Predictably, Lillian chose the security of an invisibility spell. Clement, on the other hand, used a variety of enchantments to alter his height and facial features. Darien, who lacked any skill with beguilement spells, simply wrapped his head in a scarf. Since his kingdom didn't directly border Lillian's land and they never marched armies against each other, the citizens were unlikely to recognize him.

Xanaphia relied upon her cloak, employing the disguise of a shapely redhead she had once used to seduce the knights of Buried Grove. In her disguise, she followed the others through town. Normally she preferred to walk ahead of the group but felt the sight of hardened adventurers led by a fragile-looking young woman might attract attention. If she was following, less suspicion would be roused.

Children lined the streets, using the last hours of daylight as a chance to enjoy the new-fallen snow. Several of the groups were having snowball fights. A poorly thrown snowball struck Darien hard in the side of the head as they walked. Xanaphia suppressed a snicker, but the children didn't. They laughed and pointed in obvious amusement. Darien's eyes flashed, and Xanaphia heard him muttered under his scarf. For a second, she thought he was about to attack the child, but after a pause he continued down the street.

Xanaphia shook her head. The child couldn't possibly know how close he came to suffering a potentially lethal punishment. As things stood, she wasn't certain the child escaped unscathed. She noticed every single snowball coming anywhere near him, no matter the target, seemed to swerve slightly, hitting him instead. She smiled. The kid had gotten off easy. Then again, she wondered how long the spell might last.

After a brisk walk, they reached the inn. The building looked newer and better cared for than most of the structures in town. A sturdy oak door occupied in the center of a fancy balcony atop a staircase. Clement ascended first, or so Xanaphia assumed since she couldn't see the invisible spymaster. Xanaphia followed, but Darien hung back.

"I saw an apothecary a few blocks back," he said. "I want to see if they have any useful herbs or resources."

Without awaiting acknowledgement, Darien headed back down the street. Xanaphia watched him go then turned to Clement.

"I'll stay out here also," she said. "I'm just going to linger on the balcony for a while."

Clement shrugged. Turning away, he pushed open the door and strolled inside. The door lingered open for a moment after Clement walked through then seemingly closed on its own. Xanaphia smiled. Lillian normally didn't make such careless mistakes. She probably figured no one in town was clever enough to notice. She was probably right.

The necromancer walked across the balcony and stood leaning against the rail. A couple of men carrying firewood gave shrill whistles and catcalls as they walked past. She ignored them. She didn't want to go into the inn. She felt uncomfortable in crowded places.

At the academy, she had spent most of her time in her room with her teacher. As a regent, she had rarely visited her court. She found people to be strange and incomprehensible. She didn't understand them and felt conspicuous in their presence. She feared they would see through her illusions and see her true appearance. Even worse, she secretly feared they might see through her and discover her inner fears, weaknesses, and doubts. For this reason, she disliked the living and refused to get close to anyone.

The inn was on the edge of town. A small road ran into the forest, disappearing as the trees grew thicker. She stared down the street, and her heart leapt for joy. About a mile down the road, she spotted the gate of an old cemetery.

Xanaphia raced down from the balcony and sprinted toward it. She hadn't visited a graveyard in years for fear of giving herself away. But she fondly remembered the endless hours spent exploring graveyards when she was younger, especially the Royal Graveyard in Rhoria. She longed to return to it someday but had never gotten the opportunity.

Reaching the entrance, she yanked open the gate and sprang inside. Standing among the tombs, she spread her arms, closing her eyes in bliss as she strolled along the snow-covered grounds. It wasn't the Royal Graveyard. Nor was it particularly large or impressive. But it was a graveyard nonetheless. For the first time in a long time, she felt at peace.

She whirled in ecstasy, feeling the cold touch of the grave flowing over her body like a refreshing summer rain. Spinning in intoxicated rapture, she lost all track of time. Xanaphia was at home.

A series of screams shattered her bliss. Children were shrieking in horror. Startled, she gazed in all directions, trying to determine the source of the sound. It emanated from the woods.

Leaping the fence like a hurdle, she charged into the forest, dodging through the trees as she sought the source of the disturbance. Ahead, she spotted three children racing toward her. The snow-covered adolescents had apparently been playing in the woods and wandered too far from town. Xanaphia strained her eyes to see what they were running from. At first she saw nothing.

Then she spotted it. Three large purple worm-like creatures raced through the snow behind them. Their long bodies undulated up and down through the icy ground like giant sea serpents swimming through water. Xanaphia hesitated. They were snow dragons.

Snow Dragons were massive snake-like creatures with bodies almost twenty feet in length. The gaping maws at the front of the long serpentine bodies were filled with rows of razor sharp teeth, which curved inward. Unlike most draconic creatures, snow dragons couldn't fly. They compensated for this weakness with a unique ability to move through snow as though swimming through water. The ability stemmed from intense body heat, which melted the ice in front of them as they moved. Furthermore, they possessed the uncanny ability to leap high into the air and unleash devastating aerial assaults.

Xanaphia wasn't surprised to see them migrating south with the winter snow. Still, the sight unnerved her. She possessed no previous experience battling them and knew only a few rudimentary tactics to aid her. They were cunning predators and usually hunted in large groups. The battle was likely to be a prolonged affair, and she doubted the visible creatures comprised the entire pack. More lurked beneath the surface.

The dragons were almost on top of the fleeing children. Xanaphia knew she needed to act. Racing forward, she raised her hands shouting, "Skachuk!"

The children rose into the air, landing on the thick upper branches of some nearby trees. Their newfound altitude did little to hinder the dragons though. The monstrosities sprang from the snow, snapping at the juveniles' legs. Two more creatures appeared, charging Xanaphia.

"Podneemeetez!" she said, touching her chest.

Her body rose several feet off the ground to hover above the snow. Levitation spells slowed down a person's movements, hindering mobility. Nevertheless, they were necessary when fighting burrowing creatures. She strolled toward the dragons building her magic until the air crackled. As she approached, the foremost attacker burst from the snow, saliva glistening off hooked fangs.

"Schlepuk!" Xanaphia shouted, waving her arm in a slapping motion. A loud noise of rushing wind filled the air. The creature spun away as though suffering a powerful blow from an unseen force. Still her adversaries remained undiscouraged. A second attack followed the first, followed by another and another.

"Plamya!" Xanaphia shouted, blasting the creature backward with spouts of flame. "Plamya!"

After a brutal struggle in which Xanaphia counted more than six of the creatures, the dragons burrowed into the snow and vanished. One of the children started to climb down from the tree.

"No!" Xanaphia shouted. "They're not gone!"

The boy climbed back up, and Xanaphia scanned the ground. They were regrouping, preparing to strike anew in a more orderly fashion.

Xanaphia threw off her cloak. This would be a battle to the death, and she didn't want anything obstructing her movements. She heard the children gasp at her undisguised appearance but didn't care. She had more immediate concerns. Although the spell Schlepuk batted them away, the attack appeared to leave no permanent impact upon her enemies. Even Plamya failed to make a lasting impression.

She racked her mind for some plan but came up with nothing. Tactics and strategy were never her strength, particularly if she had to make them up on the fly. Sheer brute force and overwhelming numbers were the strength of a necromancer, not strategy.

With a blast, the first creature erupted from the frost beneath her. Anticipating the attack, she leapt to the side, tumbling to a crouching position.

"Paneet!"

The spell wasn't one she used often. A gray swirling light shot from her hand and hit the monster, causing large tears in its skin. Still, it gave no indication of pain or injury. No sooner did she defend against this first dragon than five more burst from the ground in unison. One came from her left, another from her right, one in front and one behind. As the four converged on her, a fifth and smaller one sprang in a high arc coming at her from above.

"Preleeve!" Xanaphia called.

A bright-blue globe of energy encircled her body, exploding outward to strike the creatures. It collided with the first four, successfully deflecting their attack. Unfortunately, the fifth dragon was unaffected. It swooped down upon her, teeth bared and black orb-like eyes shining with the excitement of the kill.

"Tolkat!" screamed a nearby voice.

The spell caught creature in mid-air, its mouth just inches from Xanaphia's head. The force slammed the beast into a nearby tree. It rolled over, burrowing back into the snow. For a moment, everything became still again.

Xanaphia spun around to discover Darien sprinting toward her. Reaching her side, he threw off his cloak and scarf and muttered, "Podneemeetez." The enchanter rose into the air and raised his arms, prepared for battle.

"They are just regrouping," Darien said. "They'll be back."

"I know," Xanaphia said. "Have you fought these before?"

"Many times," he answered. "They are native to my kingdom. Do not use fire or physically damaging spells. The attacks may deflect them but will not hurt them. The best spells are inner damage spells like Gnev or Peetka."

"Korobeetcya?" Xanaphia suggested.

"No," he said, "they move too quickly. Keep to shorter, one-syllable spells."

Darien and Xanaphia stood back-to-back waiting for the attack. Both suspected another assault was forthcoming, and they were not disappointed. The creatures launched themselves from the ground, striking from multiple directions and angles, but Xanaphia and Darien drove them off.

This time the creatures didn't stop to regroup. Relying on a tactic of simply overwhelming their opponents with one long, sustained assault, they sprang from the snow over and over as quickly as possible. Spells flew everywhere as Darien and Xanaphia battled for their lives.

At random times, Darien would yell out instructions, indicating directions that they needed to move, different places they needed to stand, where the next attack would come from, and which creature to target. Somehow, he was always right.

After almost ten minutes, one of the dragons finally collapsed dead upon the snow. A few minutes later, a second one fell. By the end of twenty minutes, the dragons had lost half their pack. The battle grew more difficult as it grew longer. The sunlight faded, and only the slightest glimmer of moonlight crept through the trees. Xanaphia felt herself weakening from prolonged magical exertion.

She hadn't expended this much energy for many years, and never after spending a whole day marching through a blizzard. Her skin burned from the residual energy of so many spells cast in such a short period of time. Her body ached from leaping and dodging to avoid various attacks. A quick glance at Darien showed he was little better off.

Fortunately, the dragons seemed to decide the meal was becoming too much trouble. Without warning, they dove into the snow and retreated. Darien and Xanaphia watched until they disappeared from sight. Then they dispelled the levitation and collapsed onto the ground. For several minutes, Xanaphia lay on her back, too tired to move.

She heard footsteps. Townsfolk were running in their direction. She wondered what took them so long. True, the fight took place about a mile and a half outside of town, and inner damage spells weren't flashy. But the large creatures made an incredible racket as they thrashed around, slammed into trees, and shrieked in agony. Unless the entire town was deaf, someone must've heard the noise.

"Mom! Dad!" screamed the children, crawling down from the tree. A boy and a girl ran toward their parents, who knelt to hug them. A third child, also a boy, raced to his mother.

"What happened here?" a man in official attire demanded entering the clearing.

He froze, spotting the corpses of the snow dragons strewn before him.

"Those creatures came after us," one of boys explained.

"They saved us!" said the little girl, pointing at Darien and Xanaphia.

With a great effort, Xanaphia pushed herself into a sitting position, and a gasp rose from the villagers. Xanaphia looked around. Darien was climbing to his feet, but no one was looking at him. They were staring at her.

She knew they must recognize her. She seldom wore her cloak into battle, and some of them had likely fought against her armies or had relatives who fought against her. Her features were quite singular. No one could mistake her for someone else.

Women clutched children to their breasts. Men took a frightened step backward, weapons dropping from their hands. The official-looking man gaped at her, his mouth moving but no sound coming out. Xanaphia watched them in numb silence. Her doubts and insecurities rushed to the surface as she saw the fear and revulsion her disfigured appearance evoked in those whose children she had saved.

"Xana."

Darien's voice pierced her numbness, his soft tone catching her by surprise. She looked up at him. He stood above her, a compassionate expression on his face, and offered her his hand.

"Let's go," he said.

She took his hand and he lifted her to her feet. Together, they walked toward the crowd. The people parted, making a wide path. As Darien bent to pick up her cloak, Xanaphia noticed all eyes remained fixed upon her. Apparently, no one recognized Darien.

The two passed through the congregation of frightened people. No one said anything, gazing in fear and revulsion. Then the little girl broke free from her mother's grip and raced after them. The mother attempted to grab the child but the girl eluded her.

"Miss, Mister," the girl said, hurrying up to them.

Xanaphia turned and stared down in surprise. The girl was just a juvenile, probably not seven years old. Her long hair was braided, and her clothes were torn and dirty. Yet it was her eyes that caught Xanaphia's attention. They showed no signs of fear, no signs of revulsion, and not even the slightest trace of condemnation. They contained only love and grateful admiration.

"Thank you for saving us!" she said sweetly.

Startled by the unexpected display of affection and innocence, Xanaphia could only nod. Darien smiled and patted the girl's head affectionately. Then they walked from the clearing.

Once they were out of sight, Darien returned the cloak. Xanaphia put it on, her appearance reverting back to the redheaded woman she posed as earlier. Masked within the safety of her illusions, she felt more like herself again.

"Word will reach the inn we are in town," Darien said. "They will not be able to trace you because of your appearance, but they will know I am your companion."

"We'll be gone in a few hours," Xanaphia responded. "No one will act within that time."

"Probably not," Darien agreed.

They walked in silence. Xanaphia struggled to sort through the myriad of mixed emotions running through her weary mind. She felt confused and vulnerable, which in turn made her angry and defensive. Finally, she couldn't take it anymore.

"Look," she said fiercely, grabbing Darien and pulling him to face her. "Yesterday you tried to hit me with a Desecria spell. Today you saved my life. What sort of game are you playing?"

"Trust me, my actions tonight were nothing personal." Darien said, pulling his arm free and resuming his walk. "The battle was for the children. I needed your help to drive off the creatures. That is all."

"Yeah, well, don't expect me to return the favor," Xanaphia hissed.

"Believe me, I am under no such delusion," Darien replied. "But why in the world were you trying to save them anyway?"

Xanaphia didn't say anything. She didn't know why she went to the rescue of the children. She didn't normally rush to the aid of the living when she heard them scream. On the contrary, she was usually the cause of the screaming. Not having a good answer to the question bothered her.

"What do you care why I saved the little brats?" she said, hiding her unease behind a vail of anger. "You're the softy who cares about those things. Not me!"

They had reached the stairs leading up to the inn. Before Darien could more, Xanaphia raced up the steps and through the door. The common room was filled with men and women laughing and sharing stories. She suspected the clamor inside the inn had drowned out the noises of the battle outside. She was glad. She preferred Clement and Lillian remain in the dark about the night's escapade.

Looking around, she spotted Clement sitting at the bar with a room key beside him and a fresh tray of warm food. Without saying a word, she rushed forward, grabbing the tray and the key. Then she darted across the common room and hurried up the stairs. Reaching a balcony, she marched to the door with a number corresponding to her key, sprang inside, and slammed the door behind her.

Clement watched her go. Lillian had already stolen one room key and tray of food from him. What was another? Shaking his head, he turned back to the innkeeper, who appeared startled by the young woman's audacity.

"Can I get another tray of food and a new room, please?"

"Yes, sir. Right away," the innkeeper responded, grabbing a key and placing it in front of him. "That'll be room 3."

"Thank you."

The innkeeper called into the kitchen to get more food. As he did so, Clement saw Darien walk in and survey the room with obvious condescension. Clement had to agree the place was much shabbier on the inside than the outside.

The staircase leading to the inn's rooms was old and rotten. The tables and chairs looked questionable at best. The fireplace in the corner, where most of the inhabitants congregated, was so shallow that people sat several feet back for risk of getting hit by random sparks. Altogether, it was far from impressive, and the dozens who crowded into the structure made it feel cramped and uncomfortable.

Clement saw Darien spot him and cross the room to sit beside him.

"Is the food good?" Darien asked.

"Wouldn't know," Clement said. "Haven't gotten any yet. But it can't be worse than Valirian food potion."

Darien nodded. He seemed tense and edgy. Clement wasn't sure why.

"Did you find anything useful at the apothecary?" Clement asked.

"None of your business," Darien answered.

Clement shrugged.

"Fine," he said. "Is it my business why you and Xanaphia are both covered in sweat and radiate traces of heavy combat magic?"

"No," Darien said. "Where is Lillian?"

"She retired to her room about an hour ago."

"How do you know?" Darien asked. "Can you see invisible objects?"

"None of your business," Clement responded.

The enchanter scowled. At the same moment, a waitress strolled from the kitchen placing a fresh plate of food in front of Clement. She cast a glance at Darien before leaving, her eyes taking in his tall size and powerful build. She gave him a furtive smile. When he didn't return the gesture, she headed back to the kitchens looking disappointed.

"We leave in five hours," Clement said, picking up his fork and knife.

"Who made you boss?" Darien asked.

"The whole purpose of staying in town was to get a meal and an early start," he said. "You and Xanaphia have cost us critical hours with your dilly-dallying."

Darien leaned toward Clement until their faces almost touched.

"If we are slowing you down, then maybe you should go on without us and see how far you get," he said. "When your head is hanging on a wall at Junlorace Keep, at least everyone will know you made good time getting there."

Darien snatched the plate of food and the room key. Turning, he strode across the room, up the stairs, and disappeared just as Xanaphia had done.

Clement sighed.

"Can I get another room key and a tray of food please?"

The innkeeper scowled.

"You still haven't paid for the first three yet," he said.

Clement felt annoyed at being asked to pay for three trays of food and rooms, two of which had clearly been taken from him. The innkeeper should be demanding payment from the individuals who stole them. On the other hand, Clement wasn't sure if Darien and Xanaphia had any money, and anyone demanding payment from them in their current moods was likely courting death.

Clement had also failed to put up a struggle when they stole the food. The innkeeper might believe the three were in league.

"I'm not conning you," Clement said.

Reaching into his cloak, he pulled out a small pouch. Clement always kept a coin purse in his pocket, even during his battle with Sylvia. Reaching inside, he pulled out several coins and tossed them on the counter.

"Here are five royals," he said. "You can keep the change if the food arrives within five minutes."

The inn keeper's eyes went wide, and he raced into the kitchens calling for the cooks. A minute later, he returned carrying a tray laden with food.

"Your food and your key, sir!" the innkeeper said. "Our finest room. Is there anything else I can do for you, anything at all?"

"No, thank you," Clement replied regally.

The man took the coins and hurried into the back, probably to put them someplace safe. Clement frowned. Once upon a time, everyone treated him with such respect. He was wealthy and powerful. Now, Xanaphia stole food from him and Darien practically spat in his face.

Clement was a rationalist. He knew he couldn't face this challenge alone, but the thought bothered him. Once upon a time, Clement had felt invincible, believing his arsenal of spells and limitless resources could empower him to face any challenge. Yet, all of his powers had failed him against Sylvia.

"Clement the Great", they called him. Sylvia had stolen his greatness. Not because he lost his empire. Sylvia had taken something far worse from him: his mettle, his fearlessness, and his faith in his ability to overcome any challenge. She had stolen his confidence.

He felt empty without it. He felt like the orphan boy exiled from the academy so many years ago. Regaining his confidence meant more than rebuilding his empire. Only Sylvia's destruction could restore his greatness. Only her death could make him whole again.

"Ladies and gentlemen," a voice rose above the clamor of the inn.

Clement glanced toward the fireplace. A tall middle-aged man dressed in gaudy clothing held his hands outward for silence. He removed a small lute strapped to his back and sat down on a stool, placing a cup before him. The man was clearly some sort of traveling performer, and his appearance created quite the clamor in the room.

Excited children rushed to sit at his feet, and several adults withdrew coins from their purses in preparation of rewarding him. Even Clement smiled. A good story seemed like the perfect cure for his dark mood and a pleasant escape from his growing depression.

The man began singing, his voice cheerful and melodic as he leaned toward the children, adding random strums of his instrument.

I'll tell you kids a story, 'tis a story your parents know well;
A story that fills each heart with cheer, one we all like to tell;
You see, my child, a minstrel am I, and
have been for many a year;

But in young days, sought glory I did,
and threw away all my fear;

I fought beside Queen Sylvia, I held her great banner high;
I proudly served her glorious cause, not fearing if I should die;
Beside her entourage I stood, one early winter morn;
prepared to siege a mighty fort, 'ere the bugler blew his horn.

Clement's smile dropped. He knew where the story was going and looked down with determination at his food. He tried tuning out the song, but the minstrel's words pierced his brain like daggers.

Clement the Great, the castle owned,
a mighty wizard was he;
His land so large and vast it stretched up to the northern sea;
A thousand spells he knew at hand, six
hundred ways to kill a man;
against his might that day we'd stand, with Sylvia at our side.

Clement rose from the table, picking up his tray. Somehow, the story wasn't making him feel better. Directing an unnoticed glare at the singer, he strode up the stairs and into the solitude of his bedchamber.

CHAPTER 10

"That's enough!"

Cyril's shout echoed through the dungeon, drowning out Sylvia's shrieks.

She felt the grorgs remove their instruments from her body and heard the larger one rise to its feet. She looked up. No sooner did she open her eyes than a rush of hot blood flooded in, distorting her vision.

"How dare you speak to us that way!" the large grorg hissed. "We've a job from the master!"

"Your job is to persuade her to give up the tiara, not to drive her to insanity!"

"We're free to force her into submission through any means we please."

The larger grorg continued speaking but Sylvia couldn't catch what it said. The smaller one was licking the blood on her face, causing her to writhe violently. When it finally stopped, Cyril was speaking.

"Don't flatter yourself," he said. "I could lop both your heads off, and Darlyth would just send two more. You pathetic underlings are nothing to him or me!"

"Your head will be the one sent flying when we tell the demon lord you're protecting her," the other retorted.

"I'm protecting his interests, you fool," Cyril said. "She has to give the tiara knowingly and consciously to someone for the magic to take effect. If her sanity breaks, the magic becomes void! Your stone won't heal that! I can assure you death by my blade will seem merciful compared to what Darlyth will do should your overzealousness cost him his prize!"

Sylvia blinked. She could make out Cyril standing outside the cell. He was toe-to-toe with the large grorg, his hand on the hilt of his blade. The grorg's arms had raised as if preparing to strike. For a second, the two faced off. Then, the beast stepped backward giving a half bow.

"Of course, Commander," it said in a tone of bitter acquiescence. "How foolish of me to question your orders. We will leave at once and return tomorrow."

It turned to its companion. "Heal her and let's go!"

The smaller grorg looked down. Inside its claw, it held Sylvia's right hand closed in a fist around the life stone. The beast released her for the first time since the torture began, and Sylvia found she couldn't move her fingers. The bones and muscles were shattered to the point where they no longer responded to her commands.

A broken hand seemed minor compared to her other suffering. The most recent torture, which Cyril interrupted, involved using a device to force blood out through the pours of her skin. There were many others, each as excruciating as the next. Some of the blood came from hours of shrieking in pain. Her cries were so horrible that they damaged her lungs and throat until blood erupted from her mouth. Even now, she struggled to breathe from the ooze choking her airways.

The small grorg leaned close to the stone and spoke for the first time Sylvia could remember.

"Spacineeya."

A green light illuminated Sylvia's body, and the world faded. She felt herself drifting like a leaf down a cool mountain stream. The soft trickle of running water touched her ears. Gentle morning sunlight caressed her eyes. Water lilies cast their sweet aroma into the air, tickling her nose. For a moment, all was bliss. Then the sensation faded, leaving her lying on a cold floor with her wounds healed.

The small grorg yanked the stone away, handing it to its companion. The companion placed the stone back into the bag and pulled out a white bite-sized block. It held the tablet toward Cyril.

"Through us, the master orders you to give this to her before she goes to sleep!" Its eyes fixed on Sylvia, eager for her to hear. "The tablet will dissolve in her mouth, releasing a series of enchantments into her body. They will make her nerves more sensitive and enhance her experience of pain. Any suffering she feels for the next twenty-four hours will be twice as severe."

Cyril looked at the tablet and gave a bow.

"I am subservient to my Lord's will," he said. "His commands, I shall obey."

Sylvia guessed it was a customary response to such orders. When Cyril spoke again, his voice had resumed a harsh, threatening tone.

"I'll give the capsule to her after I'm done escorting you to your rooms!"

The grorg frowned. It slammed the tablet into Cyril's hand. Cyril smiled, his eyes gleaming triumphantly.

"After you," he said, gesturing toward the stairs.

The larger grorg gave a growl in the direction of his companion. Together, they slunk down the corridor and disappeared up the steps. Cyril grabbed the torch and followed behind, leaving Sylvia alone in silent darkness.

She was bound by thick chains, her arms and legs stretched wide. The position wasn't comfortable, but after hours of nonstop agony the reprieve felt like paradise. She had no choice except to lie on the floor but she doubted she would get up anyway. Her body was healed, but the memory of horrific tortures still lingered in her mind. She could hear the rough breathing and sadistic laughs of the grorgs and felt their disgusting hands touching her.

She knew tomorrow would be worse. The grorgs promised today's tortures would seem tame compared to tomorrow's suffering. The prospect of swallowing some tablet, doubling the pain, increased her anxiety. Of course, it could be some sort of placebo, but she doubted it.

Sylvia closed her eyes. When she opened them again, the room was lit, and Cyril knelt beside her. She looked at him. Neither spoke. He held up the small white tablet. Sylvia threw her pride to the wind. She clinched her jaws as tight as possible. If he wanted her to eat the pill, he would have to pry open her mouth and shove it down her throat. Cyril gave an amused smile.

"You know, Darlyth should be more careful when wording his commands," he said. "Of course, I can't break his orders, so I hereby give you the pill!"

He reached out, opened Sylvia's left hand, stuffing the pill inside.

"There, I have given it to you!"

Cyril rose and waved his hand above Sylvia.

"Oatkrevatseeya!"

The chains fell off her arms and legs. He reached out a hand, and Sylvia took it. With a tug, he pulled her into a sitting position.

"What would happen if you disobeyed his command?" Sylvia asked.

"I would spontaneously combust," Cyril answered. "My body would burst into flames, and I'd spend my remaining moments writhing on the ground as my body turned to ashes."

"Your pain would end more quickly than mine," Sylvia said, a tinge of bitterness in her voice.

"Perhaps," he agreed, "but such a sacrifice does little for either of us. My death won't free you. And, if I'm dead, I can't destroy Darlyth."

"Or enslave the world," Sylvia said.

Cyril sighed.

"Your Majesty," he said, "you need to accept the facts. The world is going to fall into enslavement one way or another. If you don't give me the tiara, you will give it to Darlyth. You're strong. But have you not thought about what you experienced today? Do you imagine that you can withstand such suffering forever!"

Sylvia knew he was right. At the same time, she also knew she couldn't give up the tiara, not as long as any hope of rescue, no matter how slim, might remain.

"I'm sorry, Cyril," she said. "I'm sure you're a better man than your master. But I can't give you the tiara."

Cyril shrugged, "Very well, is there anything I can get you to eat or drink?"

"No, I don't have much of an appetite."

She rose and glanced down at her formerly white gown, now red with blood stains. "Can you at least grant me the dignity of sleeping in dry clothing?"

Cyril smiled.

"Cheesteet!" he said pointing at her robes.

A beam of light issued from his finger, striking her robe. At first the light was pure white, but as it lingered it grew darker. The dress grew cleaner until eventually the light turned pitch black and vanished. The dress was dry and white again.

"Thanks," Sylvia responded, "I would've done it myself, but . . ."

She made a gesture toward the bracers. She opened her palm and examined the small tablet in her hand. She felt tempted to throw it away but couldn't risk the grorgs seeing it. She hid it inside the pocket of her robe.

"I wonder where Darlyth got them," Cyril mused. Sylvia noticed him looking at the bracers. "They were created after his time. I doubt someone at Kendross Keep had a copy."

"I don't know," Sylvia responded. "But if I figure out who gave them to him, I'll shove that pill down their throat! How long was I tortured?"

"Twelve hours," Cyril answered. "I encourage you to get some sleep to rebuild your courage and strength. You'll need both."

Cyril flashed out of the cell and grabbed his torch.

"Did you want to stay in this cell or go back to the other?"

"The other," she answered. "I don't think I'll get much sleep lying in my own blood."

"Understood," Cyril said. "Well, if you would please."

Cyril gestured across the hall. Sylvia passed into her own cell, and Cyril locked the door, not bothering to reattach the manacles.

"I'll have a guard bring food and drink," he said. "Once you regain some strength, I believe you'll find you're hungrier than you think."

Cyril flashed from the dungeon, leaving Sylvia alone.

Darien, Clement, and Xanaphia marched ahead in silence. At first, Lillian thought they were just tired. But as morning turned into midday and still no one spoke, Lillian questioned whether something strange had happened in town. She had retired to bed early, expecting an uneventful night. Now, she regretted her decision.

Masters of manipulation and subterfuge depended upon their ability to read others and uncover secrets. Lillian read Darien easily enough. He was an open book to her perceptive eyes. She could tell he was contemplating some dilemma. His lips moved as though having a conversation. His hands twitched at random intervals, as though contemplating two different sides of an argument. The topic of his internal debate remained a mystery, but she felt confident he would discuss the issue with everyone at a later time. He was so predictable.

Xanaphia was more challenging. She buried her thoughts and emotions deep. Still, Lillian could tell something troubled her. Her face lacked its customary scowl, and she walked with the group rather than ahead of them. Lillian even saw her stumble a few times over cracks in the road.

Clearly, something was secretly troubling her, and her attention was far from the present moment. Her secret was more appealing than Darien's.

Lillian loved secrets and knew how to use them. If someone had a secret they didn't want coming to light, she knew the art of blackmail. If someone harbored a secret desire, she used those desires to further her ends. If someone planned a political action or subterfuge, she turned the plot to her advantage. If someone schemed against her, she made the plan backfire.

Everyone had secrets. The knowledge served as a beacon of hope during her darkest hour. When Sylvia banished Lillian from the city she grew up in, stripped her of all land, honors, and titles, and even removed her name from every scholastic award won while a student at the academy, Lillian was devastated. Her decision to surrender rather than fight saved many lives and prevented the city she loved from being razed like Xanaphia's capital. She expected Sylvia to show some respect. She was sorely disappointed.

Lillian swore revenge. She would use secrets to get it. She hid inside Sylvia's hometown, tracked down Sylvia friends, pried their brains, and extracted the information they guarded. Learning about the tiara was her reward. But she remained unsatisfied. She wanted to know what happened to Sylvia's children. Where were they? How did Sylvia hide their fates? Lillian suspected that secret held the key to Sylvia's true weakness.

A hard cough by Clement brought Lillian back to the present. She looked at him. He was harder to read than Darien, but she knew him better. He was only a few years older than her, born to politically influential parents, and was her father's favorite apprentice.

She always disliked Clement. She was jealous of his skills, his studious nature, and her father's adoration of him. But after Clement's parents died, Sorin turned his back on the boy, neglecting him, abusing him, and exiling him from the academy when he defended himself. Her father's sudden change startled Lillian.

When she confronted her father with his duplicity, he responded by taking her on a tour of the city. He showed her the slums, the work yards, and the palace. He said the first had no money or power. The second had money but no power. And the third had money and power. He asked her a simple question. Where would you rather be?

He said if she wanted to be the latter, she must do whatever was necessary to get there and stay there. Others were merely pawns for furthering those ends, there to be used when beneficial, discarded if usefulness expired, and destroyed if they got in the way. The teaching had a significant impact upon her. And she remembered the lesson when her father later came between her and the throne.

By midafternoon, the road ended and travel grew harder as they plowed through the Clarin Woods. The party's pace slowed, but they remained ahead of schedule, reaching Freighton Gorge by nightfall. The gorge was one of the most formidable physical obstacles in Aurba. During Lillian's reign, it served as her eastern border and the heart of her defenses. Over a thousand feet wide with sheer cliffs on each side sporting drops of several thousand feet, the gorge ran from the nearly impassable Prafell Mountains up to the Blackguard river. It proved to be a near insurmountable obstacle to Xanaphia's expansion, especially after Lillian destroyed all the bridges.

There was only one natural crossing, a stone passage known as Riddian's Pass. Unfortunately, the company had gotten off course and emerged about three miles to the north. Levitation spells only allowed someone to hover a few feet above the ground. They might stop someone from dying if they fell, but the person still needed to scale the other side, a difficult feat even during good weather.

Unable to cross, they trekked south toward Riddian Pass, arriving just as night began to fall. The stone arch was overlooked by the tall spires of Riddian Keep. The mighty fortress was constructed by Lillian to guard the pass. Thanks to a combination of the keep's courageous defenders and the difficulty in moving an army over an archway barely wide enough for two people to walk abreast, Xanaphia never took the fort.

Lillian felt a rush of dismay over the current state of her once proud stronghold. Sylvia had naturally abandoned the fortress after her rise to power since the defense was no longer necessary. But to Lillian's consternation, Sylvia had also dismantled large portions of the stone walls for use in other construction projects. The keep was now little better than a ruin with stones strewn in all direction. Still, it provided a good campsite. Within a short time, the companions were devouring their dinners inside an old barracks.

Clement, Darien, and Xanaphia had all saved food from dinner the previous night. Lillian, meanwhile, continued flaunting the sumptuous meals provided by her multi-colored potion. She felt no guilt about doing this. Her companions always belittled her study of survival magic. Now it was their turn to bear the brunt of the joke.

"We'll enter my territory tomorrow," Xanaphia observed. "Unfortunately, my supply lines ran southward, and I used magic to spur the growth of the northern forests to hinder invading armies. Travel will be tricky. Still, if we keep our current pace, we should reach Darien's border by tomorrow night and Spiked Canyon the next day."

"We need to reach Spiked Canyon early enough to pass through before nightfall," Clement said. "The risk of an ambush is too great. I don't like the idea of traversing it after dark."

"Can we go around?" Lillian suggested.

"No," Darien said. "My directions to Junlorace Keep include going through the pass as the first step. Besides, the mountains in the area are tall and treacherous. We would lose time going over them. The canyon is the fastest way to the keep and saves us at least a day or more."

"Let's just keep with our original plan then," Clement said.

He stood up, crossing to a fallen stone slab a short distance away. Like all the stones used to construct the fortress, it was massive, standing almost four feet high and ten feet in length. As Lillian watched, Clement uttered, "Myagkeeyekamen." He waved his hand above the stone.

The gray granite shimmered and bubbled. Lillian knew the spell. It was a trick designed to turn hard stone to the soft texture of a mattress, allowing someone to sleep comfortably against an unpleasant surface.

"I thought you didn't study survival magic," Lillian quipped.

Clement shrugged. "I picked up a few spells here and there."

"I'm surprised you took the time to learn one of such limited usefulness," Lillian said.

"I find the usefulness of a spell is limited only by the imagination of the person using it," Clement replied. "In any case, I'm heading to bed."

"Not yet," Darien interrupted in a grave tone. "There is something we need to discuss first."

Xanaphia looked up from her food. Clement also seemed surprised. Lillian smiled. Just as she suspected, Darien was about to reveal the issue he was pondering during the march.

Darien hesitated before speaking.

"Have you thought about what we are doing?" he asked.

"In what way?" Clement replied. "Don't tell me you're getting cold feet."

"Of course not," Darien said. "But have any of you given serious consideration to the opposition we face?"

"Of course," Lillian said. "We're going up against a powerful cult of warriors, wizards, and demons. What choice do we have? We can either destroy the tiara, destroy Sylvia, or be destroyed ourselves."

"You are forgetting our most dangerous enemy," Darien replied. "Darlyth is awake, and his powers blanch those of his minions. His magical skills are supposed to be greater than any sorcerer who ever lived. If either Sylvia or the tiara is destroyed, he will come looking for those responsible."

"Of course," Xanaphia agreed, "But like Lillian said, what choice do we have?"

"What're you getting at, Darien?" Clement asked.

"Just this," Darien said. "The demon we encountered in the woods had no magic and was probably not one of Darlyth's more powerful servants. Yet he nearly killed us. Do you really think we can stand against the demon lord? I may not be a survivalist, but I do not intend to die if I can help it."

"What're you suggesting?" Lillian asked.

"I am suggesting we need help to survive the flight from the mountains."

Xanaphia shook her head.

"I hate to tell you this but there's no one else here," she said. "We're heading into an almost entirely abandoned mountain range where the only settlements are filled with enemies. We're all we have."

"That's not true," Lillian answered.

All heads turned to her. She understood what Darien was suggesting.

"There is someone in the mountains powerful enough to help us," she said.

"No!" Clement shouted, his face contorting with rage. "Absolutely not! I don't want to work with her. I'd rather die."

He sounded childish. Lillian felt a pang of sorrow for him.

"Clement, listen," she said, "we don't like it either."

"Then we need to find another way," Clement interrupted.

"There is no other way," Darien said. "I spent the entire march today considering every imaginable alternative. Nothing works. We need *her*!"

"No!" Clement said. "Sylvia must die!"

Xanaphia had been watching the exchange with obvious confusion. Now, Lillian saw her eyes opened wide with sudden understanding. She leapt to her feet, her hair stirring in the strange, agitated manner displayed whenever she became upset.

"I didn't come all this way to be her courier. I came here to kill her. She must die."

"She will die!" Lillian said. "She just can't die yet."

"If we kill Sylvia, the tiara becomes worthless," Darien said. "The demon lord will want revenge. He'll crush us like bugs! The only way we can defeat him is with Sylvia's help."

Xanaphia and Clement looked stricken. Clement turned away, running his hands through his hair. Xanaphia just backed away, shaking her head.

"I can steal her powers," she said, her voice filled with defiance and despair. "We don't need her if I have her powers!"

"Her powers alone mean nothing," Darien said. "Her real strength lies in the tiara. If she has not given the tiara to the demon lord by the time we get there, I doubt she will give it to you. The dagger cannot steal the tiara's magic. Without the tiara, her powers will not make a difference."

"So," Clement said turning around, "you're saying we need to get Sylvia, get the tiara, return the tiara to Sylvia, and escort her back to Rhoria. Where does killing her fall into this plan?"

"The demon lord will come after us," Darien explained. "First we destroy him, then we kill her. Xanaphia has the dagger. You have the orb. One of the plans is bound to succeed."

"And if the demon lord doesn't catch us before we reach Rhoria?" Xanaphia asked. "Then what?"

"We get Sylvia to destroy the crown," Darien answered. "If we do not destroy the demon lord, we need Sylvia. She is the only one who can rally the wizard school and the nation against his army. Once he is destroyed or put to sleep, we can get our revenge against the tiara-less Sylvia."

Clement shook his head. Xanaphia looked furious. Neither spoke. Finally, Clement turned around and walked to his bed. Without a word, he lay down on the stone facing away from his companions. Xanaphia glared at them for a moment before spinning around and walking away from the camp and into the darkness. Lillian thought they took the news better than expected.

Lillian reached into her bag, removing a small round ball. With a flick, she tossed it onto the ground, just as she had done the previous two nights. The orb expanded into a plush black sleeping bag complete with feather pillow. She climbed into the knapsack feeling the enchantments warming her body and massaging her aching joints. She took one last look around the clearing. Darien reclined against a wall keeping watch while Xanaphia lingered at the edge of her vision, staring into the night. Lillian closed her eyes and fell asleep.

Xanaphia remained wide awake. She stared into the darkness lost in thought. After a moment, she reached into her cloak withdrawing the crystal dagger. She slid her fingers along the blade, feeling the smooth cool surface. The dagger was her greatest hope for revenge against Sylvia. Yet hope was growing slimmer. One thing or another kept arising, preventing her from killing the queen. Now, she risked waiting years or perhaps decades for her chance.

She wondered about using the dagger on the demon lord, but the idea was foolish. She must hold the dagger in order to activate the magical qualities of the crystal. Otherwise, the weapon was an ordinary knife and would do little harm to a demon. The dagger wasn't large enough to hold Darlyth's powers. It would explode, and she would be killed by the shards.

As much as Xanaphia wanted Sylvia dead, she wouldn't sacrifice her life to achieve it. Clement might be content to die gloriously in battle, but not Xanaphia. She wanted to have her cake and eat it too. She didn't fear death, but she had no desire to sacrifice herself. When she died, she certainly wouldn't do so in a way that would profit others. Such selfless actions were a form of weakness, not strength.

She returned the dagger to her cloak and stared into the darkness. The night had just begun, but dawn would come quickly.

CHAPTER

11

Before the sun rose the following morning, they were across the gorge and marching through Xanaphia's former territory. Clement led the group, fueled by an inner rage that blocked all weariness. He didn't speak to his companions. He hadn't said a word since the previous night. The only time he acknowledged their existence was when Xanaphia urged him to slow down for Lillian and Darien.

His energy faded by nightfall though, and he was hardly able to stay awake long enough to finish the Valirian food potion. The night's rest proved far too short. By the early morning, they were back on their feet trekking through the harsh woods. His pace had slowed markedly along with the pace of his companions.

They had made good time so far and were ahead of schedule, but after four days of incessant marching, harsh weather, little food, and less sleep, their stamina was waning. Thorn bushes and dead vines ripped at their skin and clothing. Thick snows in these seldom-traveled areas came up to their knees and sometimes to their waists, forcing them to use magic to push through. Further, the terrain was growing increasingly mountainous and ascending the steep slopes sapped their fading strength.

They received some encouragement from the sight of the distant plateaus. Shattered Canyon was getting close. The landmark heralded the beginning of the final leg of their trek. They felt a fresh surge of energy at the sight, but it didn't last long.

By midafternoon, they were closing in on their destination. The forest faded near the foot of the cliffs, opening into a strange crescent-shaped clearing. On the opposite side, the bluffs rose over a hundred feet into the air, impossible to scale and passable only by a ten-foot-wide channel leading through the heart of the mountain. The passage was dangerous and contained no cover from prying eyes. Nevertheless, the company resolved to go through. On the other side, the forests would reemerge. From there, Darien said they would cross a large mountain lake. Junlorace Keep rested on the opposite side.

Xanaphia reached the clearing first. She was about to emerge from the trees when Clement grabbed her arm. His gaze fixed upon the cliff.

"What?" Xanaphia asked.

Clement raised his hand, pointing at the left side of the distant wall.

"I don't see anything," Lillian said.

"Zreneeyay," Clement whispered.

His eyes began to glow, and a thick purple mist issued from his pupils. It swirled and spiraled, encircling the small company like smoky snakes, the tendrils slithered up their robes to hover before their startled faces. Then, like the crack of a whip, the beams of light struck their eyes. The magic allowed them to see out of Clement's eyes. With his sharp gaze, they beheld the outline of a strange figure blending almost seamlessly into the cliff face.

"What is it?" Lillian asked.

"A demon," Darien responded.

"Do you think it spotted us?" Xanaphia asked.

"No," Clement said. "It isn't looking this direction. It's watching the canyon."

"That is strange," Darien responded. "Why is it not watching for approaching enemies?"

"Because it isn't guarding against someone going in," Lillian said. "It's guarding against someone coming out."

"That makes no sense," Darien replied.

"It's irrelevant," Xanaphia said. "Our only concern is how to get around it."

"We can't go around," Darien said. "There is no other entrance. We must go through."

"We have the element of surprise," Clement observed.

"We can't use it though," Xanaphia said. "Once we step from the trees, it will notice us, and we're too far away to attack from ambush."

"Lillian, can you make us invisible?" Darien asked.

"I can," she said, "but we will still leave tracks in the snow."

"Then we will levitate," Darien responded.

Clement waved his hand in a sweeping motion. The purple smoke disappeared, and everyone's eyes returned to normal.

"Wait a minute," Xanaphia said. "I don't mind levitating while fighting ice dragons, but if this demon is anything like the last one it's going to be moving fast. If we get into a fight while slowed down by levitation spells, we're going to get slaughtered."

"It can't be that much slower than fighting in waist-deep snow." Clement noted. "But, if we're invisible, why not just sneak past?"

"Do you want that thing waiting for us on the way back?" Darien asked. "Besides, the snow does not look deep in that area. We can just dispel the levitation spell when battle starts."

There was nothing else to do. The companions were exhausted from days of marching and on the verge of collapse from lack of food and sleep. And they were about to go into battle. Clement muttered a spell for strength while the others boosted their own bodies before levitating.

Once in the air, Lillian moved to the center of the company. Raising her arm she declared, "Chutieray nevedeimeyah!"

Clement watched as their bodies grew blurry and returned to focus. Lillian smiled.

"Right, let's go," she said.

No one moved.

"Um," Xanaphia hesitated. "We can still see each other."

"Of course," Lillian said. "I altered the enchantment to permit it. I'm sure none of us want to accidentally hit another with a spell."

All eyes went to Darien.

"After you," he said, smiling at Xanaphia.

She smiled back.

"Actually," she said, "I think you should lead. You are the strategist."

"Ladies first," Darien retorted.

"Oh, snap out of it," Clement said irritably. "This is no time for puppy love."

Darien and Xanaphia looked horrorstruck. Lillian's hand shot to her mouth, covering a smirk. Clement smiled. Turning around, he marched into the clearing.

The company advanced cautiously. Clement kept his eyes fastened upon the demon, looking for the slightest hint to suggest it sensed their presence. They were one hundred feet away. No movement. Seventy-five feet away. Still no movement.

Clement summoned his magic. He felt the others doing the same. Inch by inch they moved closer. The nearer they could get, the more damage their spells could inflict. They were within fifty feet of the cliff face when Clement saw the creature's head shift in their direction and heard a sucking noise like air being pulled through whistle. Clement understood. The creature could smell them. Its eyes focused on the spot they stood.

"Desecria!" Clement shouted, energy surging from his body as he channeled the might of his being into the assault.

"Desecria!" screamed the voices of his companions.

The massive bolts of black lightning flashed across the sky, slamming into the demon. The tendrils struck with a force so powerful the mountain trembled and pieces of rock shattered from the cliff face. The demon showed no signs of injury. With a bound, it leapt from its mighty perch, landing easy and carefree as though no spells were being cast.

Clement stumbled backward, weakened by the spell and awestruck by the might of his adversary. The others broke off their spells. All gawked at the beast standing before them. It was unlike anything Clement had ever seen.

It stood almost fifteen feet tall with arms and legs thicker than tree trunks. A round boulder-shaped head rested atop the large torso, complete with a mouth containing rows of miniature stalactites and stalagmites. Long rocky projectiles protruded from around his body like spiked armor and his fingerless hands ended in spiked fists.

"Spread out," Clement ordered, dismissing the levitation spell.

Though weakened from the aftereffects of Desecria, the thrill of battle gave him fresh vigor. He charged away from the creature, even as its mighty fist swung wildly through the air where he stood just moments before. As Darien predicted the powder was thinner in this area and Clement had little difficulty running. Still, the creature was faster.

Following Clement's tracks in the snow, the beast almost overtook him before a cry of "Perelome" and a flash of a purple distracted the creature. It turned, charging the spot where Xanaphia stood invisible. Xanaphia tumbled away as the creature's fists crashed down behind her.

For several minutes, the battle raged. The creature's speed and sharp senses matched well against his invisible opponents. Though they encircled it, rotating spells and constantly moving to avoid danger, death remained just a second away. They rained spells upon the demon from all directions, but they couldn't inflict the smallest trace of harm.

"How do we kill this thing?" Xanaphia screamed. "And why does it keep attacking me?"

The creature swatted at her, fist barely missing her head as she dodged the blow.

"Go attack Darien or something!" she shouted.

She raced to her left, dodging another blow. She was getting close to the cliff face and broke into a full sprint to avoid having her escape cut off.

"It is your stench," Darien shouted. "You smell like death. Zoobeela!"

A series of sharp swirling crescent plates spun from Darien's hand, striking the stony hide. The demon turned and charged Darien, who hastily retreated to a new location.

"I am death!" Xanaphia replied. "Smetr!"

A black crackling cone of light surrounded by large red swirls shot from Xanaphia's hand. The spell struck the demon in the chest but had no effect. Turning, it charged the spot the spell had come from, its fists catching the last strands of Xanaphia's long hair as she ducked away.

"We can't keep this up forever," Lillian said, before releasing her own ineffective spell.

"How long will the invisibility last?" Clement asked, sending out another ineffective attack.

The creature didn't charge him though. It had spotted Xanaphia's tracks and dashed after her.

"No more than twenty minutes," Lillian answered, moving in the direction of Clement as she strove to remain opposite Xanaphia. "Once the spell fades, I won't have time to recast it. The creature is too fast! We need to kill it before that happens."

"What have we tried so far?" Darien shouted.

"I've tried death attacks and elemental attacks," Clement answered firing another spell.

"I tried internal damaging spells," Xanaphia called. "Either he doesn't have internal organs or they didn't get through."

The shouts were driving the creature to frenzy. It lashed wildly at Xanaphia, chasing the sound of her voice. This time, it grazed her shoulder, sending her rolling across the snow. Fortunately, her powerful constitution and quick reflexes allowed her to recover, springing aside with the agility of a cat.

"I tried attacks designed to break rocks, but they were ineffective," Darien shouted. "Our spells just cannot penetrate the stony armor."

Catching the sound of Darien's voice, the demon turned toward him. This time, driven mad by rage, it abandoned its fists. Placing its club-like hands onto the ground, it charged the spot where he stood like a bull. The head was covered with sharp, spiky protrusions, and the creature seemed intent upon either impaling Darien or trampling him beneath its massive feet. Darien barely managed to tumble out of the way.

"I have an idea," Clement shouted. "Lillian dispel the invisibility on me."

"Are you nuts!" she replied.

"Just do it!'"

Lillian moved close to Clement, waving her hand to dispel her charm. She quickly stepped backward. The demon spotted Clement and charged him in the same manner as Darien. Clement crouched low upon the snow as the monster closed.

His focused his eyes upon a small area on the upper part of the creature's stony face. He took a deep breath. He had never used this spell in combat before. It wasn't meant for such purposes. He needed to channel the energy just right at the exact right moment. He would only get one chance.

Failure meant death. The creature was almost on top of him when Clement struck.

"Myagkeeyekamen!" he said, his fingers inches from the demon's forehead as he finished the spell.

The charging demon pulled up, rising to its feet with a shriek of pain. Its stony forehead shimmered and bubbled like the stone at the fortress. Clement let out cry of joy.

"Look out!" Lillian shouted.

Before Clement could react, he felt Lillian smash him, knocking him to the ground. At the same moment, one of the demon's fists swung through the air, right over the spot Clement stood a second ago. The attack missed Clement but caught Lillian directly in the chest.

She gave a scream of pain as the blow sent her hurling through the air. With a crunch, she slammed headfirst into the nearby cliff face. Blood covered the stones, and she slid motionless to the ground, the snow turning red beneath her.

"Desecria!" Darien and Xanaphia shouted, targeting the spot of Clement's spell.

Lightning flashed through the air. The spells tore through the soft spot created by Clement's charm. The beast writhed fitfully, its clubbed hands shooting up in a futile attempt to block the assault.

"Desecria," Clement shouted joining the attack.

He felt the spell pull at his already weakened constitution but allowed the energy to flow. His body ached, his heart pounded from the strain, and even his vision grew blurry as he fought to keep control while directing all his might into the attack.

The demon's howls grew shriller as it struggled against the assault, but the three spells proved too much. It shuttered, and its hands dropped to the side. Its eyes closed and body straightened until it became a tall, spiky stone looming above the snow. Then it collapsed onto the ground and lay unmoving.

Darien, Clement, and Xanaphia also crumbled to the ground, exhausted by their spells. Clement felt weak and dizzy, but he refused to rest. Pushing himself to his feet, he stumbled like a drunken man toward Lillian and collapsed beside her.

Lillian lay on her left side, her back pressed against the stone wall. She was still breathing, but the gasps were shallow and strained. Blood oozed from the back of her head, which had burst open. Grabbing his robes, Clement pressed them firmly against the wound like a compress, trying to slow the bleeding.

Footsteps hurried up beside him. They belonged to Xanaphia.

"Do something!" she ordered. "Heal her!"

Clement gave an angry look.

"Do you really think I wasted time learning spells that heal people other than me?" he asked. "How many non-self-healing spells do you know?"

She stared dumbfounded before turning toward Darien, who stumbled to her side. They looked at each other, but the answer couldn't be more obvious. Like Clement, neither had ever seen any reason to do something as selfless as heal another. While they could heal themselves if the need arose, in this particular crisis their skills proved useless.

Clement chided himself for not learning such spells. The only person in the company who knew them was the one in need. As headmaster, Lillian required all students at the academy to learn healing spells as part of their first year. Sylvia continued the tradition, but neither Sylvia nor any of her officers were here to help. Thinking about Sylvia drew Clement's mind back to the search party.

"The healing balm," he shouted, suddenly remembering the wooden case he found on the dead general.

His hand dove into his pocket, snatching the wooden case from his robes. He hurriedly unscrewed the lid and scooped a large handful of green goo. It was warm to the touch and felt like holding thick mud.

Darien lifted Lillian's body, while Clement rubbed the cream along the gouges covering the back of Lillian's head. He could feel the wounds sealing. The torn flesh healed almost instantly. Clement scooped another handful and covered each spot until the bleeding stopped.

The wounds closed, but Clement knew it wasn't enough. Lillian's breathing remained shallow and her skin pale. She had lost a large amount of blood. Sealing the wounds wouldn't replace it. He shook his head in frustration, screwing the lid back on the balm.

"Where did you get that?" Xanaphia asked. "Don't tell me you were carrying one in your pocket when Sylvia sent you into exile."

"I found it in General Gaheera's bag after our first battle," Clement answered. "Why do you care?"

"Just curious," Xanaphia retorted. "Don't get your robes in a knot!"

Clement looked back at Lillian feeling helpless. Piling some snow under her feet, he elevated her legs, and Darien did the same for her head. Clement didn't know what else to do. She could be unconscious for days, if she regained consciousness at all. They needed to continue their mission, but they couldn't leave her. They needed her help to retrieve the tiara.

Clement shook his head. For more than ten years he spent every night dreaming of her death. Now the one time he needed her alive she was on the verge of dying. He ran his hands up and down his face, trying to think. Why had she saved him? It was a foolish decision. Her sacrifice jeopardized their entire mission. He punched the snow in frustration.

"How many of those balms were there?" Darien asked.

"I only saw one," Clement answered. "I doubt they carried more. The green potions are the most powerful and are extremely difficult to make. The only other thing in their bags were the scrolls."

"Scrolls!" Xanaphia shouted, her head shooting up. "Do you think . . ."

Clement sprang from his sitting position, dashing through the snow toward Lillian's shoulder bag. It leaned against a stone on the other side of the clearing. Lillian must have removed it in anticipation of the battle.

Clement slid to a stop, landing in a kneeling position before the bag. Unlatching the strap, he yanked out the scrolls, tossing a handful of them to Xanaphia and another to Darien. The rest he kept for himself. Clement scanned each scroll, tossing them aside when they turned out to be useless. As he reached the end of the pile, despair gripped him. There was nothing there after all.

"I found it!" Xanaphia said, dropping her pile and hoisting a single page into the air. "The spell is basic, but it should be sufficient for our needs."

Xanaphia whirled around, racing to Lillian. Darien followed, hurrying after her. Clement jumped to his feet then hesitated. Turning around, he reached back into the Lillian's bag and withdrew a small item, which he pocketed. Then he hurried toward the fallen spymaster.

Xanaphia stood above Lillian with the scroll in her hands, looking apprehensive. Clement couldn't blame her. Trained spellcasters rarely used scrolls. He imagined the healing scroll was only there to allow the search party to heal someone should both wizards fall.

Scrolls were powerful parchments created by skilled magical scribes. Any person, even someone without magical training, could cast the copied spell as if they were the scroll's creator. They essentially became a conduit through which the creator's magical energies flowed. The idea was wonderful in theory. At one point, Clement created numerous scrolls for the commanders of his army to use in combat. But as many people discovered before him, scrolls weren't very user friendly.

Being a conduit for someone else's magical energies wasn't a pleasant sensation, even for an accomplished spellcaster. Someone else's energy flowing through one's body was uncomfortable and unnatural. It made most people want to vomit. A general or apprentice vomiting their lunch up in the middle of the battlefield did little to boost the morale of troops.

Also, the average layperson lacked the skills and focus to direct the energy. Even an experienced spellcaster could be overwhelmed if the energy proved too great to control. This drawback doomed Clement's plan. After one of his generals accidentally destroyed his own army using a spell intended for the opposing force, Clement abandoned using scrolls in battle.

Xanaphia knelt beside Lillian holding the parchment in her left hand and placing her right on Lillian's chest. The long, unnaturally white fingers blended seamlessly with Lillian's now-pale skin. Clement watched as Xanaphia read from the scroll, focusing on the exact pronunciation and rhythm of each syllable.

Emerald light radiated from the scroll growing brighter with each new word. Xanaphia closed her eyes as the page melted into a thick sparkling green mist that trickled up her left arm. Her mouth twitched as the light flowed like a long stream of thick sludge across her chest working its way to her right hand. As the first traces of light reached the tips of her fingers and slithered into Lillian's prone form, Lillian's body began glowing like a strange green lamp.

The spell complete, Xanaphia staggered to her feet. Darien grabbed her arm to steady her.

"Are you okay?" he asked in a tone so devoid of malice that Clement looked up.

"I'm fine," she snapped. "I know how to use scrolls."

Her voice sounded annoyed, but Clement noticed she didn't yank her arm from Darien's grasp. His eyes narrowed. He reflected upon their playful banter before entering the clearing, their comments during the fight, and the odd lack of open hostility toward each other ever since the night in Southgrain. Something was going on.

A twitch of Lillian's hand distracted him. Her eyes fluttered and flickered open. She gazed around, seeing Clement kneeling beside her and Darien and Xanaphia looking down upon her. She gave a loud groan.

"Ugh. I knew I was going to hell, but I really hoped I'd get a different room than you guys."

"Ha!" Clement laughed, pleased by how quickly Lillian recovered her wit. "That would defeat the whole purpose of hell, wouldn't it?"

Lillian smiled and pushed herself into a seated position. She scanned the clearing, her eyes taking in the fallen demon and the scattered scrolls. She sighed.

"You could've at least waited until I was dead before pillaging my corpse."

Xanaphia glared at Lillian.

"We needed a scroll to save your life, you selfish brat!" she said. "At least say thank you!"

She spun away and reached into her cloak, drawing out some empty vials with corked lids.

"The scroll better be the only thing you took," Lillian muttered, brushing snow and blood off her clothes.

"I wouldn't count on that," Clement said, smirking.

Lillian looked at him, her eyes narrowing. Clement's smile grew.

"Let's just say, I'll be having a good dinner tonight!"

He withdrew a large, corked bottle with swirling multicolored liquid from inside his cloak. Clement shook it a few times before Lillian's outraged face. If looks could kill, he'd be dead. But after four nights of watching her gloat over meals, Clement could hardly refrain from laughing. Returning the bottle to his pocket, he lifted his nose with the same look of superiority that so often lined Lillian's features. Then he turned and followed Darien.

"Don't worry, Lillian," Xanaphia mocked. "I'll be happy to summon a rabbit for you!"

Clement's grin grew bigger, and he hurried to catch up with the enchanter. Darien was kneeling over the beast's head, examining the chiseled features.

"Notice anything interesting?" Clement asked.

"I do not know much about demon physiology, if there is such a thing, but the body is mind-boggling," Darien said. "The skin is six inches deep and appears to be solid stone. I cannot even wager a guess how the creature could move. Everything about its biology seems impossible."

"I expect many things about demons will be strange to us," Clement said. "They've been absent from the world for over a thousand years. The magic used to create them is beyond anything mankind has achieved since the war."

"Unthinkable that no one kept any records on them," Darien said. "Did no one realize they were bound to break free eventually?"

"Foresight has never been humanity's greatest strength," Clement answered.

"Get away from my blood!" Lillian's shout interrupted the discussion.

Clement turned to see Lillian and Xanaphia having an intense argument. Lillian stood with her hands raised, preparing to attack Xanaphia. Apparently, the necromancer had scooped Lillian's blood from the snow, placing it inside vials.

"Blood is an important spell component," Xanaphia shouted back, her hand also raised threateningly.

"Use your own," Lillian retorted. "I don't want my blood to be part of your twisted necromantic experiments. I know the things you did to your citizens, the experiments you practiced on them, the ways you twisted them into horrific beasts just to suit your own whims. I'll not be a part of it! Obezareevat!"

A burst of yellow light coned from Lillian's fingers. The necromancer deflected the spell with minimal effort, striking back.

"Perelome!"

Purple light burst from Xanaphia's hand, but Clement deflected it. Arriving at Lillian's side, he grabbed her arms, forcing them down. Darien seized Xanaphia, and the men summoned a shimmering barrier between the two combatants.

"Give me my blood, you witch," Lillian screamed again.

Clement was surprised by the sound of her voice. She sounded like she was on the verge of breaking down. He wondered if the many days of hard marching, the events of the battle, and her near death were getting to her. She had never been a combatant or endured this kind of prolonged physical exertion. At least, not that he was aware of. He always viewed her as a dilettante whose love of exploring occurred at a controlled and leisurely pace within the safety of invisibility and other concealing magic.

"Fine," Xanaphia said.

She withdrew the vials from her cloak and hurled them onto the snow. They shattered against the icy surface, spraying blood across the already stained earth.

"Your blood can stay on the ground and rot," she hissed. "You can too for all I care. If Clement hadn't been so determined to save your life, you'd be rotting already, and no one in this pathetic world would lose a wink of sleep. You have no legacy, no friends. In a few years, no one will even remember your name. Why would I want your blood anyway?"

Xanaphia stormed toward the canyon entrance. Lillian collapsed onto the snow, burying her face in her hands. Darien and Clement looked at each other for a moment.

"Come on, everyone," Darien said. "We better go."

He turned and followed Xanaphia. Clement looked at Lillian. She sat cross-legged in the snow, her face hidden behind her fingers. He thought he could see tears running along her light skin.

Clement crossed to her pack a short distance away surrounded by scattered scrolls. Kneeling down, he picked up the pages, collected them all, and neatly placed them inside her bag. He stood back up and noticed her watching him. Her face lacked its normal arrogance and her cheeks were red.

He crossed the clearing, still carrying her bag, and stood in front of her. She looked up at him with a strange expression as though she had never seen him before. He offered her a hand. She said nothing but took it. Lifting her to her feet, he handed her the satchel. She took it, and without a word they followed the others into the canyon.

The canyon stretched much farther than anticipated, but they refused to rest until they escaped the gloomy confines. No one was likely to get much sleep inside. The walls often narrowed to less than five feet wide and never stretched wider than ten, which gave the path a claustrophobic feeling. The weather made things worse.

A storm was brewing. Thick black clouds obscured the night sky, barring all traces of light. Winter winds whipped through the tunnel with unnatural ferocity, and the companions fought hard to avoid being toppled. The howling gales deafened the little company, and all attempts at communication proved futile.

The hour was nearing midnight when they broke free from the crags and emerged into the bottom of a large bowl-shaped area filled with trees. The rising mountain blocked all view of the lands opposite the summit, while thick trees, wild and overgrown, formed a curtain in the sky concealing the heavens.

Despite the strategic disadvantage of camping in an area devoid of visibility and where howling winds muffled all traces of sound, the companions were too exhausted to scale the mountain. They set up camp a short distance inside the overgrown forest. Clement collected wood to start the fire while Darien and Xanaphia sat down on fallen logs, making arrangements for their respective meals. Lillian didn't stay with the company. She turned and marched into the woods.

At first, no one paid any mind to her disappearance. Clement finished building the fire, and the others ate their meals. However, as ten minutes turned to twenty and then thirty, Clement grew uncomfortable. He looked at Darien and Xanaphia. Both seemed oblivious to Lillian's disappearance. Sitting across from each other, they channeled their energy in a somewhat lighthearted battle to direct the flames of the fire away from the other. The duel increased Clement's restlessness, since the result meant he got no warmth from the blaze he had constructed.

Standing up, he cast his magic outward to feel the traces left by Lillian's feet. The task proved simple as she apparently made no attempt to disguise her movements. He followed the path into the woods. It wound through the trees, seemingly without any obvious purpose. Within a short time, he discovered her location.

She stood before a large white rose bush. Her hands stroked the soft petals of the blooms, which shined in the darkness. Their fluorescent glow illuminated Lillian's troubled face. She didn't look at him but must have sensed his presence.

"They're beautiful, aren't they?" she asked. "I've seen a number of them in this area. They appear to flower in snowy conditions rather than be killed by them."

Clement didn't say anything. He crossed to the plant and examined the leaves. They seemed to possess some unnatural magical qualities. He was wondering what potions and brews might be made from them, when Lillian turned to him with a questioning stare.

"Why did you save my life?" she asked.

"Why did you save mine?" he returned, fixing his gaze upon her.

She looked back at the flowers and stared at them for a second before speaking.

"The action was logical," she said. "We need you."

Clement stared at her, unable to imagine hearing those words from her lips.

"You need me?" He asked.

"Of course," she said. "We can't save Sylvia without you. Think about our company. Darien is a master of strategy and enchantment but he has no skill at subterfuge. Xanaphia is a great warrior but lacks strategy and resourcefulness. I'm a master of subterfuge and resourcefulness but I've no skill at combat or military strategy. Together, we compensate for each other. But if one of us is lost, we can't replace them.

"You can. Though not as strong as Darien, you're a skilled strategist and capable of weaving formidable enchantments. Although not as powerful as Xanaphia, your combat skills are almost as great. And of all the spellcasters

I've ever encountered, your skills at subterfuge are second only to mine. While we're all pigeonholed within our small areas of expertise, you have versatility. That's what made you Clement the Great. I don't like to admit it, but we need you."

She looked at him and back at the flowers with a sorrowful smile.

"If I told you that seven years ago, you would've agreed with me," she said. "Now, you stand there with a stunned expression. Exile hasn't been good to you, has it?"

Clement smiled at the somewhat comical observation.

"No, it hasn't, but where were you all these years? Surely you didn't spend all seven years researching Sylvia."

"No, you're right. I spent five years traveling and exploring in the far south."

"Studying the barbarians?"

"No, I mean the far south. I was exploring the Southern Continent."

"You mean the Great Desert?" Clement asked in surprise.

The Great Desert was the name given to the lands south of Aurba. Aurba was connected to the uncharted continent by a land bridge, but no one ever went there. A massive stretch of desolate sand and rolling dunes stretched on for untold distances. Stories told of brave adventurers who attempted to traverse or explore the region. Most didn't return. Those who did reported only an arid land devoid of all life, vegetation, and water.

"The travel was treacherous," she said. "My supplies almost ran out, but I refused to turn around. In my despondent state, I was determined to keep going until I reached the other side or died. After six months in the desert,

I emerged into a new land filled with wonders beyond the limits of my imagination."

Her voice grew soft, and her expression became distant as though swept away by the glory of a vision only she could see. Her eyes sparkled in wonder, and she smiled like a poet gazing upon her inspiration.

"White-walled cities of marble towered into the sky," she said. "Rivers of purest blue, never touched by the icy chill of winter, flowed over endless green pastures. They possessed their own history dating back many thousands of years with massive libraries to boggle the mind. They had their own magical sites, their own ancient secrets, and even their own magical system, with spells different from our own. It was like a dream come true!"

Her voice faded into a breathless whisper, her eyes gazing into the distance.

"Why did you come back?" Clement asked.

She lowered her head, her dreamy expression vanishing.

"Secrets," she said, the words issuing like a vile poison. "Secrets and revenge. Sylvia haunted me. The visions of all I lost. The memories of everything she took from me. The flashbacks of every disgrace I received from her hand. They stalked me day and night. I couldn't sleep. I couldn't enjoy my discoveries. I couldn't stay. My life would remain empty until I tasted the sweet nectar of retribution!"

Clement nodded. He understood the sentiment only too well.

"When Sylvia is dead, are you going to rebuild your kingdom?"

Lillian hesitated. She leaned against a tree, crossing her arms in thought.

"I don't know," she said at last. "Being an exile wasn't much fun, but neither was being a queen. All the work and responsibility, all the pressure of answering to the whims of hundreds of people, all the constant political maneuvering to stay ahead of my rivals, it was draining. I never felt free to explore the world or learn new things. I never relaxed. I never got to truly experience life."

Clement nodded. His dreams of revenge drove him to build an empire, but he didn't enjoy it. The life was hard. His constant battles against enemies both inside his empire and abroad cost him the lives of many friends, apprentices, lovers, and heirs. Listening to stories of a new land seemed to pierce his heart. The idea of exploring unknown worlds, discovering new magic, and uncovering new histories appealed to his passion for learning much more than the limited existence of a king.

"What about you?" Lillian asked. "Are you really going to rebuild your kingdom once Sylvia is dead?"

"I haven't thought much about it," Clement said, giving a disinterested shrug. "I'm more concerned with her death. Everything else comes second."

Lillian smiled. "Was that your plan with me? Just conquer Rhoria and then worry about what comes next afterward?"

"Pretty much," he answered, giving an amused smile. "I guess foresight wasn't always my strength either. I certainly never foresaw us standing here talking like this one day."

Lillian grinned. "Me neither. I was so intent upon killing you that I never saw much beyond that point. Of course, most of my assassination attempts weren't worth the time and money I spent on them."

"But they were so innovative," Clement said in amusement. "And you did come close a few times. My favorite one was when you sent me a marriage proposal."

Lillian burst out laughing. Clement joined in.

"Yes," she said after catching her breath. "I was hoping Darien's curse might kick in!"

"I figured," Clement replied. "Speaking of which, you may want to talk to Darien about getting rid of that. Perhaps you can ask him after this business is over."

"I don't know," Lillian said. "It might be useful. Someday I may become an advisor and control some kingdom from behind the scenes. Having a quick and efficient way of killing people could be beneficial."

"True," Clement agreed. "Maybe I should see if he can curse me. In any case, I better head back to camp before our companions get into mischief."

Lillian nodded, and Clement headed back toward the distant fire.

"Clement," she called. He turned, but she averted her eyes, gazing at the flowers. "Thanks for helping me back at the clearing."

Clement smiled. He removed her vial of swirling liquid from his pocket and held it out to her. "You're welcome."

She looked at him in surprise.

"You're giving it back to me?"

He gave a somewhat sheepish grin.

"I couldn't figure out the spells to make it work," he said.

She smiled. "Come on. I'll show you."

They walked back to the distant camp to join Darien and Xanaphia.

CHAPTER

12

Sylvia held her breath. She pretended she was dead. In the darkness, she imagined being inside a tomb and longed for death. The end of life meant the end of suffering. She'd be free. She fantasized about the sweet release and peaceful slumber of eternal rest. Life was little more than an endless string of horrific tortures. Why see the next sunrise?

She feared the loss of her sanity and prayed for her life's end but never considered relinquishing the tiara. Hour after hour, day after day, from one agonized cry to the next, she focused on her children. She felt them watching her. She could hear their voices coming from somewhere in the distance, urging her to remain strong. It gave her strength.

Torchlight filled the dungeon. She opened her eyes, wondering who her visitor might be. Morning couldn't have arrived already. She glanced at the archway. It was Cyril. She sighed and lay back down.

She felt relieved it wasn't a grorg. Though Cyril remained a dangerous potential tyrant, he was currently the closest thing she had to an ally. His nightly refusal to make her swallow the white cubes, even if done with ulterior motives, was a reminder of the goodness inherent within even the most corrupt human being. Still, she wished he'd go away. She just wanted to sleep.

Cyril said nothing, and she couldn't hear his footsteps. Finally, she opened her eyes and looked at him. He stood there, watching her from the archway. Something about him seemed odd, and she sat up to examine him more closely.

The fire in his eyes burned dim. Large bags shown beneath them as though he hadn't slept in days. He appeared ill, almost sickly, and had the air of someone suffering from a crippling ailment. She hadn't observed it when she saw him at the end of her torture session. Looking back though, the signs were there. She must've been too preoccupied to notice.

"Cyril, are you okay?"

"No, Your Majesty, I'm afraid all is not well." He strode toward her. He suddenly doubled over as though experiencing pain in his stomach. He stumbled, grabbing the bars of a nearby cell for support. He closed his eyes, taking several deep breaths as though trying to regain control of his senses. He straightened and continued. He appeared to be moving better but the signs of sickness remained evident.

"The time has come," he said. "I can't protect you any longer. Darlyth has ordered you moved to Kendross Keep."

She understood the meaning only too well. At Kendross Keep, she would be surrounded night and day by grorgs. No one would come to her rescue to stop the torture. The white pills and the promise of increased pain would become a reality instead of a fear. Cyril took a step toward her.

"Your Majesty, you must give me the tiara." There was a hint of desperation in his voice.

"I can't," she said. "You don't understand what the tiara means to me."

"You can and you must," he replied. "Do you not understand what the tiara means to this world? Do you not know what it means to your people?"

"The tiara is my life," she pleaded. "It means everything to me."

"You're a queen," he replied. "Your people are supposed to mean everything to you! Their needs are supposed to mean everything to you!"

"My people's needs don't include you!" she said, rising from the floor.

She knew her anger was misdirected but couldn't stop. All the pain she had suffered, all the rage coursing through her veins, all the frustration from the endless and horrific nightmare her life had become surged through her body. She couldn't strike back at the grorgs, but she could release her venom on him.

"They don't need you," she shouted. "I don't need you! No one needs you! The world has enough dictators, enough villains, and enough monsters ruling the helpless masses without you. I won't be responsible for adding another."

"What about him?" Cyril gestured, indicating the demon lord. "Do you not understand anything? Your people are going to die! Every human will become nothing more than livestock, kept in pins to feed his sick creations. Will you be responsible for him?"

"I'll never give him the tiara!"

"Yes, you will!" Cyril shouted, his anger matching Sylvia's. "Either willingly or unwillingly, you will relent. I'm your only hope. I'm the only one who can help them!"

"They don't want your help and neither do I. They hate you and you hate them!"

"Who cares as long as they're not demon fodder?"

"I care," she said. "I won't betray my people or my children's legacy by entrusting both to a monster!"

"How dare you!" Cyril was livid. "What do you know of monsters? You stand there in your self-righteous arrogance condemning your people to roast like chestnuts over Darlyth's fires. All in the name of your legacy. And you call me a monster?"

He inched closer to her cell until his nose almost touched her own through the bars. His voice dropped to a quiet hiss of impassioned bitterness.

"When Darlyth is killing your people, I hope he'll let you live to see the price of your arrogance. When the bloody screams of their kids echo through the night like bleating lambs before the butcher's axe, I hope you hear every cry. We'll see what you think of your children's legacy then!"

"Get out!" Sylvia ordered, pointing at the stairs.

"Fine!" Cyril whipped around, his white robes swirling behind him.

He strode across the dungeon. Upon reaching the archway, he turned around. He withdrew the tiara from his robes and tossed it onto the floor. The metal clattered against the stone as it came to a halt just beyond her reach.

"Take a long last look at it," he said. "The next time you see it will be on Darlyth's head. Goodbye, Your Majesty!"

He disappeared up the stairs. The light vanished with him. Sylvia threw herself on the floor, burying her head in her hands.

I made a fine mess of that, she thought as her anger died away.

She regretted many of the things she said. Cyril had been kind to her. He deserved better.

She looked into the darkness where the tiara lay. A dim violet glow emanated from the jewels atop the crown. It grew brighter and larger with each passing second. Suddenly, she saw the empty eyes of her children peering from the depth of the stones. She gasped and blinked. The vision was gone. All was black.

She rubbed her eyes and looked again. Nothing happened. Was she going mad? Were her thoughts and fantasies about her children causing her to hallucinate? The thought frightened her. She needed her wits in the coming days. She huddled on the floor, but the ghostly image of her children haunted her. She broke down into long, deep sobs and cried herself to sleep.

A lone figure marched unseen across the snow-covered courtyard of Junlorace Keep. Winter gales rocked the fortress, washing over the stone walls and flowing through the expansive channel before sweeping over the walls on the opposite side. The dark-red hair of the solitary soldier whipped in the gale.

Only one person would be outside in weather like this: Ladonna, second in command of Junlorace Keep. Ladonna feared no weather, just as she feared no man. She feared only one thing, life without Cyril.

Sunrise remained hours away. The guards wouldn't rotate until dawn. She had called the night watch inside to take shelter from the storm. They were busy playing cards or perhaps napping during the rare break in their strenuous routine. Everything was perfect.

Ladonna's duty was to protect the fortress. Cyril trusted her. Her men trusted her. Yet she couldn't escape Cyril's haunting message. He said love couldn't exist in a world ruled by demons. Her parents raised her to believe otherwise, but they were dead. She had only Cyril, and he'd never express his love for her as long as his people remained in danger. Though she felt misgivings about what she was about to do, she resolved to do it for the sake of love and for the sake of Cyril.

A light reached her eyes. It came from the small ovular gatehouse on the right side of the portcullis. The small outpost devoid of food, drink, or even a fire housed the two remaining sentries on duty. They snapped to attention as she entered.

"At ease," Ladonna said. "Anything to report?"

"No, Commander," both guards responded.

"Good." She scanned each in turn.

She specifically handpicked them to be on duty this night. The first was a grizzled old veteran whose body no longer responded to the fast pace of battle. The other was an excitable young teenager who posed little danger to a skilled adversary.

"All other soldiers and watchmen are in the barracks, but I can't leave the gate unprotected."

"We understand, Commander," the young guard said with customary enthusiasm. "We're honored by your faith in us. No dangers will occur on our watch!"

"Excellent," she said, smiling. "I knew I could count on you. As a reward for your service, I've brought something to warm you."

She reached into a satchel strapped to her waist and withdrew three leather wineskins. "The finest mead from the kitchen."

She handed one to each soldier and kept another for herself.

"To your health," she said, raising her vessel. "Let's drink these before the skins burst in the cold."

They drank. Warm mead trickled across Ladonna's tongue, coating her parched throat. She finished and looked around. Both men were now unconscious at her feet. Their drinks were laced with cicle, a white flower that bloomed in snowy conditions. The petals formed a powerful and quick-acting sedative. The guards would be out for a while. Ladonna tossed away the wineskin and grabbed the lantern.

General Cordor knelt behind the bush until a series of flashing lights informed him the moment had come. He moved into the open, signaling the others. Emerging from the bushes, they crossed toward the keep. He watched the drawbridge lower as they approached, the creak drowned out by the loud howl of the windy night.

A lone soldier waited on the bridge. Cordor didn't trust her. She had spotted their campsite the previous night while riding on the back of some dragon-like creature. Unbothered by the heavily armed soldiers, she landed in their midst, dismounted her beast, and demanded their business.

Five of the elite royal guard charged the petite opponent. They soon fell unconscious at her feet. Cordor had never seen a more formidable combatant. Her reflexes, strength, and speed were superior to any warrior he'd ever seen, including himself. Fortunately, Cornelius took control of the situation. She seemed wary of him. Whatever her skill with a blade, she clearly lacked magic.

Cornelius communicated who they were and the purpose of their quest. To their surprise, she revealed herself to be the commander of the fort where the queen was held hostage. She said an ancient evil threatened her people. She said it was trying to steal Sylvia's powers. The keep's ruler was powerless to disobey its orders, and she feared her people would die if Sylvia failed to relent. The story seemed farfetched, but Cornelius accepted every word.

A long discussion followed. Cornelius convinced the young woman they could save her people if she led them to the queen. She reluctantly acquiesced, indicating she must act alone. Dangerous factions inside the fort would stop her if they became aware of her betrayal. Cordor found the arrangement suspicious, but so far she seemed to have kept her word.

"General Cordor," Ladonna whispered, "thank goodness you're safe."

"Why wouldn't we be?" he asked.

"Waiting in the mountains is dangerous no matter how formidable your party," she said. "But we've no time to dwell on that. We must hurry."

She took several steps inside. Glancing in each direction, she signaled for them to follow. They hurried after her, and she led them across the courtyard.

"I disabled the guards monitoring the dungeon and relieved the night watch," she said. "We don't know how long the storm will last. The morning shift will report in a couple of hours. You must be gone by then."

"Where is she being kept?" Cornelius asked.

Ladonna pointed ahead at a stone archway. "The dungeons are down a flight of stairs on the other side. I have keys for the main dungeon but not for the individual cells. I assume you can open doors with your magic?"

"I can," Cornelius answered.

"Good," she said. "There's no time to delay."

They reached the archway, and she led them down the stairs. Cornelius descended, but Cordor hung back. Signaling the company onward, he addressed the last two men.

"Keep hidden and watch for danger. If you see anything, come get us."

"Yes, sir," they responded.

Cordor gave a nod and hurried down the stairs, never noticing the bat-like face staring down from a window overhead.

The stairs stretched downward until the sound of howling wind vanished. Still no end was in sight. Ladonna descended lightly, but the royal guard, weary from days of nonstop traveling, tired quickly. Cordor watched their stamina fade with each new level. Even Cornelius slowed as the trek continued. When they reached the bottom, only Ladonna and Cordor weren't on the verge of collapse.

"Stay here and gather your strength," he ordered as his men slumped against the cold dungeon wall. "We'll be back shortly. Cornelius?"

The high mage nodded. Together they followed Ladonna down a hallway and around a bend. Two guards lay unconscious on each side of a wooden door. Ladonna hurried forward, pulling a key from her tunic. She unlocked the door and pulled it open. Cornelius stepped forward.

"Stay here," he ordered.

"Why?" she asked, her eyes narrowing.

"The queen doesn't know you," Cornelius answered. "She might be suspicious if a stranger accompanies us down."

Ladonna eyed him with obvious mistrust. Cordor also felt uncertain about the arrangement. He disliked leaving Ladonna alone. She had proven a match for his men at full strength. Now they were exhausted and tired. She could defeat his soldiers with ease if this proved to be a trap.

Cornelius alone seemed unconcerned. He took the torch from Ladonna's hand and descended the stone staircase. Cordor followed. A short way down, a small arch opened onto a passage lined with large cells. In the last cell on the right was Sylvia.

"Your Majesty," Cordor burst out.

Sylvia heard his cry and recognized the voice. Sitting upright, she gazed in shock as her most trusted commander rushed to her cell. Even greater relief flooded her at the sight of her closest friend and confidant running behind him.

"Cordor, Cornelius," she cried. "Thank the gods you're here!"

"Are you okay?" Cordor called, grabbing the bars.

"I am now," she said, rising. Tears of joy and relief filled her eyes. "How'd you get here?"

"It's a long story," Cornelius answered. "But you can thank Cordor for never giving up on his suspicions. Otkreeteeyay!"

The door clicked open. Cordor rushed inside and threw his arms around Sylvia.

"We can also thank a young woman who doesn't want to spend her life enslaved to evil," Cornelius continued.

"One of the soldiers told us about your imprisonment and agreed to help."

Patting Cordor, Sylvia took a step back. "What else did she tell you?"

"She told us why you were imprisoned but said nothing about . . ." Cornelius gestured toward the crown.

Sylvia understood. Cornelius and Cordor knew her secret. Few others did. She preferred to keep it that way. She picked up the crown and smiled. Cyril had left it in anger, hoping to torment her. She wondered what he would think when he discovered his mistake.

She placed the tiara on her head. She'd worn it day and night for more than seven years. Now it was back where it belonged. She felt a rush of strength. She was no longer a helpless captive. She was a queen with her mightiest generals at hand. Or was she?

Doubts flooded her mind. Were these really her friends or some trick of Cyril and his demonic master? There was only one way to find out.

"Cordor," she said, "do you have the alarm amulet on you?"

"Of course," he answered. He pulled the enchanted amulet from his armor and showed it to her.

She smiled. The demon lord and his minions were unlikely to know about the amulet. Even if they did, they were unlikely to equip an imposter with one. It was useless outside the castle. Most people would leave it behind. But she'd given Cordor instructions to never take it off.

Sylvia turned to Cornelius. He was smiling, holding a small golden pendant. The circular medallion contained a series of glowing designs including books, scrolls, and arcane drawings. It was the symbol of the Headmaster of the Rhorian Academy. Only Cornelius owned the medal, and the symbols only glowed when worn by the headmaster.

"Excellent," she said. She indeed stood in the presence of friends. "Cornelius, do you know how to remove these things?"

She held out her arms. He lifted them, studying the bands.

"Are those burning bracers?" he asked. "I've never seen a pair before. I'm sorry, Your Majesty. I don't know how to get them off."

"I would've been surprised if you did. Not many do. But I'm sure someone at the academy knows."

Her nonchalance hid her disappointment. She was a spellcaster. She didn't feel comfortable without her magic. "Let's get out of here."

They hurried up the stairs. At the top they were greeted by Ladonna.

"What took you so long?" she demanded. "We don't have all night. Dawn is getting close, and the guards will be rotating soon."

"We came as fast as we could," Cordor answered. "Your Majesty, this is Commander Ladonna. She helped us find you."

"How do you do?" Sylvia said, her eyes taking in red hair that darkened as she looked at it.

"The pleasure is mine, Your Majesty," she said. "But I'm afraid right now isn't the time for introductions. We must get out of here."

"Lead the way," Cornelius said.

They raced down the hall. Sylvia's appearance was greeted by excited cries from her men. She gave a smile and a salute but said nothing. Time was of the essence. She followed Ladonna and Cordor up the winding staircase. She heard several moans from her men. She soon understood why. The stairs seemed to stretch forever. Sylvia felt exhausted by the time she reached the summit. Cordor was the strongest man she'd ever met, but he too seemed winded by the ascent.

At the top, they reached a circular alcove with no windows and only a single stone archway leading out into the center of the courtyard. All appeared quiet in the main part of the keep, but she could tell Cordor seemed agitated. He glanced around.

"I put two sentries here," he said.

Ladonna bent down and lifted a small patch of black fur. Her eyes grew wide.

"Draw your weapons," she ordered. "We must get out of here, now."

Cornelius grabbed Sylvia by the arm as her men unsheathed their swords. They dashed from the entryway, emerging directly in front of a throng of waiting archers.

Everyone froze. Their enemies had hidden behind the concealment of the alcove walls, waiting for them to emerge. Sylvia counted almost thirty men dressed in thick armor with composite crossbows leveled at the party. On each side, towering above the soldiers, stood the grorgs. They leered down at the company, their sharp teeth bared in menacing grins. At their feet were the mangled bodies of Cordor's sentries.

No one moved. Sylvia knew the enemy's superior numbers would easily crush her winded rescue party. She glanced at Ladonna.

"The winghams," Ladonna whispered, tilting her head slightly toward a distant wooden structure. "Get to the wingham pins."

"Guards, don't kill the queen," the large grorg croaked. "We need her alive. As for the rest, fire!"

Thirty crossbows twanged in unison. Sylvia's men raised their shields but not fast enough. Screams issued from her soldiers as several collapsed onto the snow. The rest charged the archers.

"Run!" Ladonna shouted, joining the fray.

Sylvia hesitated. She felt reluctant to leave her men.

"Your Majesty, they're buying time," Cornelius shouted, pulling her by the arm. "Don't let the sacrifice be in vain. Come on!"

She knew he was right. Turning around, she charged the wingham pins. Cordor, Cornelius, and two of her soldiers raced beside her. Arrows followed the fleeing company. One of her men went down. Another bolt sailed past her head.

Cornelius extended a hand behind them, summoning a makeshift wall.

"That should keep them off for a little while."

Suddenly, a black mass collided with the party. Everyone was knocked from their feet, and a scream rose from her remaining guard. She saw him hoisted into the air, impaled upon the long nails of the smaller grorg. Sylvia and her generals attempted to rise, but the grorg thrust the body away and darted toward them.

"Voplah," Cornelius shouted, a beam of green light shooting from his outstretched hand. The fiend dodged with ease.

It bounded upon Cordor, knocking him back to the ground. Its clawed hand rose to strike, but a flash of red hair announced the arrival of Ladonna. She crashed into it, knocking it off him. The two rolled away into the snow.

"Come on!" Cornelius shouted, grabbing Sylvia. Along with Cordor, they raced toward the pens.

Sylvia looked back. Ladonna stood toe-to-toe with the beast. Sylvia watched as the grorg attacked, slashing Ladonna's face and spraying blood. Ladonna responded with a sharp upper cut that sliced the grorg's arm.

Sylvia spotted the other grorg and several black armored soldiers in the distance. They were pursuing her, and catching up fast. She spun around, picking up speed. They reached the door to the wingham pen. Cordor smashed into it, bursting it open in an explosion of splinters and wood. Cornelius and Sylvia raced inside.

The room stretched over a hundred feet in every direction. Cubicles lined the walls. In the middle, a large opening provided access to the sky above. About a half-dozen winghams sat beneath, already saddled with ladders stretching up to their backs. Men and women in peasant attire stood around, feeding them and attaching the harnesses. Children stood in nearby stalls, even at this early hour, bathing unbridled winghams.

Upon seeing armed strangers burst into the room, shouts filled the air. Frightened women and children dropped their buckets and fled to nearby corners. Startled men raced to protect their families or else cowered against walls. They possessed no weapons and posed little threat to Cordor or Cornelius.

"Quick, climb aboard the winghams," Cornelius shouted, pointing toward three mounts standing at ready.

Sylvia wondered why the creatures were bridled for immediate departure. Did they always keep a few ready in case of emergency? Did the grorgs warn them to be prepared in case the rescue party escaped? She didn't know. Nor did she have time to dwell on it.

"Your Majesty, you take that one," Cornelius shouted, pointing at the smaller mount in the middle. "I'll take the one on the left. Cordor, you take the one on the right."

Sylvia did as ordered. She raced toward her beast and hurried up the ladder. Cordor did the same. Cornelius hung back. Turning toward the door, he shouted, "Strena!"

A glowing ball of azure energy sprang from his outstretched hand. It bounced along the ground until it reached the doorway. There it exploded into a shimmering blue wall. Sylvia saw the large grorg slam into the barrier and heard the angry shouts of her pursuers. Cornelius smiled and sped toward his own mount.

"That'll slow them down while they find another entrance," Cornelius shouted as he hoisted himself up the ladder. "When you reach the saddle, you'll notice there's an indention for your knees. You're supposed to ride in a kneeling position. Place your knees into the grooves and use the straps on the back rest to secure yourself to the harness."

"How do you know this?" Cordor asked.

"You forget, I grew up in the northeast," Cornelius answered. "Wingham breeding was common prior to Darien's campaign. I grew up riding them."

Sylvia reached the top of her mount and strapped herself in. The position was awkward and uncomfortable. The leg rests were soft, but the angle proved hard on the knees and she felt off-balance.

"To take off, pull upward on the reigns," Cornelius continued, not bothering to strap in. "Pull the left reign to make it fly left. Pull the right reign to go right. Loose both reigns to make it go downward. Got it?"

"Not really," Sylvia said.

"You'll catch on. Just watch me. Let's go."

He seized the reigns and lifted them above his head. Sylvia and Cordor followed his example. The winghams let out loud squawks, beating their wings and rising into the cool night air. A door burst open as her pursuers rushed into the room. The soldiers pointed overhead and hurried toward the other waiting winghams. The grorgs just glared at her, their eyes gleaming.

"Follow me," Cornelius's shouted, pointing toward the distant hills. "Rhoria is that way!"

He urged his mount ahead. Cordor and Sylvia followed. As they flew, Sylvia glanced at the courtyard below. The battle was over. Her soldiers sprawled across the ground, their armor and blood glistening in the snow. Close by, the prone form of a redheaded woman lay unmoving. They had sacrificed everything to protect her.

Yet she was far from safe. The whiz of crossbow bolts informed Sylvia the pursuers were approaching. She tried to spur her wingham but the fierce winter winds and pelting sleet hindered it. The conditions highlighted her lack of familiarity with the strange mount. It rocked and swayed in the wind. Cornelius saw her struggling and flew to her aid, while Cordor fell back to provide a barrier between the pursuers and the queen.

Their adversaries were gaining. They ducked and weaved through the winds with ease, commanding the beasts like an extension of their own bodies. Seated atop their mounts, they loaded and fired their crossbows in rapid succession. Sylvia knew she wouldn't get far.

Cornelius also seemed to recognize the hopelessness of their predicament. He moved his mount close to Sylvia's, carefully positioning them to prevent their wings from striking. He stood up, abandoning the saddle and using the reigns to balance himself.

"You Majesty, we can't keep this up!" he shouted.

She nodded. "What do you suggest?"

"I have a plan, but you might not like it."

"We're pretty desperate. Let's hear it."

"I need you to give me the tiara!"

"What?" She turned and looked at him with a horrified expression.

"Hear me out!" he shouted. "I'm a better flier than you or Cordor. If they're after the tiara, I can lead them away from you. Cordor can protect you from anyone who would follow."

"But what if they catch you?"

"I'll use Desecria on myself," he said. "I'll die, and the power of the crown will die with me. I know it was given to you by your children. I know how much it means to you. But the important thing is your enemies won't be able to steal its powers and you'll be safe in Rhoria."

"I can't let you do that!" she protested. "If I wanted someone to die, I could just kill myself."

"Don't be brash! Your people need you. They need a leader who can unite them against this evil. You're the only one who can do so. I've been in contact with the capital. The steward I left in charge during my departure is embattled on all sides by corrupt factions vying for power. Without you, the people won't be able to form a united front against the danger."

Sylvia was not surprised by the news. Seven years seated upon the throne of Rhoria had shown her the extent of corruption within the kingdom. Without a strong leader, they would fall into the same bickering and feuding that had opened the door for the rise of the tyrants. Only she had the power to unite them against the demon lord.

"Your Majesty, there's no time," Cornelius said, almost slipping as he struggled to maintain his footing. "This is the only way!"

She took off the tiara and looked at it. How many people had already died because of the simple crown? How many more would join the collection of bodies sprawled across the courtyard of Junlorace Keep?

She extended the crown toward Cornelius. He lifted his hand to take it from her. As it came within feet of his outstretched fingers, Sylvia's eyes fell upon the gems. Her heart froze. Her children gazed at her from the jewels. Their voices called to her, begging her not to leave them. She found herself frozen, unable to hand it over.

She looked into Cornelius's anxious face. She knew she must give it to him. It was her only hope. He'd never surrender the crown. He was her most trusted advisor. Her mind fell back to the day they first met, the day her men discovered him lost in the mountains, the day he converted to her cause.

Junlorace Keep! She remembered. When Cyril told Sylvia the name, she thought it sounded familiar. Now she knew why. When her soldiers captured Cornelius, she demanded to know his reason for being in the mountains. He revealed he was performing a mission on behalf of Darien. According to his story, he was returning from a reconnaissance trip to Junlorace Keep.

Of course! Cyril had told her Darien sent troops to the fort, but he said they all died. Everyone he said, except those who . . . joined the cause.

Sylvia yanked the tiara away from Cornelius's outstretched hand, staring at him in stunned disbelief. She tried to convince herself the conclusion was wrong, but all the pieces fit. All of the events of the last week made sense.

She understood how the demon lord found out about the tiara. He knew because Cornelius knew. She understood how the demon penetrated the defenses to her room. Cornelius had access to her room. He must have sabotaged them. She knew where the demon lord got the burning bracers. A pair belonged to the former headmaster of the academy. Cornelius must've inherited them when he took power.

She also understood the strange features of their bizarre escape. Why were the winghams saddled? How did they escape while the rest of her soldiers died? The answer was obvious. They were meant to escape. The rescue was a ruse, an intricate plan designed to trick her into surrendering the tiara.

Pulling the tiara away must've warned Cornelius the game was up, because he seemed to read her thoughts. He looked over his shoulder, where Cordor was winging his mount forward to join them.

"Your Majesty," Cordor shouted. He never spoke again.

"Desecria!" Cornelius said, pointing his fingers at the chest of the approaching wingham.

Black lightning burst from his hands, ripping through the beast. It gave a cry of pain and rose into the air as lightning raked across its exposed belly. Then it rolled onto its back and plummeting toward the earth. Cordor screamed, but the sound ended abruptly as the creature collided with the ground.

"No!" Sylvia shouted.

She yanked her mount to the left. It broke into a dive, striking the wing of Cornelius's steed. His mount panicked, nearly throwing him off, but he steadied the beast and dove after her. Sylvia unstrapped her harness as she dove downward.

Not bothering to lower the ladder, she sprang from the wingham's back as it settled into a small clearing near a frozen lake. A few yards away, a dense forest extended upward to the top of a tall mountain. From the air, she had seen a large canyon and a thick mass of trees on the other side. The winghams wouldn't be able to land amid such foliage. If she could reach the woods, her enemies would have to follow on foot. Perhaps she could evade her captors by hiding in the undergrowth.

"Ostanavleevat!" Cornelius called out.

A force struck Sylvia in the back. She froze, rendered immobile by the spell. She stood helpless, tiara in hand, as Cornelius's wingham swooped down upon her. The beast's talons wrapped around her, hoisting her up by the shoulders. Cold wind struck Sylvia's unblinking eyes, causing them to tear up.

"Running was pointless, Your Majesty," Cornelius shouted. "A demon was stationed inside the canyon waiting to recapture you. There was no way out."

Cornelius rose from the ground as other winghams joined him.

"Did you get it?" shouted a male voice.

"No," he called back. "The plan has failed."

"What now?" asked the other.

"We obey Darlyth's orders," Cornelius said. "I'll take her to Kendross Keep. Do any of you know the way?"

"Jason can guide you," the voice answered. "I must return her wingham and report to Lord Cyril. He won't be happy about you killing one of our beasts."

"Like I care," Cornelius retorted. "Give him your report."

Sylvia heard the winghams soar away. The wind gusted across her face and into her aching eyes. Her brief taste of freedom was over.

CHAPTER

13

Lillian sat against a fallen log. After the events of the previous day, she and Clement decided to alter how they handled watch. Both had saved the others' lives, and neither felt reason to believe the other currently wanted them dead. Under the new plan, Darien and Xanaphia would keep watch for four hours. Afterward, Clement would watch for two hours while the other three slept. Lillian would take the last two hours. The change allowed the party to break camp an hour earlier.

Neither Darien nor Xanaphia trusted the development. Aside from preventing the guards from killing each other, the additional person provided those sleeping a degree of protection from the people on watch. But as Lillian reasoned, if she and Clement were in cahoots, they could pull off their scheme during their normal combined watch. The argument was less than comforting. Both Darien and Xanaphia made a point of muttering extra protective spells before going to sleep.

Lillian didn't see the purpose of keeping watch at all. The primary goal was to prevent internal treachery. No such attempts had been made, and recent events reduced the likelihood of them happening now.

Watching for external peril was also pointless. The rising bowl of the mountains and the thick forests meant any attempt to see more than twenty yards was futile, while a blanket of pine needles obscured all vision upward.

Abandoning all pretense of performing her duty, Lillian sat doodling with a small multicolored cube. She had obtained it from the treasury of a ruthless vampire lord while traveling in the Southern Continent. She almost lost her life in the process, but the risk was worth the reward. According to legend, if the colored blocks were arranged into the correct pattern, anyone touching it could enter the dreams of a sleeping victim. The intruder or intruders would experience the subject's visions as though they themselves were the dreamer. For Lillian, such power was worth any price.

Over the last five years, she had devoted countless hours to solving the riddle. Unfortunately, the solution was proving as elusive as the secrets she sought to uncover. Only the vampire lord knew the correct pattern for the lights. Several times she thought she had come close. A few times she felt convinced she was on the verge of a breakthrough. But the solution eluded her.

The shriek of some strange animal pierced the night like an explosion. It was followed by a shout. Lillian could make out the emotion. She'd heard it many times. It came from someone who knew they were about to die.

Before she could raise the alarm, everyone was on their feet.

"What was that?" Clement began.

A third shriek sounded in the distance.

"I know that sound," Darien said, his face contorting with hatred and disgust. "Winghams!"

"It's coming from the other side of the hill," Clement declared. "Come on!"

Clement charged up the hill. Darien followed, but Xanaphia didn't. Lillian saw her turn toward the fire muttering, "Prerodnee." The camp melded into the ground, the fire pit vanishing, the ashes dispersing, and the piles of snow leveling until no trace of the campsite remained.

"Impressive spell," Lillian said approvingly.

"Thanks," Xanaphia answered, her voice devoid of its usual malice and sarcasm. "That's indeed a compliment coming from you. Shall we?"

She gestured after Clement and Darien. Lillian nodded. Together they pursued the men up the hill. They had barely taken two steps before a male voice shouted, "Ostanavleevat!"

Clement and Darien froze.

"Was that…" Clement began.

"The high mage?" Darien interrupted. "Yes."

The company hurried up the slope. The terrain was steep and the climb difficult. When they finally reached the top, they found the trees blocked all visibility. Everyone waited, listening for further traces of sound. None came.

"Lillian," Xanaphia said, "do you have a spell to detect where a noise came from?"

"Not one that'd be useful to us," she answered. "It must be cast while the noise is being made."

"What about a spell to detect the location of an animal?" Darien asked.

"Yes, but I've got to touch a piece of the species. Otherwise, it'll take me to some random animal."

Darien reached inside his tunic, withdrawing a necklace from around his neck, and flung it toward Lillian. Lillian caught it in surprise. It was a thick leather band adorned with sharp barbed teeth.

"Wingham teeth?" she asked.

"Yes," he answered.

Everyone looked at him in surprise. Lillian had never known he carried such a medallion. She was confident the others didn't either. She couldn't imagine why he wore it. Darien hated winghams. The necklace couldn't be a trophy of his kills or else he would wear it where everyone could see. Wearing it inside his clothing was indicative of a charm or memento.

She pushed the thought from her mind. She had a more immediate objective. Clutching the necklace, she closed her eyes, focusing on the teeth gripped in her hand. She took a slow deep breath, filling her lungs with cold night air.

"Eesckat," she sighed, giving a long exhale and holding her breath.

She felt the magic penetrate her pores and fill her body. A bright-yellow light issued from her skin coalescing around her hands and the necklace. A tugging sensation pulled upon her body. When she could hold her breath no longer, she opened her mouth, gasping for air.

"This way," she panted. "Follow me!"

The sun creeping over the distant mountaintops illuminated the weary face of Cyril Junlorace. He stared out the window, hands resting on his sword. His eyes didn't glow. His muscles didn't twitch. His plan had failed. The tiara was gone. His revenge was lost, and the ancient oath to prevent the demon lord's rise was broken.

The queen is a fool, he thought angrily for perhaps the hundredth time. She chose to doom the world to death rather than give the tiara to the one man who could save it. She would rather see the world burn in flames than see Cyril inflict retribution upon those whose ambivalence caused its fall.

Pain racked his body. He doubled over, gripping his stomach and catching himself on the window. He closed his eyes and waited for the pain to subside. It lasted longer each time. He looked at his desk. A goblet filled with his morning supply of blood awaited him. It had been sitting there for several hours. Cyril didn't want to drink it. He hadn't drunk his issue of blood yesterday or the day before either. Instead, he bottled them inside a couple of canteens in anticipation of visiting Kendross Keep.

He had a plan. Unfortunately, he lacked the resources to enact it. He needed accomplices, powerful accomplices, and he didn't have them. Cornelius would oppose the plan, and Ladonna lacked the necessary skill. Without help, his plot was doomed.

He stared at the cup, his reflection staring back at him. Frenzy was settling in. Agonizing pain and wild urges struck constantly. They probably contributed to his emotional outburst when speaking with Sylvia the previous night. He regretted losing control, but she was completely unreasonable anyway. He doubted anything he said would have made much difference.

He looked down at his right arm. It was moving independently, drifting toward the cup. His temper flared.

He was no animal to be controlled by his instincts. He wasn't some stupid demon bound to Darlyth's will. He was a man and could think his own thoughts, will his own will, and love with true love. He wouldn't be a prisoner to demonic desires.

He swung his left fist, knocking the cup off his desk. The right hand attempted to seize it but missed. The chalice smashed against the floor, scattering blood everywhere. Cyril turned toward the window and chastised himself for his foolishness. He should've drunk the cup. Whether he liked it or not, he was a kefling. As much as he desired freedom, he remained a prisoner. If he didn't get blood, he would lose control. Such an action was irresponsible.

"Cyril?" a soft voice called from the doorway.

He turned and found himself gazing into the penetrating green eyes of the woman he once swore to marry. Another oath in a long string of oaths he'd never get to keep. She had stayed up late carrying out orders she didn't want to obey, risking her life for the sake of a plan she never wanted to enact, and playing a role she never wanted to play. Yet she did it because he ordered her to, because he told her it had to be done, and because she loved him.

A gash ran down her left cheek. Only one creature could have left the mark, a grorg. They would claim it was an accident. Cyril doubted it. He was second in command of his master's minions, and they resented him for it. They would take advantage of any opportunity to strike at him.

The scar stole nothing from her beauty. Ladonna's presence cast a warm ray of light into the room. Her radiance was more soothing than the warmth of the sun, her voice more calming to his tense nerves than a hundred tonics.

Despite all the events of the last few days, when he looked at her, he still felt hope.

"Good morning, Ladonna," Cyril said affectionately.

"Good morning, My Lord," she replied. She smiled at his soft greeting, but her expression hardened. "The grorgs are here to see you."

Cyril's mood soured. Of course, they wanted one last opportunity to gloat. They had played along with his ruse because Darlyth demanded it. Cyril knew they didn't want the plan to succeed. They delighted in suffering. As long as Sylvia possessed the tiara, they could continue to torture her.

"Very well," Cyril said, turning toward the window. "Show them in."

She leaned into the hallway, gesturing for them to enter. A moment later, the monstrosities slouched inside. The larger grorg entered first, followed by its subordinate. The latter grinned at Ladonna and licked one of its claws. Ladonna's eyes narrowed.

The leader approached within an arm's length of Cyril, still carrying the bag of torture devices. It leered triumphantly at him. Cyril refused to give them the dignity of his full attention. He stared out the window, watching them from the corner of his eye.

"The time has come for us to return to Kendross Keep," the beast sneered.

"Don't let me keep you," Cyril said.

"The master wants you to know the queen is no longer your concern. He is disappointed you weren't able to get the tiara, but the result is not unexpected."

It paused. Grorgs possessed a strange telepathic link with their master. He could send messages and commands to them at will. They lacked the ability to send messages back, but Cyril knew his reaction to their gloating would be reported once they returned. He gazed out the window, refusing to allow the slightest change in his features. After a moment, it resumed speaking.

"The master has a new mission for you."

"I am subservient to my lord's will," Cyril said. "His commands I shall obey."

"He has lost contact with two of his minions," the grorg said. "His servant stationed north of Rhoria and the one sent to guard the canyon have fallen silent"

"You mean someone has slain them?" Cyril said in astonishment, turning to look at them. A glimmer of hope ignited in his breast. He quickly hid his excitement, turning back toward the window. "So what? Two missing demons are hardly a dent in his army."

"Perhaps not," the grorg agreed, "but he is wary of who may be slaying them, lest they become a greater threat. He orders you to investigate."

"Very well," Cyril said. "I shall investigate the matter personally."

The grorg nodded. It stared at Cyril and, abandoning all pretense of respect, growled, "I hope you meet the same fate as the demons."

The smaller grorg howled with laughter. Cyril looked at the pair and raised an eyebrow.

"Darlyth ordered me to let you inside the keep," he said. "He didn't say anything about allowing you to leave."

His voice was calm, but the words produced an instant reaction. The smile vanished from the large grorg's face, and its companion stopped laughing. They shifted uncomfortably for a moment then hurried toward the door. They never reached it.

Two howls rose and were instantly silenced. Ladonna turned toward the door, but the confrontation was over. The headless bodies of the grorgs hung in the air before collapsing. The still-blinking heads rolled along the floor. Bright-red liquid oozed from the severed necks, blending with the blood already on the floor. Towering above the corpses, sword in hand, stood Cyril.

But it wasn't Cyril. At least, not the one she knew. Ladonna gasped in horror. His normally placid face was flushed, and he wore a wild maniacal grin. His eyes were literally on fire. The flames burned his eyelids and singed his brows. Ladonna watched as he lifted his sword to his lips. With a long slow lick, the blood-soaked blade slid across his tongue as he moaned in pleasure.

The feral eyes locked onto Ladonna. For the first time in her life, she felt terrified of the man she loved. His hungry expression stared at her, devoid of sanity or recognition. He licked the blood off his lips in a threatening gesture.

Ladonna backed away, not bothering to reach for her sword. She would be dead long before she could draw it. Cyril raised his blade, and Ladonna braced for the attack. Then the flames vanished from Cyril's eyes, and the deranged smile faded. His muscles relaxed, and he collapsed to his knees. Horror gave way to concern as Ladonna raced to his side, but he raised a hand in warning.

Ladonna stopped. "Cyril?"

"Blood," he said in a quivering voice, "I need blood."

Remembering the chalice, she raced across the room and snatched it from the floor. She hurried to the neck of the larger grorg, where blood still trickled. She pushed down on the creature's back, hoping to speed the flow. When the cup was full, she dashed back to Cyril.

"Here, My Lord," she said, offering him the cup.

She shook nervously. Cyril took her hands in his, steadying the chalice as he drank. He drained the entire contents in one gulp and released her. She leapt back to her feet, getting more blood from the dead grorg before returning to Cyril again. He grew stronger as he finished the second cup and managed a feeble, "Thank you."

As Ladonna went to get more blood, Cyril, still on his hands and knees, dragged himself across the floor to the sack gripped in the large grorg's lifeless hand. Rigor mortis had frozen the fist, but with an angry tug he ripped the bag from its grasp. Wands, torture devices, and magical gadgets scattered everywhere. He rummaged through them searching for something. After a moment, his hand shot into the air with a smooth white stone. Ladonna peered at it as she offered him a third cup.

"Thank you!" he said, taking the cup from her.

He drained it and tossed it aside. Crossing to the window, he lifted the stone into the sunlight and marveled at the gentle glow radiating from its depth.

"Is that the Life Stone?" Ladonna asked in an awed voice.

"Yes," he said. Turning to her, he plunged the stone into her hand and cried. "Spacineeya."

He watched a green glow engulf her body. Her eyes grew dreamy, and an enraptured smile crossed her face. The scar grew smaller and vanished. The glow faded, and her eyes returned to normal. She stared at him in surprise. He felt a rush of enthusiasm and pride. Then he spotted the bodies of the grorgs lying on the ground. The memories of his fit came back to him.

"Are you okay?" he asked.

She nodded.

"I'm sorry," he said. "I knew I needed blood, but I didn't think killing the grorgs would cause me to frenzy."

"There was no harm done. Everything is okay."

"No, everything is not okay," he said. "You could've been killed."

"But I wasn't," she said. "I'm fine. You're fine. And I certainly don't mind seeing those brutes meet their fate."

She gave the body of the small grorg a kick. "What comes next?"

"The games begin anew," he said, moving toward his desk.

Ladonna gave an exasperated look.

"Cyril, wait," she said, «listen to me."

Cyril paused, unable to resist the plea in his beloved's voice. She moved up to him, placing a hand on his shoulder.

"I know you want revenge against Darlyth," she said. "I do too! But sometimes events don't unfold to give us everything we want. We have to satisfy ourselves with the things we get. At least, we'll get our revenge against the people. We can teach a lesson to those who turned their backs on us."

"No, we can't teach them a lesson," Cyril said, looking at her. "There'll be no one to learn it. He'll turn humanity into livestock. They'll be kept in pins and farms, bred and housed like chickens. They won't pass on lessons to their children. What would be the point? It'd be like teaching someone with no arms how to use a sword. They have the knowledge, but can do nothing with it. Humanity will know their mistake, but they can't fix it. Their suffering won't erase our pain. Then what do we have?"

"We have each other!" she said. Tears filled her eyes, and she lowered her head, trying to hide them.

Cyril reached out, lifting her chin and wiping away her tears. He bent close and pressed his lips against hers. She leaned into him. He felt her arms wrap around him and placed his hand on the back of her head. It was the first time they had kissed since before the demon lord's rise. They kissed again and again as all their bottled emotions burst from them in that single expression of love. The passionate embrace lasted only a few minutes.

Cyril pulled away and looked at Ladonna. She was holding her breath, and her eyes were closed. Her hair was the darkest red he could remember seeing. She opened her eyes and looked into his face. For a few seconds, they gazed at each other.

"I love you, Ladonna," Cyril said in a soft voice. "I wish things could be different, but I have to do this. I must do it for you. I must do it for the people of Junlorace Keep. I must do it for the world."

"What has the world ever done for us?" Ladonna asked.

"Nothing," he answered, "but the world never promised to do anything for us. The world never pledged to support us. We pledged to support it. They never took an oath to care about us. We took an oath to care about them. Though they refused to send medicine when we were sick, though they wouldn't send food when we were starving, though they didn't care if we lived or died and turned their backs upon us, we cannot turn our backs upon them."

"What're you going to do?" she asked. Her hair grew lighter. Cyril could tell she was trying to be strong.

"I'm going to Kendross Keep. I'm going to face Darlyth."

"No," she said in alarm, "you can't! You can't disobey him. What can you hope to achieve?"

"I have a plan," Cyril said.

He diverted his eyes so she couldn't see his thoughts. But she seemed to sense them anyway.

"You don't expect to return," she said.

He looked up at her. Fear and hurt reflected in her eyes.

"You're going there to die. Aren't you?"

"I am."

She rose to her full height, her eyes flashing with resolve. "Then take me with you."

Cyril shook his head.

"I can't," he said. "I need you here. Our people are in danger. They can't stay. You must lead them to safety."

Ladonna's hair turned dark crimson, and her eyes narrowed. She turned away, crossing her arms in defiance.

"And what if I refuse?" she asked.

Cyril smiled and placed a hand on her shoulders.

"You won't," he said tenderly. "I know you. Your loyalty is your greatest virtue. You take pride in it. If I give you a command, you won't disobey."

She turned toward him, her face inches from his. Tears streamed down her cheeks.

"But I need you," she sobbed. "I can't lose you. I don't want to lose you."

"Sometimes events don't unfold to give us everything we want," he responded. "We just have to satisfy ourselves with the things we get."

"What do I get?" she asked. "I'm losing my home! I'm losing you! I'm losing everything!"

"You're getting freedom," he said, stroking her hair. "You're getting a future."

"I don't want freedom!" she cried. "I don't want a future if that future is without you!"

"Ladonna," Cyril said, his voice full of compassion. "Think about our people. They're like children to us. We raised them, protected them, and trained them. They need us. We need to do what is best for them, even if it causes us pain. They deserve a future, one free from the suffering they've endured for so many generations. You can give them that future."

"But I can't do it alone," Ladonna implored. "I don't want to go on without you!"

"I'll always be with you," Cyril said, taking her hand. "I'm a part of you. I'm a part of my people. When you look into their eyes, you're seeing mine. When they smile, you're seeing my smile. When they laugh, you're hearing my laughter. I'm there in spirit. Look for me."

She dropped her head and gripped his hand tightly. Cyril understood. He couldn't imagine life without her, but he wasn't the one faced with the prospect. He would be dead soon. She was the one who must go on.

"What do you need me to do?" she asked.

Cyril smiled. Ladonna was a soldier, proud and loyal. This was how he would remember her, faithful, obedient, and devoted in both her love to him and her service to her people.

"I need you to gather everyone and load them onto winghams," he answered. "Fly to Rhoria and land in the middle of the city. That should get someone's attention. Demand to speak with the leaders of the magical academy. Tell them you're refugees from Junlorace Keep. Tell them the demon lord has awoken. Tell them he is holding the queen hostage."

"Do you think they'll believe me?" Ladonna asked.

"You just flew into the middle of the town with over a hundred refugees riding extinct creatures," Cyril replied with a smile. "At the least, I'm sure they'll listen."

"What is my objective?"

"To organize a rescue party," he said. "They must rescue Sylvia. I can get her out of the keep, but I can't get her back to Rhoria. They must come and find her. Let them use the winghams if needed. Time is of the essence. Only she can lead the people against Darlyth."

"Aren't you bound to research what happened to the missing demons?"

"Indeed, I am," Cyril said, a rueful smile crossing his lips. "I couldn't ask for a better assignment. Someone killed a stone demon and a crawler. Either could slaughter our entire fortress if I weren't here. The killers must be incredibly powerful. They would make good allies."

"Should I saddle a wingham for you?"

"No," he said, "I can't afford to take one. We're already overburdening our small force by moving the entire population of our keep. As lord, my people must come first. I and my allies will make do on foot. If you hurry, all should be well."

"Yes, My Lord."

She spoke the words with an air of finality but didn't leave. Instead, she stood there, her hand still wrapped around his. Cyril gazed into her eyes. She seemed to be fighting some internal struggle. Suddenly, she threw herself upon him in a passionate embrace. Their lips locked, and the world seemed to stand still.

The moment passed too quickly. She broke contact with him and backed away, clinging to his hand until their arms were stretched to their furthest limit. Finally, as though fearing her resolve might break, she released his hand and raced out the door. He had one last fleeting glimpse of her rounding the corner. Then she was gone.

Cyril's strength faltered. For a moment, he wondered what might have been. But there was no time for what ifs. He crossed to his desk, pulling open the drawer hiding the last piece of the golden orb. Removing the fake bottom and opening the wooden case, he held the fragment before him. A tingling sensation swept over his hand. He sensed the object knew his plan and approved. But would it work? How much magic did the stone possess? He wasn't sure, but he resolved to find out.

CHAPTER 14

For seemingly endless hours, Sylvia hung suspended from the claws of Cornelius's beast. Her robes whipped around her as the night air battered her unprotected frame. Every inch of her body ached from frostbite. Eventually, she became numb.

Unable to feel or see, Sylvia drifted into a fantasy land. The tiara floated before her. Her children's faces gazed at her. Their voices whispered cryptic tales of ancient wars and forgotten magic. Images and illusions drifted like apparitions across her mind. She struggled to comprehend the visions telling of old enemies and distant friends. Yet she was too weary to comprehend the phantasms.

She woke with an unpleasant jolt as the wingham deposited her onto a stony surface. She landed hard, tumbling along the unforgiving terrain. Jagged edges of loose gravel and cracked floor cut into her numb flesh, leaving numerous scrapes and bruises. Powerful hairy arms hoisted her into the air. The rough wheezy breath of her captors made no secret of their identity. They were grorgs.

They hauled their paralyzed victim for an unknown distance. After a while, she heard the whine of rusty metal. Then the grorgs dumped her face down onto the ground. Another loud squeal of rusted joints, and the sound of a falling latch told Sylvia she was back in prison.

The footfalls of her captors disappeared, but the sounds of harsh breathing told her two grorgs remained, keeping watch. She didn't know why. She couldn't go anywhere. Though she was eventually able to move again, she still couldn't see. Cornelius's spell had caused her eyes to dry out, leaving her blind. Her skin burned as feeling returned to her frostbitten limbs. She curled into a fetal position until the crash of the prison door caused her to start.

She turned in the direction of the sound as three figures entered her cell. Two shuffled across the ground dragging clawed feet. She presumed these belonged to grorgs. The third set of footsteps, however, bore the distinct clip-clop of traveling boots along with the rustle of a cloak.

"Pick her up," the high mage's voice demanded.

Clawed hands yanked her to her feet. Her legs proved too weak to support her weight, so they held her upright, a claw under each arm. She stared ahead, presumably facing her captor. Neither said anything. Cornelius appeared interested in her eyes. She felt his breath close to her face as he peered into their sockets.

"Well, well," he mused. His voice exuded a sadistic cockiness. He was clearly enjoying himself. "Blinded by the paralysis spell? This won't do at all. Half the fun of torturing someone is watching their horrified expression as you unleash each new torment upon them. I'll have to fix this. Glauz."

Sylvia's eyes began burning, and the blackness broke. A fuzzy orange light replaced the empty void before giving way to a collection of blurry images. These gave way to definite shapes. She could see again.

She scanned the prison, unable to remember seeing a more bizarre structure. The walls, floors, and ceilings weren't crafted from stone. They appeared to be formed from a strange orange material similar to dried clay. The surface wasn't smooth either. It was covered with numerous small bumps rising and falling, like dunes in a desert. The most incredible feature was the light radiating from them. The entire room was ablaze with an orange glow emanating from the uneven surface. The glow eliminated the need for torches and also meant there were no shadows.

She noticed the grorgs guarding her cell were different. They weren't as large or deformed as the ones who tortured her at Junlorace keep or the ones holding her arms. They stood upright, rather than hunched. Their bodies weren't as bulky, but they compensated for size with longer claws and fangs. Their hides also appeared thicker. They seemed designed for combat.

Her attention turned to Cornelius. He grinned, his eyes gleaming with malicious delight.

"Traitor," she hissed.

Cornelius laughed.

"Traitor? That is an odd accusation, don't you think? In order to turn traitor, I'd need to be on your side first."

He swaggered across the room as he spoke. Reaching the wall on Sylvia's right, he leaned against the rough surface folding his arms in nonchalance.

"Of course, I've never had much difficulty convincing people I'm on their side. When a man is as good-looking as me, women can't help believing anything he tells them. Men are the same way with an attractive lady. Somehow, when someone is good looking, people want to believe you're a good person. Add gullibility to humanity's weaknesses."

He looked at her sardonically.

"I was never on your side," he said. "Your people caught me because I wanted them to! The former masters of Junlorace Keep were clever and wise. They surveyed the world from afar, looking down upon the disgusting masses. They watched you crush Xanaphia and Lillian. They foresaw your victories over Darien and Clement. They knew you'd soon be the only one standing in the way of the Darlyth's return. They needed someone to feed them information from inside your court. They sent me to infiltrate your camp, win your trust, and work myself into a position of power. From there, I could feed them your secrets."

Sylvia shook her head. She had never questioned how her guards captured such a powerful wizard. The handsome captive disarmed everyone with his soft-spoken nature and stories of horrific trauma suffered at Darien's hands. He had convinced Sylvia he truly desired to escape his terrible past. His penitence seemed genuine, and his knowledge of Darien's defenses proved pivotal to her campaign. Looking back, she marveled at how thoroughly he had charmed her. How could she have been so foolish?

But other questions nagged at her. How did Cornelius create the power sink in her room without her noticing? How did he trick Cordor into coming to Junlorace Keep with such a small party? Where were her other generals and advisors? Why did they stay behind, and did they know about Junlorace Keep? If so, there might still be hope of rescue. She wanted answers but wasn't sure how to trick Cornelius into giving them.

"Well," Sylvia said, trying to sound hopeless and defeated, "your deception is over. You've won. Can you at least show me the respect of explaining everything to me?"

Cornelius let out another laugh.

"You're a poor liar, Your Majesty, and I'm a good one. You can't deceive me. You want information so you can find some ray of hope. It's a feeble attempt on your part."

He smiled, stroking his goatee. Finally, he threw his hands in the air.

"Okay, why not? Guards, you can leave."

The grorgs released her, and she collapsed onto the ground. Cornelius looked down at her, stroking his goatee as though contemplating where to start.

"As I said before, Lord and Lady Junlorace were great people. They were visionaries. After joining your army, I kept regular contact with them. Their son Cyril and I never got along, but after their deaths he contacted me on behalf of our master. Darlyth wanted confirmation of my loyalty. As an offering, I presented him with my knowledge of the tiara. Master was pleased by my gift.

"He desired the tiara and offered me great rewards once he gained it, but he chose not to act immediately. Master is patient. He wanted to wait until the right time. He sent me an enchanted symbol to hide in your bedchamber. When he was ready, the glyph would open a portal allowing a demon into the room. The plan worried me. The might of the tiara, combined with the protective spells shielding your quarters, made you a formidable opponent. So, I made some special modifications. I'm sure you remember two years ago when I offered to restructure and enhance the defensive spells in your room."

Sylvia groaned. She did remember. Cornelius convinced her to provide a list of the enchantments protecting her room and offered to strengthen them with a few spells of his own. Like a fool, she had said yes.

"I hid a series of contingency spells inside your defenses designed to activate the instant a demon entered your room. As an afterthought, I even added fatal paralysis spells for the guards. With your help, I was able to arrange everything perfectly. Master was most pleased."

"So," Sylvia asked unable to mask her anger, "if the demon lord is so pleased, why did you conspire with Cyril? You already said you disliked him."

"Cyril is a fool," Cornelius agreed. "He is emotional and idealistic. His desire for vengeance blinds him to the joys of servitude. But Lord and Lady Junlorace gave me the opportunity to enter Darlyth's service. I owe them much and was impressed by the way Cyril sold his scheme to our master.

"The plan involved three stages. First, your kidnapper would leave a sign. I'd pretend not to recognize it and turn it over to the magical academy. Second, I needed to eliminate the people most likely to rescue you. Search parties led by your most powerful generals would be dispatched to search for you and be destroyed."

"What?" Sylvia exclaimed.

"Oh yes," he said, amused by her reaction. Clearly, he'd been longing to tell her about the news since the moment of her capture. "Generals Gaheera, Andrus, and Alexis are all dead. I sent each with a small search party to find you. None had a chance against the demons awaiting them."

Sylvia's blood boiled. She would've charged him if she had the strength to stand. The high mage smiled. She got the impression he was trying not to laugh.

"Next, I'd pretend to receive word from the academy. I'd tell Cordor where you were hidden and lead him to Junlorace Keep. The plan was clever. Unfortunately, everything almost fell apart. The sign left by the demon was stolen, and though Cordor saw the symbol he couldn't remember it. I used a variety of vision spells on the snow and trees as we marched to jog his memory. I worried he would figure out what was happening. Fortunately, he fell for my deception, thinking his own mind was reliving the moment."

Cornelius gave a loud sigh.

"Cordor was a great man," he said, assuming a sad expression that the queen knew wasn't sincere. "It's a pity you killed him."

"I killed him?" Sylvia exclaimed. "You murdered him."

"Only because you gave me no other option. Cyril just wanted the crown. If you'd given it to me, you and Cordor could've flown safely back to Rhoria. Cyril would've slain Darlyth and taken over the world. Not as profitable for me, but I was willing to settle for a consolation prize."

"Consolation prize?" Sylvia repeated in disbelief. "And what, may I ask, is the main prize? How can the demon lord conquering the world be *profitable for you*? What do you gain from humanity being destroyed?"

"Humanity won't be destroyed, just enslaved," he explained. "Demons need human blood to survive. People will be kept around as a food source, livestock."

"Fine!" Sylvia said sarcastically. "What do you have to gain by seeing humankind become demon food?"

He bent until his nose was inches from hers.

"Everything!" he hissed. He stood back up and crossed his arms. "You don't realize the extent of Master's generosity. He always rewards his servants. He has already performed a ritual on me, granting me eternal youth. And that's just the beginning. He needs vassals to monitor his slaves. He can't trust demons. They're too animalistic. They can't understand human needs. He needs other humans to rule the flock, and that's where I come in!"

"You mean, all of this is so you can become a slave driver?"

"Slave driver is such a dull term," he scoffed. "I won't be humanity's slave driver. I'll be their master! I'll rule all humankind. Men who prove trainable will become my thralls, the most beautiful women my concubines. I'll have my own palace filled with lavish furnishings, and my palate will savor only the finest food and wines. I'll remain young forever, enjoying endless lifetimes of decadence."

"Is that all you want from life? Merely a pointless infinity of fleshly pleasures," Sylvia asked. "You want a life with no meaning or purpose. Just whiling away infinity in senseless hedonism?"

Cornelius thought for a second and smiled. "Yeah. Why wouldn't I?"

"Because slaves who rule slaves are still slaves themselves!" Sylvia responded.

"Perhaps," he said, "but slave or not, I'd rather be the farmer than the animal. Besides, I'm already a slave. Whether I'm serving you, Darien, or some other boss, I remain enslaved to someone. Even if I assume the throne, I'm still held captive by the demands of my subjects. Ultimately, one master is as good as another. I certainly get more benefits from his service than yours."

"You consider watching humanity turned into mindless cattle a benefit?"

"What is humankind to me? Men exist so I can use them. Women exist to fulfill my lusts. I manipulate superiors to my ends. I trick subordinates to do my work. The only difference between free men versus captives is how much work is required to control each."

Sylvia stared in disbelief. She didn't know how to address the narcissist. How could she even begin to speak reason to a man with such a conceited view of reality?

"I can't believe I'm hearing these words from your mouth, Cornelius," she said shaking her head. "You really fooled me. I thought you were wise."

"Oh please," he scoffed, "what do you know of wisdom? If you were wise, you'd have given the tiara to Cyril. But you squandered your chance to save humanity. You were too self-righteous, too caught up in your arrogant views on morality to hear the truths he spoke. Don't blame me for your failure."

He spoke the last words with an air of finally. Turning toward the door, he glanced back over his shoulder.

"Oh, and by the way," he added, "my name is Corineous!"

He started to walk away then stopped.

"I almost forget" he said, spinning toward her. "Ostanavleevat!"

Like the previous night, Sylvia froze in place, unable to move. Corineous, as he now chose to be called, pulled a small white tablet from his robes.

"I know you wouldn't want to forget your medicine," he jeered. Forcing her mouth open, he slid the tablet under her limp tongue before pressing the jaws shut again. Sylvia felt the chalky pill dissolve upon the closing of her mouth. The effect was instantaneous.

The slight chill in the room became magnified so the cell felt like a freezer. Her pounding heart felt like someone was punching her breast with each beat. The burning sensation in her skin stung like fire, and small aches and pains from the night before felt like knife wounds.

When Cornelius dismissed the paralysis, Sylvia's first act was to scream in pain. This proved a mistake. The rush of air escaping her lungs rubbed her throat like sandpaper, and her voice stung her ears. Closing her mouth, she rolled into a fetal position, holding her knees to her chest. Even the most mundane bodily functions felt like torture. She tried not to think what torture would feel like.

"Excellent," Corineous's booming voice stung her ears. "I'll return in a couple of hours when the torture begins. I wouldn't miss it for the world, which I'll have anyway!"

The prison door slammed behind him. Corineous disappeared into a long hallway across from her cell. A buzz echoed through the chamber as he left. Apparently, the entrance to the prison was equipped with a siren to alert the guards of approaching visitors.

Two grorgs positioned themselves outside her door. Their raspy breaths stung her ears as she tried to remain still for fear of greater agony. She lay there, curled up on the floor, dreading the coming days.

Even with Lillian's spell, locating the body of the deceased wingham took longer than anticipated. The trek down the mountain was a nightmare. The snow grew thicker as they descended. They often found themselves buried to their waists. Miscellaneous roots, sudden steep drops, and loose gravel hidden beneath the icy mass made things worse. By the time they reached the bottom, everyone was battered, bruised, and exhausted.

Ahead, the trees broke revealing an indention caused by a wingham landing. A series of deep footmarks indicated that someone had dismounted the beast and rushed toward the trees. The tracks ended after a couple of steps. None led back to the wingham.

On the other side, the snow gave way to a frozen lake everyone recognized as the landmark leading to Junlorace Keep. The body of water extended for miles in all directions with tall forests blocking visibility beyond. Lillian's magic indicated a wingham lay somewhere on the other side. They chose to levitate across the lake rather than endure numerous miles of marching to go around. Unfortunately, traveling by levitation remained laboriously slow. By the time they reached the opposite bank, the morning sun was several hours into the sky.

Clement spotted the dead wingham first. The corpse was belly up at the bottom of a small cliff. A series of dark burn marks ran across the creature's chest indicating where the coup de grace was delivered. Clement hurried forward to examine the seared flesh. Lillian joined him watching with apparent interest.

"What do you see?" she asked.

"Desecria," Clement said. "The spell leaves a pattern different from any other. Judging by the depths of the streaks, the creature was moving toward the attacker when the spell was cast. The residual energy indicates the caster was a man."

"It is domesticated," Darien observed, gesturing toward the straps. "He is saddled for a rider."

"The rider is beneath him," Xanaphia said. "I can sense a dead body."

Clement didn't question her observation. He knew necromancy well enough to understand her attunement with death.

Lillian raised a hand. "Let's see him. Podneemeetez."

She touched the wingham. It rose into the air. Clement looked underneath at the dangling body of the wingham rider, still strapped to the saddle. He recognized the broken form and shook his head. General Cordor was dead.

"Like I said, if you need to kill a Morodin, use magic on the things around him," Xanaphia said.

"Whoever killed him knew he was a Morodin," Clement added.

"I'm more interested in knowing what happened to his party," Darien said, indicating the lack of other remains.

"I agree," Lillian said. "In particular, I'd like to know where Cornelius is."

"He's at Kendross Keep," said a voice. "With the queen."

Clement spun in the direction of the voice, raising his arms. A man was leaning against a tree a short distance away. Clement wondered how the man got so close without anyone noticing. Clement summoned his magic, and the others did the same. The air crackled, but the stranger appeared unconcerned.

Clement stared at him. He stared back. The newcomer was tall, towering over Xanaphia and Darien. He wore a thick white cloak, blending with the snow. Beneath the cloak, a thick coat of chainmail glittered in the morning light. His left hand rested leisurely on the hilt of a long sword strapped to his waist.

He was clearly not human. Bright red eyes shone like fire, and he possessed a strange green tint to his otherwise pale skin.

"You can lower your arms," he said. "I've not come to threaten you."

There was a trace of amusement in his voice, which told Clement he didn't fear them.

"Who are you?" Darien demanded.

"I should ask the same of you," he replied. "When I heard someone slew a stone demon, I expected to find more than a dozen powerful wizards and warriors. Perhaps some of your group died in the battle."

"There was no one else," Darien responded. "We destroyed it on our own and can do the same to you. Who are you, and how do you know about the demon?"

"You needn't be alarmed," the man said. "I come as your friend. My name is Cyril Junlorace. I'm lord of Junlorace Keep."

"Then you're mistaken," Xanaphia said. "You're no friend of ours."

"Where is the queen?" Clement demanded.

"I've already told you," the other replied. "She is at Kendross Keep. And though you may not believe me, I am your friend. Now, I request for the last time that you lower your arms. Despite your success against the demons, you're no threat to me."

They didn't lower their guard.

The man frowned. "Fine, I'll lower them for you."

A spell rose to Clement's lips, but his adversary vanished in a blur of white light. Clement heard a scream to his left. He turned to see Lillian fly backward as though struck by a powerful force.

"Pere . . ." Xanaphia began, but with a crash she was knocked backward. Clement spotted the stranger hovering above her for a moment.

"Raz . . ." he began, but something slammed into his chest with the might of an avalanche. He bowled over into the snow, the wind knocked from him. He rolled to his knees struggling to regain his breath. The attacker stood in front of Darien, his blade pressed against the enchanter's throat.

"Now, if you please, can we talk in a civil manner?" Cyril asked, lowering his sword. "I'm not here to kill you. In fact, I need your help. If you want to save the queen, you'll listen to what I have to say."

Clement rose, and the others did the same. Clement had never seen anyone move so fast. A smile crossed his lips, and his eyes narrowed. Clement knew the history of the Demon Wars too well not to realize the nature of their visitor.

"Okay," Darien responded, taking a step away. "We are listening."

"Who are you?" Cyril asked.

"My name is Lillian," she said. "This is Xanaphia. This is Clement, and he is Darien."

Cyril's jaw dropped.

"You're kidding," he said. "You're Lillian the Insidious!"

"I hate that name," Lillian muttered.

Cyril either ignored her or didn't hear. He turned toward Xanaphia and Clement.

"You're the dark queen of suffering. And you're Clement the Great!"

"I was," Clement replied.

"And you," Cyril said, turning toward Darien, "you're Darien the Wise."

"I believe 'Dark' is the correct title," Xanaphia said, a touch of irritation in her voice.

"I'm honored to stand before you," Cyril said, addressing Darien. "You're the only regent in the last three hundred years to send us help. Thank you."

To Clement's surprise, Cyril gave a bow. Darien appeared lost for words.

"Wait a minute," Lillian said, "you killed all of the reinforcements he sent to help you!"

"No, my parents killed the reinforcements. I was just a boy. I couldn't prevent their deaths. But I haven't forgotten his help. Whether such an offer was made with genuine intent or for selfish reasons is irrelevant."

Cyril gazed at Darien in admiration, his eyes blazing.

"What are you?" Darien asked.

Cyril shook his head.

"That is a long story. I am . . ."

"A kefling," Clement declared.

Everyone looked at him. Cyril looked stunned.

Clement sighed, looking at Lillian.

"Didn't you ever listen to any of your father's history lessons? Keflings are half-human, half-demons who played a key role in the battle of Hell's Pass."

Cyril's shock vanished, and his eyes narrowed. Clement gave him a meaningful look. Both knew exactly what the other was thinking. Darien and Xanaphia didn't seem to notice the exchange, but Lillian did. She raised an eyebrow at Clement. He ignored her.

"So what do you want, half-demon?" Xanaphia asked.

"As I said earlier, I need your help," he replied.

"To do what?" Darien asked.

"To save the world."

Clement nodded. He thought that answer was coming. The others seemed amused. Darien shook his head smiling. Xanaphia grinned. Lillian burst into laughter.

"I must admit," she said, "we're not used to such requests. Saving the world isn't our forte. We're usually more interested in enslaving it."

"I can relate," Cyril said. "But under the circumstances, I have to settle for the former."

"No offense, but how are we supposed to trust you? You helped capture the queen. Your people destroyed the orbs. You set the demon lord free! Now you want to stop him?" Darien asked.

"All valid points," Cyril said. "But time is of the essence. While we speak, Queen Sylvia is suffering tortured beyond anything you've ever inflicted or imagined, and powers beyond the comprehension of humankind are focusing all their might to make her give up the tiara. She'll break sooner than she thinks. We must hurry to Kendross Keep. I'll explain everything on the way."

"Where is Kendross Keep?" Clement asked.

"About two days travel northeast from here. If we continue east for about half a day, we'll hit Old Kendross Trail. Travel is smoother along the road."

"Don't you think demons will be guarding the roads?" Xanaphia asked suspiciously.

"Not really," Cyril answered. "Demons don't make good guards because of their constant need for blood. You can't leave them standing around a place for a long period of time. Without a constant food supply, they will frenzy. Other sentries monitor the roads, but I know their appearances and locations. They won't get far. The road isn't well defended. Darlyth doesn't expect invaders. They couldn't infiltrate the keep without knowing the secret entrances anyway."

"I think you should lead," Xanaphia said.

"Fair enough," Cyril agreed. "Let's go."

He turned east, marching into the trees. Xanaphia raised her arms as though contemplating stunning him from behind. Clement grabbed them and pushed them downward, shaking his head in warning. Xanaphia shrugged, and the four embarked upon the next leg of the journey.

CHAPTER 15

Old Kendross Road had known better days. While the elevated stone walkway provided easier travel than the uneven terrain of the surrounding forests, the shattered stones were weathered, rocks slippery, and the paths overgrown. As they traveled, Cyril revealed the truth concerning Darien's former apprentice, Corineous. He told of the demon lord's release, the death of his parents, and his oath for vengeance. He explained his plot to capture the queen's tiara ending with the failure of his final plan. Lillian noticed he chose his words carefully, revealing very little about himself beyond his hatred of Darlyth.

Lillian, Darien, and Xanaphia bombarded him with questions. Clement did not. Lillian found his silence suspicious. Clement clearly knew something about the kefling that no one else did. Lillian wished she could remember all her father's lessons. But she'd lived with him for sixteen years. Could she be expected to remember every word he said? Clement apparently did. She pondered the devotion with which he dedicated each of her father's lessons to memory. No wonder he felt so stung by her father's betrayal.

Around nightfall, a distant sound of screeching and shouting filled the air. Far behind them, a swarm of winghams ascended like a green cloud into the heavens. The flock hovered above the trees before drifting westward. Cyril stopped, watching the procession glide above the forest. He stared after them, not speaking or moving until they disappeared into the distance.

As evening faded into night, the conversation turned to Kendross Keep and the queen's rescue. Cyril discussed the layout of the fortress and the location of the prison cells. He revealed the secret vault where the tiara would be stored. He outlined the resistance the wizards would meet and the keep's other defenses. By the time the discussion was complete, midnight was approaching. They decided to establish camp and begin their dinner.

Keflings, Cyril told them, only needed about three hours of sleep. If they divided the first three hours among themselves, he would watch for the rest. Everyone agreed to the plan.

Cyril joked he would be back in a flash, and so he was, his arms full of wood for the fire. The party situated themselves around the blaze while Lillian conjured food. She noticed Clement made a point of positioning himself across from Cyril and sat staring at him intently. Cyril seemed to be avoiding his eyes. Lillian distributed food to everyone. She, Darien, and Xanaphia devoured their meals ravenously. Clement and Cyril did not. Clement kept watching Cyril, who continued to avoid his gaze. Finally, Clement spoke.

"Okay, Cyril, enough games. Let's hear your true plans once we reach the keep."

Lillian looked from Clement to Cyril and back again. The two stared at each other fighting a silent battle of wills. Finally, a resigned smile crossed Cyril's face.

"The battle of Hell's Pass," he muttered, shaking his head.

"Should I tell them the story, or would you like to?" Clement asked.

"You can tell them," Cyril responded. "I'm actually curious to hear the version taught today."

"Very well," Clement said. "The Battle of Hell's Pass was the turning point in the Demon Wars. Up to then, humankind was all but beaten. Determined to end the war, the demon lord sent an army of keflings to destroy the last resistance. Keflings were strange half-demon creatures bred through an evil ritual of his own design. Darlyth treasured them as his own children. Each was imbued with unique magical properties, and he considered their army unbeatable.

"Iago the Brave assembled a force to oppose them, but they were no match against the demon spawn. In a desperate final stand, his forces retreated to a stronghold known as Hell's Pass. There a sorcerer named Artemis Kendross, the greatest spellcaster to ever live, wove a mighty enchantment. As long as the army remained in Hell's Pass, it was invincible. Unable to break humanity's hold on the pass, and with no other way to reach the settlements beyond, the demon lord faced a standoff.

"At the time, the leader of the keflings was a warrior named Redault. He possessed the most rare and unique skill of any kefling. He's the only kefling in history of the Demon Wars to possess this remarkable ability."

Clement paused.

"What was the power?" Xanaphia asked.

"He could move at exceptional speeds," Cyril answered on Clement's behalf.

"Exactly," Clement nodded. "Redault also possessed a less distorted physical appearance and a lighter complexion to his green skin. He was more emotional and intelligent than his counterparts and could even use magic."

Clement stared at Cyril. Lillian understood. The description matched him perfectly.

"The demon lord used Redault's human nature to his advantage," Clement continued. "He masked the tint of Redault's skin and sent him to seduce Kendross's daughter, Jacquelyn. At a prearranged time, Redault would slay Kendross, breaking the enchantment, and the kefling army would obliterate the human forces. Everything went smoothly. Redault seduced the young woman and was in position when the time came for the attack. But something unexpected happened."

"Redault fell in love," Cyril said, gazing wistfully overhead. "He fell in love with Jacquelyn Kendross."

Clement nodded.

"Redault betrayed the demon lord," Clement said. "The kefling army charged into the pass, believing the enchantments would come down. But Redault refused to slay Kendross. In the end, Darlyth's army was utterly annihilated. The victory turned the tide of the war."

"You sure have a roundabout way of getting to your point," Cyril said.

"I concur," Darien agreed. "What is the point of this useful history lesson?"

"The point is what happened to Redault," Clement said.

"What happened to him?" Lillian asked.

"He died," Cyril answered. "He spontaneously combusted. Before everyone's eyes, flames consumed his body. Nothing was left but a bunch of dust and a charred outline on the ground."

"Yes!" Clement answered, rising to his feet. "And we both know why he died!"

"What do you mean?" asked Darien. "What does any of this have to do with us?"

"Keflings can't disobey their master," Clement said. "The demon lord cursed them to death should they break his commands."

Clement pointed an accusatory finger at Cyril.

"That means," he continued, "either he is acting under the demon lord's orders, or he is omitting an important part of his plan. I want to know which!"

Lillian looked at Cyril. The kefling smiled.

"Well done," Cyril said. "You took a roundabout way of getting to your point, but you're right. A powerful curse keeps me from breaking Darlyth's orders. The real reason I wanted Sylvia to give me the tiara was so I could resist his curse. Since I didn't get it, I can't. The truth is I won't be leaving Kendross Keep with you. I can do more good if I stay."

"How?" Lillian asked.

Cyril reached into his cloak and withdrew a golden pebble. He held it toward the wizards.

"This is the last remaining fragment of the golden orbs that imprisoned Darlyth. It still has some of the original magic. I spent years studying it. I know how to activate its power. With it, I can trap Darlyth in his throne room. It'll buy you time to get the queen to safety."

"It can't buy much," Xanaphia stated. "Once the demon lord tells you to drop it, you'll burst into flames and die."

"I'll burst into flames, but I won't die."

"How is that?" Clement asked, resuming his seat.

"Because, I have this," Cyril responded dramatically.

He pulled another stone from his cloak and held it aloft. It was round and pure white. Darien and Xanaphia looked intrigued but unimpressed. Clement and Lillian, however, leapt to their feet.

"The Life Stone!" They shouted in unison.

Lillian rushed forward, an intense hunger like nothing she had ever felt before gripped her senses. She charged Cyril, her hand outstretched.

"Give it to me!" she shrieked.

Cyril vanished, reappearing ten feet back. The hasty retreat seemed to snap Lillian back to her senses. She noticed everyone except Clement was staring at her. She spun away, burying her head in her hands.

"You must forgive her," Clement said. "Master Sorin, Lillian's father, was obsessed with finding it. The quest was the primary reason for his interest in the Demon Wars. He viewed it as his destiny and drilled his lust for it into all his apprentices and children."

Lillian turned back toward the fire.

"My brother and many of my friends lost their lives on silly quests to find it," she said. "Father believed it would reveal all the deepest magical secrets lost over the millennia."

Darien and Xanaphia stared at her.

"You have to understand," Clement said, "before the Demon Wars, magic had evolved to a state beyond anything we've achieved since. Legend says rituals existed to make people immortal. Everything we know today pales in comparison to lost spells and knowledge of the ancient people."

Cyril shook his head. "The stone has remarkable powers but isn't as mighty as you believe. If you sit, I'll explain."

Clement and Lillian sat, but their eyes remained fixed on the stone until Cyril returned it to his cloak.

"Stories of the magic possessed by ancient wizards has become exaggerated," he said. "The only remaining source of accurate information from the Demon Wars is the library of Junlorace Keep. True, their sorcery was more advanced than today. But, as with all magic, a spell's power is defined not by the spell but by the caster. A modern spell in the hands of a powerful sorcerer is just as formidable as the ancient spells in the hands of a weak one."

Lillian reluctantly acknowledged the truth in his statement.

"Now," Cyril continued, "the stone has many remarkable powers. While I hold it, I can't be killed or go unconscious."

"So you can keep him imprisoned forever?" Xanaphia asked.

"No, even the magic of the Demon Wars had limitations," Cyril answered. "The stone won't prevent someone from dying of starvation or thirst. I'll eventually die from dehydration."

"Considering the heat you'll be experiencing, that's two, maybe three days at most," Lillian said. "What is the sacrifice supposed to achieve?"

"It'll give Sylvia time to reach safety," Cyril said. "I sent my best lieutenant to Rhoria to organize a rescue party. My death will buy time for her winghams to reach you and get you to Rhoria. I know you're powerful, but no one knows Darlyth like I do. You can't defeat him, even with Sylvia. Your only hope lies in getting back to the capital."

"If the demon lord wants the tiara, he'll come to Rhoria," Clement stated.

"Which is why the tiara must be destroyed," Cyril said. "But according to Corineous's statements, only someone with possession of the self-spell can destroy it."

"So only Sylvia can destroy the crown?" Darien asked.

"And we must convince her to break it?" Xanaphia scoffed. "She won't listen to us."

"Listening to reason isn't one of her strengths," Cyril agreed, "but she must be persuaded."

"I don't understand," Clement interrupted. "Why are you imprisoning him? Why not give the fragment to one of us? We can keep him contained longer than you."

"I'm not sure you can," Cyril said. "I've spent years attuning myself to the magic. It knows me and responds to me. Someone lacking the same attunement won't be able to command it. Any slip will prove disastrous. There'll be no second chance if something goes wrong."

"Can't the demon lord use magic though? Why not just pry the stone from your fingers at a distance?" Lillian asked.

"The magic of the orbs not only imprisons him but also forms a barrier through which his magic can't travel. He can't affect anything outside the sphere."

"Then why don't we kill him?" Xanaphia suggested. "We can stand outside the sphere and bombard him with spells. If he can't attack us, he'll eventually fall."

"If it were that easy, he would've been slain ages ago. The barrier works both ways. He can't affect anything outside and nothing outside can affect him."

Lillian tried to find additional objections. She disliked the idea of placing all their hope on someone dying of dehydration while being consumed by flames. A quick scan of her companion's faces led her to believe they shared her predicament. At last, Darien broke the uneasy silence.

"So who is the girl?"

"What?" Cyril asked in surprise.

Darien gave a sly smile.

"I may not be the most perceptive person, but I saw the way you watched the refugees," he said. "There is someone among them who you love. Redault made his sacrifice for Jacquelyn. Who are you sacrificing for?"

"Her name is Ladonna," Cyril answered, "but she isn't the only reason I'm making the sacrifice."

"Why are you making the sacrifice?" Lillian asked.

"My ancestors took an oath dedicating their lives and the lives of their descendants to protect humanity from Darlyth."

"I hardly think you're bound by such an oath," Xanaphia said. "It was taken by people you never knew before you were ever born to protect people who couldn't care less that you exist. You said yourself that Darien was the only person who ever sent help. You owe them nothing."

"Perhaps, but I choose to take the oath as my own. Though humanity may forget us and may never know the sacrifice I'm making, it's the only way to save them. Therefore, I'm obligated to make it."

Xanaphia snorted.

"Would you not do the same?" Cyril asked.

"Never in a million years," Xanaphia responded. "What do I care about humanity?"

"You fail to realize your connection to them. Your fate and their fate are combined. If they're imprisoned, you're imprisoned. What's the point of living as a prisoner when you could die free?"

Xanaphia gave a hollow laugh.

"Thanks for the thought," she said. "But if I'm going to die, I'd rather take the world down with me."

"That's funny." Cyril smiled. "If I were going to die, I'd rather take my enemies down with me. Not see them triumph through my defeat."

Xanaphia fell silent.

"So," Darien interrupted, "let us get back to the plan. Step one, you dispatch the guards and guide us into the castle. Step two, we split up, half of us going for the queen and half for the tiara. Step three, you trap the demon lord inside his throne room. Step four, we escape with Sylvia and meet up with a rescue party before Darlyth can break free."

"Correct."

"Ambitious but impractical," Darien said. "There are only five of us going into the heart of the demon lord's stronghold. His demon army is housed there, not to mention these grorgs of which you speak. I do not fear grorgs, but I am concerned about demons. One is bad enough without fighting an entire army."

"Demons won't be a problem," Cyril said. "They require too much blood to keep awake. Darlyth can't animate them without a plentiful food supply. He reawakened a few for important assignments, such as kidnapping the queen. But until recently, there's been no reason to believe the main force is awake."

"Until recently?" Lillian repeated.

Cyril shifted uneasily.

"A recent messenger to the fort noticed a significant drop in the population of grorgs. He observed less than half the number stationed there two weeks ago. I have to believe the dwindling population signifies that grorgs are being fed to the demons. Still, they won't be wandering around the halls. He'll keep them inside the barracks in the lower levels. There's no reason we should encounter them."

"Not entirely reassuring," Clement said. "What about other keflings?"

"There are none," Cyril said. "Darlyth hasn't created any since awakening. I was created by the men and women of Junlorace Keep. They wanted to curry his favor over Kendross Keep."

"The two keeps were battling to impress him before he even woke?" Lillian asked in disbelief.

"Yes. Silly, I know. Each wanted to be rewarded above the other. They sought ways to impress him, to get the upper hand. My parents felt the creation of a kefling would give them an advantage."

"And the residents of Kendross Keep didn't create one?" Xanaphia asked.

"I'm sure they wanted to, but they didn't know the ritual. My parents found the records hidden among a collection of ancient manuscripts in our library. After my birth, a servant destroyed them to prevent their falling into the wrong hands."

"That's a shame," Clement said. "Your record was likely the only surviving copy. It would've been interesting to study."

"If the record still existed, I'd destroy it myself," Cyril responded. "The world doesn't need more demons, whether pureblood or kefling."

"The point is that we will not encounter any," Darien said. "Nevertheless, the prospect of invading a fort filled with magically enhanced monsters does not sound promising. If the demon lord discovers our presence, we are doomed."

"I hate to tell you this, but even if everything goes according to plan we're still doomed," Lillian said. "Rhorian aristocracy is filled with power-hungry fools and incompetent kiss-ups with a knack for indecisive filibustering. They aren't going send help anytime soon, especially without a strong leader like Gaheera or Alexis. It'll be weeks before a rescue party comes, if one comes at all."

"If Rhoria doesn't send help, Ladonna will come on her own," Cyril answered. "She is strong-willed. She'll do everything within her power to come to our aid. She may even arrive before we reach the fort."

The rising sun was powerless to shatter the gloom hanging over Rhoria. Dark rumors spread like fire, worsening the depression cast by the queen's disappearance. Reports claimed the bodies of General Gaheera and her party were discovered along with the corpse of a terrifying unknown creature. Others claimed the remaining rescue parties had disappeared without a trace.

Trade and travel had ceased from all directions. Merchants risking treks along neighboring routes vanished as readily as the search parties. Fear gripped the city, and citizens awaited news of the impending disaster all knew was coming.

Into this dismal scene flew the refugees of Junlorace Keep. Their mounts blanketed the sky, invoking screams and cries from the on-edge populace. Women and children raced from the terrifying swarm of monstrous lizards sweeping down upon their homes. Men stared into the sky, gaping in petrified awe. Sirens and bells echoed through the city as guards rushed to their weapons and archers prepared for battle.

The mounts descended like vultures landing smoothly onto the grassy lawns and lavish flowerbeds of Rhoria's massive central park. Rhorian guards raced to encircle the landing party. Spectators lined the commons or gazed from open windows, watching in frightened anticipation. The winghams and their riders gazed at the vast force greeting them. Most of the riders were as nervous as the townsfolk, but the red-haired woman seated atop the tallest mount was not. She gazed fearless at the encircling guard and rose from her saddle.

"Men and women of Rhoria!" Her voice carried over the crowd. "My name is Ladonna, and I beseech your help. We are refugees from the mountains where a great danger threatens our city. We seek shelter and aid. I also bear important news regarding the queen. I must speak to the acting lord of the city!"

A murmur of excitement greeted her words. Either news of the queen was welcome or the people were discussing what sort of threat could chase away an army of dragon riders. Amid the fervor, a man stepped forward. He was large and muscular, wearing a chainmail coat of unnatural weigh and thickness. Ladonna guessed most men couldn't even lift the armor. Yet, he moved as though wearing a light shirt. He carried a broadsword in one hand as effortlessly as if it were a dagger and towered over the townsfolk like a colossus. Thick black hair coated his head, and a red diamond-shaped tattoo highlighted his left jaw.

"My name is Benjamin," his voice boomed over the crowd. "I'm a member of the Palace Guard. Welcome to Rhoria, Lady Ladonna. If what you say is true and you bring news of our queen, your tidings are most welcome. I shall escort you to the steward at once."

Another murmur rose from the crowd, along with several shouts and cries. Ladonna couldn't understand, but they sounded like warnings. She scanned the crowd. Something was wrong.

"Very good," she called. "I'll be right down."

She climbed off her mount. Several nearby soldiers also descended and rushed to intercept her.

"Commander," one whispered, "something is amiss. You mustn't go. Did you see their reaction?"

"I did," Ladonna confirmed, looking over her shoulder at the waiting guard. "But I have an important mission, and time is of the essence. I must take my chances. Have soldiers on guard at all times and establish a watch at night. I'll return shortly."

She turned to two of her men. "Urik, Vladimir, come with me."

She headed toward the waiting guard. Urik and Vladimir took flanking positions on her left and right. At least they could present a formidable front to any potential danger.

"Follow me," the guard stated.

Whirling around, he marched toward the distant palace. Ladonna and her companions followed. More guards, each sporting the same tattoo, joined the procession. All these soldiers, like Benjamin, were large and bulky with heavy armor and weapons. She noticed the city guards without tattoos were much smaller. They stared fearfully at the larger guards and hurried away.

Ladonna was disturbed by the behavior. She expected her arrival to cause alarm. A group of armed strangers riding dangerous beasts into the middle of town would disturb anyone. The problem was that the people seemed more frightened of her escorts than her army.

Her eyes fell on a figure lurking in the shadows of a narrow alleyway. It watched the procession, eyes locked upon her. She gazed back but could see nothing beneath the hood of its black cloak. She tried getting a closer look, but the mysterious watcher vanished into the darkness.

The procession entered a group of trees. To the left, she saw the Rhorian Magical Academy. Apprentices gazed from closed windows. No one lingered in the park, where stone benches and grassy hills were empty. No students milled about the grounds conversing or visiting. Was this normal?

Leaving the park, they proceeded through a large portcullis. More soldiers lined the entrance to the castle. Most were the colossal guards sporting tattoos. The rest looked uncomfortable beside their massive companions. Two of the large soldiers grabbed the handles on the palace doors. They opened the heavy oak structures with a casual tug.

The hair on Ladonna's arms rose, but she shrugged away her discomfort. The men must be part of some magically enhanced combat unit. With her soldiers at her side, she trusted her fighting skills, superhuman strength, and demonic reflexes to defeat any human, magically enhanced or not.

They moved through the ingress and into the main hall. The chamber was filled with fanciful crystalline chandeliers and suits of armor. They strode over marble floors surrounded by golden tapestries, but Ladonna was too focused on the perceived danger to admire the finery.

The company entered a room where a carpeted walkway ran between two long tables. A large throne with two smaller thrones stood at the end. On the largest one, a lanky woman wearing wizard robes chatted with several advisors. She was young, still a teenager, and possessed a remarkably pale face. It was the only part of her visible. Dark-green robes concealed her entire head and body except for the long raven-colored hair flowing onto the front of her tunic. She wore thin green gloves and tall traveling boots. Her most notable feature, however, was the cloth tied over her eyes. She was blind.

She looked up at the sound of footsteps echoing through the chamber and turned to face the newcomers. The leader of the procession came to a halt about twenty feet in front of her. She ignored him. She faced Ladonna with an expression of interest.

"I do not know you," she said in a soft, regal voice that reminded Ladonna of a dove cooing.

Ladonna was intrigued. "Can you see me?"

"Yes, my lady," she answered. "Thanks to my magic, I don't need eyes to see."

Ladonna's curiosity was peaked even more. "Why do you not cure your eyesight?"

"I have no eyes to cure," the woman responded. "But I don't wish to discuss my disfigurement. What business brings you to me?"

"I request audience with the current leader of Rhoria," Ladonna said, assuming an official manner.

"I'm Nimue, acting steward of the throne of Rhoria until my queen shall return to take her rightful place. Who, may I ask, are you?"

"My name is Ladonna of Junlorace," she answered with a bow. "I come seeking help for my people. We have fled our home from a great threat and seek shelter. Further, I bring news concerning the queen."

A murmur filled the hall. Nimue signaled for silence.

"Go on," she said.

Ladonna felt uncertain how much to reveal. The awkwardness of her surroundings and the strange sensation she got from the guards made her cautious. On the other hand, lying would produce no positive results. She decided to go with the truth.

"The queen is being held at a fortress known at Kendross Keep. An ancient evil plans to steal her powers and destroy Rhoria. We fled from his wrath and come bringing you warning."

Another murmur filled the hall. The steward said nothing. For several minutes, she stood staring at the ground and stroking her chin in apparent contemplation.

"These are dangerous times to trust the tidings of a stranger," she said. "Still, as we have no other leads on our missing queen, your statement warrants investigation. How many of you are there?"

"We have almost one hundred and fifty men, woman, and children along with forty winghams."

"Winghams?" The steward asked. "I thought they were extinct."

"Our village bred them and hid them from Darien's wrath."

"Very brave," the steward said. "And where is Kendross Keep?"

"Deep within the heart of the Blood Fang Mountains, Your Ladyship."

"It is quite far then. Winghams will be important. I assume you flew them here."

"Yes, Your Ladyship," Ladonna answered.

"No doubt, you carried large numbers of supplies upon them."

"Correct."

"Then we must relieve them of their burden and prepare them for departure," she said. "We shall set up camp for your people outside the city. This will be safer for my citizens and yours. Xenophobia has gripped the town over the last week. Wisdom dictates both parties be kept separate while they adjust to the change. Wilhelm. Terrance."

Two soldiers standing on Nimue's left advanced forward. The first, Wilhelm, was a normal-sized man with broad shoulders. Terrance was one of the large soldiers with the diamond tattoo.

"Wilhelm is captain of the Rhorian City Guard," the steward explained. "With your permission, I request one of your men escort him to the refugees. His men will set up a camp for your people and unburden your beasts."

Nimue gestured to the other man.

"Terrance is head of the Palace Guard. He will select the soldiers to accompany you on the mission to rescue the queen. I'm sure you wish to stay with your people, but your leadership is essential. You know the way, and I don't want my men getting lost in unfamiliar regions."

Ladonna stared at Nimue. She expected more resistance and more questions. Ladonna reasoned that after a week without any word about the queen or updates from search parties, the steward must be pretty desperate. Still, the ease with which she accepted Ladonna's story and began making arrangements seemed suspicious. Ladonna didn't know what to do about it though.

"Very well, Your Ladyship," Ladonna answered. "I'm eager to lead them to the queen."

"Excellent! If you will, please have the man not escorting Wilhelm accompany Terrance to prepare the winghams. I'll accompany you to the library at the magical academy. I wish to see what information I can find regarding Kendross Keep."

"As you wish," Ladonna said. She turned toward her men. "Urik, please accompany the captain to set up camp. Vladimir, please accompany Terrance to pick the rescue party and show them how to fly winghams."

"Yes, Commander," both men said in unison.

"Now, my lady," the blind steward said. "If you follow me, I'm eager to learn more information about the danger threatening the queen."

Nimue made a sweeping motion with her hand toward a large door to Ladonna's left. Ladonna, however, wasn't ready to have an unknown spellcaster walking behind her.

"After you, My Liege," she responded, bowing.

The steward proceeded toward the door. Ladonna followed. A guard opened the portal, revealing a wide hallway with numerous passages on each side. Several tattooed guards stood flanking the passages and doors beyond. As the steward passed, the men snapped to attention. Nimue strode past without acknowledgement. Ladonna heard the door to the grand hall close behind them.

Then the attack came. One of the tattooed guards launched himself at Ladonna. Her swift reflexes allowed her to dodge, but before she could recover more guards joined the assault. Her sword flashed through the air, but the massive warriors dodged her attacks with unnatural agility.

She was outmatched. She opened her mouth to cry for help, but a powerful blow struck her on the back of the head. Everything went black.

CHAPTER

16

Xanaphia opened her eyes. She could tell the hour was late. Everything was dark. Cyril must have let the campfire burn out. Perhaps his glowing eyes enabled him to see in the dark. She glanced around, but Cyril wasn't there.

She sat up in alarm. No one was there. Darien, Clement, Lillian, and Cyril were all gone. She leapt to her feet and summoned a ball of light. There were no signs of the camp. No footprints led in or out of the area. Even the fire pit was gone. Something strange was happening.

Looking around, she spotted a red light flickering through the trees. Then she heard it. Distant wails of anguish and lamentation echoed through the forest. She crept through the snow toward the noise and emerged onto the top of a tall cliff. Hundreds of bonfires blazed in the plains below. Horrific monstrosities towered over swarms of chained humans.

The slave drivers were horrifying. Some possessed multiple heads on top of large green scaly bodies. Others were like oozes slithering across the ground with gaping maws for mouths. She saw spider-like creatures like the one near Rhoria and bizarre tentacled beasts. Stone demons, like the ones from the canyon, wandered hungrily through the terrified captives. The number and variety of creatures was mind-boggling.

People of all types marched in procession before their masters. They paused as they reached a demon covered with grotesque protruding horns. There, each human drew a stone from a bucket. Those who drew red stones were pulled screaming and yelling from the line and carried toward a massive demon that stood butchering and filleting the struggling captives. Hungry demons watched, drooling in anticipation of the feast awaiting them.

Xanaphia noticed a small perch on the side of the cliff. Five figures stared down at the carnage. Queen Sylvia was foremost of the five. Her body was implanted on a pike, but she wasn't dead. She dangled horrified, gazing at the scene. Her arms were severed from her body, and a gag was fastened over her mouth.

Xanaphia glanced at the four figures stationed behind her. They were also on pikes, and she recognized them. One was Darien, beside him was Clement, and the third was Lillian. In horror, Xanaphia realized the fourth figure was her. She stared in surprise as her doppelganger looked at her. Their eyes met, and Xanaphia found herself transposed into the body of her tortured twin.

She felt the pain and agony of the pike cutting into her innards. She felt the gaping void in her mouth where a tongue once sat. She hung helpless, watching the pathetic human slaves below. Some looked at her and cringed in horror. She would hang in this position for years as a warning to anyone foolish enough to challenge the demon lord's might.

Xanaphia woke drenched in sweat and sat upright. She stared around the camp. Her companions slept peacefully around the still burning fire. Cyril sat a few feet away from her, whittling on a small block of wood. He looked up at her.

"Are you okay," he asked.

"I will be," she answered, still shaken. "What're you working on?"

"Just some casual carving."

Xanaphia looked at the wooden cube. A face appeared to be carved onto the side. It was Cyril. Every line, wrinkle, and crease was present in astonishing detail.

Cyril continued working on his self-portrait and Xanaphia returned to her bed. She placed her hands behind her head and stared into the night sky. The stars shone bright overhead. Xanaphia rarely dreamed or experienced nightmares. The last time Xanaphia suffered nightmares was the week before Sylvia's rise. She dreamed of being dethroned and exiled. The vision proved prophetic. She found herself reflecting on this new vision and the massive army of demons.

"What are demons?" she wondered aloud. "Where do they come from?"

"Curious about Darlyth?" Cyril smiled. "I'm not sure what I can tell you. Most records relating to early humanity and demons were destroyed during the Demon Wars. I imagine Darlyth wanted it that way. Even the ancient scripts of Junlorace Keep only reveal so much."

"What do they say?" she asked. Xanaphia wasn't really interested in history or demonology, but the conversation served as a way of distracting her mind.

"They don't provide many facts, just speculation. Most believe Darlyth was created by a corrupt sorcerer who mastered the art of crafting living creatures. He sought to engineer the ultimate weapon to destroy his enemies. He taught Darlyth the secrets of creating living creatures and of wielding magic. In time, Darlyth became more powerful than his master. He slew the sorcerer and built his own army."

"What does he want?" she asked.

Cyril stopped chiseling. He lowered the knife and looked up from his carving.

"I don't know," he answered. "He wants to rule the world, of course. But I'm not sure if he wants power for power's sake or if he possesses other motives. I know he fears humans."

She looked at Cyril in surprise.

"Do you not believe me?" he asked. "Believe it. He fears free will and all creatures possessing it. This is why he curses his creations to obey him. I think he envisions a world populated by races of his own design that can never rebel or challenge him."

Xanaphia gave a laugh.

"He is kind of like a necromancer," she observed. "Except instead of raising the bodies of the dead, he enslaves the will of the living."

"I suppose," Cyril said. "Seeing some of yourself in him?"

"Maybe, but my way is better. Undead don't need sustenance. I don't have to enslave and kill people to feed them."

Cyril laughed. "So you're saying humans and corpses can coexist peacefully."

"Exactly," Xanaphia said.

She gave a chuckle. When he put it that way, it did sound funny.

"Unfortunately, others view death as sacred," she said. "Dead bodies walking the streets make them uncomfortable. I guess they're afraid of death."

"Are you not?"

"No," she said, "I feel most at home around death."

"Then why do you scoff at dying for a cause?"

"I don't have a problem with dying for a cause. I have a problem with the cause being others. No one in this world has ever done anything for me."

"What have they ever done for me?" Cyril countered. "You're far more blessed than I. From the moment of my birth, I faced the knowledge of being an outcast, cursed to be prisoner to impulses and needs I can't control. On one hand, I'm leader of a fortress protecting an ungrateful world from a threat they no longer care exists. On the other, I'm servant to a master I loathe under the threat of death."

"And yet you want to help people?" Xanaphia asked.

"No, I want to punish them," Cyril said. "I'd like nothing better than to teach them a cruel lesson, but I have an obligation to protect them."

"Ah, yes," she said, rolling her eyes, "your ancestor's oath."

"No," he responded, "I'm obligated to protect them because I understand the threat and I'm the only one who can. Sometimes, the burden of having knowledge and power is the responsibility of using your power to act upon that knowledge."

Xanaphia looked at him, intrigued.

"I know that sounds strange coming from me," he said. "I'm no saint. My desire for the tiara led me to hold the queen hostage. I allowed her to be tortured in the hope of getting it. Still, if everyone did what they knew to be right because it was right, regardless of personal consequences, the world would be a better place. Perhaps, through my actions, I can prevent someone else from having to make the same sacrifice and protect others from the dismal existence I endure."

"And what if your sacrifice is in vain?" she asked. "What if you give up your life, endure horrific suffering, and do everything you can do but the demon lord still wins? What if the sacrifice succeeds but no one ever knows you made it. What if no one learns a single lesson and they just go about their lives with the same ambivalence?"

"At least I tried," Cyril said. "I may not save the world or change it, but I can do my part, no matter how small, to make it a better place."

Xanaphia reflected on his statement. She started to ask another question, but a loud blast sounded from Cyril's other side. Lillian rolled over, awakened by her alarm spell. Clement and Darien also stirred. Morning had come.

The party marched throughout the day. Cyril led the way, occasionally signaling them to stop. During such times, he inspected the road, checking behind trees and bushes, muttering spells and scanning the skies. A quizzical look crossed his face, but he said nothing.

"What are you doing?" Clement demanded after the third such stop.

"Grorgs!" Cyril answered, clearly agitated. "I can't find any grorgs. Along this path, there are checkpoints where Darlyth stations them. He uses magical symbols to change their physical appearance. They look like bulky elk or large pumas or massive condors lurking in the trees.

They're easy to spot because of their unnatural size and the glyphs tattooed onto their skin. I planned to eliminate them before they could report our presence, but I don't see them anywhere. All lookout posts are vacant."

"Do you think they're being fed to demons?" Lillian asked, catching up with the others. "Maybe he is waking up his army."

"Maybe he already knows about our presence," Darien suggested. "Maybe he pulled his soldiers back to fortify the keep. He could be scrying on us."

"He can't be scrying on us," Lillian objected. "I'm an expert at magical means of spying. My defenses alert me to the presence of such spells."

"Agreed," Clement added. "I also keep magic surrounding me to thwart scrying attempts."

"The demon lord wields magic beyond our knowledge," Xanaphia noted. "He may have spells superseding your protections."

"I don't know," Cyril responded. "I've never seen him use any form of scrying magic. If he could supersede your magical defenses, why send me to investigate the deaths of his demons?"

"Where does this leave us?" Darien asked.

"I know not," Cyril answered. "We must proceed with caution. Keep an eye out for any large animals on the ground or in the trees."

The march continued for the rest of the day with a few additional stops by Cyril. Xanaphia sensed his anxiety building. His agitation fed hers. She felt watchful and anxious, but as day trailed into evening she grew more relaxed. No threat appeared. Her spirits rose along with those of her companions. Travel was smooth on the road. With additional sleep thanks to the new watch schedule, better food thanks to Lillian, and freedom from trudging through thick snow, her stamina and morale were high.

The party camped around midnight. Cyril commended them for their excellent progress. Kendross Keep was only a few hours away. If they got an early start, they could reach the fortress around sunrise. He planned to attack in the early part of the morning.

The move was risky. The queen could be in the middle of a torture session and surrounded by grorgs. Nevertheless, the sooner they reached her, the better. Everyone except Lillian were unconcerned about grorgs and agreed to attack at the earliest time possible.

Cyril flashed away to get firewood while Lillian prepared the food. Soon the company was situated around a warm blaze. They ate in silence. Xanaphia started to get the impression this was going to be a quiet dinner until Darien spoke.

"There are some issues we need to discuss before our departure."

All heads rose to look at him.

"First," he said, addressing Cyril, "I know you disagree, but the rest of us feel confident help is not going to arrive from Rhoria, and you have little hope of lasting more than a couple of days before dehydration. Such a delay will not get us anywhere near Rhoria. We need more time."

"What are you suggesting?" Cyril asked.

Darien reached into his cloak and pulled out a handful of herbs and leaves.

"I acquired some supplies at the apothecary in Southgrain," he said. "I can weave an enchantment to reduce your body's normal fluid consumption, even under extreme heat. It should buy us a few extra days."

"An extra day or two isn't going to get us to Rhoria," Xanaphia objected.

"True," Lillian agreed, "but we might get close enough to find help. It'll also give Ladonna more time on the off-chance Rhoria sends aid."

"Plus, Darlyth will have to pursue you," Cyril said. "The further you are away, the longer he'll need to catch up."

"So we're looking at about four days or five at best," Xanaphia reflected. "We left Southgrain six days ago. Getting back in five days would be incredible. Reaching Rhoria in five days would be legendary."

"Perhaps a legendary feat is in our future," Darien said. "Even so, the demon lord will give pursuit once he is free. With his magic, he will catch us quickly. We must be prepared and need to know when the pursuit starts."

"You and Clement both like beating around the bush," Cyril said smiling. "You need to know when I die."

"Yes," Darien answered.

"For mercy's sake, Darien, he's going to be burning to death," Xanaphia said. "I don't think he's going to send telepathic updates on his progress."

She felt annoyed at Darien for speaking about Cyril's death as indifferently as the weather. The emotion surprised her. She hardly knew Cyril and had no reason to be bothered by the conversation. She had spoken about many people's deaths without thought or concern. Why should Cyril be any different?

Perhaps the conversation they had shared this morning was affecting her. She felt an odd connection to him. They were like kindred souls. They were both outcasts in a world that didn't appreciate or want them. She didn't feel any romantic interest in him. It was more like curiosity. She wanted to understand how he could endure so much hardship and still desire to help others.

She was still trying to understand her own actions in Southgrain. She had saved the children's lives and didn't know why. Maybe if she could understand Cyril, she could understand more about herself.

"I was never good at telepathy spells," Cyril acknowledged. "But I imagine you're proposing a different idea?"

"I am," Darien said. "I can put an enchantment on a living or once-living object you own. A light will radiate from it until you die. When it goes dark, we will know you have passed."

"A living or once-living object," Cyril repeated quizzically.

"Sure, if you have leather boots, a cloak made out of fur, anything like that will work."

"My cloak is silk and my armor metal," Cyril noted. "My boots are leather, but I would like to wear them while traveling through Kendross Keep."

"What about the block?" Xanaphia asked. "The piece of wood you were carving last night."

Cyril hesitated.

"Yes," he said thoughtfully, "I suppose the carving block will work."

"Very well," Darien said. "The enchantment will take several hours. I say we finish our food and reorganize the watch around my casting the spell."

Everyone agreed. After the meal, Darien began his ritual. Lillian, Clement, and Xanaphia watched with interest. Darien's enchantment technique was rare in modern sorcery. Most wizards considered it too complex. The various herbs and fungi were arranged around the caster, who needed to pick up each at the exact right moment. This was complex enough, but the enchanter also risked getting injured.

The items burst into flames as the spell consumed them, leaving a less skilled caster badly burned. The time required for the rituals, the complexity of the spells, and the research needed to learn how the different components interacted discouraged wizards from studying the art. The Rhorian Academy discontinued teaching it centuries ago.

Xanaphia remembered the many hours Darien spent in the academy library. He rediscovered the ancient secrets and taught himself the lost skills. As his opponents discovered to their detriment, the old techniques possessed almost limitless capabilities and the enchantments were near impossible to dispel.

Xanaphia rose. She felt tired from her poor sleep the previous night. Crossing to a soft area of snow and casting her cloak over the ground, she lay down. She didn't sleep long. More nightmares invaded her sleep. The same vision replayed over and over in different settings. In one, she hung impaled above the City of Rhoria; in another, over a distant coast; in another, a lofty plain. She again bolted upright in a cold sweat.

Gasping for air, she looked around. The night was still early. Darien and Clement were asleep. Lillian sat on guard, unaware of Xanaphia or anything else. She was reclining against a log, doodling with a multi-colored block. She kept twisting it, examining the lights and pressing various squares.

Xanaphia felt irritated at her colleague's ambivalence but shrugged it away. What should she expect from Lillian? Xanaphia pretended to be sleeping. Her watch came next, but she had no intention of relieving her companion early. She watched as Cyril snuck up on the spymaster. He stood behind her for several minutes, staring at the block.

"Interesting," he said in a loud voice.

Lillian let out a gasp and dropped the cube. She rolled to her feet and lifted her arms aggressively. Spotting Cyril, she lowered them.

"You startled me," she said, retrieving the cube.

"If you were keeping watch," he said, "you would've noticed me standing over you for the past five minutes."

"Shouldn't you be sleeping or something?"

"Sleep, really?" Cyril responded. "Tonight is my last night of existence as something other than a living torch. I'm keen to enjoy it. I spent most of the night watching the stars, but I became interested in your toy."

He took a seat on the fallen log behind her. "Can I see it?"

"Suit yourself," Lillian said.

She tossed the cube over her shoulder. He caught it and examined it.

"How does it work?"

"Simple," Lillian said, turning around to demonstrate. "Just touch a square. Different squares on different sides of the cube will change colors."

She touched a green block. Nothing happened to the touched block or any blocks on the same side. On every other side of the cube, however, seemingly random squares changed seemingly random colors.

"There are nine colors," Lillian continued. "Like every cube, there are six sides. Each side is a three-by-three grid of boxes."

"What is the objective of the game?"

"I wish I knew," Lillian answered. "No one knows. The creator never shared the secret. I'm trying to solve a riddle without knowing the question. I've studied the device for five years. I know every block by heart. I know the effects of touching each, even to the point of touching them multiple times."

"So there are nine colors but only six sides," Cyril said. "I guess that rules out making each side a different color."

"One would think," Lillian answered. "I've done so though. I've selected combinations of three colors to toss out and then set up the block to where each side had one of the remaining colors. I tried every combination along those lines, but none of them produced any results. I even set every side to the same color.

"Since there are nine colors and nine blocks on each side, logic dictates I strive for some color pattern, but I can't figure out any kind of logical sequence for the colors. There're just too many possible combinations. I don't even know if each side is going to have the same pattern or if each side is supposed to have different patterns."

"Have you tried a rainbow?"

"What do you mean?" She asked.

"The colors," Cyril said, pointing at the cube. "They are orange, red, yellow, blue, green, purple, violet, white, and black."

"So?"

"Haven't you ever seen a rainbow?" Cyril asked.

"Maybe once or twice." She shrugged. "I don't pay much attention to such things. What does a rainbow have to do with a magic cube?"

"Except for white, which sages say is the absence of color, and black, which they claim is the culmination of all colors, the remaining colors match the colors of the rainbow," Cyril answered.

Lillian yanked the cube from Cyril's hand.

"What order do colors appear in a rainbow?" she asked.

"The first color is red, then orange, yellow, green, blue, indigo, and violet."

"But where would the white and black go?"

"Don't know," Cyril responded.

"You know, one time I thought I was really close," she said. "I remember . . ."

She drifted into silence. Cyril glanced up at the stars.

"Why don't you get some sleep?" he said. "I'll watch the rest of the night."

"Thank you."

Lillian pocketed the block and crossed to her bed. Her snores soon filled the clearing. Xanaphia thought Cyril might be enjoying the solitude. She endeavored to leave him alone, but curiosity got the better of her. What thoughts went through the mind of someone who was about to die?

"What are you thinking about?" she asked.

It was his turn to be surprised. He jumped in alarm but smiled upon seeing Xanaphia. She crossed to his side, taking a seat on the log.

"Ladonna," he answered. "I miss her. We've always loved each other. Since childhood hardly a day has passed without us being together. I can't imagine life without her. I fear she'll have the same difficulty without me."

"Love," Xanaphia said, "I don't understand the concept. I've seduced lots of men but never felt any connection to any of them. Even if I did fall in love, I couldn't trust the emotion. Love puts someone at the mercy of the object of affection. Such vulnerability can only end in pain."

"Perhaps," he said.

There was a pause. Xanaphia gazed into the fire, listening to the crackle and snap of the burning wood.

"Could you do me a favor?" Cyril said.

"What?" she responded, taken aback.

He withdrew the wooden carving from his cloak. It glowed with the light of Darien's magic.

"Give this to Ladonna for me," he said. "I want her to have something to remember me by."

Xanaphia took the carving. She looked at Cyril's luminous self-portrait. To her surprise, she felt another face carved on the opposite site. She turned it over and beheld the chiseled face of a beautiful young woman.

"Is this Ladonna?"

Cyril nodded.

"She is beautiful." Xanaphia marveled more at the craftsmanship than the actual woman. "I promise the block will be delivered to her."

Cyril smiled. Xanaphia looked back at the carving. She had taken many lives throughout her lifetime. For the first time, she wished she could save one.

"Hmm." The voice of Corineous drifted through the prison cell. "I confess myself disappointed. We'll have to resort to more drastic measures."

Sylvia said nothing. There was nothing to say, and speaking was too painful anyway. Her second day of torture was at an end, but the knowledge brought no peace. Tomorrow would be worse.

Her first day under the influence of the strange white cube made days of torture at Junlorace Keep seem pleasant. Her own heartbeat hurt her chest. The agony inflicted by the grorgs proved almost unbearable. She also suffered the humiliation and taunts of her former high mage.

Corineous came to the torture sessions. They needed his healing magic to keep her alive, but he wasn't interested in watching. He wanted to participate. When her tormentors pulled out some new device, he requested the opportunity to try it first. He even challenged them to see who could make Sylvia scream the loudest.

After Sylvia survived the first day without giving up the tiara, Corineous became upset. He seemed to feel personally responsible for the failure. He promised greater suffering the next day and backed up his threat by feeding Sylvia two white pills instead of one. She had hoped the effects weren't cumulative. They were.

She writhed in anguish. Even the blinking of her eyes felt like two pugilists pummeling each other to death. She wasn't able to fall asleep, and the next day's torture was beyond unbearable. She thought her mind would shatter. Yet, her strength held.

She focused on her children. She visualized them standing above her. After a point, she could even see them, as though they were really there and actually heard their voices call out to her. It was a hallucination, she knew. It had to be. She recognized the early stages of insanity. Still, the madness gave her strength, and any source of strength was a good thing.

"We aren't allowed to kill her," a grorg hissed. "Without the Life Stone, we can't exercise our most brutal techniques."

"If more pain is needed, we can give her more of the tablets," Corineous responded.

"You want to give her three?" the grorg asked in disbelief. Even it seemed repulsed by the idea.

"Why not?" Corineous responded. "Let's test her limits!"

"If her mind shatters, the tiara is lost," it said. "You're not concerned about the pain or lack of sleep driving her insane?"

"No and neither are you," Corineous said. "This is a win-win situation for us. I like the rewards Master has promised, but I'm content should your mistress win. I already have my immortality."

"You're quite the slippery eel, aren't you?" the grorg said. "You've played every side. No matter how the dice fall, you're still a winner."

"That is my way," he gloated. "The world is my playground and humanity my toy."

Sylvia listened without comprehension. The only thought passing through her ravaged mind was a childlike plea: no more, no more.

"Still," the grorg said, "if Master thinks we're trying to break her mind, we will die. How do you intend to escape if she goes insane?"

"Are you suggesting, I give her the pills tomorrow so she can sleep tonight?" he asked.

"Yes," the grorg answered.

"Very well," Corineous agreed.

Sylvia heard the grorg slink away, the alarm signaling its passage down the hall. Corineous turned toward Sylvia's crumpled form. He gave her a hard kick, magnified by the pills.

"You got lucky," he said. "Don't worry though. You'll break soon enough."

He left, the alarm sounding his departure.

Sylvia curled into a fetal position. After an hour or so, the pain subsided. The pill's effects only lasted twenty-four hours. She felt relieved to discover taking multiple tablets didn't increase the duration.

Now that she could think again, she reflected upon the conversation between Corineous and the grorg. Corineous was involved in some other schemes. He didn't care about the tiara. Torturing her was just a perk. Whether she went insane, died from the torture, or relinquished the crown, he would be content. What were these other schemes? Did it even matter?

Sylvia knew she was about to take three white cubes tomorrow. She had almost broken today. Despite her children's images, she literally begged for death. She couldn't foresee herself holding out any longer. Despite all of her efforts over the past week, tomorrow would be the end. She knew it.

Sylvia closed her eyes. She wanted to kill herself but knew the grorgs watching the cell would stop her. She could only hope to go insane. Taking the tiara's magic with her would at least be a consolation prize. Weary from long hours of constant pain, Sylvia gave up trying to think and drifted into a world of nightmares.

CHAPTER 17

The first conclusion Ladonna reached upon regaining consciousness was that she was still alive. She based this inference on the obvious fact she was conscious. Of course, Ladonna couldn't guarantee the accuracy of the assessment. Some religions, such as the church based in Unburied Grove, spoke about an afterlife. She couldn't rule out the possibility. On the other hand, the doctrine indicated someone in the afterlife would receive a new healthy body. Since her head still throbbed from the blow that knocked her unconscious, she felt satisfied maintaining her verdict of not being dead.

Having reached her first conclusion, Ladonna began building further inferences. The rough, dirty earth under her feet indicated she was in an underground dungeon. She was also the only person there. Her holding cell was too dark to see, so the determination wasn't based upon visual evidence. Instead, she used the old-fashioned technique of calling into the darkness and listening for a response. None came.

Ladonna endeavored to get a more precise read of her surroundings. She stood and stretched her hands upward.

She couldn't touch the roof. She reached to the sides but couldn't touch the walls. She extended her arms in front of her, waving them back and forth and advancing forward. She went several steps before touching a series of thick metal poles embedded into the floor and ceiling. She pulled on the bars, relying on her strength to bend the steel. They didn't give, and she released them in disappointment.

She moved along the bars feeling for the exit. Her hands struck hinges, and she was able to deduce the location of the door. She found the latching mechanism, but there was no lock or handle. The cell must be sealed through some form of magic. She felt only slightly disheartened. She had lock picks hidden in her boots but lacked a strong proficiency in the art. She probably couldn't have picked it anyway. Defeated, she sat down with her back against the wall.

Ladonna reflected upon her conversation with Nimue. She had distrusted the steward but took a risk on the off chance she was telling the truth. If so, Ladonna might have beaten Cyril to Kendross Keep. She had hoped there was still a chance to save him. Her eagerness blinded her to the true extent of the steward's trap.

The steward had sent one of the regular town guards, Wilhelm, to escort her people outside the gates. The ploy isolated them from the normal population and prevented them from spreading tidings concerning the queen. Ladonna's disappearance wouldn't be noticed because Urik believed she was leading a rescue mission. Even Wilhelm might not know of the deceit. Meanwhile, Vladimir would collect the winghams. Once inside the castle, the steward would kill him and take control of the mounts.

The soft muffled clop of sandals striking stone echoed through the dungeon. Ladonna had a visitor. She rose to face the sound. The squeal of rusty hinges signaled a door opening, but no light greeted her. The footsteps advanced until they reached the cell door.

"Ladonna of Junlorace," a soft female voice spoke. "I hope you will be flattered to know I've heard many positive things about you. Though I've never revealed myself to either you or Cyril, I've long felt appreciation for the shelter and security you provide my people."

"Who are you?" Ladonna asked.

"Ah yes, forgive me," the speaker said. "I have little use for light. Svetlet!"

A bright glowing ball appeared and hovered in the air before exploding. The dungeon filled with light. Ladonna blinked as her eyes adjusted. Her visitor was Nimue. She wore the same green cloak and gloves, but the cloth covering her eyes was missing. Ladonna resisted the urge to gasp. Nimue possessed no eye sockets. Where eyes would be on a normal human, only flat skin flowed.

"How do you know of me?" Ladonna asked.

"My parents spoke of you often. They were Lord and Lady Westand."

"The rulers of Kendross Keep," Ladonna exclaimed.

Nimue smiled and nodded.

"I never knew they had a daughter," Ladonna said. "How did you survive the massacre?"

"My parents refused to let me attend the ritual," she said. "They believed I was too young and wanted to keep my existence a secret from the citizens of Junlorace Keep. I became upset and ran away. I didn't return home until the following night."

"Why did they keep you secret?"

"I was their trump card," Nimue said in a bitter tone. "That's all I meant to them. They planned to wait until Cyril's parent's displayed him to the master. They would retort by revealing their own kefling."

"You're a kefling? But how . . ."

"Come now," she interrupted. "Did you truly believe the servant destroyed the ritual? He saw both families attempting to incur the favor of the master and wanted to hedge his bets. He planned to receive the favor of whichever family won the competition. He gave the ritual to my parents in exchange for promises of glory."

Ladonna swore. Nimue didn't seem to hear.

"I still have the ritual in fact," she continued. "I've been improving it."

"What?" Ladonna asked in alarm.

"I'm quite a talented sorceress, you know," she said, holding her head high. "But enough about me. I want to talk about you. Why are you here? Master forbade me to reveal myself to Cyril, but I know your lord is intelligent and crafty. You're here as part of some scheme against the master. I'm glad, for I'm also conspiring against him. Perhaps we can join forces."

"Is that why you're in Rhoria," Ladonna asked.

"Not entirely. Master ordered me here to assist Corineous. He was grateful for the help. Not everyone has a shapeshifter at their disposal."

"Shapeshifter?" Ladonna tried to wrap her brain around the bizarre turn of events.

"Of course, that's my power as a kefling. Watch." Nimue's skin bubbled, and her features disappeared.

She possessed a normal humanoid build with two arms, two legs, a head, and a torso, but they were devoid of any distinguishing characteristics. When the features returned, Ladonna found herself staring at herself. Even the black hair on Nimue's head had changed a brilliant red. The experience resembled looking in a mirror except for one unique trait. Nimue still possessed no eyes.

Nimue underwent the transformation again, resuming her previous appearance. "I admit the eyes are a problem. I was born with the deformity, and it can't be healed. When Corineous needs me to perform special missions, he covers it with an illusion spell. I refuse to do so myself. I'm proud of who and what I am."

Ladonna listened in silence. She realized Nimue must be several years younger than Cyril. She was just a girl and seemed eager to have someone to talk with. She possessed no family and had spent her life keeping her identity secret. Speaking to someone with a touch of the same magic heritage must be freeing for her.

"Anyway," Nimue said, "I used my power to perform various missions. Unfortunately, Master bound me to Corineous's every command. The high mage enjoys having a servant with the ability to take the shape of any woman at any time. Especially one who can't disobey his whims."

Nimue gave a shudder, and Ladonna shook her head. She understood Nimue's meaning and wasn't surprised. Corineous felt little respect for anyone outside of himself.

"But I also received separate orders, unknown to Corineous," she continued. "Cyril's plan allowed the queen to return to Rhoria if she surrendered the crown, but Master felt she still posed a threat to him. I was responsible for positioning myself as a spy and establishing traitors within her army. Master kept the plan secret from Cyril. He feared Cyril might inadvertently forewarn Sylvia. He says your lord talks a lot."

If not for the grimness of the situation, Ladonna might have laughed. Cyril did have a knack for saying too much and leaking important information. Then again, Nimue wasn't much better. Perhaps it was a kefling thing.

"So," Ladonna said. "You're here to topple the kingdom from within."

"That's Master's plan, not mine."

"What is your plan?" Ladonna asked.

"I've no love for Master, but I can't harm or disobey him. Still, what if a kefling could harm him? As Cyril demonstrates, they're powerful enough to destroy him."

"But, how? Keflings are bound to him."

"True. The ritual binds us to his will. I can't find any way around it. Darlyth created the spell so the component would be necessary." Nimue grew excited, seeming ready to burst with anticipation. "However, I've discovered a way to create what I call pseudo-keflings. They're not as powerful as true keflings, but instead of being bound to Master they're bound to me!"

"What!" Ladonna exclaimed in horror.

Nimue apparently mistook Ladonna's horror for excitement.

"I know! I've worked on their creation ever since I became steward. I arrested several families on fictitious charges and am forcing them to take part in the ritual. I don't know if my spells have borne fruit. But, given time, I will succeed."

"But Nimue," Ladonna began, trying to talk some reason into the girl. "Having a baby takes nine months. Even after they're born, you're looking at thirteen to fourteen years before they'll be mature enough to fight in battle. Most of them will need fifteen to sixteen!"

"Ah ha!" the steward exclaimed. "Not with Darien's enchantment. If you know history, Darien enchanted his kingdom to speed the aging of his citizens. It fueled his army. Before Sylvia could dispel the magic, she needed to know how the ritual was performed. I've stolen her records and notes. I can enchant my pseudo-keflings the same way. I only need humanity to hold Master off for a few years. By then, my army will be ready."

"A few years," Ladonna repeated. "Do you really think humanity will last that long once Darlyth gets the tiara?"

"He won't get the tiara," she declared. "The grorgs torturing Sylvia still possess some memory of their lives before Master transformed them. They're loyal to me. They plan to torture her into insanity, thereby rendering the tiara mute."

"Corineous will never allow that," Ladonna argued.

"Sure, he will. What does he care? He'll still rule humankind whether they're enslaved to Darlyth or by me. Either way, he wins."

Ladonna shook her head in disbelief. She wondered if she was the only one of Darlyth's servants not plotting some scheme to kill him and take over the world for themselves.

"Join me," Nimue said.

"What?"

"You're not a true kefling, but we were both created in the same ritual. So was Cyril. We're the last of our kind. I want you both by my side!"

"Nimue, I can't . . ." Ladonna began, but the sorceress interrupted.

"Wait, listen to me." Nimue raised a hand. "I know you aren't bound to Master the way we are. You don't feel the anguish of slavery, but you do share my desire to stop him. Once he is gone, a power gap will exist. Who will fill the gap and rule the world? Humankind is intelligent but weak. They don't deserve control. Demons are powerful but unintelligent and barbaric. They have no place in the world either. The new world should be ruled by creatures who have the strengths of both and the weaknesses of neither, a truly superior race. We are that race. Keflings and pseudo-keflings are the dominant species of the future!"

"The people of Junlorace Keep are humans," Ladonna protested. "They're my people and my responsibility. I can't condemn them to a future of enslavement."

"Why not?" Nimue asked. "They're beneath you. They're inferior to you. Why waste your energies worrying about them?"

"Because they're my friends. They're my family. I must protect them. It's the right thing to do."

"Don't be stupid!" Nimue said. "When has doing 'the right thing' ever benefited anyone. Look at the world. There're hundreds of good-hearted, loyal people who treat others with love and respect. There're lonely, while Corineous can get any woman he wants. Look at the government. There're hundreds of hard-working and just people capable of ruling the country with integrity. Do they sit on the throne? No, I do. There're hundreds of people willing to use wealth, immortality, and power to make the world a better place. Do they have such power? No, Master does.

"You see, the gods favor the corrupt. When you fight for good, not only do you fight against evil, you fight against the gods. You can't win such a battle!"

"If such is the nature of the gods, I'll fight them too!" Ladonna said, defiant. "I'll never betray the love of my people!"

"You're a fool, but I'll give you time to reconsider your hasty words."

Nimue turned, suddenly gazing toward the dungeon door.

"Benjamin! What are you doing?"

The palace guard emerged from the darkness of the staircase. He held a tray of food.

"I was bringing down the prisoner's food, my lady," he answered silkily.

"Then bring down the food," she snapped. "Don't stand lurking outside the door."

"I didn't want to interrupt," he said.

He slid the food along with a canteen through a slot in the door. Giving a bow, he hurried back up the stairs.

"I thought you might enjoy some refreshment," Nimue said. "I'm sure you're hungry. You slept all day."

"What time is it?"

"Well after nightfall. How is your head?"

"Agonizing," Ladonna said.

"Sorry," Nimue responded. "I'd offer to fix it, but I'm terrible at healing magic. For some reason, the spells don't work for me. Corineous thinks it has to do with my kefling heritage. Can Cyril cast healing spells?"

Ladonna thought for a second. "I've never seen him cast one. But then he never received any formal training. His education is limited to the keep's library. The shelves are heavy on history but light on magic."

Ladonna examined her food. It was certainly not standard issue for a prisoner. Baked bread next to a large cut of pheasant. Beside both was a heavy helping of goat cheese. The canteen contained a fine wine.

"Do you always feed your prisoners such delicacies?"

"I don't want you to be my prisoner," Nimue answered. "We're allies. The enemy of my enemy is my friend. But you stand opposed to my means. I must keep you down here until I know you're on my side."

Despite Nimue's nefarious ambitions, Ladonna felt sorry for her. She lost her family, her friends, and her home on the day Darlyth rose. She was then dispatched to Rhoria, where her new master took advantage of her. She had no one to talk to and no one to trust. She seemed to view Ladonna as the only person capable of accepting her for who she was.

"Nimue," Ladonna said. "I want to be your ally. I want to be your friend. But I can't go along with your scheme."

The raven-haired teen stared at Ladonna as though heartbroken but nodded.

"You can join mine though," Ladonna continued. "We can oppose Darlyth together. You'll be a hero. You won't be an outcast anymore."

"I can't do that," Nimue responded. "I'm not a human. I'll never be accepted by humans. I'm a kefling and belong with people like me. A time has come for a new era, our era! You may not realize it yet, but you will. When you do, we'll be even greater friends."

Nimue turned and left the room. Ladonna stared after her. *Keflings are really hard to reason with*, she thought pensively. Of course, Nimue was also a teenager, which made reasoning with her even more difficult.

Ladonna thought about Darlyth. No wonder he made a point of cursing all keflings. How else was he supposed to survive creating a race where every single member wanted to kill him? But Ladonna suspected he wouldn't be easy to kill, even for a horde of pseudo-keflings. Aside from his strength and magical powers, he possessed an army of demons and grorgs. Ladonna doubted the grorgs remained as loyal to Nimue as the young stewardess thought.

Further, Nimue seemed to be relying upon her guards to enforce her reign. Would these human guards remain loyal to her in a fight? What would they do once they discovered her plan to enslave humanity? How long could she keep such knowledge a secret? Ladonna believed, given enough time, she could convince Nimue to see reason. But time was a luxury Ladonna lacked.

She finished her food and reclined against the back wall. Twenty minutes later, the light dimmed and faded. Trapped within the darkness and not going anywhere anytime soon, Ladonna started to nod off.

She was aroused by the sound of footsteps and sat up. The footfalls weren't the soft muffled steps of Nimue, nor the metal boots of Rhorian Guards. They appeared to be coming from inside the opposite wall.

The steps drew level with the dungeon floor, and Ladonna heard a soft scrapping noise. A wall was sliding out of place. Someone was using a secret door. Ladonna rose to her feet. She didn't know if the newcomer was a friend or foe. In either case, she preferred to face them standing up.

A light appeared to her left. A blue orb hovered above the hand of a cloaked figure. Ladonna couldn't make out the face, but the visitor seemed to know her.

"Are you the lady who calls herself Ladonna?" the stranger asked.

The voice was soft and feminine.

"Yes," Ladonna answered. She studied her questioner, and recognition dawned. "You're the cloaked figure who watched me from the alleyway as I moved through town."

The stranger nodded.

"Is the story true what they say?" she asked. "Do you know where Sylvia is located?"

"Yes," Ladonna said, feeling a rush of excitement. "If you want to save her, like I do, there isn't much time."

Ladonna knew the woman might be an assassin endeavoring to silence her. The possibility was just as likely as her being a rescuer. If she was an assassin though, Ladonna would die either way. If she was a potential rescuer, telling the truth was critical.

"Where is she being held?"

"In a fortress in the Blood Fang Mountains known as Kendross Keep. I have a colleague who is attempting to set her free, but he won't get far without support. I can show you the way."

"Follow me," the visitor answered. She pointed at the door to Ladonna's cell. "Oatkrevatseeya."

It swung open, and Ladonna stepped through.

"This way," the unidentified rescuer said, motioning her to follow.

Ladonna did so and found herself passing through an opening leading to a staircase. Her guide touched a camouflaged trigger point, and the passage sealed behind them. They ascended. Her guide was clearly familiar with the passage. She warned Ladonna several times of trick steps to avoid.

"Where does this lead?" Ladonna asked after almost ten minutes of ascending the stone stairwell.

"To a fake mausoleum on the outskirts of Rhoria's main cemetery," her guide answered.

"That seems like a dangerously easy way to access the castle."

"It would be," her rescuer said, "but the path is full of illusions and traps fatal to anyone deceived by them. Further, the surface entrance and exit evaporate anyone passing through unless they speak the right command word. On that note, here is the exit."

Her guide stopped next to a wall that looked like any other. Ladonna felt an overwhelming sense of unease as she looked at it. Every fiber of her being warned her not to touch it.

"How can you tell?" Ladonna asked.

"Nervous about touching it?" the woman smiled. "That's how I know. It's enchanted to make you not want to go through. The plan is to confuse unwary travelers. I can go through the passage first if you like. Just remember to say 'secrets' before stepping through."

Her guide turned toward the wall. "Secrets!" she said.

She stepped forward, passing through the solid-looking barrier. Ladonna watched her vanish. She stared at the wall and took a deep breath to steel her nerves.

"Secrets," Ladonna said, stepping forward.

The illusionary barrier gave way. She found herself standing on a marble surface. Looking back, she saw a flat white slab that appeared to be the door to a mausoleum. Row upon row of tombstones stretched for acres around her, mixed with mausoleums and other fancy monuments. The cemetery was nowhere near the size of Unburied Grove. Still, Rhoria's cemetery was easily the second largest on the continent.

Ladonna looked to her right. A collapsed iron fence outlined the boundary of the burial field while thick snow-coated trees signaled the beginning of the forests.

"My hideout is just a mile or so south," the cloaked figure told Ladonna. "Follow me."

The guide let down her hood as she led Ladonna into the nearby woods. She was young, only in her mid-twenties, with long brown hair and matching brown eyes. She wore deep crimson wizard's robes underneath a black traveling cloak and possessed a birthmark like a burning flame upon her neck.

Ladonna asked, "What would happen if someone kept going up the stairs?"

"Let's just say they wouldn't live to fix their mistake."

"That seems ruthless," Ladonna observed. "I'm surprised Sylvia would devise such a horrific punishment."

"She didn't. That dungeon is the only part of Queen Lillian's palace that survived the great fire."

"So Lillian created a passage out of her dungeon?"

"Of course. The route was designed to provide escape in case of emergency. No one would ever believe she built a secret tunnel to the surface inside the very prison where she kept her most dangerous enemies."

"How do you know about it?"

"My mentor, Robert, showed it to me. I was his personal apprentice. He taught magical trap-making and disarming at the Rhorian Academy. Lillian asked his help in designing it."

"I'm surprised she didn't kill him to maintain secrecy," Ladonna said.

"Don't be," the other replied. "The secrets he possessed would become more dangerous if he died. The necromancer, Xanaphia, possesses the power to communicate with the dead. Lillian didn't want her gaining his knowledge."

"Interesting," Ladonna reflected. "So Lillian let him live because she feared what would happen if he died?"

"Yes and no," she said. "People forget that Lillian was resourceful. Being resourceful means not wasting valuable assets. She considered Robert and his skills too important to lose. She also found his knowledge of Clement very useful during the Tyrant Wars. Robert and Clement had grown up together and served as apprentices under headmaster Sorin at the same time. I always marveled at how he and Sylvia ended up together. The two couldn't be more different in personality."

"You know Sylvia?" Ladonna asked.

"I do," the other said. "I'm one of her highest-ranking generals."

The guide stopped walking and turned to Ladonna.

"I'm sorry," she said. "I failed to introduce myself. I apologize, but we were in a hurry. I'm Sylvia's third in command, General Alexis."

CHAPTER 18

"You can't be!" Ladonna exclaimed. "Your rescue party was killed in an ambush."

"How do you know that?" Alexis asked, looking at her suspiciously.

"The same way I know where the queen is held," Ladonna answered. "I know the individuals behind the ambushes. Reports indicated they were successful."

"Indeed, they were," Alexis agreed.

"Then how did you survive?"

Alexis's face broke into a grin.

"Let's just say I'm not an easy person to kill," she said.

Alexis resumed walking. The snowy terrain was thick and overgrown. Ladonna struggled through the low-hanging branches, thorny bushes, and thick snows of the deciduous forest. Her guide was forced to stop and wait for her.

"I'm not bragging about my skills," Alexis continued. "I'm referring to my luck. I'm extremely lucky. Events around me always transpire to keep me alive in situations where others would die."

"I'm jealous," Ladonna returned. "Good fortune isn't my companion."

"Maybe I can loan you a bit someday," Alexis said. "Anyway, the ambushes were successful to an extent. I'm the only person to survive. I was saved by General Cordor. He sent messages to me, Andrus, and Gaheera. He believed there was a traitor in the castle. The three of us decided to place a bonding spell on each other."

"A bonding spell?"

"Yes, the spell connects a group of people. They can sense when the others are in immediate danger."

"Sounds useful," Ladonna said.

"Not as much as you might think," Alexis replied. "It tells you someone is in danger but doesn't tell you anything about the danger."

"And you didn't cast the spell on Corineous's search party?" Ladonna asked.

"Who?"

"Sorry. He goes by Corineous with us. I mean, you didn't cast the spell on Cornelius's search party?"

"No," she answered in an aggressive manner. "I refused to go along if he was involved."

Ladonna felt surprised. From the high mage's haughty statements, he believed everyone on the queen's council trusted him.

"You must understand," Alexis said, "I lived in Rhoria during the rule of Queen Lillian. I learned not to trust people too quickly. Robert always said, 'Put on a good face but never let them close to your back.'"

She cast a sideways glance at Ladonna, indicating the statement applied to her as well.

"Still, the high mage seemed okay until I started paying closer attention to the way he treated his students."

"What was he doing?"

"He was using them," Alexis said. "It wasn't obvious at first, but the more I paid attention, the more I realized that his every action was manipulating the students and teachers for selfish ends. He never sacrificed anything to help someone else, and never did anything that didn't give him some sort of increased pleasure or comfort, often to the detriment of those he manipulated.

"I started to recognize the same behaviors in his interactions with Sylvia, and everyone in the palace. They were all just tools to feed his desires, and his vicitims' lives were almost always destroyed in the process. Yet he somehow seemed to escape any blame or suspicion for his actions, even by those he hurt. I knew it was only a matter of time before he destroy our lives as well, and I never trusted him again."

Ladonna felt a rush of admiration for her new companion. She wasn't someone to be taken lightly. She possessed a keen sense of observation, knew how to read people, and trusted her instincts.

"But I digress," Alexis continued. "I was traveling with my search party when I felt a twinge in the bond. Gaheera was in danger. The bond fluctuated again. Andrus was in danger. Shortly thereafter, the spell broke. I realized both Andrus and Gaheera were dead. The attacks were sudden and coordinated. I suspected an ambush."

Ladonna nodded. She would have come to the same conclusion.

"I told my party that I'd catch up with them," Alexis said. "I possess a small talent at scrying and always keep the equipment with me. I pulled it out with the intention of learning what happened. Scrying spells can't show the past, but perhaps by viewing their current state I could find some clues. As I finished the preparations, I heard distant shouts coming from my own search party. I leapt to their aid, but the screams stopped. They were dead. I knew I would be too if I followed."

"What did you do?"

"I planned to return to the castle and report the incident but changed my mind. I wanted to know who planned the trap. I used magic to disguise myself and moved through the castle gathering information. It was a costly mistake."

"How so?"

"Within hours of the search party's departure, Nimue, who the high mage appointed steward in our absence, arrested a number of high-ranking officials for conspiring in the queen's disappearance," she said. "No one has seen them since. While I was roaming the castle ambivalent to her doings, Nimue amassed secondary search parties of high-ranking mages and warriors, dispatching them to bring the news to the other search parties. She has continued dispatching search parties at regular intervals ever since. Anyone who questions her finds themselves added to one. Her 'Elite Rhorian Guard' ensures none return. By the time I figured out what was happening, Nimue possessed an iron grip upon the kingdom."

"I'm astonished," Ladonna marveled. "She achieved a lot in a very short time."

"It was impressive," Alexis agreed. "Of course, her guards deserve some credit for her success."

"Who are they?"

"No idea," Alexis said. "They started appearing after Nimue took the throne. No one saw them enter the city. No one knows where they came from. They seemed to materialize out of thin air. Within hours, the force began terrifying citizens, sorcerers, and soldiers into line with her edicts. Ladonna?"

Alexis looked back over her shoulder.

Ladonna stood frozen in horror as the realization sank in. "They're grorgs."

Alexis stared. "They're what?"

"Grorgs!" Ladonna repeated. "Cyril says the demon lord uses magic to alter their appearance. The tattoos must be enchanted to make them look human. How could I have been so stupid? Jason told Cyril there was a drastic drop in the number of grorgs stationed at the keep."

"Ladonna, I'm sure this is important, but I'm completely lost. Grorgs? Demon lords? What in the name of Aurba is going on?"

"I'll explain everything," Ladonna said, hurrying up to Alexis, "but we must go. We need to reach your hideout as soon as possible."

She strode past Alexis, who turned around, racing to catch up with her. Ladonna had only taken about five steps when she heard a scream.

"Look out!" Alexis grabbed her.

Only a few inches in front of her face hung a large spider web. In the middle sat a spindly spider about the size of Ladonna's thumb. It bore a strange blue and green striped pattern unlike anything she'd ever seen. Her initial reaction was to brush it away, but something warned her against the action.

"Step back, quickly!" Alexis urged.

Ladonna took a step back, but the spider seemed to sense her presence. To her shock, it shot a thin web at Ladonna, striking her in the forehead. It crawled excitedly across toward her.

"Nasekamoye ebevat!"

A green light shot over her shoulder, striking the scurrying arachnid. It was incinerated, leaving nothing but a small whiff of smoke.

"I've never seen a spider act like that," Ladonna said.

"It was a death spider." Alexis's revulsion and hatred were unmistakable. "Clement the Great created them. They're attracted to living creatures like magnets. We thought they were destroyed after Lillian's palace burned down, but they're thriving again. We're battling a bad infestation at the academy."

"Are they dangerous?"

"The venom can kill a dragon within seconds," Alexis replied. "Your airways seal themselves. You can't speak or cast spells. Then you collapse into seizures and die."

Ladonna's eyes grew wide at the fate that almost befell her.

"Clement was brilliant," Alexis continued. "The poison is magical in nature. It's only dangerous if it comes directly from a bite. The characteristic makes finding an antidote almost impossible. My master died trying, but his notes enabled Gaheera and I to devise an anti-venom. If you swallow the potion before the seizures start, your lungs will reopen and the poison will dissipate. I keep a vial stored in my cloak."

The two resumed their walk. Ladonna told Alexis about the demon lord and about Corineous's betrayal. She explained Cyril's intentions of freeing Sylvia from the keep and her orders to organize a rescue party.

"Time is of the essence," Ladonna concluded. "We must retrieve the winghams. Once we rescue Sylvia, she can resolve everything here."

"It won't be that easy," Alexis said. "Your winghams are gone."

"What?" Ladonna exclaimed.

"They were taken to the castle. Around midday, I saw them take flight, soaring north. I don't know where they went. The plan must be to hide them so they can't be used to rescue the queen."

Ladonna shook her head. "We'll never reach her in time by foot."

"Don't despair. Saving the queen is important, but we also need to make sure there's still a kingdom when she returns. Once we secure Rhoria, we can get the winghams back."

"Perhaps," Ladonna said. "But that'll take time. Nimue will discover I escaped and come after me."

"True," Alexis agreed. "I might do well to put an anti-scrying jinx on you."

"But what about my people?"

"I know we need to protect them," Alexis said. "But I also have to worry about the people of Rhoria. I have no clue what Nimue's intentions are."

"I do," Ladonna began but stopped short.

A tulip tree stood a short distance away. There was an archway in the middle of it. The light of a blazing fire shone from within. Voices issued outward as though a party of raucous people stood inside conversing in loud tones.

The tree was tall, thin, and cylindrical. There was no way multiple people could fit inside.

Alexis advanced toward the tree, Ladonna behind her.

"Do you like my spell?" Alexis said. "I found it in Xanaphia's library and modified it. Her spell was too advanced for me to cast. I can't summon enough energy to make it work. I wish I could though. Her spell allows the creation of food inside the room and enables the caster to hide the door. Still, my version is sufficient for my needs."

They stepped through the opening. Ladonna gasped. More than a dozen men and women lingered around a bonfire. Some wore wizard robes while others wore armor. All turned toward Alexis. She signaled for silence.

"Everyone! This is Ladonna of Junlorace." She made a gesture toward Ladonna. "She commands a garrison of troops who can aid our cause. She also brings information concerning the true nature of our enemy. The danger is far greater than I expected. We must act quickly. I'll need the help of everyone here. Yeva, Kaspar, please report to me immediately. Everyone else, retire for the night. We have a busy day tomorrow."

Instant action followed. Men and women hurried across the room, lying down on various mats and blankets. A skinny girl in her upper teens with short, neatly-trimmed black hair approached Alexis. She wore the silver robes of an apprentice at the Rhorian Academy. An older man, perhaps in his early forties, followed her. He wore leather armor and a short sword strapped to his side.

"Let's speak outside," Alexis suggested.

The four filed toward the exit. A blast of cold wind greeted them. The man and woman gave an involuntary shudder.

"Sorry to drag everyone out here," Alexis said. "I wanted to talk without being overheard. Ladonna, this young lady is Yeva. She is a student at the academy and the granddaughter of an influential aristocratic family. She has contacts at both the school and among the nobility. The gentleman here is Kaspar. He is a high-ranking city guardsman. We use him to communicate with the town militia."

The man and woman nodded as a way of greeting.

"I collected a small contingent of contacts and warriors from search parties I intercepted," Alexis explained. "I wasn't always able to determine the exact moment the search parties left, but when I did I attempted to catch them."

"But aren't you one of the queen's highest-ranking soldiers?" Ladonna asked Alexis. "Why don't you just walk into town and take the throne?"

Alexis snorted. "I'm a skilled sorceress but not powerful enough to take on hundreds of massive armed guards."

"Nimue doesn't have many allies, but everyone is terrified of her soldiers," Kaspar said. "Our entire army pales before them."

"Even the magical academy is terrified," Yeva added. "She temporarily closed the school. Students and teachers are confined to their rooms and offices. She claims people inside the school were involved in the queen's disappearance. She doesn't want students putting themselves in harm's way by mingling with potential enemies. The ban is enforced by guards who monitor the school's halls. They deliver meals to the students and make sure no one leaves. Everyone knows the move is a ploy to keep us weak and divided, but they're too terrified to act."

"The school is monitored by her guards. The town is patrolled by her guards. The palace is controlled by her guards," Ladonna said, ticking off fingers. "I don't understand how she can have that many grorgs! She must've emptied the entire keep. How many soldiers does she have?"

"What are grorgs?" Yeva asked.

"I'll explain in a moment," Alexis answered. "Let's not get sidetracked."

"We can't get an accurate count," Kaspar said. "She spreads them out and keeps them in constant motion to mask their numbers. As best we can tell, there are between one hundred and one hundred fifty."

Alexis turned to Ladonna. "You know what Nimue's plans are?"

"Yes. She's using prisoners to breed a new race of half-demons under her command."

"What?" all three exclaimed.

"My little sister is one of those prisoners," Kaspar said, his eyes flashing. "You mean she is being forced to . . ."

"Calm down," Alexis said, holding up her hand. "We can't let emotions affect our judgment."

"We need to get her out," he argued. "I can't let the steward torment my sister in such a manner."

"We will get her out, but we can't act yet!" Alexis snapped. "We don't even know where they're being held. If we do get them out, she'll just arrest more people. We need to look at both the short-term and long-term implications of any actions we take."

"And," Ladonna added, "you'll need some exceptionally skilled soldiers. Grorgs are more than a match for most non-spellcasters."

"Tell us about these grorgs," Yeva said.

"Grorgs are the right hand of the Demon Lord," Ladonna explained. "Once humans, they were twisted into horrifying beasts by his dark magic. Currently, they're disguised to look like large soldiers, but in truth they're even more formidable than they appear. They're armed with sharp claws, move with unnatural agility, are incredibly strong, and possess thick hides."

"Great!" Kaspar said sarcastically. "Not only are they terrifying as humans, but they're actually supernatural monsters equipped with the kingdom's best armor."

"I doubt they're wearing armor," she said. "It's probably part of the illusion. Armor hinders their mobility, and their skin is thick enough without it. Still, they're mortal and can be pierced by a sharp blade. In the meantime, the town guard must be made aware of their true nature. Otherwise, soldiers will try attacking around the armor. They'll fight more effectively if they know it isn't real."

"Either way, we're fighting an uphill battle," Kaspar said. "Even if we rally the entire guard, our forces aren't capable of overpowering them."

Alexis agreed. "If they're as deadly you claim, the town's crippled garrison is no match for them."

"Maybe." Ladonna nodded. "But they have a severe weakness."

"What?" Yeva asked.

"Magic!" Ladonna replied. "Unlike other half-human, half-demon creatures, grorgs seem to possess the weaknesses of each race. Like demons, they lack the ability to summon energy or cast spells. Like humans, they possess no resistance to magic."

Yeva said, "If we mobilize the magic school, we can defeat them."

"Yes," Ladonna answered.

"I'm afraid I'm not optimistic about the school," Alexis said. "Our most powerful members were dispatched in search parties. The remainders are either apprentices or poor fighters."

"Not all of them," Kaspar argued. "Besides, you must fight a battle with the forces you have."

"I'd like to know how they got into the city without anyone noticing," Yeva said.

"They came in through the queen's bedchamber," Ladonna answered. Everyone looked at her. "The high mage planted a glyph in her room so a demon could enter without detection. Apparently, it's still active. Grorgs must be entering through the portal."

"A portal links Sylvia's room to the demon stronghold," Alexis repeated. "Can we use it to get to the queen?"

"No, Darlyth is too cautious. The portal is one-way and can only be activated at his command."

"Then we must destroy it," Yeva said.

"It won't be that easy," Alexis said. "I expect the glyph was hidden to prevent Sylvia from noticing. Plus the magic you're discussing is more advanced than anything I'm familiar with. If it dates back to before the Demon Wars, the glyph may be foreign to anything we know today. We'll need to research it first."

Kaspar took a deep breath. "We must free the prisoners, destroy the glyph, take the city back from Nimue, and defeat an army of monsters in disguise."

"And," Ladonna added, "we must do so within a couple of days so we can save the queen!"

She looked at the faces of the others, trying to relay a sense of urgency. Kaspar and Yeva looked at her like she was mad.

"Don't you think you're rushing things," Yeva said. "A few days? We're talking about a full-fledged revolution. What you're asking is impossible."

"Impossible or not, she is right," Alexis said. "I'm not going to relay the entire story, but saving the queen is just as important as saving the city. We need to act fast, and much of what we do will be rushed. The situation is unfortunate because we must jeopardize caution for the sake of speed."

"Here is the plan," Alexis continued. "Tomorrow is going to be a busy day. Ladonna, if I show you where your people are camped, can you speak to them without being noticed? We need your soldiers."

Ladonna nodded.

"Excellent. Yeva, I need you to get into the magical academy. Find Master Rorax, the history teacher. Tell him the demon lord has arisen. We need teachers to research the glyph and our adversaries."

"Yes, ma'am," Yeva affirmed.

"Kaspar, I need you to inform the town guard about the true nature of Nimue's forces. Do so in a way that will instill confidence rather than fear. Inform them the armor is an illusion and discuss strategies for fighting the creatures. Also, prepare for a possible attack on the castle. We can't launch an attack tomorrow, but I hope to mount some form of organized offensive the following morning."

"Yes, Commander," he replied.

"Meanwhile, I'm going to research the location of the prisoners."

The plan established, Ladonna followed the others back to the tree. Alexis, Yeva, and Kaspar curled up in mats and fell asleep. Ladonna did not. She sat against the wall and gazed into the fire. A sickening sense of failure hung over her. The winghams were gone. Without them, she couldn't reach the keep in time to save Cyril. Without them, she couldn't reach Sylvia before the demon lord recaptured her. Without them, Cyril's sacrifice would be in vain.

She needed to get them back. Nimue knew their location, but she was unlikely to surrender the information. She must be defeated first. That would take time. By then, Sylvia would be on her way to Rhoria and all hope of rescuing Cyril would be lost. Ladonna found herself facing the harsh truth. Cyril would die. Sylvia would be recaptured. Aurba would fall, all because she failed.

CHAPTER 19

The rising sun cast long, dark shadows across the face of Cyril Junlorace as he gazed upon the remnants of Kendross Keep. As a child, the majestic beauty of the stronghold always left him breathless. The stone bulwarks stood tall and strong, defying all who might oppose them, and the polished walls towered over travelers, reminding pilgrims of the site's glorious history. Now, they were nothing more than ruins.

He remembered standing beside his parents, smelling the fragrance of the fireweeds growing thick along the road. He remembered farmers and ranchers working the fields and children laughing as they frolicked in the grass. Darlyth had destroyed them all.

He wasn't satisfied with killing the inhabitants either. He took his wrath out upon the keep, as though the walls were responsible for his imprisonment. He crushed every stone structure and edifice. Only two areas escaped his carnage.

One was the farmlands. The grorgs needed to eat, so Darlyth enchanted the fields to perpetually grow crops.

He also left the front gate standing. Cyril didn't know why. Perhaps Darlyth wanted some grandiose structure marking the entrance to his lair. The rest of the keep, however, was little more than crumbling stone foundations.

The sound of approaching footsteps pulled Cyril away from his thoughts. Lillian stopped beside him.

"It looks deserted," she observed. "Where does everyone live?"

"They're located inside the mountain," he answered, turning to his companions. "Kendross Keep was built around a massive cave. The subterranean complex has served as Darlyth's home since the earliest known records. He still resides in the throne room where he fought against Kendross and the wizards of the old world. Here they sacrificed their lives to stop him. Here, we'll find Sylvia."

The histories of the Demon Wars probably meant little to Cyril's comrades. Yet, to him they meant everything. He was a part of their heritage. Today, he would take his place in their legends.

"Remember the plan," he said. "Clement and Lillian, you free the queen. I've never been to the dungeons, but the directions I provided should get you there. I'll lead Darien and Xanaphia to the crown. Then I depart for Darlyth's chamber."

They stared at him. He'd gone over the plan numerous times on the final trek but never mentioned that the structure was underground. The terms "hallway" and "corridor" could easily be mistaken for parts of a castle. He chided himself for his oversight. Perhaps the term tunnel would have given them some forewarning.

"One more thing," he added. "I don't know how many grorgs we'll encounter. The creatures are vulnerable to magic but extremely agile. They can dodge spells and kill you quickly with their claws. Use spells they either can't dodge or that keep them at a distance."

Darien, Xanaphia, and Clement nodded confidently. Cyril knew they possessed a wealth of spells and combat experience. Only one spellcaster had ever defeated them, and she needed an enchanted tiara to do so. Lillian didn't nod. Cyril understood that she wasn't a warrior and preferred the shelter of invisibility and protective magic. Such tactics didn't worked well in cramped quarters.

"Clement," Lillian said, "you know six thousand ways to kill a man. I'll keep you invisible. You take out the grorgs."

"Uncomfortable fighting in caves?" Clement said, grinning. "Don't worry. I'll handle the grorgs."

Clement stretched his arms high in the air with his hands facing inward. He closed his eyes and took a deep, steadying breath.

"Lepeetglena!" he called.

Brown light flowed from his outstretched palms, coalescing into a floating orb of energy. The globe expanded until the left side of the sphere touched his left hand and the right side of the sphere his right hand. Clement pulled his arms downward drawing the ball onto his head. The light melded with his skin, creating a bronze halo around him. Then the light flashed inward, shooting into his body.

Cyril felt intrigued, but the others seemed less than impressed. Lillian's expression indicated Clement had lost his mind. Darien held his hand over his mouth to hide a snicker. Xanaphia snorted.

"Lepeetglena?" she scoffed. "Are you planning to create a sculpture of yourself? Maybe make the demon lord a self-portrait?"

"What do you mean?" Cyril asked.

"The spell is not exactly useful," Darien said. "The charm is taught as part of a story. A king once offered a reward for whoever created the most impressive stone effigy. An ambitious sorcerer decided to design a spell allowing him to shape stone and craft a winning statue. He locked himself in his home, working nonstop until he completed it. When he came out, he discovered he had worked on the spell for three weeks and the contest was already over. The tale is a warning for wizards to avoid getting so wrapped up in projects that they forget the big picture."

"Just because someone made a mistake doesn't mean his spell isn't useful," Clement countered.

"Seriously, Clement, the spell is for sculpting statues," Lillian replied.

"Watch and learn," he said. "I used this spell in the Battle of Landsile. I've evolved it beyond anything its creator ever imagined. It's the ultimate weapon for fighting in caves."

The three wizards looked uncertain but intrigued. Even Cyril knew the story of the Battle of Landsile. The conflict was legendary. Early in Clement's military campaign, over five hundred warriors had used the ancient cavern of Landsile as a base of operations for their resistance. For five months, Clement's army failed to break their defenses. Finally, Clement walked into the cavern alone to face the entire enemy army. He walked out an hour later without a scratch. There were no other survivors. The incident shattered the confidence of neighboring kingdoms and resistance movements. Most surrendered the next day.

"If everyone is ready, let's get moving. Lillian?" Cyril asked.

"Chutieray nevedeimeyah," she said, raising her hand with a powerful gesture.

A burst of fuzzy yellow light exploded from her body, engulfing the company. The five companions became blurry and returned to focus. Lillian gave a satisfied nod, but Clement shot her a caustic look.

"Was all the fanfare really necessary?" he asked. "I don't remember the arm gesture and the explosion of yellow light the last time you cast the spell."

Lillian gave him a withering look.

"I don't remember 'Lepeetglena' requiring a massive brown ball to hover above someone's head," she snapped. "If you can over dramatize your spells, so can I!"

"All right you two, enough puppy love," Xanaphia said. "Let's go."

Lillian and Clement glared at Xanaphia as she marched away. Darien smiled and followed her. Cyril darted ahead to take the lead. He felt a touch confused about why he could still see everyone. No one else seemed bothered though, so he assumed everything must be okay.

As they approached the fortress, the trees broke. The companions reached the citadel and passed through the crumbling front gate. Cyril hardly glanced up as he passed through Kendross Keep's last-remaining structure. But his companions gazed in wonder at the ancient portal. The bulwarks stretched almost seventy feet into the sky and were armed with numerous arrow slots and other defenses. It looked intimidating, but Clement knew it was mostly for show. The fortifications never saw use. Being buried in the heart of a forbidding mountain range and forgotten by humankind served as enough of a defense.

Beneath the opening, the path became obstructed by large wooden timbers strewn across the entrance. They were the remains of the large portcullis that once barred entry to the keep. The lumber bore signs of violence and random spots of blood. The barrier was down at the time of the demon lord's awakening. Cyril remembered only too well the screams of caged citizens, barred escaped by their own gate.

Cyril guided the company around the collapsed outer walls and away from the distant ruins of the palace. He called a brief halt to give Lillian a chance to renew the invisibility spell before proceeding toward a large structure high above the keep.

The building was once a glorious sight. The stairs ascending the ruin were carved from the most exquisite white marble. The color and texture remained flawless despite the destruction of the keep and the years of harsh weather. The pearly white surface highlighted the deep-blue crystalline stone forming the fallen walls of the citadel.

The party ascended the long stairs to the sanctuary. Enormous pillars were strewn across the floor of the temple. Figures, faces, and runes circled the pillars, each hieroglyph telling the story of the spellcaster for whom it was dedicated. Cyril saw Lillian pause beside one such pillar, running her hand along the symbols. Her curious face showed a deep desire to read the stories. But they didn't have time to stop.

Cyril led them across the foundation. The height of the broken columns prevented them from seeing to the other side of the building and prevented anyone on the other side of the building from seeing them. Less than one hundred yards away, the smooth side of a steep cliff rose into the air.

The cave entrance was near at hand. Cyril raised his hand in warning. Everyone stopped, awaiting his next move.

"There should be two grorgs guarding the entrance," Cyril said. "They can't see us, but our footsteps on the loose rubble might give us away. Wait behind the pillar while I eliminate them."

Cyril vanished. A moment later, he reappeared, sword in hand, blade dripping with blood.

"They're dispatched," he said.

The party advanced forward. A large archway opened into the side of the mountain before them. It was the entrance to the demon lord's underground kingdom. It wasn't big, only five feet wide and seven feet tall at the pinnacle. The bodies of two large hairy black beasts rested nearby, blood oozing from their decapitated heads.

"Should we hide the bodies," Lillian asked.

"I don't see the point," Cyril responded. "If anyone sees the guards missing, they'll sound the alarm anyway."

"Maybe," Darien said. "But no harm can be done by making the deaths less noticeable."

He walked up to the two grorgs and stood between them. Lifting his arms above the lifeless remains, he muttered, "Razroosheneya!"

The bodies began decaying at an accelerated rate. The skin and internal organs rotted away until only white bones remained. The skeletons also aged, becoming brittle and breaking apart. These dissolved into a coarse white powder. Finally, a brief burst of wind scattered the dust, leaving no trace of the corpses. The entire process took less than a minute.

"Nice," Clement said, nodding his approval. "Where'd you learn that spell?"

"Found it on a scroll ages ago," Darien answered. "It kept my palace tidy and saved cleaning expenses."

The company continued through the archway. Cyril, who traveled the corridors regularly, was unimpressed by the structure. His companions, however, seemed captivated by the alien environment. Clement and Lillian stared in wonder at the strange orange glow emanating from the walls. Darien studied the tunnels, questioning aloud how the bizarre burrow was constructed. Xanaphia ran her hand across the rough surface, feeling the strange wavy bumps flow across her fingers.

"Incredible," she said. "The place looks like hell according to the teachings of the temple of Buried Grove."

"They probably got the idea from distant memories or stories of this place," Cyril said interrupting Darien's attempt to bait Xanaphia. "It certainly was hell for anyone unfortunate enough to be taken hostage."

The entrance zone for the cave proved to be a long passage slanting downward for more than a mile. No paths split from the main shaft, and each stretch of passage looked identical to the next. The design served to disorient potential invaders by causing them to lose track of time and distance as they descended. Only Cyril's familiarity spared him the befuddlement.

The hall expanded into in a large round chamber like a rotunda. New hallways opened to the right and the left, while the current passage extended forward. Everyone looked at Cyril.

"Avoid the left path. It's a trap," he said. "Continue straight to reach the prison. Here!"

Cyril pulled several black rock-like substances from a pouch. He tossed one to Clement.

"It's a type of chalk," Cyril said. "Numerous passages throughout the tunnels lead to traps or places you don't want to go. Marking the correct hallway saves time in case you need to leave in a hurry. Use it like this."

Cyril marked the path on the right with a large star. Clement shook his head in bemusement.

"We know how to use chalk," he said.

"Now, remember what I told you," Cyril continued. "Take the first right and the next two lefts."

"Got it," Clement confirmed. "You're sure she's being kept there?"

"Most likely," Cyril responded evasively. "Those are the only prisons I know about."

Clement and Lillian eyed him. "Most likely" was not the answer they wanted to hear, but they didn't say anything. Cyril suspected their willingness to go along with the plan hinged more on desperation than confidence. Darien seemed to notice the awkwardness of the situation. He tried to break the silence by wishing them good luck.

"We will meet you here once we get the crown," he said. The statement was not convincing. It was obvious Darien didn't expect them to be here when they returned. "If you are not here, we will come down after you." This statement wasn't any more believable than the first.

The groups broke apart. Clement marked the entrance to his hallway with an "X" while Cyril led Darien and Xanaphia down the hallway marked with the star.

Clement and Lillian's tunnel was a wide passage, with plenty of room for both to walk abreast. Lillian showed no interested in being anywhere near the front, however, and Clement found himself leading the way. They passed several hallways heading left but after almost fifteen minutes hadn't encountered a single one going right.

Clement was wondering how far the corridor led, when the path came to an abrupt end at a T. Clement marked their hallway wall with another X before he and Lillian rounded the corner. As they turned into the new corridor, they encountered two grorgs patrolling the tunnels.

The grorgs spotted them at the same time and reached for their weapons. Before they could move, however, the walls seemed to come to life. The floor of the cave shot up while the ceiling crashed down. The two sides slammed into each other, smashing the grorgs like bugs. With the same suddenness, the walls returned to their normal position. Fur and innards clung to the ceiling, and drops of blood rained down onto the flattened carcasses, still twitching in death.

"What just happened?" Lillian gasped.

"Lepeetglena," Clement nodded, smiling in self-satisfaction.

"But the spell is for sculpting statues!" Lillian exclaimed, seemingly lost for words. "How . . . It can't . . . I mean, you . . . it turns cave walls into weapons?"

"I told you so," Clement bragged. "Too many wizards are too quick to dismiss a spell just because they can't see the value. Like I said before, the only limit to a spell's power lies in the creativity of the person using it."

Lillian gaped at him.

"More relevant to me right now is how they saw us," Clement said. "I thought we were invisible."

"The spell only lasts so long. I guess I lost track of time. I hope Darien and Xanaphia figure it out."

Clement shook his head. Xanaphia and Darien were unlikely to know they were visible until someone attacked.

Fortunately, they had Cyril with them. He should be able to kill any guard before an alarm could sound.

"I'll make us invisible again," Lillian said.

She recast the spell, and the two continued down the passage. The tunnel sloped downward, and the temperatures dropped steadily. Clement knew enough about caves to expect the colder climate. The length of the hallways as well as the angle of the slope led him to believe they were several miles underground.

He was growing anxious. Their plan relied on stealth and speed. The longer they took, the greater their chances of being spotted. They also possessed no means of tracking time or knowing when the invisibility spell ended. Lepeetglena would eventually run out too. Clement started making random alterations to the corridor just to make sure the spell still functioned.

They found the first left and then the second left, their pace increasing with their sense of urgency. They all but ran down the last stretch of hallway. Then they stopped, staring ahead in stunned silence. The passage forked. One side sloped upward to the left, the other downward to the right. Clement and Lillian exchanged a look. This split wasn't in Cyril directions.

"Now what?" Lillian asked.

"How am I supposed to know?" Clement said. "Do you have any ideas?"

"Bonding spell?" Lillian suggested. "You go right, I go left?"

"Works for me. But be careful. Cyril said wrong paths are trapped. Whatever you do, don't let your curiosity get the better of you and start investigating places you don't need to go."

Lillian gave an innocent smile. Clement knew he'd just wasted his breath.

"How much longer do we have on our invisibility?" he asked.

"Not sure," she admitted.

"How do I dismiss it if I find Sylvia?"

"Close your eyes and will yourself to be seen. The spell will drop."

"All right," Clement said. "Do you want to do the bonding spell or shall I?"

"I'll do it. I'm fairly adept at them. We don't have time for a complex one though. If either of us gets into danger or finds the queen, the other will be alerted."

"Sounds good," he said. "Let's go."

Xanaphia watched Cyril march ahead of them. He held chalk in one hand and a sword in the other. The former was getting more use than the latter. The route to the keep's treasure chamber took numerous turns splitting into dozens of forks and T's. Cyril made a point of marking the correct paths with a star. Identifying them was important. He wouldn't be making the return trip.

Xanaphia was growing anxious. The adventure was taking longer than expected. Cyril admitted he misjudged the amount of time required. Capable of moving at supernatural speeds, he had never walked the halls at a normal pace.

"Could they bury this thing any deeper?" Xanaphia exclaimed in exasperation. "What's with this place?"

"Darlyth doesn't care much for visitors," Cyril joked. "About seventy-five percent of the tunnels are fake corridors designed to kill unwelcome guests."

"I understand that," Darien responded. "But why place the tiara so far from the prison?"

"Would you keep a treasure chamber near your prison?" Cyril asked. "While the odds of anyone escaping are slim, Darlyth has no reason to risk it. He placed his treasure chamber on the same side of the keep as himself and the prison on the other. Separating Sylvia and the tiara decreases the risk of losing both."

The reasoning made sense. Still, they had separated from Lillian and Clement almost a half-an-hour earlier. At some point, someone would notice the missing guards or see the chalk markings on the walls. Either way, they'd be in trouble.

They rounded a corner and entered a hall lined with doors. A few of them were man-sized, but most were massive. An ominous feeling washed over Xanaphia as she imagined the creatures living inside. Cyril led them past several large doors until he reached a man-sized one. He knelt and examined the lock, apparently looking for traps. After a moment, he raised his hand, holding his palm a few inches away from the handle.

"Otperet," he whispered.

A blue glow illuminated the doorknob. After a moment, the light faded and a soft clicking noise reached their ears. Cyril turned the knob, thrust open the door, and vanished. Xanaphia gasped, but then her senses returned. Cyril must have rushed into the room. She hurried inside and spotted him. On his left and right were the bloody remains of two newly decapitated grorgs.

"I thought he might station guards inside the room," Cyril said.

"You could have warned us," Darien responded, "instead of vanishing like that."

Cyril started to reply, but Xanaphia interrupted. "The tiara!" She pointed toward the back of the room.

A large glass display case rested against the back wall. Inside, suspended in air, Sylvia's tiara revolved slowly on an invisible axis. They crossed the room and examined the case. The glass lacked any noticeable doors or methods of entry.

"Can we just break it?" Xanaphia asked.

"I doubt it," Darien responded. "The case is probably armed with magic or traps to prevent such ploys. Where are Lillian and Clement when you need them?"

"It can't be too complex," Cyril said. "The device is supposed to be opened by grorgs after all."

"Maybe we should have questioned the grorgs before killing them," Darien suggested pointedly.

"Maybe I should have just sounded the alarm myself!" Cyril retorted.

"Maybe," Xanaphia interrupted. "We should question them now."

Cyril and Darien looked at her in surprise. She smiled as she stared at their astonished faces. She crossed her arms and gazed down her nose at them.

"I'm a necromancer after all," she declared in her haughtiest tone.

"Stop gloating and cast a spell or something," Darien said.

Giving Darien her patented smirk, she strolled across the room to the two large corpses sprawled across the floor. Reveling in the feeling of self-importance and superiority, she swaggered to the head of the nearest grorg. She grabbed it by the hair and swept it off the ground with flair. She looked back at Darien and gave him a supercilious smile before turning the decapitated face toward her own.

Her expression grew serious as anxiety and expectancy battled for control of her mind. She shoved both aside, and all thought stopped as she concentrated on drawing her life force deep within her. She needed to shield her mind and soul from potential dangers before beginning the ritual. She took a deep breath and merged her energy with the mind of the dead grorg.

The words of the ancient spell trickled from her thin black lips. She pronounced each syllable with precise cadence and enunciation, repeating the phrases over and over again. The chant flowed outward in a smooth melodic rhythm, drawing her deeper into the ritual. She knew her companions couldn't see it, but a strange black mist oozed from the monster's glassy eyes. It wrapped around her, enveloping her within its fathomless darkness. A chill crept up her spine. She was no longer in the world of the living. She had returned home to the world of the dead.

Shrill cries broke through the void. They sang to her, caressing her soul like sirens drawing her to the abyss. Some knew her from life and shrieked anger and loathing. Others showered her with affection and greeting. They were her family. She was welcome in their world as she was never welcomed in her own. They implored her to stay. She belonged here. Everyone belonged here.

Xanaphia remained firm and resolute, her focus unwavering. The soul of the grorg emerged through the nothingness, drawn to her by the spell. They were two distant beings - one dead, the other alive - but they were united by her magic. His image took form before her, but not as a monster. He was a man, young and handsome, wearing farmer's clothing. He drew nearer, compelled by her chant. He radiated fear, sadness, and pain. She closed the gap between them until their essences merged.

She cast her mind into his soul and his memories, seeking the secret to open the case. But she was careless. Her concentration faltered for just a second. With alarming suddenness, the soul lashed out at her, and she found herself overwhelmed by agony and pain. She was being transformed into a grorg. She felt her body twist and warp until her mind broke under the power of the demon lord's wrath. She heard herself screaming in agony as hair ripped through her flesh. Bones and organs deformed themselves into distorted shapes.

Cruel, wrathful voices rose from the void in celebration. Xanaphia was trapped within the body of a grorg. Her soul screamed for release. She struggled to control a broken mind shattered by the demon lord's machinations. Her body was no longer her own. She was a monster and a slave. Her very existence was agony. She prayed for death as her soul implored the gods for destruction.

Then she pulled herself together. Focusing her thoughts and concentration back to her own identity, she severed the connection with the spirit. She attempted to withdraw, but the dead surrounded her, barring her escape. The grorg's ghost rematerialized. He whispered to her. A chorus of thoughts and images projected onto her consciousness.

As her companions watched, the chanting stopped. Xanaphia stumbled and collapsed, the head fell from her hands and rolled across the floor. Darien and Cyril ran forward. She held up a hand to ward their advance. They stopped, staring at her.

She pushed herself to her feet. She staggered and found she couldn't stand. Twisting her left hand, she made an arcane gesture. The air thickened around her fingers, materializing into a wooden staff. She grabbed the walking stick with both hands and leaned against it for support, gasping for breath.

"Are you okay?" Cyril asked.

"The spell . . ." she said, straining to speak. "Not go . . . as planned . . . But I . . . found answer . . . glass case . . . can't . . . broken . . . only opened . . . enchanted word . . .' Gospodstvo.'"

Darien hesitated. She could tell he was concerned. Though Darien possessed no interest in necromancy, they had studied under the same teacher at the academy. He understood the dangers of interacting with the dead, especially if one possessed many enemies who might linger as vengeful spirits. She tried not to look at him, hoping he couldn't see in her eyes what she had experienced during her trek into the afterlife.

Darien turned and strolled to the cabinet. Holding out his hand out, he spoke, "Gospodstvo."

The glass case became blurry as though viewed through hazy water and vanished like ice melting on a hot day. Nothing remained but the tiara suspended in air. Darien snatched the jewel in his fist.

"Who's going to carry it?" Cyril asked, glancing from Darien to Xanaphia, as though expecting a battle.

"Let him have it," Xanaphia answered, gesturing toward Darien.

Darien looked at her in surprise. Although neither had discussed or acknowledged it, the battle at Southgrain shook them both. Their temporary alliance against the ice dragons and their occasional teamwork throughout the expedition had softened their animosity toward each other. Darien seemed to respect her for saving the children. Xanaphia felt appreciation for his support after the battle.

Still, little love was lost in the relationship, and Darien was not expecting her to relinquish control of the tiara so easily. Darien stared at her with obvious concern. He seemed legitimately worried about her wellbeing. On top of the unsettling confrontation with the spirits, this was too much for her. The confusing influx of emotions made her temper flare.

"Xanaphia," Cyril said. "We must leave. Are you . . ."

"I'm fine," she snapped. She forced herself upright.

Anger gave her power. She became great by burying her weaknesses and frailties. She would do the same now. Raising her head in a gesture of strength and defiance, she called out, "Let's go."

She shambled toward the door still leaning on the walking stick. Their mission was complete. The crown was theirs. She wondered if Clement and Lillian were faring as well.

Sylvia's chest rose and fell in a steady rhythm. The nightmares were over, but her lips still muttered incoherent words, and sweat rolled off her face. One large drop slithered down the center of her forehead, carving a path around her nose and into her eye. Her hand sprang up, brushing away the irritating droplet in a quick, disturbed gesture. The movement aroused the sleeping queen. She opened her eyes. The rough walls and familiar orange glow drew her back to the present. Whatever nightmares might haunt her sleep, the visions paled before her waking horrors.

She sat upright and stared around her prison. Like the perpetual darkness of Junlorace Keep, the unwavering brightness of Kendross Keep provided no means to discern the passage of time. She guessed morning was near at hand. Telling one grorg apart from another was challenging, but she felt confident the two guards flanking her door weren't the ones there when she fell asleep. The morning shift change always preceded Corineous's visits.

An intense foreboding washed over her. She remembered the plan discussed the previous night. She would receive three pills. She attempted to convince herself she could endure. She recalled her children's voices, but they sounded hollow. Instead of giving her strength, they increased her despair.

The chime sounded in the hallway. She looked up expecting to behold the harbinger of her doom. But no one entered. A minute passed. Nobody emerged from the hallway and, as best Sylvia could tell, the corridor remained empty. Did the alarm sound for no reason?

The grorgs appeared equally confused. They glanced at each other and advanced forward to investigate. They didn't get far. Giant stalactites shot downward from the roof while enormous stalagmites sprang upward from the floor. Like an iron maiden, the stone structure sliced into the trapped grorgs, impaling them upon the jagged pikes. Blood excreted from their eyes, ears, and mouths as they hung suspended like food in the jaws of a hungry giant. Then the stalactites and stalagmites melded back into the cave, and the bloody corpses collapsed into lifeless lumps of fur.

Sylvia gave a cry of alarm.

"Who's there?" she asked, staring around in terror. "Are you friend or enemy?"

"Would you believe both?" a male voice echoed against the walls.

Sylvia knew the voice from somewhere, but her mind was too weary to place it. The bitterness and hatred were unmistakable, yet it also contained relief, as though pleased to see her. She could make no sense of it.

"Right now, I'd believe anything," she answered.

Her voice cracked, and she broke into tears. The strain of the last week caught up with her. The shock of the grorgs' deaths coupled with the confusing dilemma of the unknown speaker was too much. She no longer cared if she lived or died. She just wanted it to end.

The door latch clicked, and the bars swung open. Sylvia backed against the wall as a man wrapped in dark-gray robes materialized only feet away. She looked into his face and gasped in astonishment and fear. Towering above her stood Clement the Great.

"Your Majesty," he said.

No amount of formality could conceal his hatred. Like venom, the greeting seeped from his lips, each syllable a cold mockery of the respectful address. Lines of purest loathing formed across his face. She sensed him visualizing a hundred ways of killing her. She knew a flick of his wrist was enough to turn her into mulch. She actually felt relief at the thought.

"Wait," she said. Her hand rose from the depth of her robes. "I don't know how you found me, but I know you're no servant of the demon lord. I beg you, if you have any mercy, if you're even capable of the slightest feeling of compassion, don't gloat. Just kill me and get it over with. Please."

To Sylvia's surprise, his features softened. The bloodthirsty glimmer in his eyes dimmed, and the harsh lines lightened.

"Be at peace, Your Majesty," he said, offering his hand. "You're correct. I'm no servant of the demon lord. Nor am I here to harm you. I'm here to rescue you. I've come to take you to Rhoria."

Her mind spun as she looked at the extended hand. She felt confused but accepted his hand. Clement gave a tug, hoisting Sylvia to her feet. She regarded him with disbelief.

Was this some sort of ploy? It made no sense. Clement was too conceited to serve another being, even the demon lord. He wanted the world for himself and would never accept the position of lackey. Perhaps someone disguised themselves as Clement in an attempt to get the tiara. This didn't make sense either. No one was stupid enough to believe she'd hand the tiara over to Clement faster than the demon lord himself.

Unable to find a reason for deceit, Sylvia was left to accept that her greatest enemy had traveled innumerable miles from the confines of exile in order to save her. She could only guess at his motives.

"Can you walk?" he asked, scanning her weakened condition.

As if in answer, her legs gave out, and she plummeted. Clement darted forward, catching her and hoisting her back up.

"I'm okay," she said. "A healing spell would probably restore my strength."

"Then I recommend you cast one," he said. "We don't have much time."

"I can't," she said, holding out her arms.

Clement looked at the bands.

"Dear gods," he exclaimed, "why in the name of common sense did you attempt to cast a spell with those on?"

"I didn't know what they were, okay?" Sylvia said. She received some encouragement from the frustration in her voice. The renewed hope of escape blooming within her brought a fresh surge of strength. She felt more like herself. "Look, just tell me if you know how to remove them."

"I can and I do," Clement answered. "But you should ready a healing spell. I won't lie to you. It'll hurt a lot."

"Don't talk to me about pain!" It came out more aggressively than intended or called for. "Sorry," she added somewhat bashfully.

"No offense taken," he said. "If you're ready?"

She nodded. Clement extended his hands and swept them down the queen's arms.

"Meeloserdinya!" he said.

Sylvia winced in pain as the bands ripped from her skin and fell to the floor. Her arms were free but not whole. Where the bracers burned through her skin, gaping holes remained. Veins and tendons shone briefly in the orange light before blood gushed over the wounds.

Sylvia muttered her self-healing spells. The blood ceased flowing. The pain stopped as the flesh regenerated. New vibrant skin coated the bones and tissue until not a scar remained. Within a minute, Sylvia's arms were healed.

"Thanks," she said. She rubbed her wrists in relief, overjoyed by the touch of her unfettered skin. "How did you know how to remove them?"

"Are you kidding?" Clement responded. "Sorin used to put those things on me at least once a day."

"I see," Sylvia said. "I have to admit it feels good to cast spells again."

To her surprise, Clement gave her a knowing smile and nodded. Still, he made a point of picking the bracers off the floor and stashing them inside his robes. Sylvia narrowed her eyes at him. He shrugged.

"What?" he asked, unabashed. "I'm saving your life, not applying for sainthood. These might come in useful someday."

Sylvia shook her head. She was under no illusion that Clement had decided to turn his life around and become a hero. Saving her furthered his own ends in some way. Nevertheless, she felt grateful for the help. If he wanted the evil objects, let him have them.

"How did you find me?" Sylvia asked.

"I'll explain later. Time is of the essence. We must find my companions and get out of here."

"Of course," she agreed. "Odevatseeya!"

A golden light encircled her body. It grew thicker, solidifying into a tangible cloth. A hooded woolen robe composed of golden strands manifested around her nightgown. She flipped the hood over her face, happy to escape the chill of the cavern air.

"I'm ready when you are," she said.

Clement nodded. "Good, let's get out of here!"

CHAPTER 20

Lillian wandered down a long hallway. It possessed a different atmosphere than previous tunnels. It seemed stagnant, more alien and barren. Lofty archways lined the corridor, and the roof extended higher to accommodate them. Each was well over ten feet tall. They were sealed by powerful wooden doors devoid of handles or means of entry. Either they were designed to be opened from the inside or not at all.

She paid little attention to them. No sound emanated from the doors. No movement or shuffling reached her ears. She felt no reason to believe they contained anything of interest. Cyril claimed all of the demon lord's treasures were stored in the distant vaults where he led Xanaphia and Darien. Lillian concluded they must be old storage rooms and managed to suppress her innate curiosity.

A thin layer of dust clung to the floor. It showed no signs of being disturbed for many generations. She doubted the path led to the prisons. Still, she remained dutiful to the plan and continued down the hall looking for Sylvia.

At last, she felt a tug in the air around her. Clement had found the queen.

Waving her hand, she dismissed the bonding spell. She immediately regretted doing it, but so far she had encountered no dangers. Further, although her relations with Clement had improved over the last week, she disliked the idea of being magically connected to him.

She started back, intent upon rejoining her companions. Then the noises came. Lillian froze. From behind the doors lining the hall, groans of agony and fury arose. Grotesque voices resounded with the strength of over a thousand throats, causing the whole corridor to vibrate under the weight of their screams.

Lillian backed against the nearest wall. If a multitude of monstrous fiends burst into the corridor, invisibility wouldn't protect her. Levitating into the air or climbing the cavern walls might grant her some reprieve, but even that might not be enough. She braced herself for the impending stampede.

Minutes passed. The doors remained closed. No one emerged from the rooms. The cries grew louder, but the sources of the noise remained sealed behind the large wooden barricades. Lillian extracted herself from the wall and took a tentative step toward the center of the passage, her terror giving way to curiosity. Something dwelt within those rooms, lurking behind the massive doors. They were demons. She felt certain of it.

Her father used to tell stories about them. Before his ambitions corrupted him beyond recognition, he used to sit around the fire with his kids spinning yarns about their sheer might and horrific beauty. They were a timeless testament to the unrivaled genius and unparalleled creativity of the master who forged them. Those were his words. They resounded in her ears now, drawing her back to the corridor.

She longed to see them. True, she had already encountered two, but what were two compared to the thousands filling the chamber? Does a zoologist stop after seeing two animals? Does a sorcerer stop after learning two spells? *Of course not*, she thought.

She only wanted a peak. She swirled her arms clockwise as her body drifted toward the nearest door. A stream of quiet words seeped from her lips as she drew closer. Inside the vortex of her spinning wrists, a small two-dimensional sphere of silver light took form. The flat mercurial surface grew larger as she reached her destination. She guided it onto the smooth oak surface and gazed into its silvery depth.

Images formed upon it like a window into the room beyond. Lillian gasped. A vast boundless chamber stretched ever onward beyond the limits of human vision. She could see no walls, leading her to believe all the doors led into a single room, but what a room.

Every inch of floor was covered by the mountainous forms of colossal demons writhing and squirming like the surface of a scaly ocean. They were too big to fit through the chamber doors. The demon lord must possess some form of magic to send them directly into battle. Lillian guessed these beasts were reserve units, still awaiting the call to combat they never received during the first war.

All manner of hideous beings stirred before her eyes. The shapes and forms were too massive to list, the grotesque appearances too twisted to describe, and the numbers too endless to count. Their presence thrilled Lillian with a terror beyond all words. She backed away from the door, her curiosity ceding to fear.

Like living ooze, the mass of creatures wiggled and thrashed, distorted limbs and deformed faces bobbing up and down like perverted bubbles in a grisly mire. Their gnarled hands clawed at the floor, slipping across the drool leaking from their malformed mouths. Lillian understood what was happening. They were being awoken. The demon lord was activating his horde.

The groans of the groggy demons transformed into wails of pain and repressed lust. They had slept for so long with no blood or sustenance. They were hungry. When they awoke, they would be like ravenous wolves, tearing apart whatever food they could lay their hands on. Food meant humanity!

A tentacle lashed out, striking against the door. It belonged to a strange, amorphous demon that oozed across the ground like a grisly sludge. The eyeless beast seemed to detect her presence and bashed against the wooden barrier, striving to ensnare the living flesh outside its reach. Lillian bumped against the far wall, unable to back any further away.

She stared ahead, and her mouth hung open in a horrified trance. Humanity couldn't hope to stand against these hordes. Perhaps the legendary heroes of the Demon Wars possessed a means to oppose such an army, but their civilization was gone. Whatever means of defense they wielded was lost.

A loud thud behind her caused her to leap away and shriek. The creatures in the rooms behind her apparently sensed her too and were bashing against the doors trying to reach her. Lillian pulled herself together racing away as fast as her legs could run. The demons were waking. The world was doomed.

The shadows of the forest masked Ladonna's movements as she advanced along the city walls. She hugged close to the stone fortifications so no one perched atop the battlements could see her. Thick green brambles and other thorny bushes grew along the base of the town's outer gate, providing cover as she inched around the settlement.

She was about a dozen yards from the tents and pavilions housing the refugees of Junlorace Keep. A number of disguised grorgs patrolled the perimeter. Nimue had likely discovered her escape, and Ladonna presumed her recapture ranked high among the steward's priorities. Ladonna's knowledge of the steward's secrets, not to mention the queen's fate, made her a threat to Nimue's power.

One of the royal guards strolled from the south gate. It turned left, heading straight for Ladonna. She crouched low within the branches, hiding behind the concealment of the leaves and shadows. The soldier passed just a few feet from her, marching along some predetermined perimeter.

Ladonna resisted the urge to leap from the bushes and pounce upon it. The element of surprise and her quick reflexes gave her an advantage, but grorgs were also quick. It might survive long enough to sound an alarm. That would ruin everything.

Ladonna had awoken as soon as the sun peaked over the horizon. After meeting with Alexis, Yeva, and Kaspar to plan their next moves, she headed to find her people. She knew the forces of Junlorace Keep were essential to any hope of breaking Nimue's grip on the town. Further, her soldiers' understanding of grorgs and how to fight them made them invaluable to the resistance.

Few people understood the strengths and weaknesses of grorgs like Ladonna. She had never trusted them. They were dangerous and never missed an opportunity to betray a fellow servant. This made them a threat to her people.

With Cyril's help, she had learned how the creatures moved, the ways they fought, and the nature of their weaknesses. She had developed strategies and tactics to fight them and passed these tactics on to her soldiers. Such training didn't guarantee success, but a trained warrior possessed a better chance than an untrained one. She would soon learn whether the hours of drilling and study would pay off.

Ladonna inched toward the camp. Her greatest challenge would be crossing the final ten meters, a large snowy thoroughfare devoid of trees or bushes. During most of the year, the road served as the principle trade route for merchants bringing goods from the south. As Alexis revealed, caravans ceased arriving after Sylvia's kidnapping. The lack of travelers meant no people passed to and fro to hide her movements. Without any cover, she could only hope her enemies looked the other direction long enough for her to reach the tents without being seen. She didn't like her odds.

Two disguised grorgs wandered the outskirts of the camp. She followed their movements, waiting for an opportunity to dash across the street. Minute after minute passed. No chance appeared. The guards marched and glanced one way and then another with no discernible pattern. They never looked one direction long enough for her to consider crossing the divide.

One of Ladonna's soldiers passed behind them, performing an independent patrol. Ladonna was pleased to see her charges following the orders she left them. She was less than pleased with the choice of guard. The young brunette making the rounds was Amanda. She was one of the keep's smarter soldiers but suffered from discipline problems. Ladonna normally relegated her to stationary guard duties, like watching a certain hall or corridor. Marching the perimeter of a camp provided too many distractions for her wandering mind.

Amanda strolled along: gazing at the sky, watching children play, surveying the castle walls, and doing anything but paying attention to her duties. Ladonna attempted to capture the girl's roving attention, but the effort proved futile. Ladonna may as well wave to a blind man for all the good her gesture achieved.

Ladonna searched the ground for a stone. Finding two rocks of decent size, she waited until the grorgs' heads turned again before chunking the first missile toward Amanda's feet. She reached for the second stone, planning to peg the absent-minded girl square on the forehead if the scatterbrained sentinel failed to respond to the first. Such a course proved unnecessary.

Amanda heard the stone clatter at her feet and looked down to see it roll to a stop. A confused expression crossed her countenance. Her eyes followed the presumed course of the projectile. Ladonna waved a hand before diving back into the bushes as the grorgs turned around. Surprise and recognition spread over Amanda's face, but Ladonna lacked the time to make further gestures.

To Ladonna's surprise, Amanda acted immediately. She wailed in alarm and raced up to Nimue's guards. Displaying an accurate assessment of Ladonna's predicament, Amanda positioned herself on the opposite side of the disguised grorgs.

"My son!" she screamed. "Please, you must help me! He ran off into the woods while my back was turned! Please, you must help me find him!"

The outburst caught Nimue's guards off-balance. Neither seemed to know how to respond. Even greater bewilderment radiated from the faces of the Junlorace refugees. Amanda had no children. After a confused pause, the largest guard ordered Amanda to look for the child on her own, claim their time was too valuable to be distracted over "some brat." The response was quite crude and brought an immediate reaction from Amanda. She flew into frenzy, shrieking every insult her lips could muster and even drawing her weapon.

At this point, she commanded the full attention of not only both grorgs but also her fellow refugees. The entire encampment raced over to sedate the crazed soldier. The mass of townsfolk crowding around the guards hindered visibility. Ladonna broke into a mad dash for the camp. She reached the perimeter unnoticed and dove inside the shelter of an inconspicuous tent close to the city wall.

The commotion outside continued for several more minutes before the refugees managed to subdue Amanda. Ladonna heard them apologize to the steward's guards as they carried the still struggling woman away. Normal activity resumed, although Amanda's strange behavior remained the topic of conversation.

Ladonna watched from the shelter of her hiding place. She couldn't leave. The risk of being spotted was too great, so she remained concealed within the canvas waiting for someone to approach. The first person to do so was an eight-year-old son of one of the kitchen workers. He appeared to be playing hide and seek. He strolled around the perimeter investigating potential hiding places until he stood within a meter of the tent entrance.

Ladonna checked to make sure no one was watching then leapt upon the boy like a trap door spider. Her right hand shot over his mouth, stifling his scream. Her left arm wrapped around his waist, snatching him off the ground. She dove back into the tent, the struggling lad trapped within her clutches. He fought to escape Ladonna's grip, but no mortal possessed the strength to break her grasp. Certainly no child could.

"Calm down," she hissed. "It's me."

The boy's body went rigid. His eyes darted around for his captor. Ladonna leaned forward. She felt him relax as he recognized her.

"There's no time to talk," she said. "I'm sorry to scare you, but I couldn't risk being seen. I need you to find Captain Erik, Commander Gemma, Lieutenant Urith, Sergeant Patwyn, and Corporal Urik. Tell them I'm here and have them come to the tent. No one other than those five must know of my presence. All of our lives depend upon it. Do you understand?"

The boy nodded.

"Good," she said. "Go now, quickly!"

She released the child, and he darted from the tent. Ladonna leaned back against a collection of cloths and waited. Within ten minutes, Captain Erik appeared at the mouth of the tent followed by Urik and Gemma. Finally, Urith and Patwyn arrived for the gathering. They were all surprised. Clearly, they had not taken the boy's message seriously. Nevertheless, he had somehow persuaded them to take a chance. She made a mental note to reward him later.

"I know you have questions," she told her generals. "I'll address them soon. First, I must lay out our current situation. As I do, I believe your questions will be answered."

She explained her capture at the hands at Nimue and their conversation in the prisons. She told them of her rescue and the discovery of the true nature of Nimue's guards. The revelation produced an outburst from her commanders.

"What about the academy?" stout and balding Captain Erik asked. "Surely the sorcerers are powerful enough to defeat the kefling and the grorgs."

"The academy is in lockdown," Ladonna explained. "Nimue dispatched the most powerful wizards to search for the queen. They are dead."

"What about the town guard?" joined Lieutenant Urith, a tall woman with short, layered blonde hair. "Based upon reports, Kendross Keep only contained around two hundred grorgs. Rhoria's militia must outnumber the creatures at least two or three to one."

"Based upon estimates, the steward's forces are approximately one hundred and fifty grorgs strong. The militia numbers around five hundred, but the most skilled warriors were dispatched to search for the queen. Grorgs can bring down as many as three or four human opponents if their enemies lack the proper training."

"So that's where we come in," said Commander Gemma, a middle-aged woman. Her face bore the deep wrinkles and weathering of many harsh winters, but she remained strong and disciplined, if a little rash. "Our force consists of about sixty warriors, but we do have training battling grorgs."

"Untested training," Lieutenant Urith noted. "None of our soldiers possess actual experience battling them. Most are either too young and undisciplined or too old and slow to handle such a skirmish."

"She's right," joined Sergeant Patwyn, a lanky man with long brown hair. "We'd suffer heavy casualties. Surely you don't believe our small force is capable of turning the tide in a battle."

"What is your plan, Commander?" Urik spoke over the other generals. "You wouldn't risk our lives unless completely necessary. I for one trust your judgment in these matters."

His tone was sharp and poignant. Urith and Patwyn both lowered their heads from the rebuke. Ladonna felt a rush of gratitude toward him. She could always rely upon Urik's support.

"The plan," she continued, "involves four parts. First is the preparation. Our contact with the academy is alerting the school to the danger and assigning teachers to research magical glyphs. Darlyth is using some sort of portal to transport troops into Rhoria. We must close the gateway before worse things come through."

At the phrase "worse things," her generals shifted with discomfort. Grorgs were bad enough without fighting demons.

"The second part of the preparations involves the city guard. They're being alerted to the true nature of the steward's soldiers. If the Rhorian militia fights against the enemy believing them to be normal men, they're doomed."

Her generals burst into exclamations and objections, filling the tent with a flood of mingled voices.

"Then a military strike is planned?" burst out Gemma. "When is the attack?"

"I think the move is a mistake," Patwyn cried at the same time. "Knowing the true nature of the enemy will shatter their confidence and morale!"

"I doubt their morale can get that much lower," chided Erik.

"How're they supposed to pass the message on secretly?" Urith interjected. "Once one of the steward's guards hears them relaying the information, everyone is doomed."

"That's their problem," Urik argued. "We can only answer for our part."

"But what is our part?" Urith argued back.

"I can have our entire military ready in an hour!" Gemma declared.

"How are we coordinating with them?" Patwyn asked.

"Enough!" Ladonna's angry voice broke through the den of clamor. Her advisors fell silent. She glared at them, warning them not to speak again until she finished. "The third part involves readying our troops. Grorgs are unpredictable, and I doubt the steward is in control of her army. Our soldiers must be ready at any time for an attack against our camp."

Ladonna scanned the faces of her advisors. Fear shown in their eyes. Her soldiers would be even more frightened. There was nothing she could do about it.

"Step two begins tonight," Ladonna continued. "Due to certain pressures applied to Alexis by one of her officers, I'm accompanying her on a mission to lead a rescue party.

The steward is conducting experiments on prisoners with the intention of breeding an army of half-demons. We'll free the captives before they can be subjected to further testing. I'm not in agreement with this part of the plan."

She suspected the last statement was unnecessary. Her tone made her feelings clear. The maneuver offered little upside and risked alerting the guards to the impending uprising.

Ladonna thought back to the morning conversation. Kaspar had refused to take any action against the steward unless they saved his sister first. Alexis, Ladonna, and Yeva had attempted to persuade him otherwise to no avail. He argued Nimue might use his sister as a bargaining chip, thereby compromising his loyalty. His demand was foolish and might doom their entire mission, but they needed his help.

"The third part involves a raid on the palace," Ladonna continued. "Around midnight, Alexis, Yeva, I, and a collection of researchers from the academy will enter the palace through a secret passage in the dungeon. We'll ascend to the queen's room, destroy the demon lord's gateway, and escape. This will cut off potential reinforcements.

"The fourth step will be an all-out uprising against the steward. At sunrise tomorrow, the town militia will lead a surprise attack against the steward's guards. We plan to position our soldiers to overwhelm grorgs stationed at guard outposts or in the street. They'll slay as many as they can then join us at the village commons. Together, we'll lead a full-scale attack on the palace. We'll overthrow the guards or die trying. Hopefully, the former."

"So you're raiding a prison this evening, storming a castle tonight, and leading a full-scale assault in the morning," Erik repeated, smiling ruefully. "Are you planning to get any sleep during the campaign?"

"Yes," Ladonna said. "I'll take a nap after our meeting. Wake me in a couple of hours. In the meantime, prepare our troops for battle. Oh, and give my thanks to Amanda for the distraction she provided."

"Thank goodness," Patwyn sighed. "I'm glad to hear she was providing a distraction. I thought she'd genuinely lost it."

Ladonna laughed. The sensation felt strange.

"I'd like to accompany you on the mission," Gemma said.

"I thought you would," Ladonna replied. "I appreciate your offer. You may come with me."

"I'd like to come also," Urik volunteered, but Ladonna shook her head.

"No, I can spare one general but not more," she said. "I need the rest of you here to lead our troops. But you can assist me by selecting two of our fastest soldiers to accompany me. They'll provide a means to communicate should anything unexpected occur."

"Very well," Urik responded. "I'll select our best scouts."

"Very good," Ladonna answered. "Dismissed."

CHAPTER

21

Corineous enjoyed the cool crisp air as he strode across the ruins of Kendross Keep. The sun cresting over the tall mountains cast golden rays of morning light across his handsome face. He lifted his head in ecstasy, soaking in the warm radiance. His morning stroll through the ruined fortress remained the best part of his day.

He loathed the confines of the underground maze. He was born and raised in the wide open spaces and vast skies of the Northland. His heart longed to hike lush forests or soar among the clouds. The stagnant chambers of Darlyth's halls were no place for someone like him.

His long blue robes drifted behind him as he traversed the snowy ground. Resting inside a small pocket were the three white pills. Corineous hoped today would herald Sylvia's demise. He grew weary of waiting and disliked being surrounded by grorgs and their ugly hairy bodies. He appreciated the finer things in life. Elegant surroundings, fine food, and beautiful women, these were the things with which he filled his life.

Almost a week of traveling through rugged wastelands devoid of his standard creature comforts proved distasteful to his refined senses. He longed for Darlyth's rise, when Corineous could surround himself with all the extravagant pleasures he desired.

Reaching the stairs to the ruined temple, Corineous bounded up them. He took one last breath of morning air before strolling toward the mouth of the cavern. Upon gaining the entrance, he hesitated. Something was wrong. Where were the guards?

He scanned the platform. Grorgs never abandoned their posts. Whether because of fear or a curse similar to keflings, they adhered to their master's orders. He knew better than to believe Darlyth decided to leave his cave unguarded.

Corineous strolled around the temple looking for the sentries. They were neither on the platform nor anywhere around the shattered foundation. There were no bodies, no blood, nor any other signs of violence. Perhaps, they had strolled into the main body of the fortress on some errand.

Reluctant to enter the cave before solving the mystery, Corineous retraced his earlier steps to the front of the temple. Gazing downward, he observed a line of footsteps trailing across the snow. He hadn't noticed them earlier. They didn't belong to grorgs. They were human tracks, and there was more than one. Multiple sets of booted feet left a thick trail in the icy ground leading straight to the weathered staircase.

Someone had come for the queen. They had arrived ahead of him, destroyed the grorgs before entering the catacombs, and possessed the foresight to dispose of the bodies. Who were they? They weren't one of the queen's search parties. They were dead. Even if one had survived, they couldn't trace Sylvia here nor defeat a pair of grorgs.

The perpetrators must be someone else. He racked his brain for an answer. It must be someone aware of the queen's disappearance, powerful enough to kill two grorgs before they could sound the alarm, and skilled enough to use spells capable of obliterating a body and all traces of the remains. Few possessed those capabilities.

With an unpleasant jolt, Corineous realized the truth. The infiltrator was his former mentor and regent, Darien the Dark. The inference seemed preposterous, but no other solution fit. Darien knew about the queen's disappearance. He was also familiar with both the symbol for Junlorace Keep and the location of the fortress. His former master possessed the power to vanquish a pair of grorgs, and he knew spells to dispose of the bodies. Somehow Darien had traced the queen from Junlorace Keep to Kendross Keep.

But why? Everyone knew Darien possessed a heightened sense of vengeance. Once someone wronged him, he stopped at nothing to get revenge. Still, Corineous couldn't imagine Darien embarking on a weeklong journey through rugged terrain in the middle of winter just to kill the empress. An unpleasant thought drifted through his troubled mind. What if Darien didn't come for Sylvia? What if Darien came for him?

The murderous expression on his former master's face during the confrontation in Rhoria flashed across Corineous's mind. He felt a sudden impulse to flee but pulled himself together. Corineous was caught by surprise last time. This time would be different. Darien was out of his element, walking into a maze filled with dangerous traps and monstrous grorgs. This time, Corineous had the advantage.

He smiled and raced to the cavern entrance. Reaching the arch in the cliff wall, he touched the top declaring, "Trevosheet."

The word triggered the magical alarm set upon the door. A loud, high-pitched wailing filled the catacombs. Darien would never escape. Corineous would see to that personally.

Deep inside the underground complex, Cyril, Darien, and Xanaphia froze as the corridor burst into howls.

"What is happening?" Darien asked.

"The alarm!" Cyril cried. "They know we're here. Run!"

Darien burst into a sprint. Xanaphia took off behind him but only made a few steps before collapsing. Darien turned to help her, but Cyril waved him onward. The kefling raced up beside her, scooped her into the air like a pillow, and flashed ahead of Darien. Cyril reappeared at the end of the corridor, waiting for him to catch up.

"Why not just rush her up to the surface?" Darien yelled, as he hurried up beside him.

"It's too risky," he answered. "I can't leave her up there alone. There might be grorgs, Corineous, and who knows what else. I'd rather you two stick together if possible."

The sirens continued blaring. Darien ran alongside Cyril. The kefling had slowed to a normal pace, since his bursts of speed seemed to disorient Xanaphia. Darien wondered how much longer Cyril could hold her. She didn't weigh much, but Cyril needed to leave soon to trap the demon lord. If the demon lord attacked before they were ready, everything would be lost.

Up ahead, a small black scribble etched on the wall indicated the proper route through the cavern. As they prepared to turn down the new corridor, a sound of rushing feet and heavy breathing assaulted their ears. The noises came from somewhere behind them. Cyril placed Xanaphia down on her feet.

"Keep going," he commanded. "I'll deal with the grorgs."

Cyril vanished, and Darien, disinclined to argue with him, followed Xanaphia into the new hallway. Xanaphia was moving better after ten minutes of being carried, and Darien hurried to catch up with her. The passage was a long one lined with innumerable smaller passages breaking off in different directions. Darien was only a few strides down the hallway, still trailing Xanaphia, when about half-a-dozen grorgs burst from a passage ahead.

"Step aside," Darien warned, raising his arms. "Sheguyt!"

Xanaphia leapt sideways into the shelter of a nearby passage as a massive ball of flame burst down the hall. The rolling ball charged ahead, taking up the entire corridor. There was nowhere to run. The grorgs survived just long enough to shriek in alarm as it passed through them.

At the same time, a loud scream issued from the passage where Xanaphia sought refuge.

"Xanaphia," Darien called in alarm, racing into the corridor.

The passage was silent and empty. He soon discovered why. No sooner did he step into the hall then the illusory floor gave way beneath him. With a gasp of surprise, he plummeted downward, frantically trying to grab a handhold.

A powerful hand seized his wrist. Cyril had returned. He hoisted Darien from the trap's hungry jaws, depositing him onto solid ground. Darien crawled backward in astonishment.

"Are you all right?" Cyril asked. "Where is Xanaphia?"

Nothing escaped Darien's mouth as he stared in stunned disbelief down the vacant corridor. Cyril nodded in understanding. A dark but determined expression fluttered across his face.

"I know where the pit trap leads," he said, the fire in his eyes burning with fresh intensity. "If Xanaphia is still alive, I'll rescue her."

Darien could only nod. Cyril reached out his hand and hoisted him from the floor. The enchanter dusted off his robes, regaining his composer and wits.

"Good Luck, Darien," Cyril said.

There was a hint of finality in his words. Darien understood. Cyril was saying goodbye.

Darien looked into other's face. Cyril stood calm, determined, and unafraid, his eyes burning with enthusiasm. Darien marveled at Cyril's resolve and gave a sad smile.

"Goodbye, Cyril," Darien said, extending a hand. "You taught me a lesson I will not forget."

Cyril took Darien's hand and gave a firm shake. Then he vanished in a blur of movement. Darien turned back down the corridor and raced to join his companions.

Xanaphia plummeted through the air for what felt like many miles. Caught in a free fall, she plunged downward, her black robes whipping above her head. She careened toward a distant orange surface covered with strange shapes. At first, she thought they were drawings. As she got closer, she realized they were an ocean of spikes issuing from the ground below. *So crude*, she thought contemptuously.

"Podneemeetez," she said.

Xanaphia's body slowed until she came to a smooth stop, floating upright just inches above the five-foot-tall stalagmites. She grinned at the pikes so rudely denied their victim before glancing around. To the left, the forest of needles extended for untold miles. The same held true behind her.

In front of her though, they ended after only about a hundred yards where a tall orange wall provided the nearest boundary. To her right, another break in the jungle of spears was only about fifty yards away in the form of a large circular platform with a nearby door. She proceeded that way.

As she walked, she reflected on her strange encounter in the spirit world. The dead spirit of the former guardian of Kendross Keep assaulted her brutally but not maliciously. He had inflicted upon her exposed consciousness the same tortures his living counterpart suffered at the hands of the demon lord. But he didn't do so out of spite or malevolence. Rather, the umbral beings haunting the land of the dead wanted her to experience the same tortures she had inflicted upon so many innocent people.

During her reign of terror in the Southlands, she wreaked havoc upon her enemies by transforming their still-living apprentices and friends into undead. Just like the grorgs, their shattered minds became trapped inside twisted bodies no longer responsive to their desires and commands.

The remnants of these deceased souls, wishing to subject her to the same agony, employed the grorg's spirit as a means of scolding her. They wanted to teach her, to instruct her, and to help her understand. They relayed many strange and baffling words to her afterward. These messages affected her even more than the physical suffering. She repeated them over and over in her mind, trying to make sense of the cryptic but ominous warnings. Finally, she gave up and returned her attention to the present.

She found the layout of the room quite bizarre. The platform rested like an island in the middle of the endless sea of stalagmites that continued for countless miles in all directions save one. Gaining the plateau, she noticed a long thin stone runway leading from the terrace to a large open wooden door in the nearby wall. The avenue resembled a sort of runner, stretching from the entryway to the dais.

Her eyes followed the course of the walkway from the door to the scaffold and continued tracing the trail all the way to the large circular plateau behind her. Her breath caught in her throat, and goosebumps sprang to life along her pale skin.

A forbidding archway of smooth jet stone stretched almost fifteen feet into the air. It possessed a strange otherworldly darkness that eliminated visibility inside. The absence of any discernible light gave the impression of a vast dark depth spreading forever into the unknown. She wondered how she had missed seeing the structure until now. She guessed some sort of ancient magic rendered it invisible to anyone not standing directly in front.

She didn't need to guess the source of such magic. The setup resembled a sort of stygian throne room. Only one person sat upon such a throne. She needed to get out of there and fast. She turned and took several hurried steps toward the door.

"Xanaphia."

A deep, bellowing voice spoke the name in a slow drone. It pronounced each syllable as an independent word, the last "uh" drawn out until the low vibrations faded into a distant hiss. The sound of her name sent chills up her spine. It intruded upon her thoughts, filling her brain with visions of fearsome shades whispering ghoulish messages as they drifted before her inner eyes.

"He sees you," they taunted. "He hears your thoughts. He knows your mind. He feels your fears. He senses your secrets. You can't run from him. You can't hide from him. You're nothing to him."

Xanaphia froze. Fear beyond anything she had ever felt or imagined seized her body. She stood spellbound within the inescapable grip of terrors that numbed her mind and paralyzed her senses. She couldn't move, couldn't think, and couldn't even turn around to face her captor. She didn't need to.

Like a living ballerina imprisoned upon the spindle of some wicked music box, her rigid body drifted around to face the dark archway. From within the endless void of blackness filling the ancient mound, two bright red balls of swirling fire gleamed against the dark background. The eyes rose until they almost touched the pinnacle of the stone arch. Taking a step forward, their master emerged from the confines of his lightless throne.

Xanaphia's breath froze in her lungs as her mouth dropped open in awe. The combination of all her most lurid nightmares never formed such a beast. All the maddest musings of all the maddest necromancers could never even design a creature so grotesque. From the persimmon skin oozing puss to the grotesque batty wings, from the six deformed arms to the flames burning in his eyes fifteen feet above her, his every oversized feature was hideous beyond the power of words to even describe.

The horrid appearance would've been frightening even if Xanaphia didn't know who it was. But she possessed no doubt about his identity. She stood before the hellish fiend whose diabolical schemes had brought about the destruction of the greatest age of humanity. She stood before the one whose evil inspired the trip from Rhoria and whose plans for the future Xanaphia beheld in her nightmares. Darlyth, the immortal, near omnipotent, ruler of the demons loomed above her.

Every fiber of her being screamed to run, but she remained frozen, transfixed by the magical fear engulfing her mind.

"Xanaphia," the deep monotonous drone rang out again. "I've been waiting for you."

"How do you know my name?" she stammered through the flood of emotions strangling her mind. At least she thought she did. She couldn't tell if she uttered them or merely thought them. Either way, he responded.

"Long have I watched you," he hissed. "Long have I watched your companions. I'm impressed by you. You remind me of bygone days. You remind me of my youth. The great mages of my age possessed incredible powers. They possessed the skills to use those powers to perform extraordinary tasks. You too possess astonishing powers, but you lack the spells of the ancients. If you only possessed the same spells, you would be their equals. But they have passed from history. Their knowledge and magic are lost forever.

The secrets of their power now lie solely with me. Only I remain to pass on their teachings."

Darlyth's slow, repetitive speech rolled from his tongue. Xanaphia fought to resist his mesmerizing influence as images of great magic and ancient secrets flashed before her dazzled mind. The visions beckoned to her.

"I can give them to you," he cooed. "I can even heal the poison in your veins."

A new vision swam before her. She was standing on a mountaintop beside a clear pool of water. An aura of power drifted around her so great it was almost tangible. She possessed powers and spells greater than the greatest sorcerers. She was mightier than Darien, mightier than Clement, mightier than even Sylvia with her tiara. No rival could touch her might.

She looked down at her reflection in the water. Her skin no longer bore its sickly pale appearance. Her complexion was vibrant and natural. Even her eyes had return to their true shade. The emerald, green orbs sparkled in the rays of the dawn. It was a new life of health and unthinkable power. Her dreams could all come true. She could be whole again.

A strange compulsion gripped her with the promise of tantalizing secrets and ancient might. She desired the humanity stolen by years of magical transformations and yearned to no longer fear looking in a mirror. No longer would she be repulsed by her own complexion or need to hide behind the illusions of her cloak. Her days as an outcast from human society would be gone forever.

But so would human society. The thought leapt into her mind, drawing her from the precipice of acquiescence. The sensations impressed upon her tortured mind by the grorg's dead spirit returned. So too came the haunting visions terrorizing her sleep. Could she doom humankind to such an abysmal fate? The face of the young girl she saved in Southgrain returned to her. The child's sweet expression manifested before her eyes, and she heard the soft voice saying, "Thank you."

A battle raged within her. What did she care if people suffered? She didn't owe anything to the world. On the other hand, neither did Cyril. Yet he was sacrificing everything for them. Of course, he could make any sacrifice he wanted. Just because he planned to do the right thing didn't mean she needed to follow his example.

Working with the demon lord seemed natural. She and Darlyth possessed much in common. They both distrusted humans, both delighted in filling the world with their creations. The horrific acts he performed on the guardian of Kendross Keep disgusted her, but who was she to judge him? She'd done the same thing to many others.

But she refused to do so any longer. She now knew the gruesome nature of such cruel transformations. After her experience in the spirit world, how could she continue unleashing such torments upon others? The spirits of the dead remembered their suffering. They'd repay her cruelty in kind when she joined them. Of course, she didn't need to join them. The demon lord and his minions possessed immortality. Perhaps she could live forever.

The idea made Xanaphia want to laugh. Who wanted an immortality of being alone and friendless? She never wished to live forever. She'd spent her life feeling alienated and forlorn. She was tired of it. Perhaps the reason she joined the search for Sylvia had nothing to do with revenge. Maybe she wanted to be part of a group. What if her decision to save the children in Southgrain came from a desire to do something meaningful for once?

And she had. For the first time she could remember, she felt a part of something worthwhile. Darien, her mortal enemy, treated her with respect and compassion. She chatted and joked with Clement and Lillian. Even the simple words of thanks given by the little girl in Southgrain seemed sweeter than all the empty flattery of her ambitious advisors. Could she throw it all away now?

"No," Xanaphia said. She broke free of the voices and visions. She still couldn't move, but she could speak. "I'll never serve you. I'd rather die opposing you than rule the world as your slave."

Darlyth's countenance grew dark. Like the flip of a switch, he transformed from coaxing tempter to enraged beast. The flames in his eyes ignited into massive bonfires sending black billowing clouds of smoke overhead. He puffed his chest in fury and lifted his arms into the air. Bright orange flames surged to life around his massive hands.

"Very well," Darlyth said, his voice dark and menacing. "If you wish for death, you may have it. Die if you want to!"

He flung his arms forward. The flames surged across the ground like a mobile inferno seeking to consume their victim. Xanaphia could only watch as they sped through the air to engulf her. She was going to die.

Then everything became blurry. Xanaphia was flung onto the ground, bouncing against the hard stone floor. Able to move again, she discovered she sat in a corridor just outside the demon lord's chamber. A mushroom cloud of flames surged upward from where she'd stood only a moment before.

Above her in the doorway loomed Cyril Junlorace. For a second, they gazed at each other. Cyril's eyes burned bright with the same feverish excitement she witnessed in the demon lord's face. His countenance bore a confident, haughty expression like the day he first approached them in the forests. A smug smile decorated his thin lips. For half a second, he stood above her, proud and majestic. Then the door slammed. A latch clicked. Cyril was gone.

Xanaphia rose to her feet, trembling from the dreadful encounter and her parting glimpse of the man who saved her life. She did the only thing her numb brain permitted. She turned around and ran.

Cyril gave his adversary no time to foil his plans. He whipped away from the door onto the podium in the center of the room. Flinging his hand forward, he shouted, "Zakvateet!"

A burst of white light erupted from his hand. A blazing dome of hazy energy enclosed the ancient podium and its dark inhabitant. Swirling veins of thin white lightning snaked across the surface, distorting Cyril's view of the monster within. A pulsing string of fluorescent energy connected the stone to the barrier looming no more than a few inches from the tip of his knuckles.

Standing before his sovereign, he braced himself for his master's angry reaction. Cyril couldn't imagine the pain he'd soon endure. He feared the shock of bursting into flames might cause him to drop the Life Stone in his left hand or the fragment in his right. Determined not to release either, he steeled himself for the inevitable destruction awaiting him.

Nothing happened. Darlyth stood inside the cage, smiling down on his young commander. What was he playing at? Cyril had used his unnatural speed to scout out the room while his master tempted Xanaphia. There were no other demons in the chamber. The door was locked with a latch only Darlyth could open. The demon lord could send no telepathic communications or orders to his minions. He was trapped. Nevertheless, he seemed undisturbed. Had Cyril overlooked some obvious flaw?

"My child, I've been expecting you," Darlyth said. "Indeed, your arrival is long awaited."

The fire in Darlyth's eyes dimmed as his wrath subsided. The cruel harsh tones faded back into a mesmerizing coo. The long lips curled into a sly smile, showing his many rows of fangs.

"You've always been clever and resolute," he said. "That's why I gave you command of my forces. Your craftiness and determination inspired me to award you the highest military rank of my entire army. You remind me of Redault. Even you must notice the similarities. He was strong, brave, and enterprising. He was like a son to me. You possess the same combination of strength, courage, and ingenuity. I view you like my own child. I knew of your plan and allowed you to enact it to see if you'd succeed. I tested your mettle to see your true strength."

Doubt grew in Cyril's mind. Did the demon lord know his plans the entire time? Were all his actions merely playing into his master's web of intrigue? Darlyth seemed to sense his growing unease.

"Yes," he hissed. "You give yourself too much credit. Like my minion inside Rhoria, you're overconfident. She'll be dealt with soon. Her fate is already sealed. But I wish to talk about you. You're the one I must deal with. Your plan is already doomed. It will not succeed. You hold me imprisoned, but I hold Ladonna. She's trapped, just as I am."

Cyril tried to hide his shock, but Darlyth clearly noticed his expression.

"She won't come to the rescue of your friends before I overtake them," Darlyth continued. "I shall recapture your companions and the queen prior to their arrival in Rhoria. Even if I fail to overtake them, there'll be no Rhoria by the time they return. It will be destroyed long before they arrive. I'm already awakening my hordes. They're rousing from their sleep as we speak. My minions will be fully awake by tomorrow night and at complete strength. I've already given them their orders. They know what actions to take upon waking. Tomorrow night, the portal in their room will activate. They'll enter the city through the queen's bedchamber. Each shall step into the glyph and enter the queen's palace. The city will fall. Rhoria will be destroyed."

Cyril fought to control his overwhelming sense of doom. He possessed no way of warning his companions. His thoughts went to Ladonna. She sat imprisoned in the city. The famished legions wouldn't hesitate to devour her along with the rest of Junlorace's citizens. Despair and defeat hung in front of his eyes.

"Of course, the demons are only the second wave," Darlyth continued. "The preliminary strike begins tonight. As darkness settles upon the city, the first steps will set themselves in motion. My hordes shall finish the destruction the following night. My army shall devour the city. Of course, your people could be spared. I could grant mercy to Ladonna and your citizens, but I can't do so if I'm unable to communicate with my troops. If I'm trapped in here, no one can save them.

"Repent of your betrayal, my child. Throw down the stone and atone for your error. You'll be punished. Traitorous actions must meet reproof. But your people will be exonerated. Their safety ensured. Ladonna will be liberated. Her favor restored."

Cyril hesitated. He owed a responsibility to his people. He remained their lord and Ladonna his love. They trusted him. Now, his foolhardy attempt to thwart Darlyth had doomed them all. The demon lord didn't lie. Being accountable to no one except himself and being powerful enough to do anything he wanted, he possessed no need to take such actions. If Darlyth agreed to free Ladonna and protect Cyril's people, he would keep his word.

Cyril berated himself. He never considered the possibility of Darlyth continuing to use the portal to send troops into the city. His careless neglect of such an obvious course of action proved a disastrous blunder. Xanaphia and her companions faced the certainty of capture. Even if they didn't, they possessed no other safe haven to flee with Rhoria in ruins.

The battle for the world was over before it even began. Cyril had failed to save humankind, but he could save his people. His eyes drifted to his hand, where the last fragment of the ancient orb emitted the final traces of legendary magic. When he released the stone, Darlyth would destroy it. The magic his ancestors defended for so many generations would be lost forever.

A fresh wave of courage surged inside him. He was the last heir of the historic line of Junlorace. His ancestors had battled demons, erected fortresses, and taken oaths to defend humanity for as long as their line endured, and he would remain true to that oath and his legacy. His face rose in defiance toward his master.

He couldn't guarantee his action would produce the result he wanted. But, as he had said, a person must do what is right because its right regardless of the consequences. Besides, he still possessed one advantage. He had told his companions to convince Sylvia to destroy the tiara.

Darlyth would never destroy such a powerful object. He certainly didn't believe anyone else would destroy it either. At least he could still thwart Darlyth in one small way. As long as he could claim one victory, he'd never relent.

"No," Cyril responded.

He started to say something else, but never managed. Like the head of a match struck against a rough surface, he burst into flames. The suddenness almost caused him to release the stones, but he maintained his grip.

He crumpled to the floor, writhing in agony. Every muscle in his flaming body twitched and convulsed. He tossed and turned under the intense torture of the fires erupting from him. Searing smoke filled his throat and stifled his screams. Like a living furnace, he jerked and thrashed. The smell of his own charred flesh assaulted his nostrils as he struggled to breathe with his baking lungs. Yet, the Life Stone's magic persevered. The lord of Junlorace Keep didn't die. His organs and flesh regenerated as quickly as fire burned them.

The Life Stone made the pain no more bearable, but at least it kept him alive. He possessed no time for any kind of complex thought. He focused all his attention on the idea of not releasing the stones. For the next few days, even after Cyril's brilliant mind shattered under the impact of incessant suffering, unquenchable thirst and insufficient sleep, the thought of maintaining his grip upon the stones endured. Like a mad man, obsessed with the object of his crazed desire, his determination to hold the stones became the only concept he understood and his last thought.

CHAPTER

22

Sylvia watched Clement stamp around the corridor.

"Where is she?" he fumed, kicking the ground in anger.

He seemed worried about some missing companion. This surprised Sylvia, who realized she knew very little about him. Her husband had rarely spoken about him, so most of her knowledge came from secondary sources. But freed prisoners and rebel leaders could hardly be expected to provide a neutral perspective. Aside from seeing him around the school a few times, her only firsthand experience came during their legendary battle. They were too preoccupied trying to kill each other to talk.

She questioned everything she knew about him. She saw the look of compassion and pity cross his face at the sight of her plight. Now he showed signs of genuine concern about another person. She had never expected to see such emotions in the man she once considered the evilest villain alive. She also found herself appreciating his pride, which would never allow him to submit to a life of servitude. To her surprise, she realized there were few living wizards who she'd rather be with right now.

Sylvia looked around. A corridor ran left, another ran right, and a third stretched behind them leading back to the prisons. Clement seemed preoccupied with the right passage. He stared down the hall, refusing to move from their current position.

Around the corner of the hall and racing at top speed toward the intersection, appeared a white robed figure with long blonde hair. Thick beads of sweat coated her face as she sped along the corridor, her breaths coming in short gasps. As she reached Clement, she came to a stop, grabbing her chest and panting.

"Lillian?" Sylvia exclaimed in disbelief, looking from Clement to the sorceress and back again.

She hadn't asked Clement who they were waiting for, but the last person she expected to see was Lillian. The animosity between her and Clement left the entire western half of Aurba in ruins. Sylvia's relationship with the spymaster was equally unstable. The antagonism between the two was so fierce Sylvia had fled the city after Lillian took the throne.

Clement rescuing her was strange enough. Lillian coming to her rescue was even more bizarre. Both of them working together to save her was ludicrous.

"Sylvia," Lillian acknowledged, still panting.

"Where've you been?" exclaimed Clement.

"In panic... took a.... wrong turn..." Lillian gasped. She straightened up, still panting, and gave a nod.

Together, they raced down the hallway. For almost ten minutes they ran. Sylvia didn't know where they were going, but Clement seemed confident in his sense of direction. He charged ahead. Sylvia struggled to keep pace, still weak from days of torture and malnutrition. Clement slowed down every few minutes to give her time to catch up.

They were almost to the end of a second corridor when the enemy caught them. Almost two dozen armed grorgs dashed around a corner just fifty yards ahead. Sweat gleamed off their fur and swords flashed in their hands. They were ready for battle.

Sylvia spotted Corineous following behind them. He froze mid-stride, his eyes wide and afraid as he took in the scene. Only fifty yards away stood a trio of the most formidable sorcerers of the modern age. Sylvia, the empress of Rhoria, free from the imprisoning influence of the bracers, Lillian, the former regent of Rhoria and former headmaster of the Magical Academy, and Clement the Great, perhaps the most powerful wizard of the modern era. He seemed to know how the battle would turn out. Abandoning the monsters to their fate, he raced back down the hall at top speed.

The grorgs charged ahead with reckless abandon. They galloped ahead in rows of three, a formidable force almost eight ranks deep. Sylvia saw Clement wave his hands as though attempting to activate the walls the way he killed her guards. Nothing happened. Whatever spell he employed earlier had expired. Sylvia covered for the oversight.

"Zemliya!" she shouted, summoning her magic.

A shower of sharp earthen spikes sprang from the ground, colliding into the first row of beasts. Like soaring daggers, they impaled the brutes, stabbing through the thick hides and plowing them backward into the second row of attackers. The spell did little physical damage to the second row, but the impact of their own comrades falling against them slowed the force of their charge. The third rank of grorgs sprang over the first two.

"Oodar," Lillian called, flicking her wrist as though slapping the air with the back of her hand.

The third rank was caught in midair and knocked backward by the blow. They collided with the fourth row of attackers, who were also preparing to leap their fallen allies. Clement, meanwhile, had recovered from the loss of his stone-shaping spell. Dashing toward the foremost rank of fallen grorgs, he slid across the dusty ground until he knelt at their feet. As the third row collided with the fourth, and the second row sought to shrug off the first row, Clement grabbed the legs of two fallen creatures before him.

"Fakel," he said.

The hair of the two beasts burst into flames, filling the hall with billowing smoke. In the same motion, Clement thrust his palms outward calling, "Poreev!"

As though blown by a fierce wind, the fires expanded down the hallway, encircling the remaining grorgs. Clement made a double slashing motion with his outstretched hands.

"Zola," he said. The fires died and the smoke vanished. The corridor was empty. Nothing remained in the hall except piles of ashes. Clement rose to his feet, towering over the remains of his adversaries.

"Nice combination!" Lillian marveled.

Sylvia nodded, stunned. Fakel was a simple enchantment that could only be cast upon dead bodies for the purposes of cremation. Poreev was an incantation for summoning gusts of wind. Zola was a spell for speeding up the completion of an already cast enchantment. None of them required expending much energy to cast, and none of them were very useful.

Used in combination, Clement had turned them into a single deadly attack. First, he created cremation flames. Next, he spread them to touch the living members of an army. Last, Zola caused the cremation to take place instantaneously. In less than a second, he had wiped out an entire opposing force without needing to expend hardly any energy. Sylvia could only marvel.

"Remind me how I defeated you," she said.

Sylvia immediately recognized the inappropriateness of her statement. She looked at Clement, who gave her a withering look.

"The tiara," he answered.

The response stung her like a whip. For the last week, her entire life had revolved around the crown. She'd forgotten its powers weren't common knowledge. She now realized the danger of her longtime enemies knowing her greatest weakness.

"Was that the high mage I saw fleeing down the hall?" Lillian asked.

"Corineous!" Sylvia hissed.

Hatred and rage washed Clement from her mind. She sprinted down the hall and around the corner after her former general. Clement and Lillian ran after her.

Corineous possessed a head start and was more rested than his pursuers. Sylvia charged after him but couldn't gain ground on her fleeing adversary. Behind her, Clement and Lillian fired spells at him, but he was too far away for them to launch an effective assault.

A short way ahead, a corridor led to the left. If he beat them to the turn, she knew they'd never catch him. He knew the corridors better than they did. He could lead them into a trap or else disappear and bide his time for revenge. Sylvia felt confident he'd already planned his escape. He looked over his shoulders at her, an evil glint shining in his eyes as he disappeared around the corner.

"Ostanavleevat!"

The high mage was thrown from the corridor and slammed against the wall. There he hung suspended and helpless, pinned against the rough orange surface.

Emerging from the hall, his hand held outward, fingers level with Corineous's eyes stood the powerful, green-robed form of Darien the Dark. He was drenched in sweat. His hair was matted against his face. Darien's clothes were soaked, but he smiled with an almost maniacal ecstasy, like all his dreams had come true. He took slow triumphant steps toward Corineous, his eyes gleaming with a ruthless hunger.

"Corineous," he hissed, "I have missed you. You cannot imagine how glad I am to see you. But please, allow me to demonstrate."

"Wait!" Sylvia screamed, reaching the intersection.

Stopping next to Corineous, she leaned forward against the wall, trying to catch her breath. Lillian and Clement came to a stop behind her. She looked up at Darien as she panted, her bewildered mind attempting to register the new turn of events. The scenario of Clement and Lillian working together still confused her. To believe Clement, Lillian, and Darien were all working together was insane.

She brushed the thought from her mind. She had more important things to think about. She looked at Corineous suspended against the wall, his eyes filled with fear. She reached up and removed the pendant of the Rhorian Headmaster. Placing it inside her robes, she withdrew the three pills Cyril gave her during the imprisonment at Junlorace Keep.

She held them up before his eyes to make sure he could see them. Then she pried open his mouth and stuffed the tablets inside. Placing them on his tongue, she slammed his jaw shut as hard as she could. The uncontrollable muscle twitches in his face and neck showed the pills were taking affect. She glanced at Darien and Clement.

"Would one of you care to show me the cruelest and most diabolical way you know for a person to die?" she asked, unable to repress her vengeful hatred.

Clement smiled. "Six hundred ways to kill a man," he gloated.

Miles away, in the heart of the demon lord's catacombs, Xanaphia heard the scream. She paused to marvel at the blood-curdling shriek echoing through the chamber from far above. She shrugged aside her curiosity. The effects of her visit to the spirit world had worn off, and the shock of her encounter with the demon lord was also fading. All her faculties were once again at her command.

Her supernatural physical strength and stamina served her well as she raced to escape the labyrinth. She ran as fast as a fox and darted over the uneven ground. A few times, she encountered random grorgs. They didn't survive the meeting.

She praised Cyril's foresight. Even heading to his death, he'd marked all of the corridors he passed with the same black chalk symbol. As she passed the burnt remains of the grorgs Darien slew, her heart leapt. She was getting close. Picking up speed, Xanaphia zipped down the halls.

Thick beads of sweat accumulated on her brow as she exerted herself more and more in her growing enthusiasm. She only needed to go a little further. After several more twists and turns, she recognized the distant opening of the large rotunda where the group first separated. Breaking into a sprint, she dashed recklessly forward.

She burst into the clearing only to collide with a large figure. The two tumbled against each other rolling and struggling on the floor. Xanaphia was stronger than her opponent and pinned the adversary beneath her. She summoned her energy to strike then froze. It was Darien.

"You," she panted. "I thought you were a grorg."

"How flattering," Darien answered.

"Well, you have to admit, you haven't shaved in a while," Lillian said, laughing.

"Please get her off him," Clement said, making a face. "I'm getting unpleasant images in my mind."

Lillian strolled forward to offer Xanaphia a hand. Xanaphia glared at Clement as Lillian helped her to her feet.

"You!" Sylvia exclaimed in utter shock. "You're here too!"

Sylvia felt a complete loss for words. She was being rescued by all four of her worst and deadliest enemies.

"Seriously," Xanaphia responded, "did you think these idiots survived a weeklong trip fighting demons without me?"

"Oh?" Darien asked in mock surprise. "Did you do something to help?"

Xanaphia started to retort, but Lillian interrupted, "In any case, at least we're all together again. Let's get out of here before we run into something more unpleasant than some pathetic black dogs."

"Like what?" Sylvia asked.

"I'll explain outside," Lillian responded. "For now, let's get as far away as possible."

They hurried down the tunnel toward the exit and emerged from the cave to find themselves blinded by the bright sunlight reflecting off the winter snows. They didn't linger long, eager to put distance between themselves and the catacombs.

As they hurried through the ruined fortress, Sylvia gazed at the ancient structure and the cruel destruction heaped upon the once-glorious keep. She thought about Rhoria. Could the shattered streets and decimated buildings be the future of her home? Could these people's sad fate foreshadow her people's demise?

They left the keep and ascended the steep road stretching upward from the fort. Sylvia wondered about her plight. How long would she remain free? The threat of imminent recapture hung over her head. Was she doomed to return to the prison?

Her companions might provide some protection, but she didn't trust them. Clement and Lillian loathed each other, but Clement acted concerned about Lillian's welfare while she complimented him for his spells. Xanaphia and Darien's lack of hostility proved equally baffling. Something strange had led to the current development. She doubted an alliance of her four greatest enemies was formed with her best interests in mind. She didn't know what was going on, but she was determined to find out.

The party continued up the icy road leading to the top of the mountain. The path entered thick woods. The trail was covered with ice. Sylvia stumbled and fell repeatedly upon the rocks. Her companions walked with ease over the frozen surface, but she couldn't seem to get her footing.

After almost a half an hour and four hard falls, she couldn't take it anymore. Days of starvation, dehydration, lack of sleep, and unending mental turmoil overcame her. She fell. This time, she didn't get back up.

A shadow passed over her. She looked up to see Clement. He lifted his hand, and a strange tingling sensation flooded her senses. She felt like she was floating. The sensation was no illusion. She rose into the air, drifting to the side of the road where Lillian had placed a sleeping mat. Clement set her gently onto the cushion.

When she sat up again, the sun was high in the sky. She must've fallen asleep. She looked for the others. They sat huddled around a small fire, speaking in whispered tones. She tried to make out what was said but only caught small snippets of speech. They appeared to be talking about the events that took place inside the catacombs. She heard references to the tiara and to Cyril. The mention of his name alarmed her. She already distrusted them. Knowing they were in cahoots with the scheming regent of Junlorace Keep increased her discomfort.

"All right," Sylvia said, rising. "Please don't take my words as ungrateful. I appreciate you rescuing me, but I'm uncomfortable with this entire scenario. Why are you here? How'd you find me? How do you know about the tiara? And what are your intentions?"

Darien, Lillian, and Xanaphia looked at Clement. He gave an exasperated sigh.

"What's wrong with you people?" he said. "You know how to talk! Why do I always have to do the explaining?"

Lillian smiled in obvious amusement and reclined onto the snow, pulling a small multicolored cube from her pocket. Darien cast an interested glance her direction and moved to stand over her shoulder. Xanaphia walked over to the road and stared back toward the keep, her eyes distant.

Clement threw his hands in the air.

"Fine," he shouted irritably. He turned toward the queen. "I won't lie to you. On the night of your abduction, Darien and I came to Rhoria plotting to kill you. We broke into your room right after your capture. Darien saw the cloth left on the bed bearing a symbol he recognized as belonging to Junlorace Keep. While fleeing the city, Darien and I encountered Lillian. Later, we ran into Xanaphia. None of us wanted to work together, but no one of us could oppose Darlyth alone."

"What were Xanaphia and Lillian doing in Rhoria?" Sylvia asked.

"Planning your death, of course," Lillian said. She brushed away Darien's hand as he pointed at the cube, suggesting a light for her to push.

"Is that why you rescued me?" Sylvia asked. "So you can kill me?"

"That'd be nice," Clement admitted, "but we can't. The demon lord is about to attack humanity. Lillian tells us his demon army is already awake. You're the only person who can unite Aurba against him."

Sylvia looked at them in surprise. They genuinely wanted to oppose the demon lord. These evil tyrants were abandoning their plans to kill her because they wanted to ensure the safety of humanity. The idea seemed absurd. *They must possess more sinister motives*, she told herself. A suspicion grew in her mind.

"How did you know about the tiara?" Sylvia asked.

"Lillian told us," Clement answered.

"Oh," Sylvia said, taken aback. She turned to Lillian, "How did you know about it?"

"Go get your own cube!" Lillian barked at Darien, who kept muttering suggestions for lights to press. She looked at Sylvia. "I went to school with you and your husband. Don't you think I can figure out what's happening when you start wearing a headband and your powers quadruple?"

Sylvia nodded. The explanation made sense.

"Speaking of the tiara," Darien said. He withdrew the crown from his pocket and tossed it to Sylvia before returning his attention back to Lillian's cube. Sylvia caught the tiara and examined it. Once again, she possessed the source of all her suffering and torment within her hands. The last time was a trap. Was this another one?

She placed the crown on her head before looking back at her companions.

"Thank you," she said, trying to keep her voice casual. "I'm surprised you located the object inside the maze of tunnels. How did you know where the crown was being held?"

"Cyril showed us," Clement answered.

"Ah ha!" Sylvia exclaimed. "You're in league with the kefling. Well, if you think you can con me into giving the tiara to you, you're mistaken."

"Sorry to disappoint you," Clement said, "but we don't want your tiara!"

"Yeah," Lillian agreed, "as though any of us want the demon lord coming after us. I don't know about Darien, who I'm going to kill in his sleep if he doesn't stop bothering me, but I've no desire to be tortured or suffer horrendous death."

Darien, who was just about to reach out to make another suggestion, withdrew his fist back into his robe and turned his attention to Sylvia.

"We do not want the crown," he said. "We did not take it to use it. We took it so you can destroy it."

"What?" Sylvia cried, outraged. "I'm not destroying the tiara!"

"But you must," Clement said. "As long as the tiara exists, the demon lord is going to come after you. All the armies of Rhoria and wizards of Aurba can't keep you safe from him as long as he is determined to get it. We saved you this time. Who'll save you next time? Eventually he'll take it from you. Once he gets the crown, humanity will fall. The only way to ensure a fighting chance for your people is by making sure he never gets it. The only way to do that is by destroying it."

Sylvia refused to listen and didn't want to accept the truth. The tiara was sacred to her. Destroying it terrified her. She wasn't going to sacrifice her children's legacy for some tyrants.

"Never!" she retorted. "I know what you're up to! You want me to destroy the tiara so I'm no longer capable of opposing you. The world is in peril, and you're only interested in finding ways to increase your power. You're as horrible and selfish as your friend Cyril!"

Xanaphia sprang to life.

"How dare you!" she shrieked.

Her face was livid as she spun to confront Sylvia. She charged the queen until they stood nose to nose.

"You're a self-righteous, arrogant, ungrateful . . . pig!" she yelled the words in Sylvia's face.

Her hands, one of which appeared to be clutching some small wooden figurine, flailed in agitation.

"While you stand here insulting Cyril," she said, "he is making the ultimate sacrifice, spending his final days in hour after hour of endless pain. His body is being consumed over and over again by merciless flames as he dies from dehydration, all for the sake of you and a bunch of other people, who never cared, don't care, and will never care that he even existed. And you stand here insulting him. How dare you?"

Sylvia took a step back, shocked at Xanaphia's passion and emotion. Xanaphia turned and walked away, running her hands through her hair in agitation. Sylvia watched in silence. Finally, Xanaphia strode to the other side of the road where she collapsed to her knees, burying her face in her hands. Lillian exchanged looks with Clement and Darien. Clement gave a confused shrug while Darien hurried across the street after Xanaphia.

"Sylvia…" Clement's voice was calm but firm. "We've risked our lives, stalled our ambitions, set aside our desires for vengeance, and even buried our hatred for each other, all for the sake of defeating the demon lord. If we, who everyone considers the wickedest villains to ever live, can do that, why can't you, who are considered their greatest hero, destroy a piece of headgear?"

TYRANTS, TORMENTORS AND THE TIARA

Sylvia stared at him. She pulled the tiara off her head and looked at it. They were right. As long as the crown existed, the demon lord would pursue her. She'd never be safe. The only way she could stop Darlyth from getting the tiara was to destroy it. She gripped the crown with one hand on each side. Powerful protective charms safeguarded it, but they didn't protect against the owner. A quick twist of her wrists would end all of her tortures forever.

Her eyes fell upon the three violets crystals gleaming in the morning sunlight. Her children's faces manifested within their depths. They gazed at her with sad, gentle eyes. It was the same vision she beheld in Junlorace Keep. Her breath caught in her chest. Was she hallucinating? She closed her eyes, trying to fight off the images, but their voices called to her.

"We love you! They called. We believe in you!"

Their voices echoed in her head. They filled her with hope and courage but also with a desperate hunger. She longed to hear them more. What if she never saw her children's faces again? What if she never heard their voices again? Did destroying the tiara mean destroying them forever?

She tried to break the crown, but her hands wouldn't move. She gasped and strained, trying to force herself to shatter the metal. Sweat ran down her forehead, and she clinched her teeth. Yet, she couldn't break the crown. The thought of her children stayed her hand.

"I can't!" she said, bursting into tears. She collapsed to the ground and buried her face in the snow, weeping uncontrollably.

Clement and Lillian sighed. Through the stands of hair and the blur of tears coating her eyes, she saw them glance at each other.

"Lillian, why don't you make the queen some food and water," Clement said. "She needs nourishment, and we have to leave soon."

Clement turned away. He glanced at Darien, who knelt whispering to Xanaphia, then shook his head and strode off into the woods.

Lillian pocketed the cube and rose to her feet. Using her potion, she created a full plate of food and placed it on the snow next to the queen. Sylvia looked at it but couldn't fight off her tears and sobs long enough to eat. Soon, she heard Lillian's footsteps fade in the direction of Clement. Sylvia sat alone, lost in her tears.

CHAPTER 23

No stars shone in the sky above Rhoria. Wrapped in thick winter cloaks to shield against the bitter cold, a small group of huddled figures moved unseen through the pitch-black streets. Thick sheets of freezing rain pummeled the city, creating a layer of ice upon the ground. Several times members of the assembly slipped upon the frozen surface.

Ladonna surveyed the situation with increased concern. The harsh conditions hindered their mission. Darkness favored the supernatural eyes of the grorgs, and the frozen roads hampered the mobility of Rhorian soldiers.

The arrival of a ferocious ice storm without any warning struck her as both ominous and unnatural. The weather was bright and sunny all day. The timing of the sudden shift in conditions seemed suspiciously convenient for Darlyth's minions. She felt inclined to believe some sort of magic was at work.

Alexis said there were no capable of altering the weather, but this meant little to Ladonna. She knew a monster with magical powers beyond known laws. She didn't want to think about what might motivate him to generate a paralyzing storm over the city.

Ladonna glanced at the resolute faces of her companions. Alexis led the party. She marched foremost of the company. She'd spent most of her day researching the location of the prison cells housing the victims of Nimue's experiments.

The rest of the company consisted of various resistance members and soldiers. Yeva, the teenage girl who served as the resistance's contact with the magical academy, strolled behind Alexis. She seemed unbothered by the fierce weather. She traveled with her hood off, her short-cropped black hair coated with icy raindrops. But, as she explained to Ladonna, she came from the far north and felt at home in such conditions.

Behind her marched Kaspar. He wore a thick padded-leather jerkin with a long sword strapped to his side and a stern but anxious expression. Ladonna shook her head in frustration as she looked at him. The man was an important contact and a trained soldier, but he was also a liability. His close relationship to one of the captives made him overanxious and reckless.

Flanking him were two members of the town guard, Illian and Newlyn. They were veteran soldiers. Both served in Sylvia's army during the Liberation Wars. Each wore a collection of insignia on top of his armor, honors bestowed upon them for valor and courage during their many battles. Ladonna felt they were the perfect choice for the mission.

Ladonna and Gemma followed behind. Although no longer young, Commander Gemma remained one of her best soldiers and often lamented her lack of true combat experience. She longed to employ her skills on a dangerous mission. Ladonna felt an obligation to give her this opportunity as a reward for years of loyal service.

Taking up the rear of the small company, two figures clothed in black hunting garb blended into the night. Their names were Anwyn and Daylin. Urith picked them to accompany Ladonna as runners in case she needed to send messages back to the encampment. They were excellent teammates. Although barely seventeen, the newlyweds had proved themselves to be the keep's best scouts and foremost archers.

The younger of the two love birds was the dainty-looking Anwyn. She had possessed an interest in adventure and mischief from almost the moment she could walk. The more robust Daylin had possessed an interest in Anwyn from almost the moment he could walk. Their love of mischief inspired Ladonna to train them as trackers and hunters. It seemed the best way to keep the little hellions out of trouble. Now teenagers, their talents far exceeded the capabilities of their contemporaries.

With hoods drawn low over their faces and Blackwood bows strapped over their shoulders, the young scouts drifted along looking left and right. Their sharp eyes scanned the darkness, searching for potential threats. Many years of traveling at night through the bleak Blood Fang Mountains made them well adapted to the stormy conditions.

The company followed Alexis as she ducked into an alleyway. No one spoke as they ranged down numerous back streets, wound through empty lanes, and emerged next to the magic academy. Ladonna gazed around as they positioned themselves a short distance from the towering structure. They were close to the palace's outer gates, and the stewardess's private guard patrolled the battlements.

The members of the expedition pressed against the wall of a building as they surveyed their projected path. A short trek separated them from their destination. It was a dangerous stretch with little concealment for trespassers. The back wall of the academy would provide them some cover.

The six-story box-shaped school stood between them and the prying eyes of the palace guards. They needed to keep their distance from the wall though. Thick green brambles armed with alarms designed to catch students sneaking from their rooms grew along the sides. The only break in the hedge was in the middle where a single wooden door stood against the otherwise featureless surface.

Ladonna noticed Alexis's body tense and her eyes narrow as she looked at the door.

"What's wrong?" Ladonna whispered.

"The back door is chained and locked," she said. "Why would someone bar the back door of the kitchen?"

"Perhaps some new method of controlling the students," Yeva suggested. "Where do we go from here?"

"The prison facility is located over there, about half a mile away," Alexis answered, gesturing toward a distant point on the palace's outer wall. "The structure once served as a holding cell for political prisoners and is concealed by a secret entrance. It fell into disuse about a century ago, so the stewardess probably assumes everyone has forgotten about it. I scouted the area today and saw patrols of her elite guards entering and exiting the premises. I'm confident the captives are there."

"So, let's go," Kaspar said, stomping his foot.

"Be patient," Alexis snapped. "An extra minute for the sake of caution might make the difference between your sister joining you in freedom or you joining her in the cell. Remember that. Let's move."

Alexis guided them along the back wall of the academy. She scanned the park before advancing into the open expanse. Not seeing anyone, she signaled for everyone to follow. They had barely taken a dozen steps when loud shouts and screams burst through the air. The cries bore unmistakable horror and alarm. There were coming from the school.

Everyone paused, looking behind them. Alexis and Ladonna exchanged concerned looks. The assistance of the academy remained pivotal to their plans to overthrow Nimue. If something bad was happening, they needed to know. Yeva gestured at the school, indicating her desire to investigate.

"Go," Alexis said, "but don't do anything rash and don't try to be a hero. Come back and get me if there's danger."

Yeva nodded. Turning away from the group, she darted toward the academy. The magical school was an enormous building, and the main entrance was on the opposite side. Alexis watched her go before turning back to the group.

"Hurry," she said.

She broke into a mad sprint across the open grounds. Everyone followed. After a short distance, they reached the thick bushes and trees lining the palace walls. Tall green hedges grew high under the overhanging branches of oak trees enchanted to grow in these wintry conditions. Lovestruck students often used the alcoves formed by the lush foliage to share intimate moments.

Alexis led the company through one of these small enclosures to the palace's outer wall. Striding forward, she pointed at an inauspicious brick about midway up the weathered surface.

"That brick will open the door," she said. "I'd come with you, but I can't stay. I'm worried about the academy. They're the only ones who can find a way to close the portal. We're doomed if we lose them. And freeing these prisoners will mean nothing."

She shot a poignant look at Kaspar. He held his head high in his stubborn manner, but Ladonna noticed he avoided eye contact. Ladonna turned to Gemma.

"Go with her," she said. "Make sure everything is okay. We'll meet up there after freeing the captives."

"Yes, Commander," Gemma answered.

Alexis sprinted from the alcove without another word. Gemma pursued her through the foliage. Ladonna felt dismay at finding herself as the leader of the expedition. But between her combat skills and the town guards, she felt confident they possessed enough strength to defeat any threats lurking below.

The assessment was rather optimistic, but it allowed her to leave Anwyn and Daylin outside. Confining underground hallways were poorly suited to their skills, and if something happened to them she lacked any means to communicate with her central command. She didn't want to jeopardize the connection by leading them into danger.

"Anwyn and Daylin, I want you to stay here," she said. "Hide where no one can see you and wait for us to come out. Don't put yourself in danger or do anything foolish. Do you understand?"

She added a stern look. The mischievous spirit of the two teenagers still lingered within their adventurous hearts.

Of all the times for their daredevil instincts to arise, now would be the worst. The two looked at Ladonna with the annoyingly innocent expressions they so often wore when reprimanded.

"Yes, ma'am," they exclaimed in unison.

Ladonna's eyes narrowed, but she said nothing. She turned and pressed the indicated brick. A rectangular section of wall slid from right to left revealing a small hallway. At the end, a stone staircase spiraled downward. Floating spheres of clear white light suspended at random intervals illuminated the chamber like strange torches.

Ladonna led the way, leaving Anwyn and Daylin scanning the trees for hiding places. Before she could enter, however, Kaspar blocked her. The reckless warrior drew his sword and rushed toward the stairs, leaving the others behind.

"Kaspar," Ladonna hissed.

He turned and looked at her with an obstinate expression. She met his gaze with equally unyielding tenacity.

"We're going into a guarded facility," she said. "Try to employ some semblance of diligence."

He said nothing but continued at a slower pace. Ladonna moved up behind him, drawing her sword. Illian and Newlyn followed close behind. Ladonna disliked being second in line. Her reflexes, along with the iron mail worn under her hunting cloak, made her the most likely to survive a trap or ambush.

The chain armor was particularly important. Although some grorgs felt inclined to use weapons, their primary attack remained their claws. Grorg's nails could pierce the chain shirt with a firm strike, but it would withstand the blow better than the scale mail worn by Illian and Newlyn. The coiled metal rings certainly provided better protection than the padded leather aketon worn by Kaspar.

The stairs were too narrow for multiple people to walk abreast, and Kaspar wasn't about to cede his lead. She followed behind him, wishing he would exhibit a touch more discretion as he descended. They rounded the last bend in the stairwell. There the stairway straightened for the final ten yards opening into a well-lit chamber.

The smell of blood and death struck Ladonna's senses like a hammer. Her sharp eyes darted past the door-sized opening. Long trails of dried blood flowed along the floor. In the distance, she spotted the holding cell. They were too late to help the captives.

"No!" Kaspar screamed. "Katy!"

He bounded down the stairs, all caution thrown to the wind.

"Kaspar, no!" Ladonna screamed, springing after him.

She tried grabbing him with her sword-free hand. She missed. The grief-stricken warrior charged through the opening, screaming his sister's name. He never had a chance to react to the large grorg that sprang from the concealment of the doorway. It appeared in its true form, abandoning its human disguise. The creature ambushed Kasper, impaling him in the back with its dagger-like claws. Kaspar let out a gasp of surprise, his body buckling under the force of the blow. He slumped forward, sliding off the seven-inch nails into a lifeless heap on the cold stone floor.

The grorg got no time to savor its victory. Ladonna leapt through the opening, her blade careening toward the murderous beast. The creature glanced up just in time to see her. It sprang aside to evade the blow but was too slow. The sword found its mark, slicing into the beast's right shoulder blade. It howled in pain. Ladonna prepared to finish her opponent, but powerful clawed hands struck her from behind. In her rush to rescue Kaspar, she had failed to notice a second grorg guarding the room.

Sharp nails struck her armor. It absorbed most of the blow, but the claws still cut into her flesh. Ladonna whirled to face the new assault. Assuming a half-sword position, she swung the blade upward like a sickle slicing the grorg's exposed arm. Blood spewed into the air. The fiend gave an agonizing cry, staggering backward clutching the injured appendage.

This was her strategy for battling grorgs. The nimble beasts used their agility to keep their torsos out of danger, but their overly large arms proved clumsy. They couldn't move them with the same ease they maneuvered their bodies. Since their claws were their primary weapon, wounding the arms reduced them to either fleeing or biting their adversary. The latter exposed the most vulnerable spot in their otherwise toughened exterior, their necks. That was the theory, at least. Execution remained another thing.

Having wounded one of the arms, Ladonna again found herself unable to follow-up the assault. The first grorg, now recovered from her initial attack, retaliated. It swung at her with its uninjured left hand. The fist slammed against her with the impact of a charging bull. Chain armor was designed to prevent slashing and piercing attacks and did little to absorb this blow. It landed directly upon her already torn and bleeding right side, knocking her off her feet.

The second grorg also regrouped. It sprang forward, claws raised to strike, but Ladonna was saved by Illian and Newlyn. They raced into the room with a fierce battle cry. Illian came first, his broadsword gripped in his hands. He charged the second grorg, swinging the blade in a giant arc overhead.

The grorg was prepared for the attack. It sidestepped the swipe. Illian's sword crashed against the unforgiving stone floor, leaving him momentarily off-balance. The grorg took advantage of the opening. Its uninjured left hand swung upward, the sharp claws sliding beneath the metal plates of the scale armor, entering his gut and coming out his back. The grorg then tossed him aside and turned to meet the next combatant.

Newlyn attacked in a more measured fashion. Armed with a falchion and shield, he was more reserved and calculating. He swung his blade at the monster's outstretched wrist as it flung aside Illian's corpse. The spry fiend, protective of its remaining limb, barely managed to wrench the furry mass out of harm's way. It retaliated with a swat of its claw. Newlyn deflected the blow with his shield and leapt back to the offensive.

Ladonna rolled away from the grorg still attacking her. Dodging a swipe from the brute's big hand, she tumbled to her feet and regained her balance. Attacking in a more reckless fashion than typical for her, Ladonna lunged forward. Feigning an attack against the creature's body, she let out a sharp battle cry and sprang toward her adversary.

The grorg fell for the bluff. Moving aside to avoid the blow it believed intended for its torso, it counter attacked, swinging its uninjured hand at Ladonna. She shifted her blade to intercept its arm. The combined might of Ladonna's cut met with the powerful swing of the grorg, slicing straight through tissue and bone and severing the appendage.

The grorg wailed in agony. Ladonna threw herself at it, sword thrusting toward the staggered brute. With a powerful jab, she buried her blade into its chest. It let out one last scream of rage as the blade ripped through it. After a second, it ceased moving and slid backward onto the floor, twitching in the throes of death.

A new scream filled the chamber. Ladonna looked up to see Newlyn knocked across the prison by a swipe of his adversary's hand. He fell sprawled onto his back. Lillian sprang to his rescue, but too late. The grorg leapt atop him, plunging its claws downward. The nails ripped straight through the metal scales. Newlyn let out a gasp before slumping to the floor.

The grorg turned to face Ladonna. As it rose, its momentum carried it straight onto her sword. The blade plunged into the exposed neck, tearing through veins and severing arteries. The creature crashed to the ground, clutching its throat. It writhed in helpless agony making horrific gurgling noises. Then the body stopped moving, the head fell backward, and its arms collapsed to the floor.

Ladonna sighed and slumped forward. The wounds in her back stung, but they were more annoying than crippling. She straightened up and hurried to the bodies of her companions. She checked for signs of life. There were none. Kaspar, Newlyn, and Illian were dead.

She surveyed the prison. The chamber was at least fifty feet by fifty feet. A long set of bars ran the length of the room, dividing it in half. Almost two dozen prisoners were stored in a massive communal pen. They lay strewn across the floor in grotesque angles. Their bodies were so mutilated only the clothes distinguished men from women.

Dried blood coated the walls and bars where the victims had struggled to escape the massacre. Signs indicated the grorgs carried out the slaughter with customary brutality, inflicting as much suffering and agony as possible.

Ladonna shook her head. At first, she wondered why Nimue would do such a thing, but she knew the steward didn't order the deaths. Darlyth did. He must've learned of the steward's plan and sought to shatter her ambitions. Yet, it didn't make sense. Striking against Nimue would be tipping his hand by revealing the grorgs' true allegiance. Maybe he planned to kill her too. But that didn't seem right either. Without her, he'd lose his grip on the town. There was a connection she was missing. Her mind shot back to the cries at the academy.

To her horror, everything fell into place. Darlyth didn't need Nimue to control Rhoria after tonight because there wouldn't be a Rhoria after tonight. He had coordinated the deaths of the prisoners with an attack against the town. He must've started with the academy. The school was his greatest threat. Once he eliminated it, Rhoria would fall.

Footsteps sounded on the stairs above her. Ladonna turned to see Nimue racing down in a state of agitation. Her heightened sense of smell must've alerted her to the macabre scene. She froze near the bottom of the stairs, staring in disbelief at the destruction.

"Ladonna!" she gasped. "What've you done?!"

Ladonna opened her mouth to respond but never got the chance. One of Nimue's elite guards rounded the stairs at a gallop. The illusion dropped from the beast, revealing the monstrosity located behind the enchanted façade. It charged around the corner and sprang into the air, leaping toward the steward.

"Look out!" Ladonna shouted in warning.

She was too late. The grorg landed on the stairs right behind the startled steward, its claws plunging into her back. Nimue's body lurched forward, the tips of the dagger-like nails protruding from her chest. She dangled from the brute's blood-soaked hand, gasping for air.

"A message from the master about betrayal!" it hissed in her ear.

Then its eyes locked on Ladonna.

"And you!" it hissed.

The fiend threw Nimue's bleeding body at Ladonna. She caught the girl in her arms, trying to break her fall, but she could do little more than toss her aside. The grorg sprang from the stairs, colliding with Ladonna before she could recover. The impact knocked the sword from her hands. The grorg jabbed forward with both claws smashing full force into Ladonna's armor. The attacks punctured the metal grating, the nails delving into Ladonna's gut.

Defenseless and caught by surprise, Ladonna improvised. She grabbed her opponent, and the two rolled across the ground grappling with each other. Her adversary was rested and possessed the initiative. It seized her wrists and used the momentum to hurl her toward the nearby wall. She flew through the air and crashed into the rough brick surface. Her head slammed backward as the impact jarred her body, leaving her disoriented.

The grorg tumbled to its feet, leaping upon its prey. Its claws sliced downward toward her head as Ladonna struggled to regain her wits.

"Shech!"

A red light struck the grorg straight in the back. It stumbled forward, releasing a scream of pain as its body erupted in flames. Ladonna seized the opportunity. Ilian's falchion was only a few feet away. Springing to her feet, she seized the weapon and plunged the blade through the writhing grorg's back. It spun around and stumbled against the wall, its long claws scraping the rough surface as it slid into the corner and perished.

Ladonna glanced across the room. Nimue lay on her back in a pool of blood. Her face was raised off the ground with her left hand outstretched toward the dead grorg. The blindfold had fallen off, and her breathing was strained. Slowly, her head drooped onto the cold wet floor.

Ladonna raced to her. Nimue was muttering a healing spell in desperation, but it had never worked before and still failed her now. Ladonna knelt beside her.

Nimue grabbed her arms, turning her eyeless face toward the warrior.

"Don't . . . leave me!" she gasped. "I don't want to die alone."

Her voice trailed off. Her hand drifted to the floor. Her breathing stopped. She was dead.

Ladonna stood to leave but crumpled to the floor, clutching her stomach. She rose again but fell as agony surged through her body. Abandoning the idea of standing, she crawled to her sword and wiped the blood off on her cloak. Sheathing the blade, she dragged herself to the wall and climbed to her feet, leaning against the barrier for support.

Hunched over in pain and clutching her side, she made her way up the staircase. The stairs seemed longer than she remembered. Each new step sent stabs of crippling pain through her body. By the time she reached the landing, she was on her hands and knees. She crawled across the platform and out the door.

No sooner did she pass through the sliding wall into the dark night than she noticed one of Nimue's disguised guards standing above her. Her appearance caught it by surprise, but not for long. It bounded toward her, prepared to strike.

Two twangs sounded from the trees. Long black arrows buried themselves into the grorg's head. It collapsed dead at Ladonna's feet. Ladonna pushed herself into a sitting position as two black-cloaked figures slid from the trees beside her. Anwyn and Daylin raced to her side. Anwyn pulled a small pouch of herbal cream from her cloak.

Daylin was dismayed. "Commander, what happened? Where are the others?"

"We're so sorry, Commander," Anwyn said, almost sobbing as she applied the cream to the wounds. "We did what you told us to and tried to stay out of trouble. That's why we let them enter. We didn't realize . . ."

"No," Ladonna interrupted, still gasping, "you did the right thing. I'm pleased. But now . . ."

Shouts filled the air. Some came from inside the palace walls. Others came from the nearby soldiers' barracks. Still others arose from the distant city streets. Ladonna swore angrily. She was too late. The attack had begun. Anwyn and Daylin glanced around in alarm.

"Anwyn," Ladonna said, grabbing the young woman by her tunic and jerking her around. "Run as swiftly and safely as you can back to the encampment. They're probably under attack. If not, let them know the grorgs are launching a full-scale assault on the city. Tell them to muster everyone at the village green in the center of town. Tell them to wait for me there. If I'm not there in an hour, I'm dead."

Anwyn nodded. Ladonna released her, and she sprinted into the darkness. Ladonna turned to Daylin. She could feel the cream working already. She felt stronger.

"Help me to my feet," she said. "We need to get to the academy."

CHAPTER 24

Yeva raced to the academy as fast as her legs could carry her. Sweat rolled down her face, mingling with the icy air as she charged toward the entrance. Her breathes came in painful gasps, but she refused to slow down. She felt sure something bad was happening. If so, she needed to know.

She doubted she could provide much help. She was just an apprentice in her fourth year. The first three years of study focused on learning to muster and control magical energies. Only basic spells were taught in the early grades. Most of them focused on healing. That was one of many changes Cornelius made after taking over.

Under previous headmasters, magical studies operated on an individual basis. Masters selected apprentices and taught new material at their own discretion. When the student was ready for more advance teachings, their master allowed them to progress. Cornelius eliminated the mentor system and revamped the course of study into a strict program of annual curriculums and levels.

He maintained the apprentice system was archaic. The approach permitted prodigious students to excel while the less gifted one fell behind. Apprenticeship fostered the creation of such sorcerers as Clement, Darien, and Xanaphia, whose natural talent, when unsuppressed, gave them the ability to change the world and the entire course of history. Such power was dangerous.

Cornelius's curriculum kept all students on equal footing. No student would be left behind by his peers. Teachers must tailor their teaching to the less gifted or less hard-working students. In turn, the more industrious or talented apprentices found themselves held back so the weaker ones could catch up. Cornelius argued the program ensured all students received equal opportunities to learn and thrive. Those masters who objected found themselves dismissed from the school as relics unable to adapt to the more enlightened system.

Yeva now wondered whether or not the whole scheme was a ploy to prevent students from developing their full potential. After all, as Cornelius said, truly prodigious students allowed to excel according to their natural talents developed powers capable of changing the world. In turn, they became dangerous to those in power. By limiting student growth, Cornelius ensured these gifted children and teens wouldn't threaten the status quo in which he thrived. The knowledge did little to help her now.

Yeva found herself racing into a potentially dangerous situation armed with few useful spells. Fortunately, her father had served as a combat sorcerer under Sylvia. When he died in the Liberation Wars, he left behind his old spell books and scrolls. In them, Yeva learned many spells that her classmates didn't know. Some were too advanced for her, including the ultimate combat spell, Desecria. She discovered its instructions among her father's writings and knew them by heart, though she had never cast it.

Her teachers said it was too dangerous. It drained power and life from the caster. Until she mastered her magic, using the sorcery would be a grave error. She had begged her favorite teacher to work with her, but he refused. Cornelius had forbidden the study of Desecria until a student's fifth year. Casting it was banned until the sixth. Yeva shook her head. The spell would be useful right now.

She slowed as she reached the entrance. Alexis had taught her an invisibility spell to get past the guards. She started to cast it but stopped. The guards were missing. She walked up to the porch looking for them. More shouts and screams came from inside. These weren't the sounds of some game or magical experiment gone awry. People were dying.

She raced through the doors and into the front hall. Her worst suspicions were immediately confirmed. Lifeless corpses were strewn across the hall, doors hung off their hinges, and blood flowed like rivers across the carpet. Violent shouts and cries of spells filled the air. The grorgs were attacking the teachers. She could hear the battle raging inside the distant kitchens. She needed to alert Alexis.

She turned to leave but hesitated. People were dying. She couldn't just walk away. They needed help. But they were trained sorcerers and could hold out until she returned with reinforcements. Or could they? Uncertainty gripped her.

A shriek sounded from the floor above. Yeva recognized the voice. It belonged to a first-year student who she tutored. All thoughts of returning to Alexis disappeared. She raced up the stairs to her left.

The thought of monsters attacking the students made her furious. Most first-year students were between seven to ten years of age. They were just children, many of them far from home, knew hardly any magic, and couldn't defend themselves. They'd be slaughtered like lambs.

She raced toward the dormitories. The school was built in a U-shape. Down the center of the U on the first floor stretched a long hallway lined with teachers' rooms and offices. Above them, the library, and further up, the apothecary, where various herbs and spell ingredients grew. At the tips of the U were the academy's two remaining towers, but no one used them anymore. Death spiders still populated the ancient structures, and teachers needed powerful enchantments to keep them from spreading.

Around the outside of the U, on the bottom floor, were various classrooms. The lower one's grade, the lower in the school they were housed. Yeva only needed to go up one flight of stairs to reach the first-year students.

She reached the landing and headed for the hall. More screams issued from the floors above. The beasts were killing everyone. Yeva tried to steel her nerves as she entered the passage leading to the first-year barracks. Pools of blood littered the hall, trickling from open rooms, whose splintered doors were knocked inward. The source of destruction stood halfway down the hall.

Yeva gasped. She'd never seen a grorg before. The horrid mockery of a human was covered in blood with cruel nails dripping with the vital fluids of its victims. She froze in panic, unable to speak or even think.

Fortunately, the creature hadn't noticed her. It was busy pounding on a door. As Yeva watched, the wooden frame gave way before its fists. Screams and shouts of Yeva's pupil and her roommate redoubled as the beast sprang inside.

Yeva needed to act. She shook herself from her stupor and summoned her magic, rushing after the beast. At the same time, the door across the hall from the besieged dorm opened. Two little girls wrapped in thick woolen nightgowns and cotton slippers raced from the concealment of their room, clearly hoping to escape while the creature's back was turned.

Unfortunately, the creature had spotted them. To Yeva's horror, she saw the creature spring from the bedchamber and back into the hall. Releasing a carnal scream of delight at the sight of the fleeing children, it sprang forward to ensnare the victims. They screamed, attempting to race faster. They didn't get far. Before they took two steps, it was on top of them.

"Shauleetseeya!" cried Yeva.

The spell wasn't powerful, but it was the strongest one Yeva could think of at the moment. A thin streak of yellow light burst from her hand, striking the beast. It let out a yelp of surprise but otherwise appeared unharmed. Still, Yeva had gotten the beast's attention. Forgetting all about the girls, it turned and charged toward her.

"Nosorog!" Yeva shouted, sending a large stream of gray light at the beast.

The monster leapt aside, running vertically along the wall. The spell soared beneath it. It sprang back onto the ground, continuing the charge. Yeva retreated.

"Oosherb!" she called as the gap between herself and the attacker narrowed.

Thin rays of red light sprang from the tips of each finger on her right hand. The beams shot forth in a spray of projectiles. The monster leapt against the opposite wall, twisting its body at an odd angle. The beams flew in all directions, but none hit their target.

It launched off the wall and threw itself at Yeva. She summoned her energy into a barrier between herself and the attacker. Holding out her hands, she closed her eyes and concentrated on the blockade. The shield deflected its claws, but the grorg crashed through the barrier and smashed into her body, sending her careening to the floor.

The impact knocked the wind from her lungs, and Yeva gasped for air. The grorg knelt on her chest, giving a wicked smile. Grabbing her neck, it squeezed against her airways, strangling the already choking Yeva. Its face filled with diabolical delight as she thrashed and struggled.

Suddenly, it gave a cry of pain and leapt off her. Yeva rolled onto her side, gasping for air. The beast had spun around. A small cutting knife, like the type used to carve potion ingredients, was buried in its back. It belonged to the first-year student Yeva tutored. She'd come to the aid of her mentor. Now she stood terrified before the gaze of the enraged grorg.

She attempted to sprint down the hall, but the grorg was too fast. It snatched her in its fist and slammed her into the wall. She gave a cry of pain as it pinned her against the wooden panels. She struggled, her legs kicking in panic. Yeva pushed herself to her knees, trying to gasp the words of a spell.

Before she could, the grorg's claws plunged up the girl's gut and into her chest. She went still, and her eyes rolled back into her head. For a second, her limp body dangled from her attacker's hand, and her eyes stared unseeing at the ceiling. Then the grorg ripped its claws free and tossed her aside.

Fury beyond anything Yeva ever imagined coursed through her. More than anything else in the world, she wanted to destroy the murderous fiend. Without thinking, she focused her energy on the most destructive and powerful killing spell ever designed. All her rage, hatred, and power erupted from her in a massive explosion.

"Desecria!"

Instantly, Yeva understood why her teachers forbid her from casting the spell. A cataclysmic surge erupted through her weakened body. She felt her energy and vitality ripped from her muscles, tissues, and blood to fuel the destructive might of the spell. Her own magic tore through her like razors, and her very essence seemed to be jarred from her body to fuel the merciless wrath of the incantation. The incantation quickly transformed into a scream of pain. She felt her body and mind shatter before the destructive rush of energy.

She collapsed senseless onto her stomach, but her arms remained outstretched, acting independent of her will. Streaks of black lightning erupted from her fingers, hammering into the back of the grorg. A roar of pain burst from its lips as the energy tore through its body. She saw the veins burst inside the black skin and the muscles explode from the force of the spell. It writhed in agony, its hands ripping deep gouges into his furry hide.

The dark lightning ceased. The grorg toppled dead onto the ground. Yeva watched it fall. And everything went black.

Alexis and Gemma raced through the large front doors of school. Alexis already had a plan. She had heard the screams coming from the upper floors and determined the students' barracks were under attack. The teachers would never allow the apprentices to be slaughtered. This meant they must be either detained or isolated from them. In either case, the only way to save the students was to rescue the masters.

The teachers' offices and living quarters were on the first floor. Any attempt to eliminate them must take place there. This was risky. The ground level contained the two main exits, the doors on opposite sides. An attack from one direction allowed the teachers to flee the other.

The most obvious approach involved barring one entrance to prevent escape and driving the victims toward it. As Alexis observed earlier, the backdoor to the kitchen was locked. She concluded the steward's guards attacked from the front of the school, driving the teachers toward the kitchens. The doors couldn't be opened by magic. The spell was designed to stop intruders. Now it prevented escape.

Alexis raced toward the kitchens, Gemma behind her. The grorgs' strategy had been genius. Most of the teachers lying dead outside their rooms in the hallway were the younger and more battle-oriented spellcasters. The grorgs must've surprised them and slain them first. The remaining instructors were elderly. Years of complacent life within the academy had slowed their reflexes and minds. They no longer possessed the skills necessary to deal with the unexpected threat.

Entering the cafeteria, Alexis and Gemma were greeted by a scene of utter mayhem. Bricks shattered, chairs flew, incantations bounced off the walls, charms collided with each other, and chaos reigned. Less than two dozen remaining teachers out of the school's seventy original instructors huddled in small groups launching spells everywhere. Desperation and confusion had driven all order and strategy from their minds.

Alexis spotted the grorgs. More than a dozen of them sprang and darted around the room. They had assumed their true appearance, a scare tactic that appeared to be working well on the terrified teachers.

It didn't work on Alexis though. She was a battle mage, raised in the untamed forests bordering the southern swamplands and armed with years of combat experience. She'd encountered many horrid creations during the Liberation Wars. To her, they were just more adversaries waiting to be slain.

"Perelome!" she shouted.

A bright-purple light burst from her hands, soaring straight at the back of the nearest grorg. The spell slammed into the beast as it sprang atop the prone magical defense teacher. Every bone in the fiend's body snapped into pieces with an audible crack. Its face went slack, and it fell onto the floor with a thud.

Two neighboring grorgs turned toward the sound. They spotted the newcomers and disengaged from the group. One headed toward Alexis, while the other charged Gemma. This pleased Alexis. In less than a second they'd succeeded in distracting or eliminating a fourth of the attackers.

A rush of adrenaline followed. She hadn't fought a battle in years. It was invigorating. This is what she was born to do. Now she could measure herself against the minions of the demon lord, the greatest fiend to ever walk the earth. It was like a dream and a nightmare come true at the same time.

"Shech," she exclaimed.

A ray of red light shot toward the charging grorg. It seemed to anticipate the attack. Grabbing a wooden chair, it held the object out front like a shield. The spell collided with the chair, which burst into flames. The grorg flung it at Alexis, who dodged the fiery projectile.

"Napadat!"

A crimson beam with swirling green orbs issued from her fingers. This time the grorg dove under the beam and slid on its back as the spell flew overhead. Alexis prepared to cast another, but the beast was upon her. It tumbled to its feet and snatched her by the front of her robes. With an almost effortless gesture, the beast flung Alexis through the air into a locked and frail-looking wooden door on the right wall.

The rotted wood gave way without even slowing her down. She crashed into the room, and her momentum carried her straight into a short rickety table filled with large glass beakers and test tubes. The flimsy table collapsed beneath her, and she crashed down on top of the glass containers. The bottles shattered, the shards slicing through her clothes, into her skin, and embedded themselves into her exposed palms and wrists. Only the hood of her cloak and her thick black hair saved her from worse injuries.

Before she could recover, her adversary bounded into the room. She tried to defend herself, but it seized her around the neck and hoisted her off the floor. She dangled in the air, struggling and clawing as its hands constricted around her throat.

A cold sadistic smile of delight took to its lips as her face turned red and blue. It made no attempt to finish her quickly. It seemed to savor the pleasure of watching her die. Its leering face lingered before her eyes as her vision grew blurry and her consciousness faded.

Suddenly, its grip released, and she fell to the floor. Gasping for air as the world returned to focus, she looked up to see the grorg stagger backward against the far wall. It was gripping its throat. She stared in confusion at the bizarre role reversal as her adversary choked and writhed, its eyes bulging from their sockets. A moment later, it collapsed into a corner and expired.

She shook her head, puzzled. She quickly stopped. The act hurt. The impact with the table and door had jarred her neck. Muttering healing spells for her palms, she rolled her neck backward to stretch the tendons.

All color drained from her face. Descending from the ceiling, straight toward her, crawled a whole nest of blue and yellow arachnids, death spiders.

With a shout of horror, Alexis dove out the door and skidded across the floor.

"Pocheeneet!" she shouted.

The pieces of the shattered door flew back into place, the broken fragments melding together. The lock clicked, shutting the dangerous vermin inside. Alexis's hand dove into her cloak, yanking out the bottle of anti-venom. She was halfway through the formula before her startled nerves recovered. She resealed the container and rose to her feet.

A grin arose. She couldn't help it. The irony was too great. After years of hunting down Clement's creations, the poisonous pests had saved her life. *Chalk another one up to my uncanny luck*, she thought ruefully. *I'm a hard person to kill.*

She muttered healing spells as she pocketed the vial and scanned the raging battle. Another teacher was dead, but so was a grorg. More importantly, the teachers were no longer pinned against the wall. Emboldened by the unexpected arrival of reinforcements, they had turned the tide of the battle.

Alexis rejoined the fray. Victory was at hand in the academy but far from present in the rest of the city.

CHAPTER 25

"Now what?" Xanaphia asked.

Darien looked up. They'd set up camp about half an hour earlier. He and Lillian were still nibbling on their food. Sylvia wasn't. She'd collapsed onto the ground and fell asleep as soon as they established camp. They could do little for her. She needed time and rest. Unfortunately, they lacked the first, which prevented the second.

Already midnight was approaching. In five hours they'd be on the move again. They needed to march as many hours a day as possible. Cyril's sacrifice would only buy so much time. The trip to Kendross Keep took over a week. No one believed they could double the pace on the way back. Still, they had to try. All they could do for Sylvia was grant her extra sleep by not assigning her a watch.

"If Ladonna doesn't arrive," Xanaphia repeated. "What do we do then?"

"Die," Darien answered. "The demon lord will catch us, kill us, and stick our heads on pikes!"

"Why kill us when he can stick our heads on pikes while we're still alive?" Xanaphia said, staring at the fire with a haunted expression.

Darien glanced at Clement, who gazed in a sullen matter at the small blue orb in his hands. Darien shook his head.

"I almost forgot about the violet quartz crystal," he laughed. "Wishing you could use it?"

"Yes," Clement said, "I've been fingering it in my pocket the entire walk."

"I wonder if it'll work on the demon lord," Lillian said.

"I don't know," Clement answered. "Violet quartz doesn't work on non-human creatures, but that's because they can't use magic. The demon lord can. He may be susceptible to it."

Clement looked at Xanaphia.

She shook her head. "I don't know. Violet quartz is a mystery. Centuries of magical research have barely begun to understand its full potential."

"Sylvia's husband would've known," Lillian said.

All heads turned to her. Darien started to ask for an explanation, but Clement interrupted. "I'm more curious about the blue crystals in her tiara," he said. All eyes shifted back to him.

"What do you mean?" Darien asked.

"I don't think she's keeping the tiara because of the powers it gives her," Clement said. "I saw her eyes when she tried to break it. They were focused on something inside the jewels. Her body language told me she heard something too. It was speaking to her, showing her visions. Whether real or imagined, I don't know. But to her, the tiara is alive."

"Is that possible?" Lillian asked.

"The headband could possess some control over her," Xanaphia said. "Magical objects designed to enhance one's powers can become symbiotic or even parasitic."

"But are the visions coming from the tiara?" Lillian asked. "Or is she imagining them?"

"Probably the latter," Darien said. "I am not familiar with any incantation capable of giving sentient life to an object. Longterm exposure to its magic might have caused her to develop a psychosis."

"That's the most reasonable explanation," Xanaphia agreed. "But with violet quartz, almost anything is possible. The discussion ignores my initial question though. Do we have a contingency plan for the demon lord? If Cyril unexpectedly dies—or to be more accurate, expectedly dies—before we reach Rhoria, what is our strategy?"

"I suggest running," Lillian answered. "I will. We've done everything we can to free Sylvia and get her to realize the danger. Maybe I can live out the rest of my life in some distant continent before Darlyth gets there."

"Fine," Xanaphia responded. "And what will those of you who aren't spineless cowards going to do?"

Lillian sprang to her feet in anger.

"What do you want from me?" she asked. "You want me to die fighting a futile and pointless battle against a foe I can't defeat! Don't tell me you've suddenly decided to die fighting for a cause? Admirable but pointless. You'll die. He'll live. The end!"

Xanaphia hesitated. Darien could tell she wanted to say she would fight, but doubts seemed to be clouding her mind. Choosing between death and servitude was one thing. Choosing between dying and running away was another.

"Look," Darien said, "I do not know what I will do when the time comes. None of us can know for sure how we will act until we are there. Discussing it serves no purpose. Let us just go to bed and get ready for the morning."

The women shrugged and turned away. Lillian unfurled her magical bed while Xanaphia prepared to take watch. Darien rose and crossed to stand behind Clement. The sorcerer still stared with a pensive expression at the crystal. Darien placed a hand on his shoulder.

"You will get your chance," he said. "Be patient."

He gave Clement's shoulder a squeeze.

Hours later, Sylvia woke. She rolled over and looked into the sky, reflecting on the proceedings of the previous day. She still felt unsure about her new allies. Lillian had provided food and nourishment but also gave her a cold shoulder. Xanaphia seemed content to just pretend Sylvia wasn't there. Clement behaved cordially, but Sylvia sensed him picturing her death a thousand times over in his mind. Even Darien seemed friendly out of necessity rather than desire.

Sylvia rolled over. A tray of food sat on the ground beside her. Apparently her companions had prepared a plate of fruits and breads in case she awoke. It was thoughtful of them, and she felt a small twinge of guilt for insulting them earlier. Sylvia pushed herself upright and glanced around.

The tyrants appeared to have formed a barrier around her. Clement slept to her left on some sort of magically altered surface, while Darien slept on her right. Xanaphia slept at her feet, twisting and muttering. She appeared to be suffering from nightmares. Sylvia could relate. She couldn't remember the last time she had a peaceful sleep. It'd been many years, perhaps since before her military campaign.

Darien slept on her right opposite Clement, and an empty sleeping bag rested above her head. Her comrades were either trying to protect her by surrounding her or trying to ensure she didn't escape.

Sylvia scanned the clearing for Lillian. With all the emotions and stress of the past few days, the last thing Sylvia wanted was to be left alone with her thoughts. She welcomed any form of distraction, even speaking with an old and hated rival. She spotted the spymaster a short distance away fiddling with a multi-colored cube.

Grabbing an apple from her tray, she rose and crossed the campsite toward her white robed companion. Lillian didn't notice. She appeared oblivious to everything except the small block. She was muttering to herself and pressing lights with great excitement.

"Is this your definition of keeping watch?" Sylvia asked in a derisive manner.

"Bite me!" Lillian retorted, not looking up.

"Fine," she said. "I just thought you might want to pay some degree of attention to what's happening around you."

Lillian lowered the cube and gave an exasperated sigh.

"Good point," she said, sarcasm oozing from her lips. "Let's see."

She glanced to the left, holding her hand above her eyes and squinting in the mock gesture of someone trying to spot an object in the distance.

"Hmm, I see darkness," she exclaimed with false enthusiasm. She repeated the gesture looking to the right. "Oh! And I see more darkness!"

Sylvia rolled her eyes as the spymaster continued her angry demonstration by peering ahead.

"Oh! And look at that, more darkness." Lillian lowered her hand and picked up the cube. "Glad I got that taken care of."

Sylvia shook her head. "I guess your manners haven't changed much in the last seven years."

"Go kiss a grorg!" Lillian responded, not looking up from the block.

Sylvia laughed. She couldn't help it. The entire situation struck her as humorous. She'd spent the last seven years surrounded by flatterers and sycophants. It was an odd feeling to have companions who not only didn't like her but who felt no reservations about showing it. For the first time in a long time, she found herself needing to earn the favor or attention of someone else.

"Look," Lillian said, "do you mind leaving me alone? I'm almost finished solving this thing."

"What is it?" Sylvia asked.

"None of your business."

"I just meant, what'll it do once you solve the lights?" Sylvia said.

"Please reference my previous statement!" Lillian reiterated in a dull tone.

Sylvia shook her head. Striking up a conversation with Lillian might be more difficult than anticipated.

"All right," Sylvia exclaimed, throwing her hands into the air. "I just wanted to chat. You could try being a little civil."

"If you don't like my attitude, why don't you just take away all of my property, titles, and possessions, exile me from my home, and remove my name from every honor I ever earned. Oh wait! You already did that!"

The bitterness in her voice struck Sylvia like a fist. She gaped in speechless silence, unsure what to say. Her actions clearly stung Lillian, as they were intended to, but what else could she have done? Her former classmate was an evil and corrupt leader. She had controlled her people through manipulation, assassination, blackmail, and disease. Lillian deserved punishment, even if Sylvia was somewhat overzealous in carrying it out.

On the other hand, Lillian possessed reason to feel resentment. First of all, she had treated Sylvia's husband, and in turn Sylvia's family, very well. During Lillian's reign, Sylvia had fled the city and lived in hiding, fearing retaliation or assault. No such attack ever came. But Sylvia's husband, Robert had refused to run. Lillian rewarded him with a significant promotion and large pay raise. She made sure he got the apprentices he wanted, lived in the best housing, and received the utmost security. She even spoke of making him headmaster before his passing.

Lillian also put up no resistance to Sylvia's army, accepting the demand of unconditional surrender. The decision prevented months of war and thousands of deaths. Yet she had received the same harsh retribution dealt to Xanaphia. Sylvia had to admit her punishment wreaked more of jealousy than justice. Still, she couldn't change the past.

Sylvia sat down beside her old schoolmate.

"I never thanked you for the courtesy you showed following Robert's death," Sylvia said. "Thank you."

Lillian lowered the cube and gazed at her, as though unable to imagine hearing such words from her lips.

"Why did you do it?" Sylvia asked. "You gave Robert a lavish burial normally reserved for kings. Why'd you always treat him so well?"

"You should know why," Lillian said. "Robert was the world's greatest expert in violet quartz crystal. His research was hundreds of years ahead of anyone else. Only Xanaphia compares with his knowledge. Whatever techniques your children used to craft that tiara, I'm confident the crystals are the source of its power. I'm further confident that they learned how to construct it from his notes."

Sylvia diverted her eyes.

"I didn't want to lose such a valuable teacher," Lillian continued. "I knew Xanaphia would stop at nothing to get his knowledge if she found out about him. So I kept him close to me, where my spells and spies provided him some protection. The royal burial I granted him included rituals to prevent Xanaphia from contacting him in the world of the dead, and the Royal Cemetery seemed the safest place to safeguard his remains."

Sylvia nodded. "How much do you know about the tiara and my children?"

"Not much," Lillian answered. "I know they gave you the tiara as a gift. I know they haven't been seen since. I know little else."

She looked at Sylvia as though expecting some explanation, but Sylvia felt no desire to continue the conversation along those lines.

"I know you hate me," she said. "And I understand your anger over your exile. But what else could I do? You couldn't stay in Rhoria."

"I didn't want to stay in Rhoria!" Lillian barked, springing onto her feet. "If you'd taken the time to talk with me or even meet with me, I would've told you so! I just wanted to collect my possessions and leave with dignity."

The bitterness in Lillian's voice startled Sylvia. She stared at Lillian in shock as her former schoolmate raged.

"But no!" Lillian continued. "You couldn't take the time to speak with me or negotiate. You just stripped me of my possessions, banished me with only the clothes on my back, and ordered me gone before you arrived at the castle."

"I acted inappropriately," Sylvia admitted. "I allowed my spite to get the better of my judgment. I'm sorry."

Lillian stared in apparent surprise at the other's admission. After a while, she sat back down and picked up the cube. Sylvia waited until Lillian's temper cooled before speaking again.

"Do you believe we'll reach Rhoria before the demon lord catches us?"

"No," Lillian said in a matter-of-fact manner.

"So, Aurba is doomed?" Sylvia asked.

"Unless you destroy the tiara, yes."

"But I heard your comments while we marched today," Sylvia pointed out. "You said the demon lord's armies are unstoppable. You said humankind can't hope to resist them."

Lillian lowered the block and stared into the night with a thoughtful expression.

"So what difference does destroying the tiara make?" Sylvia continued. "Either way we will fall."

"You lack faith in the world," Lillian responded.

She turned toward Sylvia, and their eyes locked. Lillian gave a small compassionate smile.

"You've always been held back by your fears," she said. "In school, you possessed far greater talent than most students, but it never manifested because you lacked a willingness to take risks. You refused to experiment or delve into dangerous or little-understood areas of magic. In time, you fell behind other students who possessed enough faith in their talents to explore the unknown.

"Look at us," Lillian continued, gesturing at the other sorcerers. "We achieved our greatest accomplishments from taking risks. Xanaphia dedicating herself to necromancy, the most dangerous and unpredictable form of magic in existence. Darien chose to pursue a branch of enchantment and spell casting considered so archaic no one taught it anymore. Clement took spells relegated to the trash dumps of sorcery and transformed them into unstoppable weapons. I researched areas of survival magic and subterfuge considered worthless by my peers. Even your husband, Robert, dedicated his life to performing risky and potentially fatal experiments on violet quartz in an effort to learn its secrets. Think of the things you might have achieved if you had demonstrated the same willingness to step outside the box and take a chance."

Sylvia opened her mouth, but Lillian went on. "After I assumed the throne, you fled before my imagined wrath, but why? Seriously, I killed almost a hundred people to secure my path to the throne. If I wanted to kill you, why wait until after I became queen? But you let your fear and doubt get the better of you. It cost you many years with your husband."

That stunned Sylvia, and she shook her head trying to process the revelation.

"Cyril told us what happened at Junlorace Keep," Lillian went on. "You only needed to give him the crown and save the world, but your doubts and fears paralyzed you with indecision. You missed your chance. Now you have a second one. You can destroy the tiara, but fear and doubt stay your hand."

Silence fell between them.

"You say I lack faith," Sylvia said. "What am I supposed to believe in? Myself? My magic? Both have their limits."

"Then believe in the world," Lillian suggested. "The world has a way of working things out. Do you think it's coincidence that Clement, Darien, Xanaphia, and I are here? What're the odds that the four greatest sorcerers to live in the last thousand years would all be born in the same generation? What're the odds that it coincides with the rebirth of the demon lord? What're the odds we all happened to be in Rhoria on the night of your kidnapping? All are astronomical. The only valid explanation is to believe something bigger than us is at work."

Lillian's eyes sparkling with passion. "Destroy the tiara," she pleaded. "Give the world a fighting chance. Let's see what happens. The world may yet have another bizarre twist or two up her sleeves if you just give her the opportunity."

Sylvia stared in open-mouthed surprise. She couldn't believe those words came from Lillian's mouth. The stout survivalist who never missed a chance to flee from danger was telling her to be brave. A sorceress who always had a dozen contingency plans for every scenario was urging her to have faith in a higher power.

Lillian also seemed shocked. She hesitated as though struck by the weight of her own words. Her mouth hung open, and her brow knitted in a look of confusion and bewilderment. She leapt to her feet in obvious agitation and strode away from Sylvia without another word.

"Are you okay?" Sylvia called.

Lillian didn't respond. She hurried to where Clement slept and gave him a firm kick.

"Your watch," she said before striding away at top speed into the forest.

Clement rose with a puzzled expression as Lillian disappeared. Then he spotted Sylvia.

"Oh, she was talking to you," he said. "No wonder she's in a bad mood."

"Good morning to you too!" Sylvia retorted. "Are you the last watch?"

"I am," Clement answered. "But if you're up, I'll gladly go back to sleep."

Sylvia ignored the statement. She expected to remain up the rest of the night but still wanted someone to distract her mind.

"I guess you hate me also," she said.

It was a poor way to start a conversation, but she couldn't think of anything else to say. Clement seemed amused.

"Of course," he said. "We all do. As I said, we put aside our hatred to see the demon lord destroyed."

He rose and crossed the other side of the clearing, where he knelt beside the campfire. Picking up wood from a pile of branches, he tossed a few into the blaze and prodded the embers.

"If the demon lord and the tiara are destroyed, what then? You'll kill me, won't you?"

Clement hesitated.

"Yes," he said. "But neither of those is close to happening."

"I suppose not," she admitted. "But if they do, at least I'll die knowing the world is safe."

Clement shrugged. Sylvia watched him in silence for a couple of minutes.

"All of you hate me," she said at last. "But I think you hate me more than the others."

She waited for him to speak, but he said nothing. He just stared into the fire.

"I guess that's fair," she continued. "I hate you more than the others also."

"Because of your husband?"

"Yes," she said, her voice filled with emotion. "You took him from me!"

Again, Clement neither spoke nor looked at her.

"I didn't get to see him much those last years, but at least he was there," she said. "There's something comforting about knowing someone loves you and thinks about you, even if you can't be with them. He came to visit every couple of months and spent a week or two with me. We exchanged letters all the time. We even sent magical baubles with messages to each other. When the letters and messages stopped, I was worried. I sent my best friend Gaheera to the capital to check on him.

"The next day, I received a message from his favorite apprentice, Alexis. He was dead. I fell apart. I was a complete wreck for almost a year. His death left a void in me that no one could ever heal. Even now, I still suffer eternal loneliness. I wanted you to feel the same emptiness and desolation that haunts my every waking hour. I wished for you to experience the same eternal bleakness and vacancy. I don't know why I'm telling you this, other than I suppose I need you to understand why I did what I did. It amounts to little more than vengeance, but at least I carried out my retribution in a righteous manner."

Sylvia looked at Clement. He just gazed into the fire, saying nothing. She felt a rush of irritation. She wanted him to acknowledge her. She wanted him to say something.

At last he spoke. "If your life is nothing but eternal emptiness and desolation, rest assured that when the demon lord is defeated I'll remedy both of our problems."

Sylvia gaped at him, stunned by his callous response.

"Don't mistake me," Clement added. "I'm sorry Robert died. He was a great man and a talented sorcerer. But people die in battles. He knew the risks associated with staying in Rhoria and chose to take them. In the end, he was a casualty of war."

"A casualty of war," Sylvia said in disbelief. "He wasn't a soldier! He was just an innocent civilian trying to make an honest living in his hometown."

"Battles have collateral damage," Clement said, looking at her for the first time. "Don't act like you don't understand, and don't act so righteous. How many innocent civilians died trying to make an honest living during your campaign?"

"What do you mean?" she demanded. "I didn't attack villagers or . . ."

"You didn't have to," Clement interrupted, rising to his feet. "How many battles did you fight on people's farmland? How many people in neighboring towns died because your armies destroyed their crops? You set up hospitals for your sick and wounded in villages. How many innocent people died from the diseases your men carried into their cities? My soldiers and apprentices you slew in combat were husbands and wives, mothers and fathers. How many innocent people died or starved to death because you killed the source of their family's income?"

"I was fighting for a cause," Sylvia argued. "I was bringing those people freedom and peace."

"Noble!" Clement said sarcastically. "My soldiers and apprentices fought for a cause too. Some fought to fulfill their dreams of becoming famous warriors, great generals, or powerful sorcerers. Others just performed their jobs to earn paychecks to feed their families. Still others fought because they believed in my empire and in me. You don't view them the same way you view your own soldiers. Still, noble or not, they fought for a purpose. To believe otherwise discredits their sacrifice, even if that sacrifice proved in vain.

"You judge me for your husband's death, but there are lots of Sylvias out there who judge you for the deaths of their husbands, wives, children, or parents. So you can take your talk about righteous retribution somewhere else. In the end, your justifications are nothing more than a mask you use to cover your own atrocities."

Clement sat back down and gazed into the fire. Sylvia thought about it. She had always seen herself as a liberating hero. Most people considered her a savior. But Clement was right. Her military campaign left many orphans, widows, and widowers behind. Many of these victims likely bore grudges against her for the loss of their loved ones.

"Listen," Clement said, looking back at her. "You're not the only one who's suffered losses in your life. I lost my family and found myself wrongfully banished from my school and my home. The pain is great. I understand the desire for revenge, but this isn't about revenge. The demon lord is threatening humanity. You must let go of the hurt. Use it to give you strength. Think of how many innocent people will die if you don't destroy the tiara. Let your sense of loss give you the power to prevent others from suffering the same fate."

For the second time in the same night, Sylvia found herself confronted by wisdom from someone she believed to be shallow and evil. She looked at him.

"You confound me, Clement. How can you be so cruel one minute and so wise the next?" She paused. "You know, I remember you from my school days, though I doubt you noticed me. You always exemplified honesty, hard work, excessive pride, and possessed a more brilliant mind than anyone in the school. That was before you allowed anger, hatred, and vengeance to turn you into a monster. Yet at times like this I can catch a glimpse of the old you somewhere behind the dark façade. I sense the truth in leaving my past pain behind me, but I'll ask you this. Can you leave your past pain behind? Can you let go of the pain caused to you?"

He gave no response. She waited for several minutes, but he said nothing. She sensed the conversation was over and rose to her feet.

"I know you wanted me to kill you," she said, "but consider this. If I killed you, who would've saved me from the demon lord? Lillian seems to believe the world possesses some sort of guiding intelligence. Maybe she is right. Perhaps everything happened so we'd develop the skills necessary to be right here, right now, as the world's last hope."

She strode away, leaving him alone by the fire.

The grorg army marched in procession down the empty streets of Rhoria as the first rays of dawn stretched over the city. The corpses of the fallen lined the roads and blood coated the cobblestones. The smell of death tickled their nostrils while the buzz of flies filled their ears. They ignored both. Their minds were focused on their dark purpose, to destroy the last remaining bastion of resistance.

Ladonna stood before them. Her sword, her hands, the sleeves of her tunic and even her hair were drenched in blood. Sweat coated her face. Her eyes were bloodshot from lack of sleep, but they glittered with fierce determination. She stood motionless, her chainmail glistening in the dawn like a guardian angel defying her foes.

The day was the end of a long night for the red-headed warrior. After Alexis and Gemma retook control of the academy, Ladonna met up with her soldiers. Battle raged throughout the city by now, and Rhoria's forces were too dispersed to repel the attack. They needed a unified front. Following Alexis's initial plan, she had chosen to establish a stronghold at the central park and sent parties of runners into the village crying for everyone to regroup there.

The tactic was risky. It involved townsfolk leaving their homes and shelters, exposing them to attack. But since the grorgs were already forcing their way into houses, citizens faced just as much danger staying in as going out. In the end, more people reached safety than Ladonna dared to hope. Some escaped while the beasts occupied nearby houses. On other streets, husbands, fathers, mothers, and sometimes even courageous children sacrificed themselves for their families and friends. Ladonna's runners made valiant stands against the pursuing grorgs, buying time for the Rhorians to reach safety. Ladonna herself led several forays to drive off pursuing grorgs.

At first, the grorgs didn't attack the square. They were too scattered to mount such an offensive. Instead, they focused on preventing others from reaching it, particularly soldiers, strong men, and those capable of wielding weapons. Ladonna understood. As long as the people reaching the square were civilians, they were no threat. The grorgs could finish them off later. That later was now.

Satisfied with the destruction of Rhoria and confident in their victory, sixty grorgs marched toward the park. They spread out as they reached a walkway that separated the green from a circle of tall flat-roofed stores. Ladonna stood before them. On her left stood Anwyn; on her right stood Daylin. Behind them, fifteen soldiers from Junlorace Keep and ten Rhorian militiamen guarded almost three-hundred civilians. Most of these were women and children.

The townsfolk shuffled nervously, and Ladonna heard babies and adults both crying. She remained strong and statuesque before the enemy.

The lead grorg spoke.

"At last, the great Ladonna is at our mercy," it hissed in triumph. "Cyril isn't here to save you this time, little girl. You can't win this battle."

"Take a step toward these people, and I'll slice you to pieces," she said, lifting her sword.

"Fool child, failed kefling," the grorg huffed. "You know the powers of the master. You can't hope to confound his might. Fortunately, he bears you no malice. You're the last of his children born before his awakening."

Ladonna's eyes widened at the implication. Cyril was dead. The grorg's knowledge of his death meant his plan to trap the demon lord had either failed or was anticipated.

"He wishes to offer you a reprieve," the grorg continued. "We're here to destroy Rhoria, not Junlorace. Stand aside, and your people will be spared."

"Speak your lies to someone else," Ladonna said. "You'll not harm these people."

The grorg gave a harsh laugh.

"I knew you were too foolish to accept Master's offer," he gloated. "Very well, die along with them. Do you think your rabble can compete with our superior might, speed, and intelligence?"

Ladonna mimicked the other with her own mocking laugh.

"Ha! You may have superior might and speed, but intelligence? Don't make me laugh. If you really had 'superior intelligence,' you would have checked the roofs of neighboring buildings before positioning your army between us and them."

The hyena-like grin on the creature's face dropped. With a worried glance, it looked back at the two-story shops encircling the square.

"Now!" Ladonna screamed, hoisting her sword.

Atop the roofs rose over fifty Junlorace soldiers and thirty Rhorian guards, all armed with readied crossbows. Four dozen robed sorcerers, some apprentices, and some masters stood intermingled with them. The soldiers in the commons dropped to their knees, yanking their own readied crossbows from the concealment of the high grass.

"Fire!" Ladonna screamed.

Arrow and spells filled the clearing. The grorgs howled in surprise and terror, slamming into each other in their rush to escape the ambush. Some charged the attackers on the green while others attempted to fly down distant streets. None escaped.

The battle was over, but the worst was yet to come.

CHAPTER 26

Inside the academy, Alexis, Ladonna, and a small group of advisors gathered around a wooden table. The sun setting over the distant horizon signaled the end of a long day. After the destruction of the grorg army, the remaining grorgs had fallen back to the palace. A contingent of guards established a watch to prevent a counterattack while civilians and soldiers alike searched the village for survivors. Priests supervised the transportation of dead bodies to the town cemetery while sorcerers treated the injured and dying.

Ladonna found herself in charge of both the Rhorian and Junlorace military forces. Alexis believed Ladonna was better suited for working with the soldiers, while Alexis coordinated the sorcerers. The increased workload meant Ladonna got no sleep for the second day in a row, although she managed a brief catnap before hurrying to the academy to meet with Alexis and her officers. Together they struggled to develop some plan of attack against the grorgs' remaining stronghold.

"I don't understand why the grorgs didn't escape." Captain Eric said. "They could've easily fled to safety instead of trapping themselves inside the palace."

"Perhaps they believe they can still win," Commander Gemma suggested.

She hobbled around the table on a wooden crutch. A grorg had managed to slice off her left leg during the battle at the academy. The injury could be treated, but regenerating limbs required several days of regular treatment.

"I don't know," Ladonna said, pacing the room. "Our intelligence indicates they've completely barricaded themselves inside."

"They boarded every window large enough for a man to pass through and sealed every doorway," Phorus said. The retired Rhorian captain was an old and decrepit man with a lilting voice few could listen to for an extended period of time. "They went so far as to collapse the corridors with magical explosives."

"Hardly the type of behavior one expects from an army planning a counter assault," Alexis observed. "Maybe they're waiting for reinforcements."

"Possibly," Ladonna said. "But if they've closed off every entrance, how do they plan to get out once reinforcements arrive?"

"And how many reinforcements can they possibly expect?" Captain Eric asked. "We've counted over a hundred grorg bodies, and there are likely more slain inside the palace that we can't count. Kendross Keep doesn't have an unlimited supply."

"Cyril never performed a full count of the grorg population," Ladonna said. "Estimates ranged anywhere from one hundred and fifty to one hundred and eighty. Scrying indicates fifteen grorgs are currently inside the palace. This means as many as sixty might remain available for reinforcements. That would make a formidable force."

"But we're still left with the question of how they plan to get out of the palace," Gemma argued.

"That's the problem with making a structure impossible for enemies to enter," a young orange-robed sorceress named Julianne quipped. "You also make it impossible to get out. Maybe the brutes didn't think that far enough ahead."

"No," Ladonna said, "they have their weaknesses, but stupidity isn't one of them. If they plan to counterattack, they'd leave themselves a way to do so."

"So we're left with a quandary," Eric concluded. "They sealed every entrance and exit. They aren't trying to escape. And even if reinforcements come, they can't counterattack. We know they're waiting for something, but we don't know what."

"Maybe they want to escape back through the glyph," Gemma suggested. "Lord Octha, are there any indications the portal in the queen's room can operate in reverse?"

A golden-robed sorcerer looked up from his pile of random papers and notes. A short, well-built man, he taught defensive magic at the academy. His rescue by Alexis when she entered the cafeteria proved fortuitous, for he was the teacher researching the magical glyph in the queen's bedchamber. At the moment, he was preoccupied with reviewing the papers, and hearing his name seemed to have caught him off guard.

"Hard to say," he stammered. "Information on the subject is limited, as such magic has all but vanished from our world. I was able to find some information in writings by early sorcerers and historians, like headmaster Sorin. However, I'm still limited to speculation. But none of my notes indicate the portals work in reverse. It seems they're designed to travel only one way."

"Ladonna said as much in our first discussion," Alexis acknowledged. "But we can't take anything for granted with the demon lord. If his magic is as great as legends say, then perhaps he can reverse the flow of the portal."

"True," Ladonna said. "But if so, why aren't they inside the queen's room waiting for it to activate?"

Alexis shook her head.

"Does the demon lord possess any other minions he can send through the gate aside from grorgs?" Phorus asked. "Perhaps ones who can walk through walls or even smash through them?"

"Not that I'm aware of," Ladonna responded. "Unless he started turning the animals into monstrosities or created some new creatures from scratch."

She froze. A horrible thought had occurred to her. She looked at Alexis, whose eyes went wide as though sharing Ladonna's revelation. Dread filled the room as everyone waited for them to speak.

"Am I coming in at a bad time?" a quiet voice asked.

All eyes turned to see the silver-robed form of Yeva standing at the cafeteria entrance.

"I'm afraid so, my child," Phorus said. "But come in nonetheless."

She hurried into the room. She was still a little unsteady on her feet and stumbled as she walked. But color had returned to her skin, and her usual enthusiasm remained in place.

"What did I miss?" she asked.

"I believe," Alexis said, "Ladonna is about to inform us the demon lord's demonic horde is awake and about to attack."

All of the advisors and sorcerers started speaking in unison as pandemonium filled the room. Yeva alone said nothing, staring in surprise at the chaos unfolding before her. Amid the confusion, Ladonna raised her hand for silence. Eric and Gemma fell quiet. The rest of the company took a little longer..

"Yes," Ladonna said. "That's the only explanation which makes sense."

"I thought the survivors destroyed the demon lord's army after his imprisonment," Julianne objected.

"Not all of them," Octha answered. "Humanity slew the demons involved in the battle, but according to legends he housed a massive army of reserves inside inaccessible chambers in the heart of the citadel. To prevent them from killing each other, he kept them in a deep stasis. Stories say they still await their master's call to action."

"The stories are true," Ladonna stated. "I haven't seen them, but one such creature kidnapped Sylvia while others butchered the search parties."

"But surely he isn't sending his whole horde," Gemma objected, as though the number of demons coming made a difference. "Maybe he is just dispatching one or two. Sending them all is a bit of overkill, don't you think?"

"I do," Ladonna responded. "But he may not. The monsters haven't eaten in a long time, and I've seen how demonic creatures act during blood lust. He may feel the best course of action is to release his beasts into the city and let them gorge themselves on the people. Afterward, they'll be ready to carry out his next assault."

"So you're saying we're all about to die?" Julianne asked.

Alexis rose to her feet. "No, she's saying we must close the portal and must do so now! Octha, have you learned how to seal the gate?"

"How hard can it be?" Yeva asked in a sarcastic voice. "The glyph is just some sort of drawing or painting embedded onto the ground. Why don't we just drag a knife through it and break the circle."

"Because wizards are smart," Octha said. "They aren't going to risk losing a whole army of soldiers by allowing any fool with a butter knife to ruin their spells. They protect their devices. In the case of these glyphs, if you destroy the symbol, you destroy everything else as well!"

"What do you mean?" Alexis asked.

"If one of these markers is physically harmed, the symbol explodes with the force of a lightning ball decimating everything nearby."

"Then how do we destroy it?" Ladonna asked.

"Sources claim the portal can be sealed by a series of dispelling rituals," Octha said. "The spells involve an enchantment technique no longer taught at the academy. But if we assemble enough teachers, I believe we can complete them in a satisfactory manner."

"Will the demon lord know when the portal is dissolved?" Alexis asked.

"The creator knows when the glyph breaks, but no one else does," he answered. "In fact, the glyph on the other end remains active. Anyone entering becomes teleported into oblivion. I found several stories about sorcerers using the symbols as traps to dispose of disloyal servants or intruders."

"But even if we can destroy it, we don't have a way to get into the palace," Eric pointed out.

"True," Phorus agreed. "All entrances and gates are sealed. The creatures must be aware of the demon lord's plan and are making sure we don't thwart it. I'm still mystified how they knew to seal off the secret passage in the dungeon."

"They probably deduced the path's existence," Ladonna said. "They know I escaped somehow."

"Maybe we can scale the walls?" Julianne offered.

"Maybe," Alexis acknowledged. "But climbing the battlements is tricky. We'll run into a host of anti-thievery spells. There might be another way though."

She trailed off and stood scratching her chin in quiet contemplation.

"Well, what?" Octha asked.

Alexis began pacing in thought.

"On the night of Sylvia's disappearance, Darien the Dark and Clement the Great infiltrated the castle," she said. "No one knows how they entered. They must've used a secret passage, but Cordor had guards stationed near all known secret entrances. They must've used one unknown to us. This inference alone means little until we take into account that Cornelius knew such a passage as well. He often gloated about his 'personal entrance.' Again, the knowledge alone does little for us.

"Everything changes though when we consider the events following Sylvia's kidnapping. Darien and Clement got into a battle with Cornelius in the park near the school. None of the students on either side saw Darien or Clement prior to the confrontation. The two even surprised Cornelius by their sudden appearance. At this time, the alarm was sounding and Cornelius had left the academy in a hurry to reach the queen's chamber. Yet he went the opposite direction from the nearest entrance. There was no reason for him to be in the area where he encountered Darien and Clement. The only sensible explanation is to conclude Cornelius encountered them on his way to the secret entrance, and they encountered him on their way out of it."

"So," Ladonna said, "the secret entrance to the palace..."

"Must be on the wall nearby the site of the battle," Alexis finished.

"Then we have a way in!" Yeva exclaimed.

"I think so, but I need to know for sure before we make a move," Alexis said.

"I'll go with you," Ladonna said. "In the meantime, Eric, Gemma, I need you to select a company of soldiers for the mission."

"Why aren't we doing an all-out attack?" Gemma asked.

"We don't want to attract attention," she answered. "Once the grorgs know we're inside, they'll move to secure the queen's room. I prefer destroying the glyph in secrecy. Once the portal is closed, we can finish off the rest of Darlyth's minions."

Gemma nodded.

"Octha," Alexis said, "I want you to select a company of six wizards young enough to move quickly and quietly through the palace but powerful enough to cast the necessary spells."

"I'll go!" Yeva declared, and Alexis whirled around.

"No, you won't!"

"Why not?" Yeva asked indignantly. "I risked my life a dozen times on missions for you and the city. Why shouldn't I be allowed to go if I want?"

"Because you're too young to cast the necessary spells," Octha said.

"Ladonna and her soldiers can't cast spells either!" Yeva argued. "But they're coming to provide protection, and I can too!"

"You aren't a battle mage, my child," Phorus chided. "Your powers aren't developed for this type of combat."

"General," Yeva pleaded to Alexis, "I've always done everything you asked me."

"Except return to me when you saw there was danger at the academy," Alexis said pointedly. "I'm sorry. You can't come."

The teenager gave a loud huff and marched from the room.

Alexis watched her go and gave a sigh before turning back to her officers. "You have an hour. Choose your companions and meet us in the park."

She gave Ladonna a nod. "Let's go!"

An hour later, a dozen figures assembled on the spot where Cornelius had survived his encounter with Darien and Clement. Six of them were soldiers led by Eric and Patwyn. The rest were sorcerers led by Octha. Alexis and Ladonna surveyed them in silence.

"From this point forward, no talking," Alexis declared. "We scouted the path. It should be clear. But the future of our world depends upon this mission. So let's be cautious."

Alexis led the company into a set of large bushes.

Cries of surprise escaped the lips of the company as they passed through the illusionary greenery and emerged in front of a blank wall. Ladonna and Alexis pushed against the flat surface as they'd done when searching for the passage earlier. The wall gave way, revealing a small room filled with brooms, dusters, and other cleaning supplies.

The company soon found themselves meandering down halls and corridors. Ladonna felt uncomfortable as she traveled down the unfamiliar twists and turns of the massive facility. She trusted in Alexis guidance though. If Ladonna judged her character correctly, the general had spent more time inside the walls than her house and probably knew these halls as well as the architects.

Ladonna scanned for signs of trouble. At first everything seemed alright, but after a while Ladonna became suspicious. On multiple occasions, her sharp eyes picked up a strange displacement in the air behind them. At other times, her superior hearing detected the sound of footsteps and breathing. She couldn't see anyone, but she became convinced someone was following them.

When Alexis guided the company through a large illusionary mural of hunters chasing a white stag, Ladonna decided to test her suspicions. She waited until she'd pass through the false wall before tapping Alexis on the shoulder and signaling her desire to hang back. Alexis nodded and continued. The rest of the company did likewise, filing past her in pursuit of their leader.

Ladonna pressed herself against the wall and waited. She didn't need to wait long. A strange distortion of light passed through the canvas in front of her. Ladonna gave it no time to realize its mistake.

She sprang from the wall and seized the invisible stalker. It struggled and let out a cry of panic as Ladonna slammed it against the side of the corridor. The victim was light, relatively small, and appeared to be wearing long silk robes. Ladonna frowned.

"Yeva!" she growled. "We told you not to come!"

The rest of the company turned around to see the disturbance. As they did so, the invisibility spell fell away from of the young silver-robed apprentice. She gazed at Ladonna with obstinate eyes but shrank before the furious gaze of Alexis.

The general strode toward her, furious. Energy crackled from her raised hands.

"I should paralyze you and leave you lying in this hall like a statue!" Alexis glowered.

"But what if a grorg should enter the hall by accident while you're gone?" Yeva said.

"You'd be to blame for your own death," Alexis retorted.

Her fingers were inches from Yeva's face, but Yeva held her ground.

"Maybe," she said. "But the creatures would be tipped off about someone being inside the palace."

The two faced off for a second. Then Alexis lowered her hands, a look of intense irritation on her face.

"Fine," she snapped, "but if you ruin this mission…"

Alexis shook her head, seemingly unable to come up with a good conclusion to the statement. Instead, she just strode away with an expression that made her soldiers quake. Yeva beamed with excitement. She almost skipped down the corridor after the irate commander. Ladonna shook her head.

Teenagers, she thought.

The group exited through another false painting and after several more twists and turns arrived at a corridor lined with decorative suits of armor. Each looked exactly alike and even held identical halberds in their hands. Alexis took great interest in them, and Ladonna heard her counting them with deep concentration.

Ladonna saw nothing spectacular about them except for one suit that had a slight smudge under the visor, as though someone had recently lifted the hood. She was about to point this out to Alexis when the sorcerer stopped in front of it. Reaching forward, Alexis lifted and dropped the visor. An odd circular blue light appeared on the wall to the left. Alexis pressed it with her forefinger, and the wall vanished to reveal a steep staircase extending upward for several stories.

Alexis advanced into the passage and waved for the others to follow. A second coat of armor stood inside. Once the company had entered, she lifted and lowered the visor on this coat. The doorway vanished and the wall reappeared.

"This passage," Alexis whispered, "is one of the greatest secrets in the castle. You mustn't tell anyone else of its existence. The tunnel is known only to the queen and her highest advisors . . . oh, and her two greatest enemies, Clement and Darien."

Alexis gave a small shrug and led the company up the steps. About three quarters of the way up, she stopped to guide them around a trick step. At the top, they found another suit of armor sitting conspicuously beside a blank wall.

"The door I'm about to open will take us straight to the queen's room," Alexis whispered. "Her chambers are less than a dozen feet to our right. Guards are positioned in front of the doors. We must take them out before they can alert anyone. Sorcerers up front please."

The spellcasters shuffled to the front of the formation. The plan was simple. The moment the door opened, they would burst into the hallway, fill the corridor with spells, and slay the grorgs before they knew they were under attack. This part went as planned. Alexis opened the door, and the sorcerers sprang from their concealment. Spells filled the hallway. The grorgs were obliterated before they even got the chance to turn their heads.

Ladonna and her soldiers followed. A long corridor lined with doors ran to the left and to the right past a large set of open double doors with two dead grorgs lying in front. This was the queen's room. The company hurried inside, except for Ladonna and Commander Eric, who propped the bodies of the grorgs upright against the wall. Only a complete idiot could mistake them for being alive, but the ruse might fool an inattentive grorg if it was far enough away.

Satisfied, they proceeded into the room. Everyone was standing around as though expecting to see a giant rune in the middle of the floor. Ladonna shook her head.

"Cornelius placed the glyph inside the room years ago" she said. "He would've hidden it somewhere that Sylvia would never see it."

"But don't the creatures have to come out of it?" Yeva asked.

"Not necessarily," Octha answered. "If something is resting on top of the symbol or in front of it, the creatures will just appear on the other side."

"Which means it could be anywhere," Alexis observed. "Spread out and search the room. If you notice anything suspicious, report it immediately."

The bedchamber was massive and filled with hiding places. A four-post bed stood against one wall while various cabinets, dressers, and armoires collected dust along another. The only place devoid of decoration was the opening where a window once led to a large balcony with a carved stone handrail. The window was gone, replaced by a newly constructed wooden frame still awaiting the glass.

The crew spread out across the room. The soldiers scoured the inside of wardrobes and cabinets while sorcerers levitated furniture to peek underneath. Ladonna lifted a mirror and looked behind the glass. Meanwhile, Alexis raised her hand above the mattress and muttered, "Rentgenov."

A cone of light spread downward from her outstretched palm. The light reached into the bed, revealing the insides of the cushion, from the bunched up feathers to the silk lining. She scanned the innards looking for some indication of the mysterious marking. Yeva watched her with apparent interest. Extending her own palm, she whispered, "Rentgenov."

A cone of light identical to the one summoned by Alexis burst from her hand, and Yeva gave a cry of surprise that drew angry looks from the rest of the company. She gave a somewhat bashful apology before turning excitedly to Ladonna.

"I can't believe I was able to get the spell to work," she said, practically bouncing.

"Great," Ladonna said, trying to mask her frustration. This was a serious moment, and the girl's antics were a unwelcome distraction. "Why don't you use it to wander around and see if there's anything on the floor?"

Yeva seemed delighted by the suggestion. She spun around, gazing at the dirty and cracked paneling underneath the dark-red carpet. Small insects and ants strolled below, exploring the aging structure, and she muttered with excitement as she studied them. Then she gasped.

"It's here!" she screamed, bouncing up and down as she pointed at the floor.

Just a short distance inside the door, underneath the carpet, rested a strange marking. It was small, no large than the size of her hand. A V in the center of a circle, with the bottom of the V being in the middle, the tips of the V on the outside, and a squiggly line going up the middle. Ladonna had never seen anything like it but knew it must be the glyph.

Pulling out her sword, she started cutting through the carpet. Other soldiers joined her, and they soon uncovered the unusual symbol.

"How do you think he got it there?" Yeva asked.

"The same way we did," Alexis answered. "He cut the carpet and used a mending spell to disguise it. Now, let's get rid of this thing."

Alexis stepped away and signaled for Yeva to do the same. Ladonna and her warriors followed suit.

"Excellent," Octha exclaimed, pulling some papers from his robes and distributing them to the other sorcerers. "The ritual will take about five minutes. Everyone, focus."

He froze and stared with an expression of horror at the glyph. All eyes followed his gaze. The symbol was glowing.

"Draw your weapons," Ladonna screamed, but it was too late.

A massive monstrosity appeared in the center of the room. It stood over nine feet tall with three short stubby legs supporting a large bulky midsection. Like a human, it possessed a large head resting on top of a short flabby neck, but the similarities ended there. Six ten-foot-long tentacles, each almost three feet in diameter, sprouted forth in a circle around its body, and a ring of eyes encircled its head. A wide mouth filled with rows of razor-sharp teeth gleamed at the horrified onlookers, and dark-purple skin formed a thick and scaly armor around it.

The demon struck so fast even Ladonna couldn't react. Tentacles flew everywhere. One of the appendages shot forward, wrapping around the closest sorcerer and yanking him off his feet. Another smashed into Yeva, sending her flying into a bookcase, its shelves collapsing under the force of the impact. The same tentacle struck Alexis, sending her sprawling over a bedside table. Other tentacles struck other sorcerers, scattering the robed figures across the room. They collided with the warriors, who sprawled onto the floor.

Octha's papers flew into the air in a disheveled mess of parchment. Screams and shouts filled the room. Soldiers and spellcasters stumbled over each other trying to regain their footing. Others screamed in terror as tentacles snatched them off the floor. The apprehended sorcerer shrieked as the beast whipped the helpless man up into its mouth. Teeth sank into the man with a sickening squish, and it drank deeply of the blood gushing from its struggling victim.

Into the flailing mass of tentacles and panicked companions sprang Ladonna. Her sword flashed as she brought the blade down with all her might onto a tentacle grasping a nearby sorceress. The attack did nothing. She stared in surprise as the blade bounced off, leaving only a slight cut in her enemy's tough exterior.

"Desecria!" screamed Alexis, regaining her footing.

The black lightning streaked through the air, striking the demon in the chest. It twitched and took a small step backward but didn't even release its meal. It must've felt both Alexis and Ladonna's blows though, because it retaliated immediately.

A tentacle struck Ladonna from behind, snatching her off the ground by the waist. She tried swinging her sword at it, but the powerful tendril slammed her into the ceiling and flung her like a rag doll across the room. She crashed through the wooden window frame and skidded across the balcony into unforgiving stone railing. Knocked temporarily senseless, she barely registered a glimpse of Alexis soaring out of the room and colliding with the barrier beside her.

Screams sounded from everywhere. Spells flew around the room. Blades swung through the air. Tentacles crashed into victims. Bodies flailed in the creature's grasp, and, amid all the confusion, the symbol glowed anew.

"The glyph!" Octha's voice sounded from somewhere inside. "We must seal it!"

Ladonna rose to her feet and lifted her sword. As she did so, her eyes fell upon Yeva. The girl had emerged from beneath a large pile of fallen books and was observing the chaos surrounding her. Her eyes fell upon Ladonna. For a moment, the two made eye contact. Then, without the hesitation, Yeva sprang toward the beast. Ladonna saw her hand rise above her head, gripping a small dagger Ladonna recognized as the one found next to Yeva's body at the academy. Yeva held the weapon high to strike, but she didn't attack the demon.

"No!" Alexis screamed.

It was too late. As the indistinct figure of a second demon appeared inside the chamber, the knife fell. It slashed across the outer ring of the symbol, cutting the paint. An explosion ripped through the room. The heat of the flash burned out Ladonna's eyes, and the blast made her ear drums burst. Her flesh burned as though fiery hands ripped her skin from her body. She was lifted from her feet and soared through the sky like an arrow.

Her flight ended abruptly as she crashed into a stone surface. The air was knocked from her lungs, and her bones and skull shattered. Her consciousness faded, leaving nothing but a broken, unmoving mass of flesh and armor falling into the brambles below.

CHAPTER

27

Darien, Clement, Xanaphia, and Lillian again found themselves sitting around a fire in the heart of the Blood Fang Mountains. The day's march had pushed everyone to their limit. They'd made good progress, but the strain was catching up with them.

Sylvia had collapsed onto the ground before they even finished collecting firewood. Clement muttered self-healing spells on his aching legs and back. Darien crushed various herb and roots in his hands as he performed enchantments to recharge his stamina. Lillian expressed her weariness by devouring her plate of food so quickly Clement doubted she took a breath between bites. Xanaphia curled up on the ground, expressing herself too exhausted to eat. At which point, Lillian ate her plate as well.

Clement took a break from his healing spells and glanced at the queen. She twitched and thrashed in the throes of intense nightmares. Unintelligible moans issued from her lips, which moved as though speaking to someone. Sweat ran down her face, and the tiara shifted in her hair. The blue gems seemed to glow in the firelight.

"What do you think she dreams about?" Clement asked.

"I do not know," Darien said. "Whatever it is, it is not pleasant."

Lillian glanced at Sylvia, and her lips broke into a mischievous grin.

"Want to find out?" she asked.

Darien and Clement looked at her in amazement. Even Xanaphia sat up as Lillian removed the mysterious multi-colored cube from her robes. Every side looked identical, and Clement noticed an eerie green luminescence radiating from within. The light shimmered and fluctuated as though threatening to disappear at any moment. The colors on the cube were arranged in a rainbow pattern with the first square white and the last square black. Only one square remained out of place.

Lillian gestured for everyone to move close. They did so. Clement sensed her excitement as everyone gathered around. Lillian lifted her right forefinger about an inch away from one of the glowing lights on the cube, her hand quivering with anticipation.

"Everyone get ready to touch it," she whispered.

She jabbed her finger forward, striking the block. The deviant square changed to match the pattern on the other sides, and a green light burst from the cube. It showered everyone in a deep emerald glow before coalescing into a thick cylindrical beam that shot toward Sylvia.

Sensing the moment at hand, Clement, Darien, and Xanaphia each placed a finger on the cube. The world around Clement swam out of focus. He felt his mind wrenched from his body and his consciousness drifting toward the sleeping queen. It entered her body through the forehead. He lost track of his identity as he melded with her mind. He wasn't witnessing her dream; he was the dreamer. He was Sylvia.

Sweat poured down Sylvia's face as she raced through the thick tangled woods of the far southeast. It was nighttime, but no moon or stars shown through the trees overhead. A faint glowing turquoise apparition danced just out of reach before her. Clement recognized the specter as Sylvia's husband, Robert. Sylvia was dashing after him, her hands outstretched in a desperate attempt to reach him. But no matter how fast she ran, her husband's ghost remained just beyond her fingertips.

"Sylvia, come to me," Robert's voice echoed.

"I'm coming," she cried.

"Come back to Rhoria," he called. "I thought you loved me."

"I do love you," she sobbed, racing onward.

"Why did you abandon me? You could have saved me! I needed you!"

"I'm sorry!" she pleaded.

The image drifted further away from her, disappearing into the trees.

"No, come back!" she screamed.

Bushes and thorn vines reached out at her, wrapping around her and cutting into her skin as she fought to overtake her vanished husband.

Then the forest cleared. She stood before a beautiful wood cabin decorated with flowering vines rolling up the sides. The shutters and door were closed tight, but Sylvia could still see inside as though the walls were transparent. It was a typical peasant home. There was a stone fireplace with a large kettle resting upon the hearth beside a brick oven.

A number of straw beds lined the left side of the cabin, and a massive wooden cabinet filled with magical tomes sat on the right.

Something was odd though. The table wasn't in its normal spot. It had been moved to the very center of the cabin. A silver headband lined with diamonds rested on it. There were three circular openings at the top, one on the left, one in the center, and one on the right. A violet quartz crystal rested in each. Underneath the tiara was a piece of parchment containing a note scribbled in untidy scrawl. A twelve-year-old boy stood before the left crystal. Next to him, a young girl of nine stood in line with the middle crystal, and a boy of six stood in front of the right one.

The children lifted their heads in unison to look at their mother. Their bodies radiated the same blue glow as the earlier apparition of her husband. Their faces wore the gentle and loving expressions she always remembered when she thought of her babies. They flashed the tender smiles that always greeted her upon returning home and looked at her with eyes that could brighten her darkest days. She longed to hold them, to kiss them, to hear their laughter, and to touch their skin. Then the daggers rose.

"No!" Sylvia shrieked.

She tried to run toward the house but couldn't move her feet. A feeling of terrified apprehension gripped her. She must reach her children. She struggled and screamed, but her feet refused to budge.

Her oldest son gave a loving smile. He was her first born, the treasure of her family. He was a brilliant and gifted magical prodigy like his father. His voice was soft and filled with compassion, although it echoed in an eerie manner.

"It's a gift, Mother," he said. "You no longer have to grieve for dad. You no longer need to feel afraid."

"Michael!" she screamed, tears streaming down her face. "Michael! No!"

The dagger fell. It sank deep into his chest. His face froze in momentary astonishment, and he crumpled to the floor. The crystal in front of him erupted with blue light. Next the girl spoke. Her voice was gentle and sweet. She was Sylvia's only daughter, the girl she desired for so many years.

"It's what you always wanted, Mother."

"No," Sylvia pleaded, "don't do it. I don't want it!"

"You can save the world," she said. "You can get revenge."

"I don't want revenge!" she screamed, falling to her knees in despair. "I want you! Don't leave me! Erin, please!"

The dagger plunged into the girl's tender frame. Her eyes went wide, and blood trickled from her mouth. She fell to the floor. Again the blue gem flashed with energy. The six-year-old looked at his mother. His face was so delicate. He was her youngest child, her littlest angel.

"No," she moaned through torrents of tears. "Please, gods, make him stop! Stephen! No!"

"We love you, Mommy!" he said in his childlike voice.

His dagger fell. All three crystals exploded with light.

The walls became solid again. Sylvia found herself walking toward the cabin. She held a small picnic basket in her hands. She'd spent the day in town, selling her trade as a healer. Inside the basket was an apple pie, a special surprise for her children. The dessert was their favorite. She picked it up on the way home just for them.

As she approached, she realized something was not right. The windows were dark and bleak. No smoke came from the chimney. Where were her children?

"Michael?" Sylvia called. "Erin?"

None one answered.

"Stephen?" she called again, a note of fear in her voice.

Her children always answered her call. Something was wrong. She dropped the basket and raced inside. The room was pitch-black. The fire must've burnt out hours ago. She summoned a ball of light and gasped in horror.

The house looked just like the previous dream. The table sat in the center of the room with the tiara and the note, but Sylvia paid it no mind. Her eyes were fixed on her children lying on the floor. They looked peaceful and calm, as though sleeping. But they weren't asleep. Their eyes stared at the cabin roof, and daggers protruded from their chests.

"No!" Sylvia shrieked.

She raced to them, pleading with the gods for them to be alive. She went from one to the other, muttering every healing spell she knew. It was pointless. The children were dead. She threw herself on top of their bodies, weeping uncontrollably. Wrapping her arms around them, she lifted them to her breasts and wept. Behind Sylvia's back, unobserved by her, the violet gems glowed and the faces of her children appeared inside.

Green light flooded the scene. Clement found himself detached from Sylvia. He floated away from her body and back to his own. The cube went dark, and everything became still. No one said anything for several minutes. Clement spoke first.

"Dear gods!" he said, aghast. "Is that what she dreams every night?"

Lillian's mouth hung open in wordless horror.

"So," Xanaphia said, "she believes her children live inside the tiara."

"Do they?" Lillian asked.

"No!" Xanaphia snapped. Her aggressive response unsettled everyone. "The crystals hold magical energy, not souls. They might've placed a portion of themselves in the jewels, but it isn't truly them. It's just a shadow."

"Sometimes a shadow is enough," Darien said. He was holding the wingham-tooth necklace in his hands and wore a strange unreadable expression.

"Regardless," Xanaphia said, "the tiara must be destroyed. This is bigger than children or lost spouses. The entire world hangs in the balance."

"True," Clement agreed, "but we aren't going to achieve anything sitting here discussing it. We have a long day ahead. Let's get some sleep."

No one argued. Xanaphia and Lillian rose to their feet.

Lillian's face froze in shock and revulsion.

"You've got to be kidding me," she exclaimed.

She was gazing at the block. Clement glanced at it. The lights were mixed again. The intricate pattern she'd worked so hard to create was gone. She gave a snort of disgust and slammed it into her pocket. Clement couldn't resist the urge to crack a small smile at her expense. He rose from his seat and noticed Xanaphia watching Darien with concern. The enchanter sat with his head hung low, still fingering the necklace.

"Are you all right?" she asked.

"I will be," he answered without looking up. "I think I will take first watch though. You can go second."

She gave him a quizzical look but merely shrugged and walked away. Clement watched her lie down on the snow beside Sylvia. She seemed just a troubled as Darien.

"She will destroy the tiara," Clement heard her mutter as she closed her eyes. "Somehow I'll find a way."

A cold breeze brushed Sylvia's face, waking her from her sleep. She opened her eyes and rolled onto her left side. The night seemed unusually dark. She sat up in surprise. The campfire was out. The only light came from the infinite ocean of stars overhead.

She glanced around the campsite. Darien slept only a short distance to her left, and Lillian dozed at her feet, but she saw no one keeping watch. She was about to check on Clement and Xanaphia when a sound caught her attention. She looked up and watched in horror as Corineous emerged from the nearby bushes.

"You should've given the tiara to Cyril," he said.

Sylvia gasped. He couldn't be here. He was dead. She must be dreaming, but she knew it wasn't a dream. She was awake, and Corineous stood before her.

"You aren't worthy of the crown," he continued. "If your personal desires mean more to you than the welfare of your people, you're no better than me or the tyrants surrounding you!"

Sylvia raised her hands to attack, but Corineous vanished. Her husband stood in his place.

"Robert?" she gasped, lowering her arms.

"You *are* better than the tyrants," he said gently. "You possess the power to save your people. Let go of your fears."

"I can't," she said.

Her eyes began to fill with tears as she gazed at him.

"I need you," she said. "I can't do this without you!"

Her husband disappeared, replaced by her oldest son, Michael. His eyes were bright, his voice consoling.

"Yes, you can," he said. "We believe in you. We always believed in you."

"No," she cried, tears began rolling down her cheeks. "I don't want to lose you again!"

Her son's features blurred. Stepping over the sleeping form of Lillian was General Gaheera. Her black hair flowed in the cold breeze. Her face bore a harsh expression, and her tone was cold.

"Want?" she repeated in disbelief. "Is this the woman I fought beside during the war? Did our fellow soldiers want to die? Of course not, but they did so anyway. They sacrificed themselves for us. They sacrificed themselves for the greater good."

Gaheera transformed as she spoke. Her hair grew shorter, and the feminine features vanished. General Cordor loomed above her.

"I made my sacrifice for you," he said. "So did General Gaheera! And Michael! And Robert! How many more lives would you throw away to compensate for your weakness?"

"I'm sorry!" Sylvia wailed. "I didn't mean for this to happen! I didn't know things would come so far!"

Cordor faded. Cyril appeared. The kefling's eyes glowed in the dark.

"Only you can set things right," he declared. "You must destroy the crown. Do so for your people. Do so for everyone who died to give you this chance!"

"I can't." She buried her face in her hands.

"You must," he argued. "You have a responsibility. You can't shirk your duties. You are the queen!"

"Stop," she cried. "Please stop."

"Xana! Enough!" Darien's voice broke through the building tension.

Darien had leapt to his feet. His face was red with anger, and he glared at the form of Cyril standing before them. The kefling's image shivered, and Xanaphia towered above Sylvia wrapped in her enchanted black cloak.

"No!" she howled at Darien. "It isn't enough! Don't you understand? She's dooming us all!"

Xanaphia looked completely crazed. Her eyes were bloodshot, and she trembled as though suffering from a nervous breakdown. Her voice was cracked, and her breathing was strained.

"All of her friends died for her," she shouted at Darien, causing Lillian and Clement to stir from their sleep. "All her family died for her. We're next. You don't know what I've seen. You don't know what I know. The entire world will be enslaved, and all because of her!"

Xanaphia pointed an accusatory finger at Sylvia, whose mouth hung open in breathless shock. Darien stood firm, his expression unyielding. Xanaphia stared back, her breath slowing as she looked into his calm, steady face.

"Xana," Darien said, his voice quiet and compassionate, "go to bed. I will cover the rest of your watch."

Xanaphia stared at him for a moment, lowered her gaze, and marched away into the woods. Clement and Lillian glanced around in confusion. Darien raised a hand to signal everything was okay. They shrugged, lowered their heads back to the ground, and fell asleep.

Darien watched Xanaphia stroll into the forest. She stopped at a nearby tree and lay down facing away from the party. After a while, her breathing slowed and she fell asleep. Darien sighed and turned toward the extinguished campfire.

"Shech!" he said with a dismissive flick of his wrist. A red beam burst from his fingers, igniting the pile of dried limbs and twigs. He turned to Sylvia. "Are you all right?"

She nodded, trying to regain her composure. Darien pulled a handkerchief from his cloak and handed it to her. She wiped her eyes with the linen while Darien tended the fire.

"Thank you," Sylvia said, offering the handkerchief back.

Darien took the cloth and gave her a reassuring smile.

"Are you going back to bed?" he asked.

"I can't sleep," she said, shaking her head.

"I cannot imagine why you would want to," he responded.

He sat down beside the fire and pulled a pouch from his cloak. He opened the pouch and withdrew a large leaf, which he placed in the center of his hand. Selecting a few random fungi and roots from his collection, he crushed them and piled them onto the leaf. Sylvia rose and crossed the clearing to sit beside him.

"I guess she woke you," Sylvia said.

"No," Darien answered. He checked to make sure the others were asleep and gave a small smile. "Do not tell the others, but I do not actually sleep."

"What?" she asked in surprise. "You don't sleep at all?"

"No," he responded. "I enchanted myself early in my reign. Instead of going unconscious, my body falls into a trance. I get the same rest as if sleeping but remain aware of everything happening around me. My eyes are closed, so I can't see, but I can still hear. I heard the conversation and drew myself out of the trance."

Sylvia gave him a wry smile. "So you've been eavesdropping on all of the conversations happening at night."

"Maybe," he answered evasively. "I might have caught your discussions with Lillian and Clement. And I might have overheard Lillian and Xanaphia's conversations with Cyril."

"I guess I've been warned," she said.

"Anyway," Darien continued. "How long have you suffered from nightmares?"

"Ever since my first night with the tiara," Sylvia answered. "But they've gotten worse."

Darien nodded. "Losing your family is difficult. I lost my wife and children too."

Sylvia looked up in astonishment. "I never knew you took a queen or had heirs."

"I did not," he answered. "This happened before I founded my kingdom. You would not have heard about it. I do not believe there are any people living who know. Even Xanaphia does not know, although she caused my family's death."

"What happened?"

"One of her apprentices took an oath to find and kill me. My wife, Mesha, came from a family of wingham keepers. When the killer discovered me, we were out in the field training a new brood. Rather than attack me directly, he cast a spell sending the winghams into a killing frenzy. My magical skills allowed me to survive, and I eventually destroyed the murderer, but the winghams killed my entire family."

"That's why you drove them to extinction," Sylvia said.

"I wanted revenge," he admitted. "I still wear the teeth from the winghams who killed my wife and children. My willingness to resort to any means and any measure to get revenge is well documented. I forged my empire with the sole purpose of getting revenge on Xanaphia. When I came into conflict with Clement and Lillian, I wanted revenge against them too. I told myself I was protecting my people, but things spiraled out of control. I became the monster I was trying to fight."

"I'm surprised to see you getting along so well with Xanaphia," Sylvia said.

"Me too," Darien agreed. "But on the way here she risked her life to save some children. I started wondering if there was more depth to her personality than I ever considered. Maybe there is a greater and better person hiding beneath her hard exterior."

"I'm starting to think there's more depth to all of you than I ever considered," Sylvia agreed. "I wish I'd taken more time to learn about you. I allowed myself to get swept away by my overzealous nature. I became too eager to punish and destroy."

"All that time the greatest danger to humanity was inside your own camp," Darien said.

"True," Sylvia nodded. "Corineous."

"No, I mean you."

"What?" Sylvia said, feeling a surge of indignation. "How can you make such a statement? I never harmed my people! I rule with fairness and justice. I know the tiara is dangerous. I know I possess my weaknesses, and I admit I made some bad decisions, but I never performed any action designed to harm humanity."

Darien gave a small laugh before turning to her.

"You really do not understand, do you?" he asked. "How could you spend so much time talking with Cyril but still not learn anything?"

"Like what?" she said defensively.

He shook his head and looked into Sylvia's eyes. His face showed no malice or hostility. Sylvia realized he wasn't trying to insult her. She took a deep breath to calm her nerves and decided to be less defensive and pay more attention.

"Cyril and Xanaphia sat up talking every night while he was with us," Darien said. "I eavesdropped on their conversations. In doing so, I learned something from him that you missed."

"What?" Sylvia asked.

"The greatest dangers confronting humankind today are not tyrants, tormentors, or even your tiara," he said. "There will always be those misguided people whose desires lead them to do wrong, but the worst threat confronting humanity is not those who do evil. The true danger is those who can prevent evil but do not.

"Apathy. Lethargy. These forces allowed the demon lord to return. If left unchecked, they will destroy humankind. The world is filled with people who can prevent evil from happening but choose not to. Whether because of fear, laziness, or an unwillingness to make sacrifices, they sit back and rely upon others to fight for them. One day, things will go too far. There will be no one else to atone for their negligence. By then it will be too late."

"You think I'm one of these people?" Sylvia asked.

"Your Majesty," Darien said in a soothing voice, "you did incredible things during your ascent to power. But all of them were founded upon the sacrifices of others. I do not know what events were taking place in your home to inspire your children to choose to die the way they did. But, tell me, if your children did not sacrifice themselves to create the tiara, would you have led the campaign to free the world from oppression?"

The answer didn't require much thought.

"No," she admitted.

"Exactly," Darien said. "You lived in safety while evil and tyranny flourished, war raged, people suffered, and innocents died. As long as you remained unaffected, you did nothing. Only after those close to you died did you act."

Sylvia felt inclined to scoff at hearing a tyrant chide her for not overthrowing him sooner. Still, she recognized the truth when she saw it.

"But how was I supposed to defeat you without the tiara?" Sylvia asked.

"You could not," Darien replied. "Not in a one-on-one battle, but your military campaign was not a one-on-one battle. It was a war fought with armies. No sorcerer can defeat an entire army on their own, even with your tiara. Okay, Clement might be able to, but my point is that your strength came not from your tiara but from your leadership. Your courage rallied the people. Your strength and charisma attracted the soldiers and resources necessary to overthrow our regimes. They were always there. They just needed someone to unite them and spur them to action. You possessed that power. You just needed to use it.

"That is why we need you now. We can get rid of the tiara at anytime by destroying you, but the demon lord would still remain. The people need someone to unite them against the threat. But, again, you're relying upon others to make sacrifices for you. When Cordor came to Junlorace Keep, you held the crown in your hands. You only needed to destroy it to receive your freedom. Instead, you relied upon your soldiers to sacrifice themselves for your escape. After you got taken to Kendross Keep, Cyril sacrificed himself for you, but you will still not destroy the tiara. You are relying upon our protection."

She gave a sigh. "Everything depends upon me destroying the crown. But I can't do it. Do you think the demon lord believes I'll destroy it?"

"No, I do not," he answered. "I doubt the idea ever crosses his mind. From Cyril's description, he is obsessed with power and control. He feels no concern for anyone else, so he is incapable of understanding the idea of sacrifice. Giving up something valuable or special for the sake of another is beyond his comprehension. He would never destroy it."

"Well," Sylvia said. "I guess we share something in common."

"I disagree. Your children believed in you, and we do as well." He smiled. "You look surprised. Would we waste so much time trying to convince you if we thought the effort futile? You just need to believe in yourself. Your children made the ultimate sacrifice, giving up their lives for you to free Aurba. Now, you must make the ultimate sacrifice a parent can make, giving up their lives again to save the world."

"I don't know if I can," Sylvia responded.

"I think you just need a few nights of rest to clear your mind." Darien folded the leaf into a pouch around the various crush powders and liquids. He waved his hand over it and muttered a quiet incantation. The edges of the leaf fused together into a small capsule, which he offered to her.

"Hold it in your mouth while you sleep," he said. "You will have a peaceful night free from dreams."

Sylvia rose and took it from his hand.

"Thank you," she said, her voice filled with gratitude.

He nodded and turned back to the fire. Pulling his bag of ingredients from his cloak, he returned the unused portions.

"Where did you get all those supplies?" Sylvia asked, intrigued.

"We passed an apothecary on the way here," he answered. "I robbed it."

"You what?" the queen gasped, appalled.

"I needed the supplies," Darien said with an unabashed shrug. "I am an outcast. I have no money."

He tossed some wood into the fire. Sylvia smiled. She had to admit that the tyrants were very interesting people. She popped the green capsule into her mouth and strolled back to her bed site. For the first time in years, she would sleep in peace.

CHAPTER 28

"The lake," Darien called. "Fortune has smiled on us. We are on the correct side."

They stood on the crest of a tall mountain where the trees still remained thin enough to allow visibility. Sylvia gazed down upon the land below. The winter forest and frozen lake spread out before her in a breathtaking panorama.

"I remember landing in the snow over there in my attempt to escape Corineous," she said, pointing into the distance. "I almost reached those trees."

"We know," Clement said. "We heard the commotion but couldn't get there in time. The snow was too thick."

"Speaking of which," Darien said, "I am not looking forward to going through it again. We will lose a lot of time if we are forced to levitate."

"We don't have any choice," Xanaphia pointed out. "To the right is Junlorace Keep, no point going there. We could try the left path. It may lead to Buried Grove."

"Unburied grove," Darien interjected.

"Would you stop that?" Xanaphia snapped.

"Regardless," Clement interrupted, "the town offers no refuge from the demon lord, and we'll lose time from the diversion."

"Not as much as we lose trying to trudge through the snow," Lillian said. "That's probably how Corineous beat us to the keep."

"The straight line through the canyon is the shortest distance," Darien said. "On the other hand, the conditions place us at a severe disadvantage."

"If the snow is the problem, I know a spell to help," Sylvia said. All eyes turned to her in surprise. "General Andrus designed an enchantment for our campaign in the north. Watch. Topeetna!"

She waved her hands over the uneven ground. A bright-blue mist issued from her fingers, encircling everyone's legs and feet like an odd turquoise cast. With a bound, Sylvia leapt off the path and onto the deep snow. Instead of sinking, her feet landed firmly on top. She appeared to be walking on solid earth. She stomped playfully, pressing her boots hard against the powdery surface, but didn't sink in.

Cries of delight issued from the others as they too leapt from the road. Sylvia felt a rush of pride. For the first time in the entire expedition, she'd done something useful. She'd finally found a way to benefit those who spent so much time protecting her. The few hours of undisturbed sleep gave her a sense of clarity so long missing from her life. She'd never realized how badly her nightmares affected her until she got the chance to escape them.

The company continued through the mountains for several hours before reaching the entrance to the canyon. The winds proved lighter than their first trip, although the tunnel remained unpleasant. Lillian cast invisibility on the company as they exited, but the precaution proved unnecessary.

No demons guarded the exit. The corpse of the slain demon still lay on the ground, and Sylvia called a halt to examine it. Her only experience with a demon had lasted less than thirty seconds, and she was intrigued by the ancient creature. Clement and Darien watched impatiently. After only five minutes, Clement declared the break over.

As evening approached, the sun broke through the clouds for the first time in almost a week. The daylight brought new life to the company. Conversation flowed freely, and it wasn't the usual talk of dark tidings. It took on a lighter and more pleasant tone. They laughed and told stories. They joked and shared anecdotes. Even Xanaphia joined in the fun.

Sylvia laughed along with them. She'd never imagined strolling through the woods and chatting with her enemies like old friends. Traveling with them felt different than traveling with her subjects. They didn't seek her favor. They didn't want political gifts. They felt no need to hide their true natures or put on a false face. She could be herself around them without any concern for political ramifications or masking her words. She felt free.

She even dined with them that night. Conversation remained light-hearted as they looked ahead. Darien reported that Freighton Gorge was only about four or five hours away. At their current pace, they should reach it sometime in the morning. They might even reach Rhoria the following day. The plan was incredibly optimistic, but in the beautiful night following the pleasant evening anything seemed possible.

When the meal concluded, Darien rose to face Xanaphia. His somber expression broke the jovial proceedings.

"Xana, I think you should take last watch."

"Why?" she asked. "If this has to do with last night..."

"No," he interrupted, "this has to do with the last week. You've suffered from violent nightmares, and you can't possibly be getting much rest. Both you and Sylvia would benefit from an extended night of deep, dreamless sleep. These pouches will provide you with both."

Darien withdrew two leaf wrapped packets from his cloak. He must've made them while keeping watch the previous night. He handed one to Sylvia and the other to Xanaphia. Sylvia snatched it so fast she startled Darien. Xanaphia seemed less certain. She examined the capsule with obvious reluctance before accepting it. Finally, she did so and gave Darien a small smile.

"Thank you," she said.

Sylvia marveled. Stories claimed Xanaphia resented help from others and never said thank you. Sylvia reflected on what Darien said the previous night. Perhaps Xanaphia was a deeper person inside than she let out.

"Well," Xanaphia said, rising, "midnight is fading. I better retire if I'm to get the full benefit of the sleep. Good night."

She strolled away and lay down on the snow. Sylvia also rose, thanked Darien for the pill, raised her cup in salute, and headed for bed. She made a point of distancing herself from Xanaphia though. She didn't want anymore experiences like the previous night.

Clement watched Sylvia until convinced she was asleep. Then he turned back to the others. Lillian and Darien were discussing the pills.

"I hope those don't become standard issue," Lillian said. "You'll ruin my cube."

"No," Darien chuckled. "I am out of the ingredients. They will have to do without until we reach Rhoria."

"Speaking of which," Clement said, "what do you think will happen to us when we reach the capital?"

"I do not know," Darien said. "She knows we tried to kill her and that we are only helping her because of the demon lord. She might throw us in prison. On the other hand, she cannot hope to defeat Darlyth without our aid."

"I'm not worried about prison," Lillian replied. "There's no jail or dungeon capable of holding me. Besides, I pity anyone dumb enough to try arresting us."

Darien chuckled, and Clement gave a smile. Arresting any one of them would be a challenge. Arresting all of them together would be legendary.

"I'm more nervous about what will happen if we aren't arrested," Lillian continued. "We have a long battle ahead of us."

"True," Clement agree. "Even if we win, there won't be much of an Aurba left to rule. What greatness is there in ruling an empty ruin?"

"Clement, when are you going to learn?" Lillian asked. "Greatness doesn't come from ruling a kingdom. Forging empires or slaying enemies may attract praise and admiration, but they won't restore confidence or pride. The only way to regain your greatness is to find it inside you."

"Then why are you so worried about your lost honors and titles?" Clement retorted. "You know what you've done and achieved. Just because the rest of the world doesn't know doesn't mean you didn't do it. The fact is outward symbols of our accomplishments are important to all of us."

"I do not know if I need any outward symbols anymore," Darien observed. "Once Sylvia is dead, I think I would be happy to settle down, find some apprentices, and retire into a life of quiet teaching."

"You want to retire to teaching?" Lillian asked. "Where did this come from?"

Darien shrugged.

"Speaking of retiring," Clement said, "I think all of us should do so for the night."

He pocketed his dining utensils and strolled away.

Lillian stood up and looked at Darien.

"See you in an hour and a half," she said.

"Looking forward to it," Darien joked.

Together, Lillian and Clement headed for their beds and the short night ahead.

Sylvia woke hours later feeling refreshed and energized. She couldn't remember the last time she felt so rested. She stretched her arms high above her head and gave a loud groan.

"Those pills are quite amazing, aren't they?" a voice addressed her.

Sylvia glanced in the direction of the speaker. Xanaphia sat in front of the fire only a short distance away. Sylvia felt a rush of apprehension but pushed herself upright to face the necromancer.

"Yes, they are," she said. "Are you feeling better?"

"I am," the other replied.

Xanaphia gestured for Sylvia to sit beside her. Sylvia rose to do so. A strong icy wind nipped at her skin as she crossed the camp. A storm was moving in, and the prospects weren't good for the next day's travel. Snow was already starting to fall. Xanaphia picked up a canteen of water from beside the fire and offered the heated beverage to Sylvia, who took it.

"I want to apologize for last night," Xanaphia said. "My actions were uncalled for after everything you've gone through."

The apology caught Sylvia off guard. Just like accepting help or saying thank you, apologizing wasn't a normal part of Xanaphia's nature.

"No need to apologize," Sylvia said, taking a sip of water. "I understand what you were trying to say, and I don't believe you were entirely wrong."

She glanced at Xanaphia's hands. The necromancer held a small wooden carving of a man's face, which emitted an eerie white glow.

"Is that Cyril?" Sylvia asked in astonishment.

"Yes," Xanaphia confirmed. "And on the other side is his love, Ladonna."

Sylvia studied the bust of Ladonna's face. The carving was masterful, with each line and wrinkle appearing in perfect detail. It was an impressive tribute to both the talent of the artist and the deep affection he felt for the subject of the piece.

"Cyril's last request was for me to take it to her," Xanaphia said.

"He must've meant a lot to you," Sylvia said.

"He did," Xanaphia answered. "He presented the world to me in a different way than I had ever looked at it before. He possessed a unique conviction, a sense of right and wrong different from anyone I've ever met. He possessed no incentive to do good and no outside pressure to conform to any code of ethics, yet he chose to do so anyway."

Sylvia reflected upon Cyril. Like so many people, he faced a crossroads. Down one street, he could gain safety and power by supporting evil. On the other side, he risked losing everything for the sake of doing right. In the end, he chose the latter. Not many would.

"He was a remarkable man," Sylvia agreed. "He gave me every opportunity to surrender the tiara. I've been told by both sides that I was wrong for not doing so. Maybe I was, but I felt he was dangerous. He possessed so much anger, resentment, and hostility toward the world. But he also demonstrated mercy and compassion by ending my torture sessions early and refusing to give me the white tablets. Perhaps I became too preoccupied with seeing him as an enemy. I forgot to see him as a human. I guess I did the same for all of you."

Xanaphia gave a reassuring smile.

"You aren't the only one," she said. "We did the same with each other. I think traveling together was an eye-opening experience for us all."

Sylvia returned the smile. The two sat in silence for a moment before Xanaphia broke eye contact and glanced back at the carving. She gasped in alarm. Sylvia's smile faded.

"What?" she asked.

"The light is gone," Xanaphia answered.

Her eyes were wide with shock. Sylvia looked at the block. Xanaphia was correct. It was no longer glowing. Xanaphia leapt to her feet, shouting for the others.

"Wake up! Wake up," she screamed.

They stirred and shook themselves awake with questioning looks. All eyes fell on Xanaphia. She was leaping up and down waving the carving in obvious agitation.

"The light is out!" she screamed frantically. "The light is out!"

For a moment, no one moved. Then chaos erupted. The tyrants leapt to their feet, scrambling over each other to collect possessions and get ready to march. Sylvia didn't understand, but she sensed the urgency in the situation. She dashed forward and collected her equipment.

"What is happening?" she asked.

"Time is up!" Xanaphia explained. "The demon lord is coming!"

The scent of charred flesh filled the chamber along with the remaining wisps of black smoke. On the floor, a large pile of ashes signaled the spot where Cyril had been. On the ground beside the ashes sat the small fragment of the golden orb along with the white glow of the Life Stone.

Darlyth looked at the golden pebble with disgust. How could something so small and insignificant foil his plans? He learned about it from watching Cyril speak with his companions. Their feeble anti-scrying magic was far too weak to block the ancient powers at his command.

He had felt no need to stop his insubordinate general. In fact, he felt a certain degree of pride for his child's fearless nature. Darlyth had already set his plans for the destruction of Rhoria into motion and didn't believe Cyril's sacrifice would alter them.

He hadn't anticipated the failure of his grorg army in Rhoria. The destruction of his glyph had ruined everything. He felt the connection snap, but the fragment prevented him from stopping his army from entering the portal. He stood helpless inside his prison while his entire horde marched into oblivion.

His anger swelled. He took pride in his creations. He'd forged thousands of them. Each was special to him. He hated losing them. Fortunately, they could be replaced. With the power of the tiara, he'd make more. The new ones would be twice as powerful, twice as deadly, and his spells to control them would be twice as effective. They wouldn't even think about breaking his commands. He'd fill the world with the mightiest assortment of creatures ever imagined.

Together they'd reduce humankind to nothing more than fodder. He'd never fear any creature again. He would be immortal, the creator of all creatures, the wielder of all magic, and all living beings would be bound to his will. He'd live forever in safety and security, spreading his creations to the end of the world. He only needed the tiara.

He raised his foot high above the two small stones. He pictured the faces of the four sorcerers who dared to defy his might. They reminded him so much of Kendross and the ancient spellcasters of old. They possessed the same fearless audacity and tenacity. Now, they'd meet the same fate. He brought his foot down with all of his might and lifted it again. Only crumbled dust remained of the once mighty magic. Darlyth had wiped it from the world forever. Sylvia and her companions were next.

—⚬—

Everything was blurry. For several moments, Ladonna saw nothing. She heard sounds, but they seemed faint, as though coming from far away. She tried to move, but her muscles defied all attempts at arousal. Gradually, her surroundings swam into focus. The strange shapes swirling overhead proved to be hands with bizarre multi-colored lights flashing from their fingers. They belonged to healers. Two stood on each side of her, chanting incantations.

"General," called one, breaking her chanting, "she is waking."

A robed figure detached from a nearby wall, drifting across the room to join them.

"Well, well," a female voice joked. "And you said you weren't lucky!"

It was Alexis. Ladonna blinked as the smiling general came into focus. She attempted to push herself upright, but pain surged through her battered frame and muscles collapsed beneath her weight. Alexis placed a restraining hand upon her and pushed her back onto the bed.

"Relax," she said. "You're still weak. You shouldn't be alive at all, but the healers are fixing you up. In the meantime, you might try a simpler task, like talking."

Ladonna's throat felt dry, and her lungs were tight. She opened her mouth to speak but only managed a low groan. She kept trying until her lungs loosened enough for a feeble, "You're alive."

"Yes, I'm a tough person to kill, you know," Alexis replied. "Like you, I was on the balcony when the explosion happened. I saw the knife go down and summoned my magic like a shield. It didn't hold long, but it prevented me from being torn to shreds. Instead, I was hurled into the air, landed in a fishpond, skipped across like a stone, and crashed into the opposite bank. I don't remember anything else. The healers found what was left of me lying in a heap atop a pool of blood."

"What about the others?" Ladonna asked.

Alexis shook her head.

"You and I are the only survivors," she said. "We only survived because we were on the balcony and got blasted away from the destruction. Even the palace didn't survive. The explosion destroyed the entire wing and caused the outer walls to collapse. Repairs will take years."

Ladonna scoffed. It sounded extraordinarily optimistic. The demon lord had almost wiped the city from the world, and the conflict remained far from over. Discussing rebuilding at this point was rather silly.

Alexis seemed to realize the ridiculous nature of the remark and gave a faint smile before continuing, "I have no clue how you survived. They found you entangled in a thorn bush at the bottom of an outer wall. Your skin was melting, and just about every bone was broken, but somehow you were still alive and breathing. Perhaps your demon blood provides you with a measure of supernatural resilience."

Ladonna shook her head. She was lucky to be alive but couldn't help thinking about those who had died. Junlorace Keep was a close-knit community. The people were family, and her officers, like Urith and Eric, were like siblings. Their losses weighed heavily on her mind.

She thought about Yeva. The child was so young, so talented, and so brave. She died a hero's death, but that brought little consolation. Too many had died hero's deaths in the last few days. How many more were still to come? Ladonna wondered if Alexis was thinking the same thing.

"I'm sorry about Yeva," Ladonna said.

Alexis looked away. Their last exchange had been unpleasant. Ladonna suspected she felt some guilt.

"She knew what she was doing," Alexis said. She gave a dismissive wave, but Ladonna noticed she still hid her face. "She was hardheaded, much like her father. In the end, she saved Rhoria."

Ladonna flexed her hands. The muscles were healing fast, and she decided to try sitting up again. She positioned her arms behind her back and gave a hard shove. Two of the neighboring healers abandoned their spells to provide assistance. She was soon upright.

She glanced around the chamber. It was small with a thin curtained window and a few torches providing the only light. The dark tinge of the sun's rays coming through the window hinted of thick clouds and overcast skies. On the wall opposite the window, a tall wooden door stood beside a long table. Ladonna's armor, sword, and other equipment sat atop it. The healers must've removed them after her rescue.

"How did the healers reach us?" she asked.

"You can thank Commander Gemma for that," Alexis answered. "She assembled a rescue party without our knowledge and spent the night watching the palace. After the explosion toppled the outer bulwark, her forces rushed inside accompanied by healers. They found you first and me shortly thereafter."

"Did they slay the remaining grorgs?" Ladonna asked.

"They didn't need to," Alexis answered, shaking her head in evident confusion. "No grorgs remained alive inside the fort. Our forces discovered only piles of ashes in the center of charred floors."

"Ha!" Ladonna laughed. "The demon lord ordered them to protect the symbol. They should've been more careful. They probably thought all entrances were sealed. Again, their overconfidence proved their flaw."

One of the healers broke from casting spells to stand behind her. Ladonna felt the woman's fingers run down her spine, checking the success of the treatment. Another healer lifted Ladonna's left arm, pressing on different spots and asking if they hurt.

"How long have I been out?" Ladonna asked.

"More than thirty hours," Alexis said.

Ladonna shook her head in frustration.

"Thirty hours lost," she moaned. "I don't see how we can hope to reach the queen in time by foot. We need to set out at once."

Ladonna started to jump off the table, but Alexis lifted a restraining hand.

"Calm down," she said. "Give them a few minutes to finish your leg muscles or you'll find yourself on the floor. Besides, we won't be going by foot."

"What do you mean?" Ladonna asked, not daring to hope for what she wanted to hear.

"A messenger arrived yesterday from a small northern village called Pleasant Lake," Alexis explained. "They requested help battling a force of small dragon-like creatures that settled in a large cavern north of the city. The beasts, mysteriously equipped with mounts and saddles, are feeding off the local livestock and creating panic among the ranchers."

"My winghams," Ladonna exclaimed. "You found them!"

"Yes," Alexis smiled. "I sent a group of your fastest soldiers and told them not to rest until they returned with the beasts. I expect them back soon. Your soldiers are well disciplined."

Ladonna smiled. She could receive no higher praise than a compliment on the quality of her personally trained soldiers.

"Have you assembled a rescue party?" she asked.

"I assigned the task to Gemma," Alexis answered. "Her hand-picked squad stands ready whenever the mounts arrive. To be honest though, I don't know when they'll make it. A blizzard swept in last night, and the conditions aren't conducive to flying."

"My riders can fly in any weather," declared Ladonna. "I have complete faith in them. I can't say the same about our chances of finding the queen."

"True," Alexis acknowledged. "She could be anywhere. We don't even know what path she's taking to get here. She might try crossing the mountains toward Freighton Gorge, but she doesn't know the territory. She's more likely to head toward Unburied Grove and more familiar paths."

"That may depend on her companions," Ladonna noted. "Even if we pick the correct path, we still have to see her. Visibility will be difficult in the thick forests and bad weather."

"Such a large area to find something so small," Alexis agreed. "I feel I should come along. My magic might help, but I don't know how to fly."

"Don't worry about that," Ladonna said. "My mount wears a companion saddle for training new soldiers. You can ride with me."

Ladonna flexed her legs, testing the joints and muscles. The healers examined them with minute care to make sure they were fully healed. Suddenly, the door to the room burst open. A young lad raced into the chamber.

"They're here!" he shouted. "The dragons are here!"

Ladonna sprang from the bed, landing unsteadily on her feet. She stumbled forward, catching herself on the shoulders of a nearby healer.

"Where are they?" Alexis demanded. "How many are there?"

"Four of them. They're in the park in front of the academy." The child raced from the room, apparently eager to see the magnificent animals again.

Ladonna stumbled toward the nearby table.

"My armor," she called. "Someone help me get this on!"

"I'm going to alert Gemma," Alexis declared, dashing toward the door. "Meet us in the park in five minutes. We depart immediately!"

CHAPTER 29

The sorcerers struggled against powerful headwinds as they raced across the snowy ground. Everyone knew their chances of reaching Rhoria vanished when the light did. Still, they had to try. They planned to march straight through the night with no breaks for either food or rest.

They found themselves looking over their shoulders as they hurried through the thick woods. They didn't know how quickly the demon lord traveled or from what direction he'd come, but they hoped to spot him before his arrival. They didn't want to be caught off guard. The fastest method of pursuit was flight, so they scanned the skies and listened for the sounds of rustling branches.

After four hours of travel, they reached Freighton Gorge and the Pass of Riddian. The narrow stone archway spanning the fifty-foot drop was dangerous at any time but particularly in this weather. Fierce winds whipped through the canyon like the rapids of a monstrous river. Snow and ice coated the bridge, making the crossing even more treacherous.

Lillian struggled to keep her balance. At one point, she slipped, and only Clement's fast reflexes saved her from an otherwise deadly fall. Sylvia also found herself unable to maintain her footing against the malevolent flurries. Xanaphia fell back to provide assistance, and the two fought against the brutal winds until they reached the other side. There, a tall slippery stone step represented the return to normal ground.

Darien positioned himself atop the rise, and Clement helped Lillian up to him. Clement climbed up behind her while the men lifted Sylvia over the barrier. The weary queen stumbled away from the gorge following Lillian toward a massive stone block the size of a house. The fallen piece of an old tower provided momentary protection from the wind, and Lillian rested against it as Sylvia hurried to join her.

Meanwhile, Darien and Clement leaned over to assist Xanaphia. The necromancer lifted her arms to grasp the hands of her comrades but never got the chance. The ground beneath them exploded. Rocks and snow blasted upward from the earth as a geyser of hot steam erupted into the air. The quake threw Sylvia and Lillian onto the ground. Darien and Clement were hurled backward into the air.

Riddian Pass shattered. The stones crumpled and crashed into the depth below, carrying Xanaphia with them. She attempted to utter a levitation spell, but an avalanche of thick snow and rocks cascaded down upon her as the cliff face collapsed. She barely had time to shield herself inside her magic before being swept away by the debris. She tumbled and flipped, bouncing and rattling against the rolling stones. When she finally stopped, she found herself buried alive beneath tons of rock and snow.

She fought to maintain the small capsule of protective magic surrounding her as the weight and pressure built. To her surprise, her first thought was about the welfare of her companions. Something bad was happening overhead, and they needed her help. The thought seemed comical. She was buried alive inside an inescapable icy prison, and all she could think about was reaching her comrades. Yet, she knew they needed her. Clement might be clever, but in a straight fight she was the more powerful combatant. Darien might provide some assistance, as he did against the snow dragons, but she was the true muscle of the party.

An idea occurred to her. She thought about the ice dragons. They burrowed through the snow by surrounding themselves in extreme heat. If she could funnel enough warmth into the shield surrounding her, she could melt the ice and snow. She could then use her levitation spell to ascend the cliff and a telekinesis spell to move the rocks out of the way.

It would require a legendary feat. She needed to maintain enough concentration on her shield to prevent getting crushed. Meanwhile, she needed to focus on melting the ice and moving aside heavy rocks. Finally, she'd have to keep her attention on levitating upward. Nobody could possibly sustain all three spells at once. On the other hand, nobody could concentrate long enough to absorb magical powers from a violet quartz crystal — nobody except Xanaphia. A smile crossed her lips. It was time to test the full limits of her power.

Atop the precipice, Darien called out Xanaphia's name. He climbed back to his feet and dashed ahead. Clement also rose while Lillian and Sylvia pushed themselves upright.

Everyone prepared to rush to Xanaphia's aid. Then they froze.

A geyser of lava erupted from the ground. The steaming molten liquid struck the cold morning air and began to solidify. The exterior transformed into hard scaly flesh covered with large pustules oozing green slime. The falling droplets of slag merged and attached to the central stalk to form six tree-like arms. The top of the fourteen-foot geyser became a head spiked with a crown of tall horns. Billowing black steam rose from hollow eye sockets like a dark cloud obscuring all light. The demon lord had come!

His coming was like a scene from an apocalypse. The earth trembled as though racked with pain. Trees shook in the fury of his roar. Lightning flashed from his closed fists as he reveled in the ecstasy of his own magical might. Clement reacted first.

"Desecria!" he shouted.

The black lightning struck the monstrosity in the chest with the fury of a hundred charging bulls. Darien, Lillian, and Sylvia also joined the attack. Their bolts hammered into Darlyth's face and eyes with an explosion that sent shockwaves through the nearby forest.

The spells did nothing. Darlyth made no attempt to defend himself. He seemed to take sadistic delight in watching them drain their bodies to the verge of collapse. Deep mirthless guffaws burst from his throat, mocking his attackers.

Finally, Darlyth struck. He flung his two bottom arms outward, sending a tsunami of transparent energy rippling across the earth and sky. Darien tried to dive beneath the wave, but the impact caught him and launched him spiraling backward. Sylvia also tried diving out of the way only to be thrown into the hard stone slab behind her. Clement tried to block the attack with a hastily summoned shield, but his defense shattered, and he was launched into the unforgiving surface of a large pine tree. The impact knocked the wind from his lungs, and he crumbled onto the ground.

Meanwhile, Lillian took cover behind the enormous slab on her right. Even it couldn't withstand the force of the wave. It buckled under the blow and flipped on top of her. Thinking quickly, she focused all her energy on catching the tumbling block. To her surprise, she succeeded. It hovered in midair just above her. She sprang to her feet, launching it toward the demon lord. He merely batted it away with one arm, shattering the brick to pieces.

Lillian looked around and gasped. She was the only one still standing. Lillian dove for the shelter of a nearby tree, but Darlyth caught her mid leap. An invisible hand seized her body and held her suspended in the air. Then it flung her backward into the thick forest. She summoned her magic, but the shield shattered as she slammed like an arrow into the base of a nearby cedar. The collision knocked her senseless, and a loud crunching noise came from her arm as the bones snapped. Her momentum caused her to spiral around the tree and she skidded to a halt on the other side.

Clement regained his footing. Realizing the desperate nature of the situation, he called upon his last resort. He wrenched the small crystal orb from his cloak and prepared to activate it. He didn't know if violet quartz would work on Darlyth. Even if it did, the orb lacked the capacity to hold the demon lord's power. Once the gem exploded, no magic could protect him. He would die. *So be it*, he thought.

Darien spotted Clement and nodded. Leaping to his feet, he started bombarding Darlyth with every spell he could think of as fast as his lips could utter them. Sylvia joined the assault, hoping to provide a distraction. They failed.

Darlyth spotted the threat. His amused grin faded. He recognized the danger and didn't take it lightly. Six beams issued from his hands heading toward Clement. Darien and Sylvia tried to bat them away. They succeeded on the first three. The rest found their marks. Clement was blasted onto his back, and his body burst into flames.

The ball flew from his outstretched hand and rose into the air. Another ray struck the crystal at the peak of its arc. The gem flashed, and a fine white powder drifted toward the snow. Darien and Sylvia gasped. They'd never seen magic capable of destroying violet quartz.

Clement didn't see it. He was too busy muttering spells to put out the fire engulfing his body. His agony was far from over though. The demon lord gestured upward, and Clement shot twenty feet into the air. He was only there for a second. The demon lord flicked his wrist, and Clement was slammed face down into the hard surface below, vanishing into the snowy depth. The flames died, and he lay there twitching uncontrollably.

"Enough of this," Darlyth's voice boomed.

The hollow eyes locked upon Darien. His time was up. Darien braced himself as a bolt of blue light crashed through his defenses and into his chest. Waves of electricity shot through him. He twitched and thrashed then shot backward like an arrow. Everything went black as he ricocheted from one tree to another before disappearing into the foliage of an overgrown fir.

Sylvia panicked. Abandoning the battle, she attempted to flee into the woods. An invisible fist seized her before she could take two steps. It snatched her from the ground, and she drifted back to Darlyth. The invisible hand brought her face-to-face with the beast. The two floated upward from the ground until they hung together above the trees.

"Give me the crown, mortal" he cooed, assuming the mesmerizing tone he had used against Xanaphia and Cyril. "Surrender the tiara to me!"

"Never," Sylvia screamed. "Desecria!"

She pointed her unfettered arms at him. The black lightning soared from her fingers, but the spell remained just as ineffective as the first time.

"You and your friends are no match for me," he continued. "You're mere mice to be crushed before my power. If you won't relinquish the tiara, I'll take you back to my keep and pry it from your broken soul while your companions watch on stakes! Now, give it to me!"

The unseen hand gripping Sylvia constricted, and the breath was squeezed from her lungs. There was no more time for thought. She needed to act. She reached up and pulled the crown from her head. She could hear her children talking to her. She looked into the gems. They were watching her.

"We believe in you." It echoed through her ears. "We love you! Be brave!"

Tears filled Sylvia's eyes. She would be brave. Her hands twisted, and the metal band snapped in half.

"If you want the tiara, then take it!"

She flung the pieces at him. Darlyth's eyes flared with surprise and rage. Flames burst from their sockets. The invisible hand released her, and she plummeted. Her right leg gave way as she crashed onto the ground. She heard the bones break and the demon lord scream. Both were drowned out by the shrieks from the tiara.

Above her, the violet quartz crystals in the tiara shone like the sun, releasing a dazzling blue light. Glowing apparitions of her children erupted from the crystals. They writhed and screamed, their semi-transparent bodies jerking and thrashing as they rose into the air.

The agony in their cries wrenched at Sylvia's heart. Her hand reached upward in a desperate wish to touch and sooth her suffering babies. Then with a final shriek their bodies exploded in a flash of azure light. The crystals vanished. The light went out. Sylvia gazed into empty air.

In the distance, Lillian pushed herself upright with her good arm, gazing at the spectacle. The tiara was destroyed. They'd thwarted the demon lord's plans. Now was the time to flee. She gazed around. The trees grew thick, and she was beneath Darlyth's notice. She could turn invisible and escape to a distant continent. Without the tiara, maybe someone could stop him.

Lillian started to run then hesitated. Darien, Clement, and Xanaphia remained behind. After everything they'd endured together, she couldn't abandon them now. But she wasn't abandoning them, she told herself. They knew she planned to run. She'd told them so. Still something inside told her to stay and help them. Lillian shook herself. She had a broken arm and wasn't a fighter. Now didn't seem like a good time to change. She broke into a sprint heading away from the fight and her companions.

Meanwhile, Darlyth drifted back to the ground. Sylvia looked up as he landed on the edge of the cliff before her. The fires burned in his eyes, and streams of billowing black smoke swirled above his head. He leered down upon her as flames engulfed his hands.

Sylvia crawled backward as fast as her arms and legs allowed. Her broken right leg dragged across the ground as she scrambled for dear life. Darlyth swung his arms forward one after one. Fireballs erupted from his hand with each thrust. They soared through the air at Sylvia. She couldn't block the attacks, but she could deflect them. She waved her hands back and forth using her magic to knock the balls off course. They rained down upon her in an endless succession. Ice and dirt exploded everywhere as they crashed into the earth. They were getting closer each time. Her magic was failing.

Darlyth swung his four lower arms forward together. The globes merged into a single ball of flame roaring toward her. Sylvia tried to redirect the attack. She couldn't. It was too large and too powerful. Without her tiara, she lacked the skill to stop it. The inferno soared toward her, and she watched as death arrived.

A short distance away, Clement lay face down in the snow, muttering self healing spells just to stay alive. His body was broken. His mind was defeated. All seemed lost.

It was then that his strength surfaced, the kind of strength that can only be found in the heart of someone who was once the greatest in the world. It was a power is born of pride, a pride which demanded not only the respect of others, but the respect of himself; founded in confidence, a confidence that remembered every time he faced overwhelming odds to stand triumphant; established through dedication, a dedication which drove him on an unending quest to excel beyond their predecessors, and cemented with resiliency, a tenacity that spurred him to overcome obstacles capable of crushing lesser champions.

The power flooded through him like a tidal wave, coursing through his blood. Strength surged through his muscles, and the dynamic confidence missing from his life since his defeat at the hands of Sylvia returned. Like the fires of the phoenix, the weak, uncertain, defeated man of the last seven years was burned to ashes, and in his place rose Clement the Great, the exiled orphan who had become the mightiest sorcerer of the modern era.

Clement plunged his hands into the ground and pushed himself to his feet. He saw the massive ball of flame streaking toward Sylvia. She attempted to deflect it but failed. She was going to die. She lacked the power to save herself. She was not Clement the Great.

"Udaryat," he said, batting his arm. A glowing fist composed of blue energy manifested before Sylvia. It slammed into the flames, shattering them the same way Darlyth crushed the stone. Sylvia gave a gasp and collapsed from shock and pain.

The demon lord's face, flushed with the excitement of the kill, darkened, and his eyes narrowed. He turned to see Clement striding toward him. Darlyth released a growl of rage. Swinging his arm through the air, he launched a massive wall of force similar to the one he had used at the beginning of the battle. Clement was ready for it. Borrowing an idea from Lillian's earlier evasion tactic, he flicked his wrists palms upward in a circular motion.

"Moroshnoye, Moroshnoye, Moroshnoye," he said.

One after another, large walls of thick ice sprang from the ground. The force of the tsunami shattered the first two but weakened with each collision. When the spell smashed into the third wall, the defense buckled but held. The remainder of the wave passed around him. Clement dismissed the wall and continued advancing toward his enraged foe.

The demon lord's fury increased. He flung his arms wildly toward Clement. A massive bolt of green lightning crackled across the ether. Deadly icicles fired from the ground like a barrage of arrows. Two spheres of red fire sizzled through the sky, and a boulder covered with spikes vaulted into the air. All shot straight toward Clement.

"Zakvateevat!" Clement exclaimed extending his arm toward the lightning.

The bolt struck his hand. He closed his fist and spun like a dancer. The lightning encircled him like a shell of crackling light. Little tendrils of energy burst from it striking the approaching icicles, blasting them from the sky. Then Clement clapped his hands together. The two globes of fire swerved, colliding with the boulder and each other. All exploded in a flash of dust and smoke. The lightning field surrounding Clement faded, and he continued striding forward.

The demon lord's wrath burst from his body in a roar of hatred. No one except Kendross had ever dared to stand alone against him, and like Kendross this pathetic mortal possessed the audacity to stride fearlessly toward him. Memories of imprisonment flashed through his mind. He saw his legendary rival reborn in the face of the loathsome sorcerer. Every cell in his body screamed for Clement's death, and he directed all of his might upon the man's destruction.

Darlyth launched a barrage of destructive spells beyond anything Clement had ever imagined. Clement summoned his magic into a shield before him and focused all his might upon it. The shield held, but the spells didn't stop. They hammered against his defenses in a rapid and endless succession, growing more powerful with each new spell. The force threatened to topple him, and Clement braced against the attacks as his feet slid backward through the snow. It was no use. He felt his shield giving way before the might of his opponent. Finally, it failed completely.

Darlyth sensed its collapse and thrust all his arms forward in unison. A mountain-sized blast of dazzling white fire erupted from his body. Clement summoned more walls of ice, but the spell plowed through them without weakening.

Clement attempted to redirect the flame, but it remained intent upon its course. A smile crossed Clement's lips. He was a warrior. This was how he wanted to go. He'd put up a good fight. Now, he would die.

A shield of radiant energy formed in front of Clement. Then a second barrier appeared, followed by a third. The assault shattered before the combined might of the three enchantments. Stunned, Clement glanced around.

Lillian emerged from the woods to his left. Her shattered right arm hung at her side but her left hand was held toward her ally. Her white robes swirled in the cold winds, and her eyes were locked upon the demon lord. There'd be no retreating today. Today, she'd face her fears. Today, she'd stand beside her companions. Today, she'd have faith in the world. If she died, so be it!

To Clement's right appeared the green-cloaked figure of Darien. His face and arms were covered with deep cuts and gouges. Blood stained his robes and clothing. Yet he stood shoulder to shoulder with his companions. He no longer cared about revenge. He no longer cared about the past. He stood beside his former enemies, not as a reluctant companion dragged here by fate but as a warrior standing with his allies.

Sylvia came after him. Her leg was broken, but she didn't fall. She hobbled toward Clement, her eyes flushed with determination. He'd saved her life twice in the last week, just like so many others had saved her life. This time, she'd return the favor. No one else would die in her place. She'd face her fears. She'd become the hero everyone believed she already was.

Four of the greatest sorcerers of the modern age faced the most powerful being to ever exist. Ten days ago, they were mortal enemies. Now, they were a team — united in the face of overwhelming evil. Their fates were intertwined. They'd live together or perish together. If the latter, they'd die as allies, as comrades, and perhaps even as friends.

Maddened beyond the point of rational thought, the demon lord summoned the most powerful magic he knew. The entire continent shook with the upheaval. Torrents of rocky spikes exploded from the ground like enraged bees swarming toward the companions. Innumerable lightning bolts streaked from the sky like a rainstorm of electricity showering upon them. Fire spewed from his hands so hot the entire forest burst into flames for miles around. The ice evaporated and the grass previously buried in wet snow ignited from the heat. These flames too erupted toward the company. Fissures formed in the earth between the demon lord and his enemies.

The four summoned their shields, uniting them into a fortress of magical energy. They closed their eyes and leaned against the barrier in an instinctive effort to divert every ounce of power to the bulwark. Earthquakes rocked the countryside, collapsing fortifications and cracking the foundations of distant houses. The crash of spells echoed for hundreds of miles like the wrath of the gods unleashed upon the world. Flashes of lightning illuminated the sky with the brightness of the midday sun, blinding the wingham riders racing toward the light they knew they'd never reach in time.

Spells crashed, lightning streaked, fire slammed, but the shield held. Their muscles spasmed. Beads of sweat turned to blood. Breaths grew strained. Yet they didn't fall. Darlyth screamed with rage. He focused all his concentration, all his magic, all his might, and all his energy upon the annihilation of his foes. His shout filled the sky and his body quivered with adrenaline.

Sylvia couldn't hold any longer. Her shield cracked, and she collapsed from the strain. A moment later, Lillian's shield shattered, and she joined the queen on the ground. Darien followed. Clement felt his shield buckle. Any second, the defense would fail. He opened his eyes, determined to face death head on.

The earth behind the demon lord erupted with rock and debris. Rising like an angel of death came Xanaphia. For the first time in his life, Clement understood why Darien feared her more than any other sorcerer. Her hair swirled behind her as though caught in the center of a tornado. Her pale skin bulged with red and blue veins pulsing through her flesh. Her red eyes burned within her sockets almost as bright as the flames in the demon lord's. Her razor sharp teeth flashed in the lightning as she screamed in rage. Power seeped from every pour of her body, so great the air around her crackled with energy matching Darlyth's fury. She rose into the air, her hand gripping the violet crystal dagger.

She'd come in time. They needed her, and she wouldn't let them down. She would finish this battle forever. She would make a difference. She'd do something meaningful. She knew her fate was sealed, but after years of meaningless existence she'd finally found something worth dying for: friendship.

Darlyth sensed her presence. He attempted to pull his magic back to himself. It was too little, too late. Xanaphia slammed the dagger downward with all her supernatural strength. The weapon plunged up to the hilt in Darlyth's back. The absorption spell activated upon contact.

The dagger glowed. Then it exploded. Shattered crystal shards ripped through the demon lord like knives cutting through butter. Other fragments slashed through Xanaphia, tearing her clothes and flesh. She dropped from the sky, landing like a rag doll at the demon lord's feet.

Darlyth screamed his outrage, clawing at his skin with his many arms. Beams of red light spewed from his body, and he fell to his knees shrieking into the sky. The flames in his eyes turned into a bonfire, which engulfed his body. With a final flash of red energy, he exploded, showering the charred ground with a layer of ash. The demon lord was gone.

CHAPTER

30

Silence filled the air. Clement stood alone. Lillian and Darien lay on the ground, breathing heavily. Sylvia was unconscious. Darien picked himself off the ice and raced toward Xanaphia's lifeless body. Skidding through the ashes, he came to a sliding halt at her side.

Clement felt a hand reach up and grab his robes. He took the hand and lifted Lillian from the ground. She cradled her broken arm. They both looked at the silhouette of Darien leaning over Xanaphia.

Clement sighed. He thought of everything Xanaphia and Darien went through together. From children competing for a master's favor to the years of bitter warfare and the strange friendship they developed at the end. They were the only ones who truly knew each other. Clement imagined the loss felt like losing a sibling, no matter how strained the relationship.

Clement gestured for them to join Darien. Lillian hung back. She turned toward the flaming trees and ran her fingers through the air. The flames grew smaller until they vanished. She turned back to Clement. Together, they crossed the clearing toward Darien. All three stared upon Xanaphia's fallen figure in quiet reverence. Her eyes stared into the sky and blood trickled from her lips.

"Hard to imagine she's gone," Lillian said. "After all the mean things we said to each other over the years, I'd like one last chance to speak to her. Just to say thank you."

Darien nodded. There was nothing more to say. Ultimately, silence seemed the best tribute.

The sorcerers began muttering healing spells, treating their wounds. For several seconds, they stood in silence, allowing their bodies to recover. Finally, Lillian broke the quiet.

"So," she said, "Darlyth is dead. Now what?"

As if in answer to her question, a moan issued from the other side of the clearing. Sylvia was waking up. Clement's face darkened. Grim determination outlined his features. He looked at Lillian and Darien. They stared back at him, their faces resolute. They knew what was next, and they turned toward Sylvia as one.

Sylvia had just finished healing her leg when she saw them approaching. They were stoic. Apprehension arose. The demon lord's death signaled the end of their alliance. She didn't attempt to flee nor fight. Without the tiara, she posed no threat to any one of them, let alone all three. She merely watched and waited. Lillian stepped up to her right. Darien stopped at her feet. Clement strolled up to her left.

Clement's arm rose from his side. His fingers drew level with her face. Her breath caught as she awaited the final spell. His hand hovered in the air for an instant. Then Clement acted. His hand flipped palm upward, and he lowered it toward Sylvia's shoulder.

Sylvia gazed at his outstretched hand in silent shock. She took it, and he lifted her to her feet. She gazed into his eyes with a stunned expression, unsure what to think or say.

"I thought you were going to kill me," she said at last.

Clement shook his head.

"There's nothing I can do to you that's worse than what you've already suffered," he said. "Besides, I already got back what I wanted."

He turned around and strode across the clearing toward Xanaphia. Sylvia looked at Lillian and Darien.

"What about you?" she asked.

"I think the time has come to leave the past behind," Darien said. "Today is a day of new beginnings."

"For all of us," Lillian agreed.

They turned and strolled back to Xanaphia. Sylvia followed. She walked up to the body and knelt down. She'd never forget their last conversation. She reached into Xanaphia's cloak and extracted the small wooden carving.

"Should we bury her here?" Clement asked.

"No," Darien answered. "She'd want to be buried in a cemetery. She should rest in the place where she felt most at home when alive."

The others nodded. They gazed at her in silent reverence, until the cry of a large animal broke the silence. Swooping down from the dark gray sky came four large reptilian beasts. The winghams circled as they settled down into the clearing.

"Sylvia!" shouted a voice from atop the nearest mount.

A red-cloaked figure leapt from its back and raced toward the queen.

"Alexis!" Sylvia shouted.

Beaming, she sprinted toward her companion. They met in the middle, wrapping each other in a tight hug.

"I was told you were dead," Sylvia said.

Alexis chuckled, breaking the hug.

"Me?" she asked incredulously. "Die? You should know better than that!"

"What about Gaheera? Andrus?" Sylvia asked.

Alexis's smiled faded. She shook her head. Sylvia's mirth vanished, but she dismissed her disappointment.

Sylvia said, "At least I still have you. I want to hear all about what's happened in Rhoria since my departure."

"I'm not sure you do," Alexis responded. "The town is in ruins, and most of the citizens were massacred. There'd be no Rhoria at all if not for our hero here."

Alexis gestured toward the approaching form of Ladonna. The red-headed warrior strolled nervously up to the queen. Sylvia felt a rush of mixed emotions. Ladonna served in the scheme that resulted in the deaths of a platoon of her soldiers. On the other hand, she aided Cyril in the plan to prevent the crown from falling into the demon lord's hands.

Alexis felt the tension and stepped away, looking between the two. Ladonna drew her sword and extended the pummel toward the queen. She knelt down, lowering her head.

"I know I wronged you," she said. "Many good soldiers died in the scheme where my actions played a central part. I ask no forgiveness for myself. I would obey my lord's commands again were I given the chance. I only ask mercy for my people."

Sylvia took the sword and slid the blade from Ladonna's outstretched hands. She lowered it to the soldier's left shoulder, resting the weapon upon the bright mail.

"Ladonna of Junlorace," she declared. "As penance for your crimes, I appoint you high commander of my personal guard. As Cyril sacrificed himself for me and for all the people of Rhoria, I pass our futures into your care and commission you with ensuring his legacy lives on to the end of our days. Arise, Commander."

Sylvia lifted the sword, and Ladonna rose to her feet. Ladonna's face remained stoic and unemotional, but gratitude shone in her eyes. Sylvia smiled and returned the sword. Ladonna was much like Cordor, loyal and proud. She would make a great commander.

"What happened to the demon lord?" Alexis asked. "We saw the battle and . . ."

The general gasped.

"Your tiara is gone," she exclaimed in alarm.

"The tiara is destroyed," Sylvia said. "So is the demon lord. Let me introduce you to my saviors."

Sylvia gestured at the three sorcerers lingering uncertainly around the fallen form of their comrade.

"Meet, Clement the Great, Darien the Dark, and Lillian the . . ."

"Please don't say insidious," the spymaster interrupted.

Sylvia gave a grin.

"Resourceful," she finished wryly.

Alexis advanced toward the three.

"Alexis," Lillian said, giving a small nod.

"Your Majesty," the other replied, "it is good to see you again."

She turned to Darien. "It is an honor to meet you off the field of battle."

"It was an honor to have met you on it," Darien replied, tilting his head in a respectful bow.

"All of Aurba owes you a great debt," Alexis declared, taking a step back.

"But in particular, I'd like to thank you," she said, turning to Clement.

Clement looked shocked.

"Why?" he asked.

"Long story," she said. "But believe me when I say I owe you my life."

Clement looked bewildered, but Alexis didn't elaborate.

"My friends," Sylvia addressed them, "please return to Rhoria with me. I owe you more than I can ever repay. I hereby revoke your exiles and offer you any reward you might ask, up to a fourth of my kingdom."

She looked at their faces, but they merely stared back at her. No one said anything. Sylvia's smile faded.

"Lillian?" she asked anxiously.

"No, Your Majesty," Lillian said. "I'm free and I'm happy. Perhaps you could restore my titles and honors if you like, but I won't be here to see it. I have a world to explore, and a new life to live. I wish you a long and glorious reign."

Lillian gave Sylvia and Alexis each a small bow. Then she turned toward Darien and Clement.

"Goodbye," she said. "And thank you . . . for everything."

She shook Darien's hand and gave Clement a quick hug. Then Lillian turned away and vanished. Sylvia stared in shock at the unexpected turn of events.

"Clement . . ." she began.

"I'm afraid not, Your Majesty," he answered. "There's nothing for me in Rhoria, and I don't need a kingdom. I'm tired. I just want to go home. Long life to you and to all the people of Aurba."

The greatest sorcerer of the modern era lifted his hand in a quiet salute before turning to Darien.

"Goodbye my friend," he said. "A month ago neither of us fathomed the idea of working together. Now I can't imagine what it'll feel like not to have you around."

Darien smiled.

"Send me a bauble sometime," he joked. "Do not be a stranger."

Clement laughed. He turned away and strolled into the woods.

"Darien," the queen asked tentatively.

"I ask no boon," he said, "though I will return with you to Rhoria. Sounds like the town will need some help rebuilding. Perhaps I can lend a hand."

Sylvia smiled in relief. Ladonna cleared her throat.

"We should be on our way, Your Majesty," she declared. "The people are eager to see you."

"One more thing," Sylvia said. "I had one more companion."

Sylvia gestured toward the deceased body of Xanaphia.

"She'll be coming with us to be buried in the Royal Cemetery," Sylvia said. "She also gave me a request."

Sylvia strode toward Ladonna. From the pocket of her cloak, she pulled Cyril's wooden carving. She held the sculpture out with trembling hands.

"Cyril's last request was for you to be given this," she said, "Xanaphia swore she would make sure you received it. In her name, I give it to you."

Ladonna took the tiny mold. She stared at the intricate carving of her own face and the face of her beloved. Tears filled her eyes. Clutching it to her chest, she fell to the ground. For the first time since leaving Junlorace Keep, she wept.

Alexis knelt beside her and hugged her gently. Anwyn and Daylin dismounted from their beasts, crossed the clearing, and bore Xanaphia's body back to a wingham. A few minutes later, the procession started back to Rhoria.

—⚙—

Three weeks later, Sylvia sat at the head of a long table inside the magical academy.

"Honestly, Your Majesty, I feel we should consider moving our capital," declared General Gemma, recently appointed commander of the Rhorian home guard. "The Grorg War cost us over ninety percent of our population, and rebuilding is taking too long. I'm just not sure the process is worth the trouble."

"I disagree," a male voice declared from the hall.

Everyone spun around to face the newcomer. Darien strode inside. His dark-green robes were disheveled. On his chest bounced the small golden medallion signifying Headmaster of the Rhorian Academy. Alexis followed him, her robes sparkling with the bright red of wet blood. Behind both of them came Ladonna.

"High Mage Darien, report!" Sylvia declared.

He gave a low bow before speaking.

"Thanks to the help of the winghams, we tracked down the two rogue demons," he said. "The roads to the south and west are now open."

He strode to his seat at the high table.

"You know, demons are much easier to kill from the sky when they can't fight back," Alexis said, taking her own place at the meeting. Sylvia smiled.

"So," she said, "only my kidnapper remains. He won't be able to hide forever. We'll track him down. At least the roads to the city are open."

"Which means," Darien added, "once word gets out to neighboring villages, people will flock here. I can enchant the surrounding farmlands to increase fertility. Construction on the new palace and the monument to Xanaphia and Cyril will mean many jobs for skilled artisans and laborers. Between the high-paying jobs, plentiful housing, and bountiful farmland, people will rush to the capital. I haven't even mentioned all the applications I'm receiving from teachers eager to take up posts at the magical academy."

"Nor the number of warriors and soldiers vying for prestigious military openings," Ladonna added.

Clement watched the scene playing out in his fireplace. Having helped save Rhoria, he felt inclined to monitor events happening throughout the city. He maintained a constant scrying spell on the queen and her commanders.

Right now, he was only half-listening. His primary interest focused on the collection of spell books surrounding his chair. One of them sat open in his lap, and he held a quill in his hand. He scrawled random notes into a journal as he studied the book.

Then, his head rose as he felt an alteration in the room. Like water disturbed by the sudden ripple of a fish passing beneath, the air changed. The magic surrounding him swirled and tingled in reaction to the presence of a second energy source. A smile stretched Clement's lips.

"Didn't your parents teach you to knock?" he asked.

"Didn't your parents teach you not to steal?" a female voice retorted. "Honestly, was there anything in the Junlorace library you didn't take?"

The lithe, white-robed figure of Lillian manifested to Clement's right. She brushed off a small amount of dust and flipped through the top pages of a random tome.

"Not much," Clement said with a smile. "How did you find me?"

"Darien," she answered. "Or perhaps I should call him High Mage Darien. I visited him to have a certain curse removed. He has an odd view of a quiet life of retired teaching."

Clement chuckled. He set aside his book and rose to face her.

"I suppose I should ask what brings you here. I figured you'd be halfway to the southern continent by now."

"I would," she said, "but the last time I went there I almost got killed by a vampire lord. I'm pretty skilled at sneaking around, but there are a lot of dangers down there that I'm not prepared to handle."

"Oh ho!" Clement said. "So you want a bodyguard to provide some muscle should you find yourself in a tight spot."

"Maybe," Lillian replied silkily.

She placed her hands behind her back with an innocent expression. She moved toward him, swaying and giving a seductive look Clement knew to be well rehearsed.

"Or maybe I could use someone to keep me company," she said.

Clement roared with laughter, and even Lillian abandoned her effort to keep a straight face. Together, they buckled over in a fit of raucous cackling. After a moment, Clement straightened up, grinning at his companion.

"Are we leaving right away?"

Lillian looked at him with delight. Her eyes sparkled, and her smile stretched from ear to ear.

"Yes!" she exclaimed, nearly bursting with joy. "We just need to pack your books."

"Then let's go," he declared, picking up tomes and tossing them into a newly enchanted bag of his own design.

Packing his belongings didn't take long. Together, Clement and Lillian set off into the snowy woods in search of new adventures, new magic, and a new life.

www.ingramcontent.com/pod-product-compliance
Lightning Source LLC
LaVergne TN
LVHW041222080526
838199LV00083B/2153